I0818003

A STORM OF IMMORTALITY

J. WINT

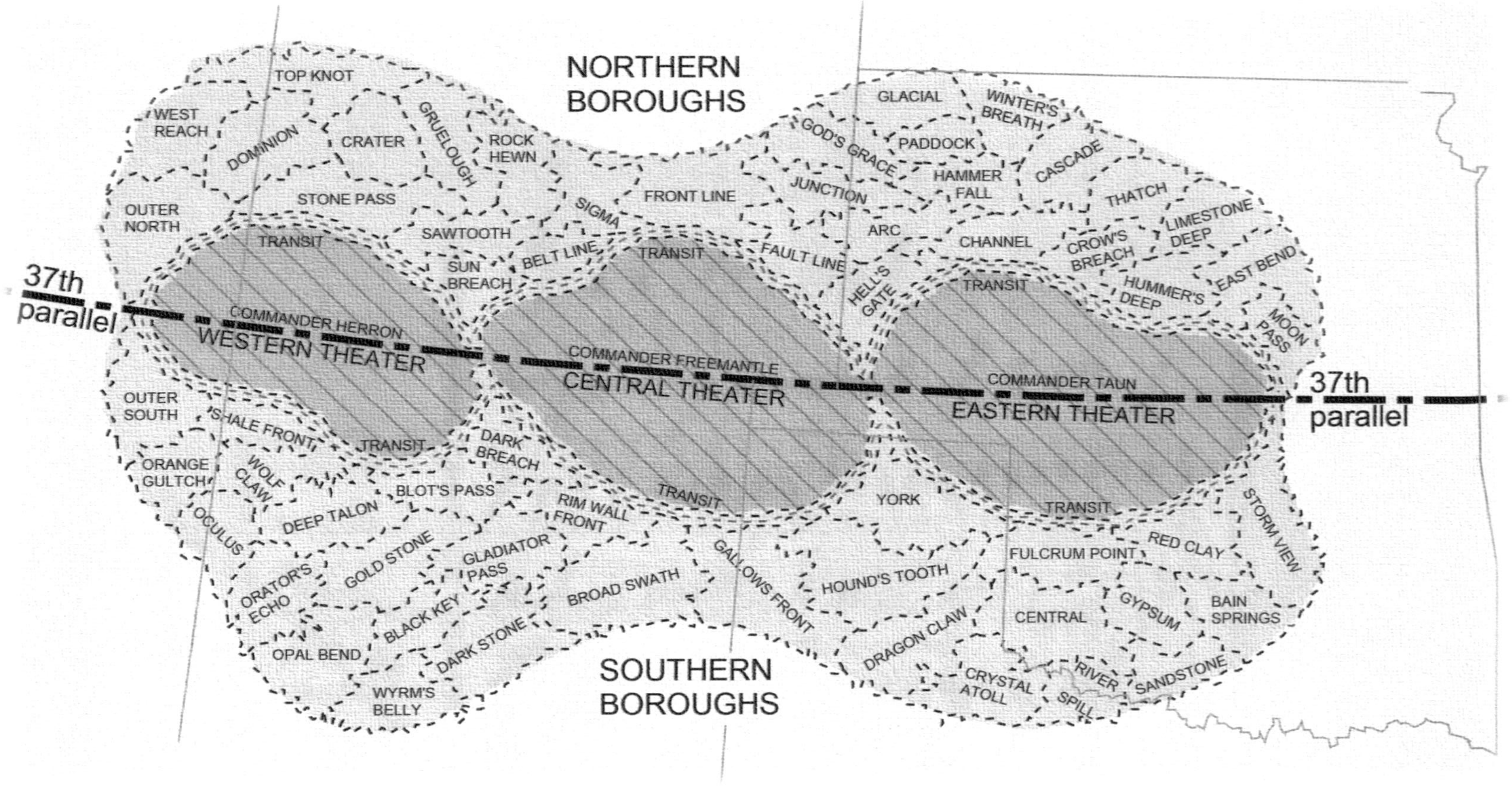
NORTHERN BOROUGHS
SOUTHERN BOROUGHS
37th parallel
37th parallel
WESTERN THEATER
COMMANDER HERRON
CENTRAL THEATER
COMMANDER FREEMANTLE
EASTERN THEATER
COMMANDER TAUN
TRANSIT
TRANSIT
TRANSIT
TRANSIT
TRANSIT
TRANSIT
WEST REACH
TOP KNOT
DOMINION
CRATER
GRUELOUGH
ROCK HEWN
STONE PASS
OUTER NORTH
SAWTOOTH
SUN BREACH
BELT LINE
SIGMA
FRONT LINE
FAULT LINE
JUNCTION
GOD'S GRACE
GLACIAL
WINTER'S BREATH
PADDOCK
HAMMER FALL
CASCADE
ARC
HELL'S GATE
CHANNEL
THATCH
LIMESTONE DEEP
CROW'S BREACH
HUMMER'S DEEP
EAST BEND
MOON PASS
OUTER SOUTH
SHALE FRONT
ORANGE GULTCH
WOLF CLAW
OCULUS
DEEP TALON
BLOT'S PASS
DARK BREACH
RIM WALL FRONT
ORATOR'S ECHO
GOLD STONE
GLADIATOR PASS
BLACK KEY
OPAL BEND
DARK STONE
WYRM'S BELLY
BROAD SWATH
GALLOWS FRONT
YORK
HOUND'S TOOTH
DRAGON CLAW
CRYSTAL ATOLL
FULCRUM POINT
CENTRAL
RED CLAY
GYPSUM
BAIN SPRINGS
RIVER SPILL
SANDSTONE
STORM VIEW

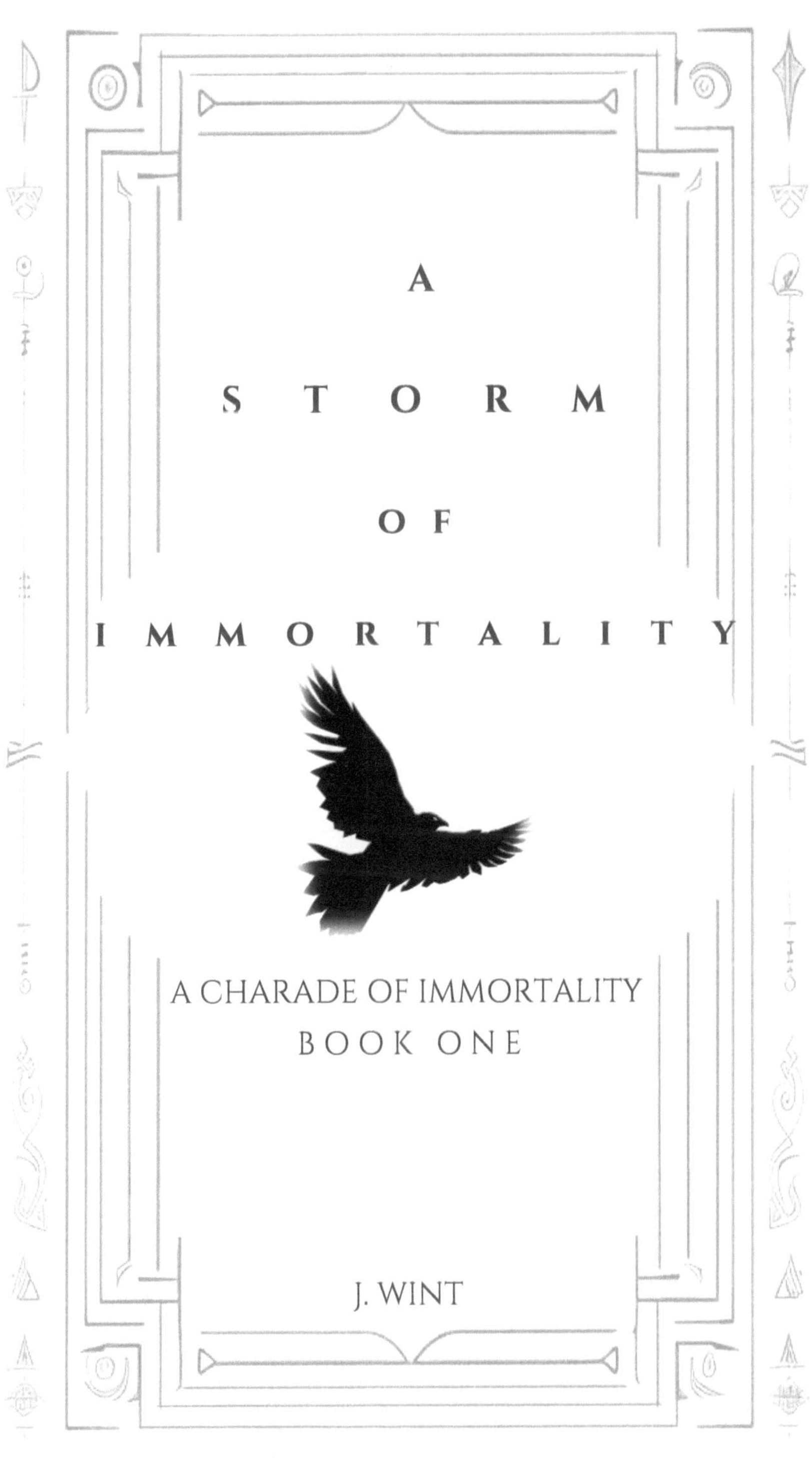

A STORM OF IMMORTALITY

A CHARADE OF IMMORTALITY
BOOK ONE

J. WINT

FOR DAVE

ISBN: 978-1-7363029-8-9

Edited by CAROLINE BARNHILL
Artwork by SIENNA GRAPHICS

A CHARADE OF IMMORTALITY:

BOOK ONE: *A STORM of IMMORTALITY*

BOOK TWO: *A SHROUD of IMMORTALITY (forthcoming)*

BOOK THREE: *A RAGE of IMMORTALITY (forthcoming)*

THE SKYLIGHT SERIES:

BOOK ONE: *THE PRISM EFFECT*

BOOK TWO: *THE SKYLIGHT FALLOUT*

BOOK THREE: *THE HELIOGRAPHI MEMOIRS*

BOOK FOUR: *THE SERPENT EFFECT*

BOOK FIVE: *(forthcoming)*

www.theskylightseries.com

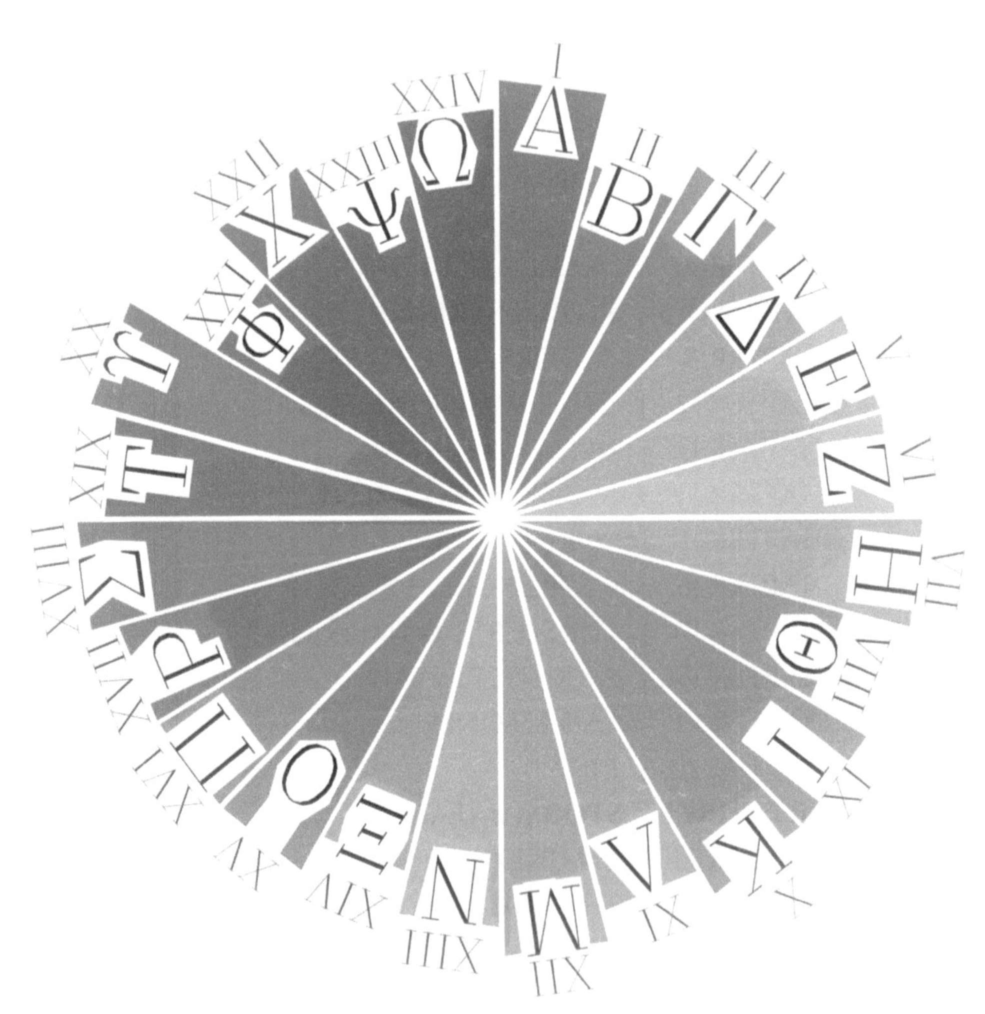

PART ONE:

STORM FRONT

"You may not realize it,
but you have the ability to change
the tide of war through the smallest act of bravery."
—Commander Gorgan Freemantle

THE DAY OF THE NAIL | **CHAPTER 1**

JUNE 15, AD 2186

M

The long line of citizens shuffles forward.

The collective sound of thousands of feet moving in unison resonates through the vast cavern. With so many people crammed together, I feel constricted, suffocated almost. It makes me anxious.

Dust particles glide across the air, dancing around me in a surreal haze. Above my head, the blurry light from the shale ferns illuminates the floating dust in a sickly hue. Their genetically modified stems cast a cold, bioluminescent glow that somehow manages to cut through the sooty haze. The ghoulish green light matches the nauseous feeling in the pit of my stomach.

I'd been standing in line the entire morning.

Waiting...walking...*worrying.*

The hewn stone floor had worn a hole in the sole of my boot about the size of my palm. A rock had wedged its way under my foot hours ago. I hadn't bothered to remove it, thinking the distraction might keep my mind off what was about to happen.

The distraction hadn't worked, though.

The crying around me makes my situation impossible to ignore. Still, the constant moaning had gone on so long that it sounded like white noise in the background now. A buzzing sensation—*like being shellshocked, perhaps*. I no longer flinch at the children's confused stares or the wailing that cuts through the commotion.

This is my home. This is the ARC Borough.

That thought makes me want to laugh despite my situation. The fact that I even bother to call it a home is hilarious. This old cave system beneath what was once known as the Great Plains of North America is, in fact, home to millions of drifters, vagabonds, and beggars. Rather, citizens, I should say, if I'm being polite. The ARC is a mining pit, first and foremost. Then it's a home. The minerals here are a far more precious resource than the inhabitants. Minerals are worth killing for.

The sound of a hammer dropping onto an iron nail rings out. Its metallic ping echoes around the chamber, followed by a scream. The line inches forward. The sound of scraping feet diminishes back to moans.

I'd known for years this day would eventually come. As a child, the rumors seemed like a myth. Some fairytale story told by toothless men gathered around campfires. Some even called it a lie.

The Day of the Nail.

Such a thoughtful name. I find myself wondering who had crafted the poetic phrase.

It's a day that occurs once every year in all the boroughs and districts of this subterranean society. The boroughs are so populated with citizens that it's taken eighteen years for my own day to come. *It'll be here before you know it, young Brindall*, my pa had once said. That was ten years ago, just before he'd been drafted into the Coffin Wars of 2176. I never saw him again.

The hammer drops, and another scream rips through the cavern. The line shuffles forward. The sound of scraping feet lingers.

Soon, my younger brother, Ben, will face his Day of the Nail. My mother, Joyce, has already gone through hers and been cleared. Every citizen is required to face this trial before the age of twenty-four.

Right now, it's my turn, and I must be brave...*for Ben,* I tell myself. I can't let him see my fear, even though he isn't here. I know he looks to me for strength since our father is gone. I do what I can to fill that need. I work the graveyard shift in the mines to provide enough rations for my family. The precious metals, ores, and the occasional rare-earth find keep us alive. By day, I help with the local militia. Ma doesn't like it, but the added credits help cover us when the mining doesn't. Besides, the local militia is the first step to joining the Frontline War against the Southern Coalition. I almost prefer the fighting to the mining, though the sonic chisels and pickaxes are hard on my joints. Being in the militia is a nice change of pace. With all the warring clans and raids, it's every borough for itself. Even though we're all part of the Northern Coalition, the neighboring boroughs will raid minerals if they can, especially for the rare-earth.

Hammer. Scream. The line scraping forward.

I look down at my arms. Scars run the length, mostly from fighting in the militia, though some of it's from mining. My broad shoulders are a constant reminder of a lifetime of swinging a pickaxe. My skin is pale from the lack of sunlight. I brush my long, brown hair back, trying to rake the dirt and mining soot out. I don't need to look in a mirror to see the grime and filth on my face. I just need to look at the citizens surrounding me to understand that a shower and good hygiene are things only the 'Elites' are privy to.

The hammer drops again, and a higher-pitched scream issues forth this time. Maybe a child or perhaps someone's mother or sister.

All of this is for one thing.

The Skylight System.

Minerals, especially rare-earth, are needed for the floating space station in the earth's atmosphere.

The human race's greatest hope, so they say.

Someone named Christian Albright. That's the name I hear in whispers from other citizens. The one responsible for its creation. Also, the reason for the Day of the Nail.

The hammer drops. Another scream. I inch a bit closer.

I hate living in this subterranean borough. But life underground is the only way to survive the storm called the Unbalance. The massive storm has ravaged the Earth's surface for decades, the topography is no longer recognizable. Cities, nature and everything that was once green have been erased. Living below ground is the only option now. Much of the continent's population has migrated to these boroughs, creating the world's most densely occupied region. Food and resources are scarce, and trips to the surface are dangerous. But I often wonder if I would take that risk. If I ever got the chance to flee, would I make the run for freedom?

The hammer, the nail, the scream…

The line shuffling forward.

That sound is the only thing I need to hear. Yes, I would flee, assuming I could manage to remove the signature collar from my neck. I tug at the iron ring, something that's been a part of my life since birth. Every citizen wears one, thanks to the Elites.

I'm close.

I can see the dais through the haze now. There are several tables set upon the stone shelf, backlit like skeletal remains in the dusty light. Each of the three stations has an old wooden table and two rickety chairs on either side. On one side sits a burly man. His right arm bulges with muscles. I can tell this man has spent a lifetime hammering nails into poor souls. So much so that he does his job with little remorse. *Just a job*, I can almost hear him growl.

I feel fear then. Real fear. A cold shiver runs through my body at seeing the man. Like some executioner standing before me on judgment day. But I set my jaw and quickly sweep the feeling from my mind. Surely, I will pass this trial, just like my mother did. Then,

I can get back to life as normal: swinging a pickaxe and fighting in the local militia. Taking care of my family.

But what if I don't pass?

That thought creeps into my mind and roams around, trying to poke holes in my resolve.

What then, young Brindall? the roaming question asks, and I think of my father and what he told me so many years ago. Will I be dragged away from my family at the age of eighteen? I've only heard rumors of what comes next. It's been decades since that's happened, though, maybe longer.

Another loud bang rings out, metal on metal as the nail penetrates flesh. The scream interrupts my thoughts. Then, somehow, I'm next in line. My tall frame is standing over the wooden table. I feel my arms tremble as adrenaline courses through me. I stare straight ahead at the burly man.

Nothing to worry about. I repeat this over and over in my head.

The burly man is wearing some loose-fitting graphene armor and looks at me, then motions for me to sit. I take a deep breath, step forward and stop behind the rickety wooden chair. He places a calloused hand on my shoulder and forces me to sit. I look down to see the fresh blood splattered on the stone floor. Gore and leftover flesh are stuck between the table's cracks. It looks putrid in the greenish light of the shale ferns.

"State your name and cell block," the burly man barks as he arms away some sweat from his bald head. I look into his eyes and see there's no sympathy in his expression or tone. He's blocked out all emotion—I imagine it's the only way anyone could do such a job.

I lean over and show him the coded tattoo on my shoulder.

The burly man scans the tattoo and repeats it out loud to the high-ranking military officer standing next to him. "B. Harper, block 6A." Then he cuffs my wrist with an iron ring and chain. He cinches the chain down and tethers it to a hook anchored into the stone floor. "You know how this works, first the left, then the right hand."

I glare at him and smirk, despite his serious tone. *Yes, of course I know!* I want to scream at him.

If my left hand awakens, they will kill me instantly. If my right hand awakens…

Once again, I'm shocked at how casually burly man goes about his business. I realize there's no sense in holding him responsible for any of this. I close my eyes and prepare myself. It feels like hours pass as I sit there, waiting for the hammer to drop. I see my brother, my mother, my father. I think about my miserable life here in the ARC Borough. Then I somehow find a calm within me and slow my breathing.

Nothing to worry about.

The hammer finally drops. I feel the iron nail pierce my left hand. My eyes snap open to see blood well almost instantly. As much as I try not to, I cry out in pain. My muscles tense, and my left bicep tries to curl instinctively. I want to bring my hand up, wrench it away from the source of pain. But burly man uses his other hand to hold the chain tight. This is the nicest thing he can do for me. It prevents my arm from moving or ripping through the nail and causing more harm. Spots dance in my vision, and I feel my stomach lurch in an attempt to reject that morning's gruel.

"Steady, lad," the burly man says, trying to calm me—a rare moment of empathy, I assume. "We're almost there. Hold tight."

He unclamps the iron rung, then shifts his chair over. He clasps the iron cuff about my right arm and pulls the chain tight again.

"Bite down, lad. It'll help," he says and tethers the chain to the floor.

Despite the pain, I manage to do as he says. I don't close my eyes this time. I won't close my eyes because…

…because you need to see this, a voice whispers.

Then I watch the hammer fall. It seems to drop in slow motion. Burly man's forearm flexes and veins bulge as he brings the hammer down. I hear the shrill ping of metal on metal and feel the iron nail pierce my palm.

And I wait for the pain to erupt.

But this time, it's different. There's a haunting split second where I feel nothing.

Then a searing pain shoots up my arm, much, *much* greater than before. Yet somehow, it's not as painful. I feel my body begin to float, as if gravity lets go of my being. I'm outside of my own physical form now, outside of my soul, I think. Perhaps this is what an out-of-body experience is? The ground below my feet falls away, and the space around me explodes outward. There's a fire in my chest. It burns intensely, so hot and fierce that I can barely breathe. That fire flows in my veins, into my extremities. I feel my head pounding, threatening to explode. I envision my life unfolding before me like an old reel-to-reel film. In fact, I sense there are eons of lives, and not just mine. Thousands of other memories rocket by, ghostly images that flow through my vision. Joy, anguish, rage.

Decades, centuries, millennia.

In the blink of an eye, it's over.

I can hear burly man screaming at me, and I look down at my palm. The iron nail has melted away, burly man's arm is on fire and a bright turquoise light streams from the open wound in my right palm. In the middle of that blinding light is a symbol in the shape of the letter M.

AN UNEASY ARRANGEMENT | CHAPTER 2

M

I sit up with a start, and my vision takes its sweet time to focus.

I'm in a dark holding cell, lying on a stained cot. The greenish light from the shale ferns cast a dreamlike glow about the room, and there are iron bars on one side. The musty smell of wet dirt stings my nostrils as I reach out to the cold stone wall to steady myself.

I'm familiar with stone patterns, especially the ARC Borough's colors and striations. I can tell immediately I'm in a different location by the hewn rock walls in the room. The broad striations of limestone alert me that I'm further north, near the more affluent regions of the ARC Borough.

I swing my legs over the edge of the cot and let my bare feet touch the cool stone floor. It's then that I feel something different about the signature collar around my neck. It's not as bulky and feels much lighter. The old iron collar I'd grown up with has been replaced.

My head starts to pound as I try to make sense of what's happening. My mind races when I recall the hammer, then the nail—then burly man's arm on fire and his screams.

I see a stone pitcher of water on a wooden table. I lurch from the cot and grasp at it. I down the water so quickly that it drips from the corners of my mouth. I try to drown the dirt caked in the back of my throat. Then I notice the bright turquoise glow streaming from my hand, and I drop the pitcher in shock. It shatters on the stone floor. The sound echoes around the small holding cell.

I ignore the broken shards near my bare feet and hold my hand to my face in awe—*in fear*.

No…no. *NO!*

This can't be real!

I practically scream out loud. Panic sets in again as I look at the wound. The hole in my palm is about an inch wide, and the wound has been cauterized. There's dried blood down my arm. I assume it's mine, but it could be mixed with burly man's. I try to convince myself that the bright glow of turquoise light streaming from the hole must be an illusion. And what's the deal with this symbol, this letter M? I'm almost convinced this *is* an illusion, or some cruel joke.

The turquoise light bathes my face as I stand there, too stunned to move or breathe.

I hear the sound of approaching feet and crunching gravel from down the corridor. Two shadowy figures stand just beyond the bars of my chamber. One fumbles with a set of keys, and I can see his hands tremble as he finds the right one. He unlocks the iron gate, and it groans in protest as they step inside the cramped cell.

It's the same military officer from the Day of the Nail. Following close behind him, almost using him as a shield, is an older man in a dingy gray suit. I guess he's in his late sixties. He has gray stubble on his chin and neatly trimmed gray hair to match. Though the suit has seen better days, owning one is considered a sign of prosperity. I assume this man is some important dignitary.

They stop in front of the wooden table and stare silently at me.

The man in the suit kicks at the shards of the broken stone pitcher. "Do you know me, youngster?"

I hear, or rather *sense*, the slight hesitation in his voice. There is a hint of fear in his tone. Odd, I think, that I can sense this now when I couldn't before. I shake my head at the man in the suit. "No. I don't know you, or where I'm at or why I'm here."

The man in the suit looks at the soldier next to him, then nods. The soldier steps aside, and the man approaches me. I stand my ground. I'm at least a foot taller than he is. He looks up at me with his dark gray eyes. A nervous smile creases his stubbled face.

"My name is Grior," he says and holds his hands behind his back. "This is General Nem, of the local militia. You're familiar with the local militia, I believe?"

I nod.

"I imagine this is quite a shock for you," Grior continues. "You woke up this morning, probably expecting to go through the Day of the Nail, then go home and continue your life. Well, that's not going to happen."

"What's going on?" I ask. "Why am I in this cell? I've done nothing wrong. What's happened to me?"

"We're very fortunate!" Grior says. Then I see genuine satisfaction in his expression. His eyes finally light up, and he claps his hands in a sideways motion. His shrill voice echoes around the cell. "The ARC Borough has finally produced one. You, Brindall… you are a chosen one. You are an Immortal!"

"An Immortal? I…I can't be," I stutter in shock. "That's not possible!"

The man holds out a hand and points at my palm and the light flowing from it. "Do you need more proof than this? You're young, but you've heard the legends, no doubt?"

"I don't want this. I can't have this right now. My brother, my mother…they need me—"

"The ARC Borough needs you!" Grior raises his voice. "The North needs you. This hasn't happened…not in a lifetime have I seen this. You are a miracle, Brindall. You can help us. You can *save* us. You *will* save us."

"My family, though, they rely on me."

"Yes, they do. And now, so do all the citizens in the ARC. You are the most important person in all of the borough."

"What does that mean for me, for my family?" I ask. I feel lightheaded again, and my pulse quickens.

"Look, there." Grior points to the wall behind me, and for the first time, I notice an old circular chart. Grior walks close and holds a light to it. The chart is round, roughly carved into the rock wall. I wonder if the crude artwork was done by a former prisoner, one with way too much time on their hands. It's so rudimentary that one might assume it was some prehistoric cave painting composed by an ancient civilization. Around the perimeter of its circumference are twenty-four equally spaced pie-shaped sections. Inscribed inside each section is an odd-looking symbol. Of the twenty-four symbols, I recognize one immediately. It's the M-shaped symbol matching the one in my own palm.

"Yes," Grior whispers when he notices my gaze. It almost sounds like a hiss in the cramped holding cell. "That is your symbol!"

"What is this chart?"

"It is knowledge passed down through the years. We have documented these twenty-four symbols over the decades." Grior finally steps up to me and grasps my hand, holding it up to the light of the shale ferns. "They match…there! You are the M, no question about it. See, near the bottom? On the right side of the chart, just barely. Your right hand is *awakened*. You belong in the North," Grior says and turns to face Nem. "We must start immediately. There is no time to waste."

I pull my hand back from his grasp, unsettled by his touch. "Wait. I have a life. I need to get back to my—"

"Wrong!" Grior snaps, his voice harsh for the first time. "Your life is no longer yours."

"I don't understand."

"Listen to me, Brindall. This is a sign. This is reality. It's not happenstance that you're here. Therefore, you will fulfill your responsibility."

"What are you asking of me?"

"You know what Immortals are meant to do." Grior poses this as a statement, not a question.

I know what Immortals are meant to do. I'd heard that much in the legends. They are used to kill.

"I can see that you don't want to believe it," Grior says, his eyes alive with excitement.

It's all a mistake! I keep repeating this over and over in my head.

Grior holds up a small electronic device. It's smooth, about the size of his hand. "This is a holopad," he explains. "It's linked to the new collar around your neck, which contains a special mental signature device. It's made from the strongest material known, reinforced graphene. If the signal it emits is broken, you will die. But if I press this button, the signal is also broken and, well…"

I feel the collar again and give it a quick tug.

"Uh, I wouldn't tug too hard, Brindall." Grior taps the holopad tentatively.

I'm familiar with the mental signature collars, of course, as are all citizens. But I know Grior isn't lying. This type of collar is reserved for high-profile prisoners and criminals. I'd seen what happens when a prisoner disobeys, too. It could incapacitate, disable…or kill. It was not a pleasant way to die.

Grior watches my expression. "Good! I see that you are aware of the consequences. And one more thing, youngster. If you try to escape or don't do as you're told, your younger brother will be the first to die. Let's move on," Grior says in an almost jovial melody.

Grior walks on without a second thought, and Nem follows close behind. They lead me out of the holding cell and into a lower portion of the complex. The air grows warmer as we descend, and the strata color shifts to deeper maroons and magentas. The musty smell of wet earth diminishes slightly. Soon, we're standing inside a larger chamber. Below are cages where I assume other prisoners are being held. Grior appears to be not only the governor but also the chief negotiator, if that's a fair use of the word.

"We're going to train you," Grior says. He folds his petite hands neatly into his gray vest and beams at me.

"Train?" I ask and look around the space, though I don't see anything other than the cages.

"Not here, Brindall. Your training will begin in a place that's well hidden and for good reason. We can't have the Southern Coalition knowing where we house our greatest assets now, can we?"

"Then why did you bring me here?"

Grior lifts his chin toward the dozens of cages beyond. I look closer, and I can see the citizens within, most of them too weak and emaciated to even acknowledge us. I realize then that Grior is trying to intimidate me.

"You know of the Frontline War? You know why we battle the South, I trust?"

"To guard our territory," I answer, lifting my shoulder in a half shrug.

"That's partially true, yes," Grior replies. "But more territory means more areas to mine. If we can take more, then we will mine more. The ARC Borough is ours, and we will defend it. But we are but one of many vast boroughs in the North. All of those boroughs contribute to the Frontline War."

I knew there were other territories, though I'd never been outside of the ARC Borough. It is forbidden to leave. Grior is giving me more information right now than I've ever had before.

"Our future is mining and always has been. Ores, minerals...*rare-earth!*" Grior's eyes light up when he says this, a greedy lust that's hard to miss. "Mankind will move away from this place, but only the side that wins. Hopefully, a time will soon come when we will no longer live in these dreaded caves. There is a place amongst the stars. It can be ours, if we win the war, win the contract. That reality is within reach, and you can help us achieve it. Wouldn't it be nice to live in a place where nature thrives? Trees, plants, wildlife? We can have that again, if we hold more territory than the South, and time is running out."

I stare at Grior, then look at Nem. "I have no idea what you're talking about."

"We must defend the North from the South, but we must also win more territory than them. That is how the contract will be won. They have armies, they have Immortals. They are fighting, right now as we speak! Territory is being lost, minerals."

"You expect me to go off to someplace I've never heard of? To fight for people I don't even know, people I don't care to know? Maybe even die, for the sake of land?"

"I didn't expect that you'd be excited about it. I imagine your attitude will change, though, if you know you're fighting for the lives of those you love."

I narrow my eyes at Grior, but my heart skips a beat. "Are you threatening my family?"

"You will lead our armies, Brindall. You will learn the ways of the Immortal. You will help the Northern Coalition win this contract."

I don't really know what contract Grior is talking about. But the thought of dying in some far-off place just to acquire more territory, more minerals, makes me queasy. I can't just leave my family behind. They will not survive without me. "What are you offering?"

Grior smiles, his yellow teeth dull in the green light of the shale ferns. "Your family will remain unharmed. I will ensure that they are taken care of."

"Even if I die?" I ask and watch him closely, trying to detect any hint of dishonesty.

"Of course," Grior answers. "Are you not excited to fight for your homeland? I would think it an honor just knowing that you might save us all: give us a chance to live on the Skylight System."

"We seem to be surviving as it is. The ARC Borough has made it this far."

"You have not seen what I've seen, youngster. Nem is a veteran of multiple wars. The Coffin Wars of 2176. The Desolation Wars of 2180. We were lucky then. We are in the midst of another major war, and it's building quickly. Many have died, and many more will. This might be the final great war, the last push for territory. It may well determine who prospers and who is left behind."

"It's not right that this falls on me," I say. I hear the desperation in my own voice now. I feel uneasy again, realizing I'm trapped. If I say no, I have no doubt this man will follow through on his threat to my family. I pull at the collar again. "What choice do I have?"

"I sympathize for you," Grior says, and for the first time, I sense that he truly does. "Other Immortals have gone before you, younger in age even. But what's done is done. Your Day of the Nail is over, and you are an Immortal now. Whether you agree with it or not, you must accept this fate and move forward. If I must force you to action, I will not hesitate. You will fight as the ARC Immortal, or you will die. Make no mistake, Immortal or not. You can be killed. And I will personally see your family follows you into that shallow grave."

WAR ACADEMY | **CHAPTER 3**

BEHOIM

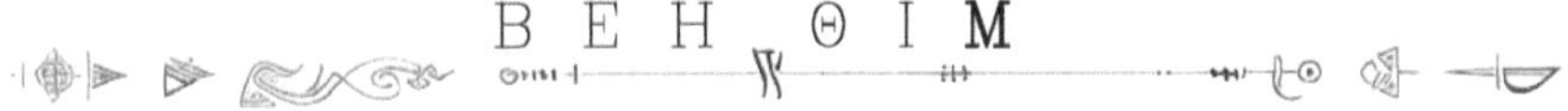

I spend the rest of the day considering from my cramped cell. It's dark and foreboding inside the small iron cage. I'm offered some cold gruel and dirty water but decline, even though my stomach rumbles with hunger. Most of the time I keep my back turned from view and propped against the rusty cage, contemplating. I struggle to find sleep that night as I think about my younger brother and my ma.

What Grior said still rings inside my head—*you are an Immortal now. You must accept this fate and move forward.* I'd known very little about Immortals before the Day of the Nail. However, I'd known about the battle at the frontline. Several of my friends and neighbors had been drafted, shipped off and never seen again. Watching them being rounded up like animals struck close to home. But now that I'm front and center of this very situation, things have taken on a whole new perspective for me. I'm afraid, more for my family than myself.

I swing my legs over the stone bench and stare down at the hole in my palm for the thousandth time. I carefully push my finger through the open wound, half expecting it to melt. As odd as it seems, I feel no different…at the moment. I'm still tired and afraid. I'm still hungry, sad and confused. The prospect of fighting in this war leaves my gut tied in knots. If this is what being an Immortal feels like, then I would rather have my former life back.

But regardless of my situation and the fear I feel, my thoughts keep drifting back to my family, especially my brother, Ben. I imagine him waiting by the door, as he always does, sitting on the dusty porch and drawing pictures in the dirt as he waits for me to come home. I try to think of what I will say to him, struggle to explain what will happen to me. I know then that I won't be able to find the right words, not ones that he will understand.

Grior and Nem return early in the morning. Grior holds the control device in his hand, his finger hovering unsteadily over a button as he watches me. I can somehow sense that Grior wants no more to force a decision from me than I do. His nervous attitude is evident as he stands there from behind the bars of my cage. Even knowing his reluctance, I still have no desire to test my luck or risk harm to my family. If I try to run or fight, Grior will use the collar. Then he will go after my family. I am certain of this.

"Good morning, youngster. Have you made your decision yet?" Grior stands behind Nem, his voice trembling slightly. I sense the fear and excitement in his tone.

I wait, eyeing them both. Inside, I feel anger at my situation, though. I realize what I'm about to do. I have no choice but to agree to their demands. I calm my emotions and keep my expression steady, though. "I want your word that nothing will happen to my family," I say and stand tall as I face them behind the bars of my cage.

"I give you my word," Grior says without hesitation.

I continue to watch him but let out a silent sigh of relief, hoping neither of them notice it.

Grior places his hands behind his back, a smile on his face now. "If you become the ARC Immortal, our champion, then your family will be well taken care of."

"When will I return home?"

Grior chuckles and looks at Nem. "I don't think you understand, Brindall. You are an Immortal now. After you are trained, you will have enhanced abilities. You will know things and accomplish things that others may only dream of. You cannot simply leave this role. You'll serve until the war ends or until you die."

I feel my mouth drop open in disbelief. My eyes grow wide in shock, and I don't care if Grior or Nem notice. My head lulls forward and hits the bars of my cage. I barely catch myself before my legs give out. I hadn't considered this part of the bargain, but now it makes sense that they would never let me go. I am viewed as an asset, one that will take resources to train, no less. Of course, the Northern Coalition would expect me to fight to the end. The shock settles in as the two men watch me silently, no remorse on their faces.

"You are too valuable to work in the mines anymore," Grior says. "As for your family, I will arrange a visit before you leave for training. You will soon begin to notice things in a different light."

"How do you know? I thought you'd never met another Immortal before?"

"I haven't…in person. But I know the traits. I've heard the stories from neighboring boroughs. There are other Immortals out there. You will not be alone."

I place my hands in my pockets, then look down at my worn boots and dusty trousers. The life I have known isn't much, but it's what I'm used to, and I feel reluctant to let go. Am I really prepared for war? One I know nothing about?

"If you help us win this war, only then can you return to your family. You can live in the Skylight System with them. If we win, Brindall, you will live like a god amongst the stars."

I look up at Grior and Nem and detect a split second of fear in them both. Was it because they were afraid that I might reject their offer to fight? Did they fear me and who I'd become? As much as I hate to give in to this man, I already know I have no other option.

"Alright, Grior. You win."

Later that day, I'm allowed to meet with my family. I'm brought into a small holding cell with a stone table. Thankfully, Grior agrees to remove my chains, for Ben's sake. I sit, hunched over the table, and talk in hushed tones, trying to calm Ben. My ma is on the verge of tears. But she understands that she needs to remain composed for Ben. The look I give her reinforces that fact.

"It's not fair," Ben says, and his high-pitched voice echoes around the cell. He balls his tiny fists as he stares at me, his eyes red. I can see that he refuses to cry, though. His anger is overriding his fear, for the moment at least. "You should be coming home. Why are they making you do this, Brin?"

Mother looks at him then to me for help, unsure what to say. All I can do is grip Ben's tiny shoulder and give him a gentle squeeze. "Hey, don't you give up on me now, got it?"

Ben holds up my right hand. He stares at it through his puffy red eyes. I can see that he's confused and unnerved at seeing the turquoise light and the hole in my palm. "You're still the same ol' Brin to me," he whispers. "I don't care what they say you are."

"That's my guy," I say and give him a playful shake.

"Are you sure about this, Brin?" my mom asks, and I know she's thinking about Father. "It seems dangerous."

"There's no other choice, Ma. Grior's forcing me to do this. I have to go."

"I don't want you to go away!" Ben pleads. "Not like Father did."

"It doesn't work that way, Benji." I tussle his hair and do my best to make light of the situation. Ben may be young, but he isn't fooled. "I know this is confusing," I continue. "It's going to be hard for me too. If there was something else I could do, you know I would."

Mother grips my shoulder and then runs her hand through Ben's thick, curly hair. She pulls us both into a hug. I notice how her gray eyes look so tired, hopeless. I know she's worried as much for Ben as she is for me. Leaving to fight in this war, this so-called *game* for territory, wasn't in the cards for any of us.

I eventually pull back from her. "Try not to worry about me, Ma. I'll be fine. I always manage a way, right? Grior has promised to take good care of you both, as long as I stick to this agreement."

"For how long, though?" she asks. "Did they say when you'll return?"

"As long as it takes, I guess. It's supposed to end soon, I hear. Though, I don't know when. There'll be training, and some combat they say. I'm not sure what to expect, but I'll try to write and let you know how things are going. How does that sound?" I give them both a weak smile.

Nem steps into the cell and places a hand on my shoulder. I feel his strong grip and understand that he doesn't enjoy what's happening to me any more than I do. "It's time."

I give my mom a hug. Then I kneel and grip Ben by the shoulders and look into his eyes. I hold him steady until I have his full attention. Ben's eyes begin to water, but he doesn't look away. "Take care of Mom, Benji, you hear me? I need you to be strong."

Ben wipes his eyes but nods. He hugs me one last time, and I feel an ache in the pit of my gut. Hopefully, this isn't the last time I'll see him, but a disturbing voice in my head begins to whisper, and doubt creeps in. When I leave the cell with Nem, I don't look back. I hear Ben begin to cry.

That evening, I'm herded onto a packed transport and sent on my way out of the ARC Borough.

The highspeed transit glides smoothly along the charged rail so fast that my stomach lurches. I try not to think of Ben as I'm pressed into the back of my seat. The sound of the electrified rail sizzles from below, and I grip the arms of my chair nervously.

As I adjust to the g-forces, a display in the seat's headrest in front of me begins to play a hologram. What I assume is a newsreel from decades past shows historical footage of the Unbalance. Over the years, the unnatural storm had grown in size and intensity and blanketed most of the planet's surface. In turn, the human race had been forced into subterranean dwellings like the ARC Borough. What I didn't know was that there were some thirty boroughs, all linked together through a tunnel system. This was what made up the Northern Coalition. The entire North American continent's population had mostly relocated to the boroughs, creating huge masses of overpopulation. I scan the three-dimensional map in amazement. Suddenly, I'm learning things I'd never known before and wonder if the Coalition has purposely kept these facts hidden from most citizens. I'm beginning to see how vast the underground network is and how small my previous world once was.

Moving through the caverns, I get glimpses of the storm clouds above through openings in the cave's ceiling. These are areas where I assume crews had overmined in years past, causing the earth to collapse. The debris had been cleared long ago to make way for the rail system, perfect since that territory could no longer be mined. I begin to understand how valuable the underground land really is. Like connected dots, the vast peepholes in the ceiling give me brief glimpses at something I'd only heard tales of. The Skylight System. Through the storm clouds, I can see the floating outline of its framework. Like some hollowed-out moon in the earth's atmosphere, its enormous steel belts look like some giant's denuded ribcage. I count nine belts surrounding a small glowing orb that shines like a miniature star. Some areas of the belts are lit up, where I assume construction is taking place. According to Grior, the Skylight System is the driving force behind all the wars and minerals. Apparently, whoever controls the most land will win some sort of contract. I don't understand how something as trivial as a patch of dirt can cost so many lives, though, including my father's.

But it was as it always had been—humans fighting over resources. The video lays it all out for me. I can clearly see how past generations simply couldn't figure it out, leaving future generations to clean up the mess. This tribal nature had continued over the past century and a half, splitting the North American continent into two factions along the 37th parallel—the North Coalition and the South Coalition. As fate would have it, I'm now entangled in the middle of this conflict. But now that I am involved, I'm eager to learn more.

"Approaching classified boarding station," a computerized voice chirps over the intercom.

"Better hold on," a guard seated next to me says. "Deceleration is a bit bumpy into the Fault Line Borough."

The transit bounces a few times, rattling my teeth, then slows so quickly that I'm thrown forward into my harness. It constricts around my chest and torso with such force that I struggle to breathe. The transit lowers slightly, then skids to a halt. I'm unbuckled by the guard, then pushed into a line with others and filed out. We step onto a boarding platform, which is crammed with hundreds of other people, most wearing military fatigues.

I stand in awe as people surround me, talking and chatting like I don't exist. I assume most of these people are coalition employees, though I see a few peasants dressed like myself. Above, a high, domed ceiling arches over the entire subterranean port city. I wonder how on earth it's held up, since I can see no cables or structure. It's like magic is supporting the massive dome. Beyond, I see traces of lightning flashes: vibrant blues and yellows that literally zap the stasis dome and dissipate immediately. The surface is white, a milky texture almost, and buzzes with static. Although it is translucent, no rain seems to pass through it.

Around the enormous circular pit are the city's walls, with hundreds of openings carved into the stone. This borough is, without a doubt, on the higher end compared to the ARC Borough. The citizens are less gritty. Their clothes are actually clean, and I'm amazed to see no dirt on their faces or hair. Missing is the constant sound of mining. I've become so accustomed to hearing the sonic chisels and low booms that it takes me a second to adjust to my surroundings. The technology is a step up as well. Glass facades cover the perimeter of the pit, indicating high-end office buildings, I assume.

Large tunnels lead out from the space, and all manner of transits are boarding and departing the platform. I assume now that this city is a transportation hub. I even see some flying vehicles, known as skiffs, zipping by overhead. Though they're mainly large frigates loaded with materials, some are smaller private transports, and very expensive. I watch the skiffs exit directly through large airlocks in the stasis dome, which spiral open into the stormy skies beyond. I can only assume their destination is to the Skylight System.

Soon, I'm escorted off the large boarding platform by a dozen or so guards. I feel like a convicted prisoner with the cuffs around my wrists. Wealthy citizens stare at me with looks of disgust. I struggle to understand all the precautions since I'm still wearing the signature collar. That alone is enough to prevent me from fleeing.

Another group of armed guards approaches us, and I'm handed off to them. These guards wear a different uniform and badging, ones that look more official. They lead me to a small cavern along a narrow thoroughfare, and the sound of transports fades away.

We walk along a thin highway made of strengthened graphene, which is something rare in my district due to the cost. Its thin, transparent surface is reinforced with carbon fiber and allows for longer spans. I'm marched through another chamber that opens up to a smaller stasis dome some twenty meters overhead. Like the larger one, this one allows some diluted light in but keeps the wind and rain out. We walk across a roughly hewn stone dais that's polished to a mirror finish. Our group finally comes to a stop, and we wait silently.

I want to turn to the guard next to me and ask what's happening. I feel a nervousness in the pit of my stomach again, that same uncertain feeling I had on the Day of the Nail. I think how long ago that feels already and realize that my journey is only beginning.

We continue to stand in silence, and I begin to notice more detail about my surroundings. The dais is about twenty meters in diameter, with walls reaching up to the dome above. The space beyond seems to be divided up into smaller rooms, similar to an apartment. Around the middle of the space are several old rugs and a library of books off to one side. Beyond is a kitchen and a table and chairs with what looks to be several sparring mats next to it. Around the perimeter are sleeping quarters and a firepit in the center of the complex.

Several people enter the space with an armed escort of guards wearing the same uniform. I count three boys and two girls who, I guess, range in age from early teens to perhaps late teens. It's hard not to notice their right hands, which are like mine. I see the holes with a glowing light from them. The colors range from red to yellow to green. The guards remain silent as a woman enters the space. She walks up to our group and dismisses the guards.

I watch the lady approach and how she seems so confident in her motions, her directness. Her gait is brief and measured, though her age is probably sixty years or greater. In contrast to the higher-class citizens I've seen here, she wears a dirty robe that looks to be silk but is stained from long use in this dusty environment. Her light cloth boots are also dirty and worn and frayed around the hems. Her hair is a dove gray, tied into a topknot, and her face is touched with subtle age lines. She has dark skin and a stern gaze that seems to stare into my soul. I feel a sense of authority and wisdom from her presence that

I cannot explain. Yet despite her air of command, I also detect an underlying, motherly nature.

"Good day to you all. My name is Miss Henak," the lady says. Her voice is low and unwavering, warning us not to question her. It reverberates in the large, cavernous space, meandering off into a light echo. "I will be your instructor over the next few weeks," she continues. "This war academy will be your home until I deem you are ready to move on. You are Immortals now. I guess we will see if that is true, won't we? At some point, you will face other Immortals on the battlefield, and you may find yourself in a fight to the death. Will you be prepared for such a battle? I'm here to make sure you are. Your training will not be easy, and I will not be lenient on you."

I feel my hands start to sweat at that. *A fight to the death with another Immortal?* That thought still hasn't sunk in. I'm beginning to understand the possibilities as I stand there among the other kids. I wonder how many Immortals are out there and what their level of training is. I wonder if these kids are also instructed to fight for their homes and families, too. Have they been threatened like I have? Are they also worried that if they lose, their families will be sacrificed?

Miss Henak walks in front of us. Then she stops and takes each of our hands to examine them. She carefully looks at each, inspecting the glowing holes. "Hmm…letters…symbols. Yes, I see that we have a variety here. Reds, greens, yellows…all of the colors align, as they should. Follow me!"

Henak leads us to the center of the complex and into the stacks of books piled on the stone floor. Surrounding the ten-meter-wide pit are several walls with large maps, charts, and other documents pinned up. I've never had an education, but I know how to read well enough. However, some of the symbols on the charts look to be written in a different language.

Henak pauses in front of one large wall. Etched into it is the same chart Grior showed me. "Do any of you recognize this chart?" Henak waits for an answer, her hands held behind her back.

I look at the other five kids, who glance at each other in confusion. I almost say something, but then decide to keep quiet. There's no sense in drawing attention to myself just yet.

"No matter," she says. "Let's get introductions out of the way, then we'll go over your schedules. Left to right…you first." Miss Henak motions to a tall, dark-skinned boy, and he steps forward. The hole in his hand glows a light green with a round-looking symbol floating within. His black, curly hair hugs his head like a tightly knit sweater, and matching scruff covers his chin. He's tall with broad shoulders, likely from years of working in the mines, like me. He grins as he faces her. It's a smile so infectious that the rest of us can't help but smile back. It makes me wonder how someone living in such conditions like this can find anything to be happy about.

"Name's Vernault Steward. Friends call me Vern, though. I think it's okay to call me Vern here, I hope. I'm sixteen and live…*lived*, in the Gruelough Borough in the far northeast, in case you're wonderin'. I've a mother and two sisters." Vern looks at Henak, and she motions to the next in line. Vern takes a seat on the old rug, still smiling.

The next kid stands. A girl, some fifteen or sixteen, I guess. She has red hair and pale skin, and the wound in her hand glows yellow with a letter H. She's athletic in build, narrow-waisted, and has a strong upper body for a girl. Like the rest of us, she wears dirty trousers, a ripped poncho, and worn-out black boots. I can see now that access to showers and bathing is rare in other boroughs as well. The girl has a worried look on her face, sad almost. Her skittishness is hard to miss. She tugs at her knotted, red hair, running her fingers through it and trying to flatten it down in a presentable manner as Henak stares at her with hawkish eyes.

"Go on, dear," Henak prods. "We won't bite you."

The girl still hesitates, then places her hands behind her back and clears her throat. "Grishum Carter. My name is Grishum, but I go by Grish. I'm from the Crater Borough in the middle." I notice her accent as she speaks but can't quite place its origin. She continues. "No family, they're all dead. That's all I have to say." Grish quickly sits down and pulls her knees to her chest and buries her face.

A few seconds pass before Henak motions to the girl next to her. She steps forward, flashes us a quick grin and places her hands on her hips. The light from her hand is illuminated in a dark orange color with the letter B. As I watch her, it feels like a ray of sunlight is shining down from the heavens, and I'm suddenly at a loss. Something in her kind expression takes my breath, and I can't turn away from her. She's tall for a girl, with blonde hair in ponytails and inquisitive greenish hazel eyes that exude confidence, unlike Grish.

"My name is Shiloe Van Saint. I'm not really excited to be here, honestly. I'm from Hammer Fall, in the north. I work as a balancer, or I did. That's someone who counterbalances mining loads on frigates. I have a younger brother. Mother and Father died long ago. I like to paint. Anything else?"

Henak holds her gaze, as if assessing Shiloe's directness. "Thank you, Shiloe. That will be all." The blonde-haired girl takes a seat on the mat and looks straight ahead, not bothering to address anyone else.

Henak nods to the next kid, a large boy who is broader and taller than any of us. He has scars on the side of his face and neck, and his hand glows a light orange with the letter E. I can already see that this kid has been trained as a pit fighter, which is a sport for entertainment. Usually, the guardians or parents train their kids for the extra money. I'd known a few in my own district. Life expectancy for paid fighters isn't great, and the ones who managed to survive their youth normally had permanent disabilities or psychological side effects. It's a horrible way to live, and I feel a moment of pity for the boy. I'm suddenly thankful that I'd never been pressed into it.

"My name is Pendrake McLeary. I go by Drake." Like Grishum, he, too, has the same thick accent, though it's a bit slurred, thanks to the scarring on his right cheek and neck. I guess that he's close to my age, maybe sixteen or seventeen. The boy tugs at his dirty shirt, scratching the area of scars beneath his iron collar. "I'm from the same borough as Grish. My father makes me do it for the money, so don't bother askin', cause I can see the looks already. These scars are from him, not the fightin'. Don't feel sorry for me, that's all I ask. Being here is the best thing that could've happened to me. I'm happy right now, haven't been this happy…well…never, I suppose. It's great to meet you all." Drake says this without a smile or any emotion, though, and plops down on the mat.

I see the others smile at Drake. It makes me realize that some of them are probably happy to be away from their former surroundings or families. Not everyone has loved ones like I do, which makes me think of Ben and my ma again.

But Miss Henak doesn't smile as she looks at us. "You may not be grinning for long. If you think this is a good break, or some sort of good fortune, you're mistaken." She turns to the next boy and motions to him.

He is short and skinny, almost wiry, reminding me of a feral cat. His right hand is lit in an emerald green with the letter I. He seems to be the youngest in our group, perhaps in his early teens. He wears a pair of glasses, and the wire frames are bent in several places. He has wavy, reddish-blond hair, though it's hard to tell the actual color from all the soot. His cheeks are flushed bright red like he's just finished a race.

"My name is Tripp Collins. I'm from the north central area, Top Knot Borough. We mine a lot of rare-earth in that area. Everyone works in the mines where I'm from, but I'm in the accounting offices. I hate where I live. I don't like my parents." Tripp doesn't wait for

Henak to dismiss him. He turns and sits down and crosses his short legs.

Henak doesn't seem to mind. She finally walks over to stand directly in front of me. She looks up into my eyes, as if trying to probe my thoughts. I watch as she crosses her arms and taps her lips with an index finger, considering for several seconds. I continue to wait for her to say something, and the silence becomes a bit uncomfortable. I wonder what she's thinking, wonder if I'm in some sort of trouble perhaps.

Eventually, she straightens and places her hands behind her back. "Brindall Harper of the M class. What do you have to say?"

It takes me by surprise that she knows my name, and I hesitate for a split second as I look down at the lady. "I…I go by Brin. I have a younger brother and a mom. My father died in the Coffin Wars a long time ago. I live in the ARC Borough. It's not far from the front lines, actually." I stand patiently, waiting for Miss Henak to dismiss me. She finally nods and motions for me to sit.

"You've all lost someone close to you," Henak says. She folds her hands before her as she paces in front of us. "These wars have gone on for too long. They have taken a toll on us all. It isn't fair that you face such a trial, and I'm afraid it is only beginning—"

"Pardon me, Miss Henak," I ask, hoping that I won't be reprimanded for the interruption. "What is it that you all expect from us?"

Vern suddenly speaks up. "Yeah. I wanna know what's going on. We get hauled off like prisoners, taken away from our families, with no explanation, then we're told we have to fight in some war we barely know about. What gives, man?"

"Just because we have glowing holes in our hands, we have to fight?" Shiloe says. "Vern's right. We've been threatened, our families threatened. There's more to all of this—"

"That's quite enough for now!" Henak says in a raised voice. It's subtle but loud enough to make us all go silent. "I will answer those questions soon. What I can tell you is that you are here to learn, and it is my job to teach you as much as I can. Whether or not I agree with your situation isn't important. Just know that this is a safe place, shared by all the Northern Boroughs. Consider this a neutral borough, if you will. Here, you will learn more about who you are and what you are expected to do. However, it's a short period of time, and you'll be pushed to your limit. There's a lot to take in and very little time. How much you learn depends on you alone. It is your responsibility, and I cannot help you once you leave this place. If you wish to help yourself, your family and those who live in the North, then you must stay focused. The two weeks we have together is precious time. Don't waste it." Henak walks among us and stops to stare at us as she talks, reminding me of a stern schoolteacher. "What I can promise you is this! You will face an array of deadly mech units. You will face other Immortals who will be out to kill you. If you expect to survive, you will pay attention to what I have to say."

"How come we're limited to just two weeks then, if this is so important?" Shiloe asks.

"That is all the time we are allowed. The collective North funds this operation, and they are anxious to get you to the battlefield. Your daily routine will be balanced between meditation, physical training and learning traits specific to you. You will not spend much time sleeping, there will be time for that after the war."

"Meditation?" Drake asks.

Henak ignores him. "You will practice and live here during this phase of your training. Consider this your new family. Your lives will depend on that bond if you want to defeat the other Immortals."

"Other Immortals?" I ask. "Do you mean the ones from the South?"

"Oh, yes. There are more." Henak moves over to one of the walls and brings up a three-dimensional hologram. It's the circular chart again, and she points to it. "Here, we see twenty-four symbols, yes? All of you have a symbol; look on the right side of this chart. Do you see?"

We all look around at each other and the glow coming from our right hands and the symbols.

"You've heard about Immortals," Henak continues. "What you haven't heard is there are two *types* of Immortals. Those on the left side of this chart and those on the right side. Those on the left fight for the South." Henak pauses again, letting that sink in. "You all must work as a team if you expect to defeat the opposing Immortals. The more you train together, the stronger you will become. The winning side takes all, in this game. Territory is the key, and whoever holds more of it at the Winter Solstice deadline will receive the contract. The prize, you ask? The right for our people to settle on the Skylight System. The others will be left behind. Who wants to be left behind?"

Of course, I'd already heard some of this from Grior. Apparently, the others hadn't, based on their shocked expressions.

"So, that's what this war is all about?" Shiloe asks. "The right to move to the Skylight System?"

Henak gives her a stern look and crosses her arms. "Do you want your family left behind? Your friends? Do you want to be left behind?"

Once again, we all look around at each other but say nothing.

"You asked what is worth dying for. The answer: the hope of moving to the Skylight System for you and all of us in the North. There isn't room for both sides. That's a battle worth fighting. That's why you are here. That's why this training facility exists and why the North Boroughs pay a hefty price to develop Immortals. You all represent our greatest hope, our greatest asset. There's a large investment placed upon you all, and the North will expect a lot from each of you in return. More territory equals more resources. We must win that contract. You fight and win, then the prize for us is great."

"No pressure, right?" Vern jokes.

"This is no laughing matter," Henak says and lowers her gaze at him. "Ahead is a deadline, and very soon, you all will begin the game of your life. I have only a limited time to train you to the best of my ability."

"Is this really a game?" I ask. "I don't understand why it's referred to as one."

"This is for keeps, man," Vern chimes in. "But it's no game. And whoever calls it one is wrong, at least in my book."

I ponder the gravity of it and everything Henak's told us. A group of teenage kids who've just learned of their new abilities are being thrust into a war they know nothing about and are expected to fight to the death to attain territory for people they don't even know. In return, assuming we don't die, we're granted the right to move to the fabled Skylight System. It sounded great, if we weren't being asked to sacrifice our lives. It appears as though the aspirations of the entire Northern Coalition will fall upon our small group. The six of us will decide the fate of millions of people. But I already know that not all of us are making it out alive.

"What exactly is it inside of us that makes us special?" I ask.

"No one knows, to be exact," Henak answers. "We know that it's a light, an inner spirit of some sort. It grants special powers and abilities to its host. Your physical form is reinforced by this inner light. But you can still be harmed or even killed. And when that happens, the inner light will find another host, one that suits its preference. That light cannot be extinguished, even though the host can. I intend to show you as much as I can, so be patient. More knowledge is coming. We start first thing in the morning."

A GATHERING OF IMMORTALS | **CHAPTER 4**

B E H Θ I M

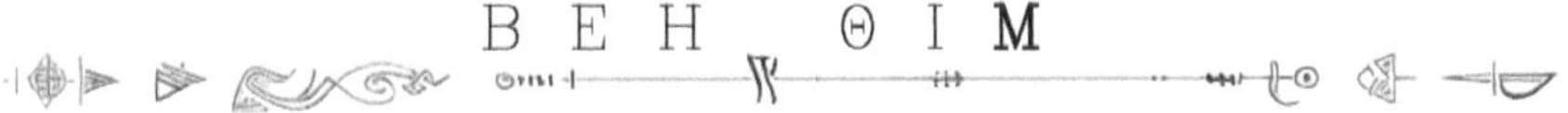

The six of us are placed in the small apartments positioned around the perimeter of the training facility. The proportions of the apartments are uncomfortable, with tiny spaces and roughhewn stone walls springing up from the cobbled floor. But the open ceiling helps lessen the cramped feel and allows me to see the dome above. The intermittent flashes of lightning strobe into every crevasse of the training complex, an ominous reminder that there's no place to hide.

I stay up late into the night, sitting at a rickety old table in the living space while gazing out the translucent stasis dome. I think about my family, mainly Ben, and wonder what he might be doing at that moment. It helps keep my thoughts off of what's to come. But the day's events keep creeping back into my thoughts no matter how hard I try to evict them.

What will happen if I fail?

What will become of my family, and will Grior really uphold his threat toward them? Soon, other thoughts float into my head. Will mining for minerals no longer be required once the Skylight System is complete? If the North loses and we're left behind, what will become of the ARC Borough and our way of life? But my thoughts keep returning to my family, especially Ben.

A movement to my left breaks my thoughts. I turn to see the blonde-haired girl from that day's orientation enter the living room. She walks over and stands in front of me, then pauses, as if she's about to ask for permission to sit. Instead, she pulls out a chair, plops down and rests her chin in her hands and stares at me.

"Brindall, right?" she says. It's direct, no pleasantries or formalities. I can tell immediately that this girl, Shiloe, is a no-nonsense type of person. I know the type, not that it bothers me, though.

I return her stare and somehow sense that her attitude doesn't match her personality. Despite her outward directness, I can detect kindness. Though she's hidden it well, I understand why: kindness is considered a weakness in the boroughs.

"You can call me Brin," I say and hold out a hand.

"I'm Shiloe," she says and hesitates for the first time. But she shakes my hand anyway, somewhat awkwardly.

I look around for the others, but everyone's already gone to bed. "Couldn't sleep?" I ask with a slight tilt of my head and a bit of sarcasm.

She chuckles and wrinkles her forehead. "Kinda difficult after hearing what Miss Henak said, don't you think?"

I grin in agreement. "What area are you from again?"

"Hammer Fall. It's not far from the ARC Borough, I think."

"I couldn't say. I don't make it out much. Remind me what a balancer is. I've never heard that term before, don't think we have any in the ARC Borough."

Though I'm not much for small talk, it's nice to have someone to chat with. Besides, it's something I'll have to get better at, and I might as well start now.

Shiloe crosses her arms. I can see that she, too, is simply trying to make conversation, probably to keep her mind preoccupied. I'm not the only one worried, it seems.

"It's someone who weighs mining loads," she says. "The weight of each frigate has to be balanced out perfectly before it's shipped. Otherwise, it could throw the frigate's flight path off or even wreck the skiff. You probably do have balancers, and you just didn't know it. But why don't you be honest with me, Brin? You don't really care where I'm from or what I did in my borough, do you?"

I'm caught off guard by the abrupt change in tone, but I shrug it off. "No, not really. Why not just say what's on both our minds? We're afraid. It's okay. I don't mind saying it first, if that helps."

She gives me a long look, then smirks. "Directness. See? That's better. You'd think, after all I've been through, this wouldn't bother me as much."

"Well, it's not every day that you find out you're an Immortal. I would call you crazy if you weren't worried. It's been tough on all of us. But this is new, and new can be scary. None of us are prepared for what's happening right now. I don't mean to sound harsh, but we'd better get used to it. This is our new life, whether we like it or not."

Shiloe pushes her lips to one side as she stares at me. "My, Brin. Why don't you tell me what you really think? So, you're a calm one, I get why Henak knows your name now."

"What's that supposed to mean?"

"She's already singled you out. Now I see why. Anyway, I believe her when she says we're all dead unless we work as a team. I normally keep to myself, but I can see the writing on the wall. I'm going to step outside of my comfort zone because I'd prefer to live. After our introductions, I knew you were the one to approach first."

I return Shiloe's matter-of-fact gaze, my arms still crossed. I wonder if she has a point—was Henak already singling me out? Then I stand and walk out of the tiny living room. "Follow me. I want to show you something."

Shiloe narrows her eyes in confusion before standing and following me.

I walk to the central space, working my way around the books stacked on the floor. I stop in front of the circular chart on the stone wall and point at it with my chin. "What do you make of it? If there really are twenty-four of us out there, people they call Immortals, how come I only counted six of us today? Does that mean there's the same amount on the opposite side?"

"Good question. I guess we're gonna find out soon. Something tells me we'll know more at the end of this two-week training session."

"Yeah, maybe." I step closer to the chart, beginning to notice more detail now. "It's like a clock or something. See? There are twenty-four Roman numerals, like daylight and nighttime hours. One through twelve on the right half, and thirteen through twenty-four on the left."

Shiloe stands next to me, peering in behind my shoulder. Then she reaches out and traces the strange symbols next to each Roman numeral with her fingertips. "You're right. There are warmer colors on the right half and cooler ones on the left."

We stand there next to each other as lightning flashes continue from above. It's the closest I've ever been to a girl, alone, anyway. I feel suddenly awkward standing near her and clear my throat. "How old were you, when you heard about the legend, I mean?"

"Fairly young, when my mother was still around. But it wasn't until a few days ago that I found out more. I passed through the Day of the Nail. Afterward, I woke up on the transport with no explanation and this new collar." She gives it a frustrated tug, and it beeps with a warning.

I watch Shiloe as she speaks, still trying to determine if I can trust her or the others with my life. She notices my stare and starts to say something but then shakes her head and takes a deep breath.

"What's wrong?" I ask.

"Well, I don't know…I mean, we just met, and I don't want to come off sounding weird."

"Are you talking about our senses?" I say. "Yeah, I've felt it too. Maybe that's part of becoming an Immortal? I guess we could ask

Miss Henak. Sounds like she's worked with other Immortals before. I think it's all tied together somehow."

"Maybe," Shiloe replies. "Not sure I trust her or anyone just yet. Don't you get the sense there's something more they're not telling us?"

"Who? Miss Henak?"

"And this Northern Coalition. They're lying to us, Brin."

Shiloe has picked up what I've also noticed. Her senses, like mine, are somehow heightened now. I'd detected subtle wavers in Grior. I got the same vibes from Henak too.

"I get what you're saying, Shiloe. There are things they probably don't want us to know. But I think we can trust Miss Henak. We may not have a choice. Eventually, we're going to have to trust each other too. We won't survive if we don't."

Early the next morning, Miss Henak wakes us and leads everyone to the center of the complex. I'm beginning to see that this will be our main gathering space. It's the same area where Shiloe and I had talked the night before. The books, charts and maps are informational tools that I assume she will use to train us.

Henak pulls up the same three-dimensional hologram with the chart. "I mentioned yesterday that you are all known as Immortals," Henak begins as we sit around on the worn rug in front of her. She is dressed in a dark cloak today, her hair pulled into a bun, her eyes just as stern as the day before. "There are two distinct groups of Immortals: those on the right half of this chart and the other twelve on the left half. You are different from those on the left. We know that you all share similar abilities, but the color of their light falls opposite of the spectrum you see here. The darker colors, or the evening colors, tend to lean toward those unethical moral values, as far as we can tell.

This type of mannerism can be harmful to you, or your 'inner light,' I should say. Does this make sense?"

The six of us look around at each other in confusion. Grish, Drake and Tripp sit across from Vern, Shiloe and me. I finally look at Henak and speak up. "Sorry, Miss Henak. I don't think we follow you. Are you saying that if we do bad things, we could be harmed?"

"You host an entity within you. For reasons unknown to us, this entity has selected you for a specific reason. It resides in you because of who you are. Your essence is partial to it. If that tendency or persona changes too drastically, then it may decide to leave. If that were to happen, your essence would fade, and you will eventually die."

"So. Don't do bad things," Vern says in a half-joking tone, though I catch a hint of concern in his voice.

"That's not exactly what I'm saying," Henak says, folding her hands in front of her. "I'm saying to do the things that feel right to *you.* You'll know when it's the right decision because your inner voice speaks. If you've not experienced that yet, then just wait. It will."

"The same holds true of the opposing Immortals, I assume?" Shiloe asks.

"Indeed. So, don't expect any sympathy from them. Now, here are your symbols, and the ones that we know of on the South, at the moment." She selects a portion of the hologram. "All of your symbols have a name. They were once known as the Greek alphabet. Whatever knowledge was attached to that explanation has been lost to time. Thanks to the great storm, The Unbalance, much of the knowledge we once knew was wiped away."

"These symbols were once an alphabet? That's interesting," Tripp says, and I can see his attention perk up.

"Yes, an ancient language," Henak continues. "Now, on the right side, there are your six symbols—Beta, Heta, Iota, Lamba, Mu, and

Epsilon. There are also Immortals in the South, though we don't know which ones and how many. Any Immortal on the left, had they been discovered on the Day of the Nail here in the North, would've been killed immediately."

I'm shocked to hear this, though it makes sense now. I'd known that had my left hand 'awakened,' I'd be dead right now. Life is unfair, especially in the boroughs. But some citizens who'd faced the Day of the Nail were no more than children. That meant even a toddler, if identified as an opposing Immortal, would have been executed. Of course, I'm sure the South has similar rules as well.

Henak moves on with little remorse, it seems, as though this is simply another reality of war. "Now. Your main source of knowledge will come from this book." She holds up an old, tattered book with leather bindings. It looks to be ancient, and it's practically falling apart. "This is called the Book of Vishmu. And everything we know about Immortals is written within. Some of this knowledge is ancient, and we cannot interpret it completely. But some of it we do understand. Be gentle with this, please," she says and hands the book to me.

I leaf through the worn tome. There are pages missing, which I assume were lost to the ages. Within the remaining pages are more charts, math and other strange languages. I wonder how on earth Henak means to teach us such complex things.

"You will regain your energy through meditation, or Vishmu, which is an ancient practice," Henak continues. "Some of you might have experienced something similar on the Day of the Nail, after your conversion ritual."

"Conversion?" Grish asks. "The Day of the Nail was a…a conversion ritual?"

"Essentially, yes. You got it. You will meditate twice a day in that area over there." She motions at some old rugs on the opposite side of the complex. "Here, we will spend time studying Vishmu, much of it from this book, but not all of it. And over there, you will practice your physical training, combat and fighting abilities." She directs our attention to the opposite side, where I see some sparring equipment. Then she claps to regain our attention. "Now, I don't want you all to think that fighting is the most important part of this because it isn't. Your sparring ability is just part of the larger picture. Honestly, it is, in fact, less important than Vishmu and meditation. Got it?"

"Can I ask another question?" Grish says. She pushes her red hair to the side and gives the mental signature collar around her neck a tug. "When do these come off?"

Henak gives Grish a long look, and I can see some hesitation in her stare, and perhaps a bit of sympathy. "I'm sorry dear. They cannot be removed until this war is over."

TRAINING DAY | CHAPTER 5

I watch the others as Miss Henak delivers the bad news. Drake, Shiloe and Grish stand in protest while Tripp and Vern remain seated with stunned looks on their faces.

"You're kidding, right?" Vern says as he scratches at his dark, curly scruff.

Shiloe stands with her hands on her hips, looking at Henak in disbelief.

Drake towers over Henak but remains silent, as if the thought of continuing to wear the signature collar is still sinking in.

Through all the commotion, Miss Henak simply holds her hands behind her back and looks at each of us, though I can see her stern gaze begin to soften.

"So, let me understand this," Grish says and crosses her arms. "We're expected to fight to the death to help the North seize more territory, which in turn will offer more resources for the Skylight System. And yet we're to be treated as prisoners while we battle?"

"I'm sorry to say it, but yes," Henak says. "I hate to break the news to you like this. It's not my decision, you understand. The backers of this program are afraid you might run off. We can't afford that."

The room remains silent as I glance around at the shocked expressions. Everyone finally sits down, and a subdued quiet settles in. Even though I'd already heard this from Grior, I still feel a moment of injustice and frustration.

"There's no sense in bickering about it." Henak claps, drawing our attention. "You must focus on your training now. That is the only thing you have control over. Now, we are going to work on psychic communication today. That's how you will learn to talk to each other, and this can be accomplished over great distances once you perfect it. Brindall, you and Shiloe. Come and sit here." She guides us to an area near the meditation rugs. I sit down cross-legged opposite Shiloe, a bit apprehensively.

"I want you both to visualize the other one, standing at the end of a long tunnel. Close your eyes, then lengthen out your thoughts. Let your breathing slow, then focus energy on the other side of the tunnel and on the person you see there. Got it?"

I give Henak a confused look, not sure if she's joking or being serious. But joking doesn't seem to be her style, and I'm beginning to realize this. I glance at Shiloe, and she returns my confused look but tries to keep a straight face. I can see that she isn't buying this mumbo-jumbo either. Regardless, I do as Henak says and close my eyes and slow my breathing. I focus, trying to visualize Shiloe sitting at the opposite end of a long tunnel. Eventually, I sense her presence. Then I can see her, though she seems hazy and hard to grasp, like there's a thick mist between us. I call out to her using my thoughts. Surprisingly, I can hear her voice answering me. It seems to magically appear in my mind. But her voice is muffled, as if there are mountains of blankets clogging the tunnel. I focus, and the haziness seems to lessen. Occasionally, I can hear a stray word, or perhaps a random thought, but they're muffled, and I can't understand what Shiloe is trying to tell me. Several minutes pass before I snap out of my trance, my eyes wide. Shiloe stares at me with the same expression of surprise and shock.

"How did that just happen?" she asks, her voice trembling with excitement.

I shake my head at her, too shocked to respond.

"I see you two made a connection, and on the first try!" Henak says and stands to greet us. "That's excellent! Very well done. The more you practice, the clearer your voice will become, and you can achieve greater distances. Every practice session and meditation with Vishmu will increase your psychic capacity and expand your abilities. I recommend you do it as often as possible. Next two, let's go!" she snaps.

Shiloe and I continue to practice with Vishmu while Miss Henak gives instructions to Grish, Vern, Drake and Tripp. After several more hours, we can all communicate with ease. Soon, I'm forced to close my mind from all the chattering.

"Okay, onward!" Henak barks and leads our group to the sparring mats. She straightens her cloak and pins her gray hair into a bun. "Here we are, the physical training part. Now, I want you to all understand one thing. Vishmu cares not about physical attributes. Sound confusing? Good! Because it is. Brindall, you're what…6'-4"? And Shiloe, 5'-7" perhaps?"

Shiloe and I look at each other and nod back to Henak.

"Brin. I will bet that by the end of the day, Shiloe can best you in a fight. What do you think?"

I give Shiloe a sidelong glance. "Maybe I should spar with Drake, Miss Henak. We're about the same size."

"Nonsense. Come over here, both of you." Henak grabs me by the elbow and guides me onto the mat. She positions Shiloe opposite me. "Now, Brindall, stand there. Shiloe, I want you to remember how you used Vishmu to speak to him. Can you do that?"

She nods, but I can see her biting her lip nervously. "No problem, but how will that—"

"Don't be concerned, dear. I'm going to tell you. Everything surrounding us emits quantum fields. Think in terms of energy, frequency and vibration. Imagine it at your very fingertips. Focus that energy onto your subject, whoever or whatever that may be. It isn't hard if you only think of that. Got it! Good, let's go!" Henak claps before we can ask more questions.

Shiloe relaxes her shoulders, and they droop forward as she gives me a defeated look. But then she shakes her head and shrugs, as if committing to the challenge. I still can't believe I'm being asked to fight someone half my size. But before I can prepare myself, Shiloe rushes forward and grabs me under one arm. I'm caught completely off guard, and she lifts me, turns her upper body, then slams me to the mat. I feel the air escape my lungs from the impact, and stars erupt in my vision. I lay there on my back, stunned. Shiloe stands over me with a grin on her face.

"There! You see! It's that simple. Focus. Energy!" Henak claps her hands, then snaps her fingers at us. "Pair up, all of you. Let's go."

Our group does so with Grish and Tripp first, followed by Drake and Vern. We take turns sparring with each other. By the end of the hour, I can feel my sides bruised and battered. I know I'll be sore in the morning, but the new abilities I'm learning excite me, and I ignore the pain.

I grin at Shiloe, and she grins back at me as we continue to spar. Her face is red and covered with welts, but I can see that she's not ready to quit either. It's our first sparring session together, and I'm already feeling drawn to her spunky attitude. When Henak finally breaks training, we all moan in disappointment, not wanting to stop.

"Let's move on to the next," Henak says, ignoring the complaints with a grin. "More of that tomorrow. Now…it's time to meditate. This is how we will end our training days. I would recommend that you do this even after your training here is complete. Once in the morning, once in the evenings, and as often as you can beyond that. There is no limit to meditation. It is the one thing that will expand your Vishmu abilities quicker than anything else. Your powers depend on this, and you will be weak without it."

We all follow Henak to the rugs. She lowers the lights and sits, facing us. Above, lightning clashes through the clear dome, continuing to light the space with intermittent flashes. An occasional thunderclap rolls in the distance as we wait anxiously.

"This session will be similar to your Vishmu training. You will let your inner light go now, let it run free. It needs time to release, decompress, recoup. You will observe only, understand? What you see here will be difficult to comprehend. Stay calm, don't panic! This is what your inner light needs, got it? Now, relax…slow your breathing and let go. Give your inner light permission to roam, let it run wild."

I relax, then slow my breathing like I'd done with Shiloe during our psychic speech training. After a few minutes, I began to feel something stir deep in my soul, as if part of my being is pulling away. It's an odd feeling, one I struggle to understand. I'm trusting in Henak now and try to focus on what she's told me. Oddly, I feel like I had on the Day of the Nail—like I'm standing on the edge of existence, and there is nothing else around me. Perhaps I was standing at the creation of time or witnessing the beginning of the universe. Whatever it is, I know that I'm simply there as a witness, an observer, as Henak warned. What I see is beyond comprehension. I give my inner light permission, and it immediately bursts from my being, like a child running off to play at recess.

I follow as it gallops across the cosmos. I can see the others, too. Shiloe's light, I think, and it matches the color of her palm—a reddish-orange glow. It's like some cosmic supernova, exploding with immense power as it races across existence. I watch the others too, racing from galaxy to galaxy. Our lights zip around stars and other strange phenomena that I can't explain or comprehend.

Eventually, I hear someone, or something, calling to me, and my inner light begins to return to my being. I reel it in, and the turquoise light starts to compress back to its normal size. Time seems to slow down, and eventually, my eyes flutter open. Then, just like that, I'm sitting on the rug and trying to regain my bearings. For a split second, I feel nauseous, my head spinning as reality comes into focus.

"Easy does it," Henak says and places her hand on my shoulder. "It takes time to regain your senses. Just let it happen on its own, got it?"

Before long, each of us is back to our normal selves, breathing heavily and trying not to pass out. First Shiloe, then Vern, Grish, Drake, and Tripp last.

"What just happened?" Shiloe gasps. She looks pale, her eyes still trying to focus.

"Something miraculous, I dare say." Henak pats her shoulder. "That is something you must get used to. The more often, the better. This is what recharges your inner light. As energy is expended during the day, while using your abilities, the greater the demand it will require to recharge. Your meditation will become vital as your powers grow."

I feel completely spent as I sit there and try to remain calm. But this last session has been somewhat earth-shattering for me. In a word…*mindboggling*. The realization finally hits me that very few people have ever witnessed such a god-like experience.

"Let's call it a day! Off to bed, all of you," Henak bellows and claps her hands. "At it again tomorrow, bright and early." She shuffles us off to bed like a mother hen.

But after she leaves us in our dorm rooms and the lights are turned out, I wander back to the gathering space in the center. The others are already there, sitting on the rugs under the dome's stasis field, ready to talk about the day's events. I sit next to Shiloe, already feeling like I know her—more than I want to admit, actually.

"Do you miss your families?" Tripp asks and brushes his wavy, reddish-blond hair from his brow. He leans back on his elbows, his legs kicked up. I notice how his red cheeks are still flushed from the day's training, which seems to be a constant trait with Tripp. In a way, Tripp reminds me of my brother, Ben. Maybe it's his small stature, though he carries himself in a more mature manner, like the rest of us it seems. Thanks to the situation we've been shoved into, we are being forced to deal with things other kids our age will never have to face.

Next to Tripp is Vern. He lays on his side with the rug bunched under one arm. His large hands tug at his dark scruff, trying to straighten out the curls. "Kinda, I guess. I'm sure they miss us too, though." Vern seems to finish all his sentences with a chuckle. It's light, a quick vibrato that sets us all at ease. He's an imposing figure with his tall, broad frame, but he expresses himself in such a lighthearted manner that it feels so disarming. I can tell immediately that we'd get along great.

Grish and Drake sit on the same rug, leaning against each other. It's somewhat of a miracle to me that two Immortals can be from the same borough. They seem to be alike in many ways, though they aren't related. Both speak in what I think is considered an old Irish dialect, and at times, they even finish each other's sentences.

"It hardly seems fair, don't it?" Tripp says.

Vern looks at him, pulling his gaze from the stasis dome and the lightning beyond. "I assume you mean it's not fair we're stuck here with you?" he jokes, giving Tripp a playful nudge. But once the laughter dies down, Vern grunts in a more serious tone. "No, it ain't fair, Tripp. But why don't you tell me why you think it should be."

Tripp looks at Vern, then at each of us. He sits up, brushing his sandy-red hair back. "It's not fair this happened to me. I don't want to be here. I should be back at my desk, doing my accounting."

"So, it's numbers, is it?" Vern says, joking. "Is that your superpower?"

"What? Can't you tell?" Tripp says and stands. He flexes his thin arms, trying to show off what little muscle there is.

That draws a laugh from the group. Drake and Vern both stand and pick him up and place him on their shoulders. They start prancing around and lifting him up and down like some conquering hero. Tripp laughs, then smiles and raises his arms over his head, basking in the momentary glory. Everyone claps and hollers, except for Grish, who remains seated.

Eventually we sit, and I look at Grish. Her quiet nature strikes me differently than the others. She's reserved, that much is easy to see. But I sense inside her is a unique person, waiting to emerge, and I'm determined to get her out. I finally nudge her, and she glances over at me, which is more of a scowl, I suppose.

"Your turn, Grish. Let's go." I hold out a hand, giving her the floor to speak.

The others start clapping and cheering. Vern hoots until Grish finally stands and brushes off her trousers, then gives a forced curtsy.

"Speech!" Shiloe shouts, cupping her hands around her mouth and whistling.

Grish purses her lips in frustration as we all wait a few long seconds before she speaks.

"I'm going to try and be as polite as I can. I don't really like these people. In general, I'm shocked that you're all so positive about this. They're using our families against us as leverage. But since I don't care about mine, they have no leverage over me. They can only threaten my life, which honestly, doesn't really bother me. And, at some point, I might just test them on that."

We all grow silent.

I realize that Grish isn't joking.

"Come on, Grish," Drake says. "It ain't that bad yet."

"Really? How could it get any worse?" she retorts. "We're essentially slaves," she says. She tugs at her collar, and it beeps. "And soon, we'll all be forced to fight and kill other humans. Ever think about that, Drake? You claim that you want to help others, but in a short while, you're gonna be slaughtering people by the thousands. Still think it ain't so bad?"

Drake's face turns ashen as the blood seems to drain from his features, and he clenches his jaw. I watch his massive arms bulge and flex beneath his torn jerkin.

"Yeah, that's what I thought," Grish continues. "Any of you actually think this through? They are going to use us as weapons, a guided missile, to inflict as much damage to their enemies as possible. Then, when we've all gone insane, or we're dead, they'll find another immortal to replace us."

The mood suddenly goes from cheerful to dark.

"Well," Vern says and claps. "Maybe we shouldn't be here, but we are."

"Tell me something I don't know," Tripp says, and I can hear the frustration in his voice. "I heard people telling me I'm a miracle, that I'm some sort of blessing. So, everything's on us now? Do I have that right? Millions of people are counting on us to win. Come on! I'm not buyin' any of this. There's something they aren't telling us."

"I figured that out, too," Shiloe says. "Wasn't that hard, either. I can see you guys sense it as well."

I watch the others nod in agreement and hold out my hands. "That may be. Perhaps Miss Henak knows something we don't, but she's obviously trained other Immortals before. She can help us."

"Do we have a choice?" Tripp asks. "I guess it doesn't matter if these people are lying to us. We're stuck in the middle of this war now."

"Henak's in on this, Brin," Shiloe says and lowers her voice. "Whatever's going on, she knows."

"You're probably right," I say. "But she also cares about training us to be the best. I sense that too. If there is some conspiracy, then it doesn't necessarily mean she agrees with it. Maybe she's just tasked with training us? I don't think she's a bad person. So, we should focus on our training right now, conspiracy or not."

"But seriously? Us, leading an army?" Tripp says and his voice cracks, sounding like a squeak.

"Or maybe we'll end up being assassins or spies?" Vern says. "Whatever it is they expect us to do, it still seems weird to be here. Last week, I'm workin' in a mine. Now, I'm some sort of immortal being. It's all wrong. Something isn't adding up."

"If we're who they say we are, then we can't change it," I say. "We have to accept that and focus on being a team. We're away from our families. I don't know when I'll see my brother or mom again. We have to rely on each other now that it's just us. This is our family. What do you all say? Can we agree to that?"

"I mean, I've only just met you all," Shiloe says. "This is our first real conversation. If we are some sort of ancient race, as Henak says, then I guess that makes us family, in a sense. I don't see any harm in trusting each other. I don't get a bad feeling from any of you."

"Same here, man," Vern says. "I may never see my family again. I miss them already. If this is it for me, then I don't want to die alone. I don't like to think about fighting others, possibly killing them for the sake of land. But I guess if I don't, my family's as good as dead. We're all in the same boat, it seems."

After a brief pause, I stand up and hold out my hand. "I'm in for the family we have now. I say we make a vow to fight and protect each other, no matter what happens. Who's in?"

Shiloe pulls herself up by my shoulder, and I wince from the bruises from all the sparring that day. She smiles, gives me a shove, then places her hand over mine. "I'm in."

One by one, Vern, Grish, Drake and Tripp clap their hands on top of ours.

"We got each other's backs," Shiloe says.

“That’s right!” Vern replies, and Grish, Tripp and Drake all look up through the clear dome above and at the moon. Soon, we’re all howling like lunatics and laughing.

We continued to chat throughout the night, no one wanting to go to bed or be alone. Vern is full of jokes and soon has us all bellowing with stories about his youth. Hearing him laugh helps break the tension of the day. I haven’t felt this good in a long time, maybe my entire life. Being with the others helps me forget the struggles of my past and what’s to come, if only temporarily. I’m here with a group of kids I barely know while preparing for the fight of my life. And yet, I’m laughing my head off. It's the break I feel we all need, regardless of the dire situation.

Eventually, as the conversation lags and the night hour deepens, I know what’s on everyone’s mind. Tomorrow will be more training, and before long, we’ll be thrown into a war that we’ve only heard tales of. The entire weight of the Northern Coalition rests on our shoulders, and I have no idea if I’ll ever come home to my family.

SIGMA | **CHAPTER 6**

BEH ΘIM

Like the morning before, Henak rouses us early from our warm beds. I'm tired from staying up late into the night, as I'm sure the others are too. I massage my muscles. They ache all over, and I can feel bruises and welts from yesterday's sparring.

When I leave my quarters, I peer through the stasis dome above at the persistent storm that crashes outside. There's no sunlight to greet us as we prepare for the day, though I'm happy to see the clouds, nonetheless. Getting a glimpse of sky, no matter how stormy, is a welcome sight compared to the dark caves, dirt, and rock I'm used to seeing. Just a hint of that dark sky raises my spirits.

I meet the other five in the chow hall for more of the lukewarm gruel prepared for us. It's runny, the consistency somewhere between water and syrup. It tastes better than the gruel back home, though, and I shovel down a few bowls of it.

That day's training is more of the same. We start with meditation, followed by Vishmu and more of the psychic telepathy. Then physical combat training, which is everyone's favorite. We take a quick break for lunch, then more meditation.

Henak pushes all of us to our limits, both mentally and physically. She introduces additional maneuvers, each one more difficult. We fight through each challenge, including longer Vishmu and meditation sessions. Later, we all sit in the small library and study more about our heritage, at least what's available about our immortal background. But there's little to share, it seems, since Henak doesn't have much knowledge to give. I find myself wondering if what she is sharing with us is even correct. I think about Shiloe's comments the night before—is Miss Henak withholding information, or is she simply that limited? It's obvious that someone must have taught her, which means there's more we don't know.

Over the next several days, our training sessions grow longer and more difficult. We spar against each other, learning new moves. We work on speed, agility and strength training. At the end of the first week, we're a group that no one would want to mess with. But I also know that what we will face on the battlefield will be more dangerous than anything we've seen in the comfort of our training facility. I envision armies of troops with great weapons of war and armored vehicles. I imagine killer mech units, rumored to have abilities rivaling our own. I assume the opposing Immortals will be hardened and vicious and ready to fight to the death. If we want to survive, we'll have to be stronger, faster and smarter. We must be ready to kill. We must learn to work as a team. Unfortunately, our time with Henak is running out.

That night, after our training session, the six of us gather in the center again. Vern and Drake find some chunks of coal for the firepit. Soon, we have a blaze going and lean back to catch occasional glimpses of the Skylight System above. It glows like a fractured moon, its nine orbiting belts encircling the core as it nears completion.

"What do y'all think?" Vern says and nods at the system through the intermittent cloud cover. "Will we ever get a chance to live there?"

"As long as I'm away from my family, I don't care where I'm at," Tripp says. He's curled into a ball, like a fox, and trying to stay warm, his cheeks flushed. Next to him is Grish, who has her knees pulled up, as if she's also fighting off chills. Her red ponytails are poking out from beneath her hood as she stares straight ahead, seemingly lost in her own world.

"What do you say, Grish?" I ask, trying to bring her into the conversation. "What are you hoping for?"

Grish blinks, as if waking from a dream. "Hope? Really? You all think that's even on the menu?"

We all stare at her in the dancing firelight. I'm a bit caught off guard by her terse comment.

"Go on," I say. "What do you mean by that?"

She rocks back and forth, gripping her knees a bit tighter. I watch her pale skin flush in frustration. "You're all bein' too naïve. They don't care 'bout us. We're just pawns, pushed around on a battlefield. We'll be on the front lines soon enough. How long do you think we'll last there? Our life expectancy doesn't look good in my book."

"She's got a point," Tripp says. "Things are bound to get worse, and we've got no idea what we're really in for."

"Let's keep our chins up," I say. "We're going to war, like it or not. Our option is to lean on each other or die alone. I need you guys if I want to get back to my family. Help me do that, and I swear I'll do everything I can to help you all as well."

"Can we just change the topic?" Grish says without looking at me. "I don't want to think about war any more than I have to."

I nod and clap my hands on my knees. "Fair enough. What should we talk about? Vern's lovely hair?"

That draws a chuckle from the group as Vern stands and prances around the firepit, patting his dark, curly hair. Then Drake stands and falls in, following him around and mimicking him. Soon everyone is laughing, including Grish and Tripp.

"Why are you so happy?" Tripp asks Drake. "You're a pit fighter, right?"

Drake rubs at the scars on his face as he looks at Tripp, then at the rest of us. His deep voice fills the open chamber as he faces Tripp. "Isn't it obvious? I'm lucky to be alive. I mean, I should've died years ago. Somehow, that didn't happen, and now I'm here, away from all that, talking to my new friends. What's there not to be happy about?"

"Or, one might argue, out of the fryin' pan and into the fire," Tripp continues.

"Well, I guess I don't see it that way. I look at this as a second chance at life. I'm just happy to be away from my father." Drake rubs again at the scars along his neck. "When I was a kid, I was forced to fight against my will. I hurt a lot of people smaller than me. I didn't want to do it, but my father made me. I hated that feeling of picking on weaker kids. I made a promise to myself that if I ever got out, I'd do my best to help others. You have that too, Brin. I see that light in you, maybe you just don't realize it yet, but I think Henak does—"

"So, what are you saying, Drake?" Grish says and crosses her arms. "You think being kind and docile is gonna save us?"

"Why do you think we're here?" Drake says. "We were all chosen for this. We have to help these people. I'm doing this, alone if I have to. I don't care what anyone says, I'm here for a reason. I want peace, something I never had growing up. Maybe now I can give it to these citizens. At least, I'm going to try and do that. I owe it to them."

"Well, maybe I don't want that responsibility," Grish says.

"You've got an opportunity to help others who need it, and you won't?" Drake asks, his brows coming to a point.

"Why should any of this be on me?" she asks.

"So? You prefer the easy way out, Grish?" Tripp says. "Is that it?"

Grish looks away. "That isn't what I said."

"You don't have to say it," Tripp says. "I can see that's what you want. That's just who you are, isn't it?"

"Well, it's better than complaining that everything isn't fair all the time, huh?" she retorts.

Tripp turns away, his skin flushed, and I can see he's upset, but he doesn't say anything.

"Let's keep it positive, okay?" Shiloe says and holds out her hands.

The conversation was teetering and about to turn sour.

Tripp sighs, then turns to face Vern. "Same question. How can you be so cheerful in a hellhole like this?"

Vern lifts the corner of his mouth, considering. "Dunno, I guess. No real reason. It's just how I've always been. Life of the party, man." He stands again and shakes his hips at the fire, a little shimmy dance, then takes a bow.

"I would've never thought the two biggest guys in our group would be the class clowns," Shiloe says with a chuckle.

"And I never would've thought the two smallest people here would be the grumpiest," Vern replies with a grin toward Grish and Tripp. "People come in all shapes and personalities. Surprise, surprise."

"And Shiloe's the eldest? Am I right about that?" Tripp says.

Shiloe rolls her eyes at that but shakes her head. "Hey, I'm no babysitter. Don't look at me to lead this group of hooligans."

"No, I think that's gonna be mister handsome over here," Vern says and gives me a shove.

I feel my skin flush and give Vern a go-to-hell look. But he gives me another playful shove. Almost immediately, Drake and the others are there, pushing me around and swooning. Soon we're all rolling around in the dirt and laughing.

We talk through the night again, continuing to ask questions and make small talk. There are no awkward moments now. We're comfortable around each other, like we've been friends for years. At times, we erupt in laughter at Vern or Drake. At other times, we break out into singing as we stare up at the storm. We share stories about our homes and our childhoods. Grish and Tripp don't share much at first, but slowly, they begin to open up. Though we're still getting to know each other, our accelerated friendship is quickly solidifying.

The one topic we all avoid is our time with Miss Henak. No one wants it to end. We've grown comfortable here, and I can tell that everyone wants to stay. Like a warm, cozy bed, I want to curl up and hide from what's to come. But I know that security blanket will soon be stripped away.

On the fourteenth day of our time with Miss Henak, we are essentially trained killers. I feel pretty confident that we will be able to survive whatever challenge lies ahead; at least, I hope so. As far as our team goes, I'm beginning to see each of our strengths now. Shiloe is by far our most talented fighter. Tripp and Grish are stealthy. Like tiny assassins, they tend to move in from the side or behind their opponent, while Vern and Drake are bruisers, with a straight-ahead tactic. Although more training with Miss Henak would be welcome, the day had finally come for us to move on to the next phase of our journey.

"What should we expect, Miss Henak?" Vern asks.

We lay around on our meditation mats, having just finished that evening's training session. I wipe sweat from my forehead and lay on my side, ignoring my bruised ribs from sparring with Shiloe.

"That, I cannot say for certain," Henak says. She stands in front of us, her hands behind her back. I notice how relaxed she's become lately. In the beginning, she was stern and direct with us. But now that we've completed our training, I wonder if perhaps she views us as peers, at least to some extent.

"I can tell you that this is just the first phase of your training. Past Immortals are usually assigned to units. They will likely ease you in through basic assignments at first. You will all see action soon, and it will push you to your limit. I hope I've done my part. I will miss you all."

"Miss Henak," I say and lean forward, placing my elbows on my knees. "I...*we* were wondering if there's anything else you can share about Immortals. I get the sense there's more we aren't being told."

Miss Henak glances around at each of us as if considering what she should say and how to say it. "Of course, there's more. There's always more, isn't there? You're not blind, obviously, and I'd be disappointed if you didn't suspect something. I would tell you more, but I feel it isn't my place, frankly. However, I can say that answers are coming if you will be patient. Use your abilities wisely, and practice, of course. There are secret powers you all possess that have yet to be realized. Some are beyond my ability to teach you. Only in time will you achieve your greatest potential, got it?"

"Is that all you can tell us?" Shiloe asks.

"I'm afraid so, my dear. I wish you all the best. Now, off to bed! You've a big day tomorrow."

As usual, we sit around the firepit that evening and talk about the day's events. But surprisingly, little is said that night as anxious feelings occupy our thoughts.

What will tomorrow bring? I wonder. *What type of assignments will we be given, and what new dangers will we face?*

One by one, Tripp, Grish, Drake, and Vern slip off to bed, and eventually, Shiloe and I are alone. She sits across from me, her chin on her knees as she stares into the fire. Her blonde ponytails are tangled from sparring that day, her hazel eyes red and glossy from exhaustion, and perhaps, some emotion.

"You okay?" I ask, trying to draw her attention.

She doesn't look at me right away and takes a moment to compose herself. "Yeah...I think so," she says. "I like it here. I only wish we could stay with Henak, you know?"

I give her a quick nod. "Yeah, me too. It feels safe. Maybe the safest I've ever felt. That's odd to say, considering."

"I know. I feel close to you—to the group, I mean." Shiloe straightens, and her skin flushes a shade of pink. "It's odd that we've all grown so close in such a short time, right?"

I smile at her, wanting to say more. I want to tell her how much I like her, too, but I stop myself and simply nod.

"I just hope we're together, tomorrow, that is," Shiloe continues. "I know Henak says we're a team, so I assume we'll be placed together. But…what if they do split us up? I'll miss you…everyone, that is."

I lean back and stretch my legs. "I wouldn't worry about that right now. Something tells me we aren't splitting up just yet. Maybe at some point. But right now, I think they want to continue our team building."

I notice her take a deep breath and seem to relax.

"I hope you're right," she says.

There's something in her tone that sounds different, a slight waver of concern maybe. But she quickly turns away before I can say anything else. Then she stands and walks back to her sleeping quarters.

"Good night, Brin."

Henak allows us to sleep in the next morning. We're up at a decent hour and eating breakfast. There is no training today, but we all go through our meditation ritual out of habit anyway.

At midday, several Northern troopers enter the training facility. They wear the same insignia-clad uniforms and hold the control devices for our signature collars at the ready. We're rounded up and funneled toward a waiting rail transport. I quickly notice that this time, we aren't chained like before. Miss Henak waves encouragement as we march onto the waiting transport. I think I see her wiping her eyes, but then she quickly turns and leaves.

Once onboard, several more troops, along with General Nem, join us. The troops look on with nervous expressions as we're seated along benches. Several stare at our palms and the light streaming from them like we're diseased mutants. Nem displays the same stoic expression as he looks me over, almost like I'm a different person now. But he remains silent, all the same. There is no sign of Grior.

The transport hovers just above the charged rails, then it accelerates through an opening in the cave's wall and into darkness. I sit next to Shiloe and close my eyes, trying to relax as the transport bumps along at high speed. Shiloe's fists are balled, her knuckles white as she stares straight ahead. Tripp and Grish have the same anxious expression on their faces. Even Vern and Drake, with their normally happy-go-lucky attitudes, are quiet and reserved.

I begin to sense that our rail is heading in a southerly direction.

Toward the front line.

I send a psychic message to the others, already knowing they're aware of the same thing. We're traveling into the danger zone, an area that runs the length of the dividing line—the 37th parallel. That's where the fighting is the worst. If this war—this game or contract or charade, whatever it is—should be decided, that's where it'll take place. That's why the Northern Coalition wants us there so badly.

Thirty minutes later, the military transport slows and lowers in through another airlock. Smaller, more maneuverable transports and skiffs zip in and out as we enter a much larger port this time.

As our transport docks, the six of us are escorted across the boarding platform and toward a nearby command facility. As we walk, I take in the new surroundings.

Compared to the last secret borough where Henak trained us, this one is much larger. The main stasis dome seems to float miles above and the storm clouds and lightning crash into it and redirect around the sphere. The air space inside the dome is packed with flying skiffs and transports, something only wealthy citizens can afford. The large earthen walls that make up the perimeter of the city rise up hundreds of meters to the edge of the stasis dome. Thousands of structures that look to be apartments are cut into the walls like tiny pods and cantilever out. The main thoroughfares crisscrossed through the space, impossibly thin and elegant. Below are tall buildings that nearly reach the stasis dome overhead. The reinforced graphene roads carry the thousands of pedestrians and vehicles with no sign of stress. Citizens, all dressed in military uniforms, hurry along. The noise level inside the city echoes around the vast rotunda as loudspeakers blare announcements. Projected onto the dome's underside is footage from the battles, which I assume is the front line. There are charts and graphs showing real-time information, statistics and other data about the war's progress.

Our group is ushered downward through a massive vector accelerator and eventually into a hardened bunker-like structure. Nem leads the way to a boardroom and holds the door for us. We all sit around a large conference table made of stone. Vern and Drake sit slouched and relax while Grish and Tripp hunch near each other, darting glances around nervously. Shiloe sits next to me, calm and collected. I use my psychic speech to communicate with them as we wait.

This boardroom is similar to the last one. The large table is surrounded by dozens of executive chairs, and the walls are crowded with holographic displays. The images we see are the same as the ones on the dome's underside. The battle rages in a large, open canyon, perhaps several kilometers wide. The sky above is filled with lightning, matching the fury of the ongoing war. Tanks and other vehicles launch rounds of artillery, and tracer bullets light up the air.

Soon, the heavy wooden doors swing open, and several people march into the room. The group stops near the head of the conference table and surveys us with stern looks. There are two women and two older men, all wearing military fatigues and badges. The men look to be in their mid to late sixties, and the women much younger. There's an uncomfortable silence as we wait.

"Welcome to the Sigma Borough. I hope your trip was acceptable," one of the men says. He is lean and looks surprisingly spry for his age. His cropped gray hair is cut in typical military fashion—high and tight. His face is weathered with soft carelines. His cheeks are peppered with gray stubble. The man's dark, cavernous eyes seemed to search my soul as he meets my gaze. I'm forced to look away after just a few seconds under his intense stare. His piercing ice-blue eyes hold a mysterious power, it seems. He looks at the rest of our group in the same manner, almost like he's trying to read our thoughts.

In stark contrast, the other man seems much less intimidating, almost friendly. His gaze and aura feel safe to me, approachable and warm. He is slightly taller with a pencil thin nose and dark skin. A long scar runs the length of his jawline. Like the first man, he, too, is remarkably fit for his age and has a gray beard.

"Well?" the first man asks us again. "Was your trip acceptable?"

"Acceptable isn't the word I'd use." Grish is the first to respond in her typical gruff tone. "We're not here by choice."

The man smiles at her. "My apologies for that, Grishum. My name is Gorgan Freemantle. I'm the Supreme Commander for the Northern forces. This is my second-in-command, Triton Mothe. Also, Lieutenant Guinn and Captain Lewin," he says and motions to the two women. "They will be your intel team and are here to assist on your mission. Before we move on, do you have any questions?"

We all look at each other, bleary-eyed and uncertain. It's been a long day already, and it appears we're just getting started. I can tell that everyone wants to laugh at Gorgan's comment. *Of course, we all have questions, and a lot of them!* But no one speaks up, either too tired or too intimidated to say anything at the moment.

"Very well, there will be time for questions later, should you have any. Please, follow me then." Gorgan Freemantle abruptly turns and leaves the room, followed by Triton, Guinn, and Lewin.

The six of us stand, somewhat surprised at the quick departure, and follow. I fall in behind Shiloe and take note of the facility as we walk. The complex is heavily armored, and I guess that we're deep inside the Northern Coalition's main headquarters.

"If he really is the Supreme Commander, this must be the main hub for our entire faction," I whisper to Shiloe.

She nods over her shoulder and whispers back. "We've got to be close to the front line. I think that was the 37th parallel I saw in that war footage."

Everywhere I look, there are armed guards. The walls around us are reinforced concrete and steel, a bunker designed to withstand any bombardment, I assume. But I can still see glimpses of Earth in some areas, which is a mix of red clay, sandstone and gypsum. Shiloe is right, we must be very close to the 37th parallel. *But how close?*

Freemantle leads our group deeper into the complex, across wide thoroughfares and causeways. I peer over the edges and down onto large open bays with soldiers training below. I hear shouts as drill sergeants bark orders at the troops marching through exercises.

We finally come to a halt in front of a massive pair of steel doors, some three meters wide and just as tall. The doors swing open, and we're ushered inside. Then they close behind us with an ominous thud that echoes down the hardened tunnel and into silence. We continue to follow Freemantle through a series of corridors. Eventually, my head is spinning as I try to keep up with our location. But we've changed directions so many times that I'm completely turned around now.

We finally end up in another boardroom, though this one has more technology. I assume this might be more of what's considered a 'war room.' By the looks of it, this may be the nerve center where all the Northern Coalition's major decisions are made. Along one wall is a live stream showing the ongoing battle and footage of the most intense fighting. I watch as strange looking mech units march across the battlefield. Some are smaller and more maneuverable, while others are large, almost like giants in stature. More data and stats are broadcast along the bottom of the display like a ticker tape. What I'm seeing is the war as it's unfolding in real time. It's the front line at the 37th parallel, the war that we've all heard so much about. The chaos I see makes my heart race. I feel my palms grow clammy. I clench my jaw, and my fists tighten involuntarily. Soon, I know we'll all be thrown into that chaos and destruction. We'll be in the center of that raging battle.

Fresh recruits for the grinder, I think to myself. Pawns being pushed around the battlefield, as Grish had said.

How long will any of us possibly survive in all of that? But as I watch the live feed, I feel a split second of empathy for those who are already there. I feel sorrow because I know the men and women are dying at that very moment, all in the name of territory. And not just the Northern soldiers either, but those fighting for the South as well. I think about their families and the heartache they must feel, worrying about their loved ones and if they'll ever return home.

I settle into a plush, black chair behind the stone table, but my eyes don't leave the scenes on the displays, unable to pull away from the spectacle. Freemantle waits, seemingly wanting us to witness the carnage, as he stands to one side patiently. I feel as if he wants to baptize us in this moment, this harsh realization of what is happening near us right now. Perhaps this is his way of breaking us in.

Better to expose us to the shock of it right now, I muse to myself. *Then we can get on with it.*

It's then that I understand something. Gorgan Freemantle is a seasoned commander, and this isn't the first time he's broken Immortals into this war. I also understand that if he takes it easy on us and coddles us, it might mean the difference between life and death. This is serious business, and he is using a 'shock tactic' to prepare us.

When Freemantle finally speaks, there's no emotion in his voice. "I wanted you six to see this firsthand, not because I'm trying to frighten you, but because I need you to see the truth of what's happening out there. This battle is real, and lives are being lost every second. If the South takes more territory than us by the Winter Solstice, not only will it hold sway over the future of the human race, but more people will die. This 'game' that we refer to is actually a contract, one that can only be won through the control of territory. You six are here to help us win that. Now that you are Immortals, we expect great things from you."

"No pressure, huh, Mister Gorgan?" Vern says with a slight chuckle.

Freemantle turns to face him and the smile on Vern's face quickly fades away. "When you address me, it's Commander Freemantle."

"Right…sorry, Commander Freemantle," Vern says, but I can see Vern's hand shaking under the table as it rests on his knee.

"I'm not sure we're really prepared for any of this," Grish says.

"None of us are," Freemantle says. "The men and women fighting now have been rushed to the front line. Many of them are volunteers who know they will not come home. Our troop surplus is low. This long war has depleted our supplies, resources and citizens. Still, brave men and women step forward. So many lives have been lost."

"But…we've only been training for a few weeks," Tripp says. "We need more time to prepare, a lot more time—"

"Most of those troops you see have had less than a week to prepare," Freemantle says. "You six need to understand that you *can* save lives. And the sooner you're out there, the more you can help those citizens. You may not realize it, but you have the ability to change the tide of war through the smallest act of bravery. You will make a difference, believe me."

Triton steps forward and folds his hands behind his back. "As we speak, there are Immortals leading the Southern forces, and they are on the move. Just today alone, we have lost a full percent of our territory. The longer we wait, the greater the loss. Lives are important, but so is territory."

Freemantle turns and pulls up a three-dimensional map. The hologram centers over the large stone table so that we can see it with greater detail. He highlights an area that shows the 37th parallel. Along the bright yellow line, we get a satellite view of the battle in real time. To the south of the yellow line, I see the territory is shaded a bright red color, and to the north, it's a royal blue. The imaginary line meanders, with little inconsistencies running the length of it. A large projection on the far eastern portion of the line is bulging into the north, which is our territory. The amount of lost land doesn't look like much, but it's obviously the one percent portion Triton is talking about.

"You can bet there are Immortals there," Freemantle says as he points at the area. "If we don't counter soon, that network of underground territory could fall. Once it falls, it could be lost for good."

"But it seems so small compared to what we're seeing on the map," Tripp says. He sits forward, his hands tucked under his arms. His cheeks blush bright red when Freemantle levels his gaze at him.

"Remember, Tripp. The contract goes to the side that holds the most territory. Only a tenth of a percent is enough to decide this war. That lost area may look insignificant, but a snowball can cause an avalanche." Freemantle stoops low in front of Tripp, holding his gaze. "When momentum is gained, it's hard to stop. We need to plug that gap soon, or our line may give, and the floodgates may open up."

Triton steps to the head of the table and leans against it with arms crossed. "Just a few days ago, we considered giving you all a bit more time to ease into this war. But at the moment, we need to stop the bleeding in that area. This is what our war looks like. We're sending you all in now, within the hour, in fact. Prepare yourselves."

We all look at each other in shock. Vern, Grish, Drake and Tripp stand immediately and begin speaking in raised voices. Shiloe looks to me with concern, her eyes wide and her skin a bit pale. I can see her knuckles bleached white as she grips the edge of the table.

"You're joking, right?" Grish says. She runs her hands through her red hair and rubs her forehead nervously.

"This is a live drill," Triton confirms. "Practice runs are over, I'm afraid. Our time has run out."

"We're dead," Vern slumps back in his chair and kicks his tactical boots up on the table. "Can I get a last meal first?"

"Hold on," I say and stand to face Triton and Freemantle. "We understood this might happen at some point, but you know we still need a bit more training. Seems like a forced error to rush us in right now. A mistake could cost you Immortals. If we're as valuable as you say, wouldn't it be smarter to give us at least a little more time?"

The others nod in agreement as we wait for an answer.

Triton considers for a few seconds longer. "This isn't my decision, Brindall. I don't make those high-level calls, and unfortunately, even the Supreme Commander Freemantle doesn't either. We answer to the Northern Coalition Council, and they've vetoed our request for more time. We tried to buy you as much as we could with Miss Henak. I'm sorry."

I stare at him in shock and try not to show my dismay, but I imagine the look on my face isn't very convincing. I turn to

Freemantle. "Is this true? Is this 'Council' really above the Supreme Commander?"

"The Council overrides my decision, I'm afraid," Freemantle replies with his hands held calmly behind his back. "Yes, they are concerned about the men and women that are dying as we speak. Their greater concern is the danger of losing the entire Eastern Theater of territory if we don't act now. There is no time left. I'm sorry."

I feel a sudden nervous chill shoot through my entire body. My guess is that the others feel the same way. We're about to go into battle, and this will be nothing like our previous training drills. We won't be just fighting, either.

We'll be leading the charge.

I feel the collective stares of Vern, Drake, Grish, Tripp, and Shiloe boring through me. I sense their fear and confusion. They look to me and wait for my decision.

I finally nod, take a deep breath and look back to Triton and Freemantle. "Tell us what to do."

Triton claps me on the shoulder and smiles broadly. "I said I deliver orders, but I also provide support. I wouldn't leave you without some assistance. Lieutenant Guinn and Captain Lewin will guide you in the trenches. I also have these to give." Tyberius walks over to a metal safe. He punches in a code, and the vault door swings open with an electronic beep. Inside are what look to be reinforced suits of armor. They are a strange color, dark and worn and weathered, as if they've already seen battle. I immediately wonder how many previous Immortals they've served.

"These are yours," Triton says and hands out the armor. "It has an active camouflage interface and will provide some cover. These are very valuable; guard them well."

The upper body portion covers my neck and shoulders and extends down to midthigh. The suit is lightweight, and it doesn't hinder my movements. In fact, I feel like I'm wearing normal clothing. The helmet is tight when I slip it on, but it automatically adjusts to fit me. It's also a bit worn, a hand-me-down, like the rest of the armor.

Once I pull the helmet on, the visor activates. I can see a digital screen that displays my vitals and other information about nearby heat signatures, sounds, movements and communication with my group.

"There's just one problem," Vern says. "We don't have a weapon. Wouldn't a railgun be handy?"

"These suits are for defensive purposes," Triton says. "Sometimes subterfuge is more effective than weapons." He walks over to Vern and pulls his visor down a bit lower. Suddenly, Vern's body flickers, fades, then disappears. It's as if someone's pulled a gossamer screen in front of him. The others let out a gasp of amazement.

"That's a neat trick," Vern says and whistles. He lifts his visor and magically reappears.

Triton claps him on the back. "As I said, used properly, these will give you a tactical advantage. But as you can see, you're still slightly visible, and if you move too quickly, you can be detected."

Then Triton does something that shocks us all. He pulls a small railgun from his vest, aims it at my chest and fires. It happens so quickly that I have no time to react. I brace for the impact. But the round hits my breastplate, and the body armor absorbs it. Then, the spent round drops to the stone floor with a dull clink.

Everyone looks at me, then to Triton, then to their own armor.

"Ok, now I'm impressed," Vern chuckles. "What's next? Do these suits fly?"

"I'm afraid not yet," Triton says with a grin. "We're still working on that. This is reinforced graphene armor. It can withstand heavy railgun fire and will protect you, at least to some extent."

"So, do we get a railgun or not?" Grish asks. "Armor is nice, but how do we fight back?"

"Have you learned nothing in your training?" Freemantle says. "Your hands and your mind are the only weapons you need—"

A red light blips above the main screen and draws our attention. Guinn taps Triton and whispers to him.

"Your transport is here," he says. "It's time to go."

Before we can ask more questions, we're being escorted out of the war room and through the tunnel system. Minutes later, we're all seated on a sleek-looking skiff. The small aircraft has a tubular-shaped cargo hold with portal-like windows running the length of the hull. A metal bench lines each side, and a harness strapped to a bar above dangles beside each of us. Next to me sits Shiloe and Tripp, both gripping the strap anxiously. Across from me, Vern and Drake talk in hushed tones as Grish sits with her head bowed and eyes closed, taking in steady breaths.

"Good luck," Triton says. "Be aware and pay attention. Work as a team, and you will survive." He hammers the side of the skiff, and the door slides shut.

The small craft lifts from the platform and wavers slightly as it passes through the airlock above. Then it rockets up and into the storm. I feel my stomach lurch, not used to flight. My heart rate spikes as I grip the harness. I sense the others are just as anxious, and I calm my nerves. Like in the war room, I realize they're looking to me for guidance. Knowing that helps keep me calm. I need to remain steady for their sake.

Lieutenant Guinn and Captain Lewin sit in the front seat near the pilot and co-pilot, chatting urgently as the skiff maintains a low altitude over rocky terrain. Old twentieth-century cities lie in ruin below us, steel skyscrapers rusting and twisted in the constant rain like ancient bones exposed to the elements. The wind tosses us around like a small ship in an angry sea. We're jostled violently by the storm's turbulence as we zip along.

Lewin turns to look at us and raises her voice to be heard over the thunderclaps. She holds up a small display. "The nearest outpost is here! Once we drop you, report to Commander Glenn. He's your contact for this mission in the Eastern Theater." She hands me the small device. The screen shows our frigate, and I note our destination, a glowing green dot some ten kilometers away. I nod to Lewin, then sit back and try to relax.

I turn to look at Shiloe. Her eyes are shut, and I can tell she's in Vishmu, meditating. I decide to do the same.

As soon as I close my eyes, our skiff yaws into a steep bank. My eyes snap open, and I reach for the harness with both hands. When I look to the front of the skiff, the entire cockpit is missing, along with both pilots, Guinn and Lewin. Our transport is on fire and hurtling toward the rough terrain below.

FIRST ASSIGNMENT | CHAPTER 7

My harness constricts across my chest, and the air escapes my lungs. Our skiff slams to the ground, ripping a hole in the side of the hull. Through the large opening, I see the ground cartwheeling past. The skiff continues to roll several more times along the rough terrain and pitted craters. It eventually settles on what appears to be an old, asphalt highway and stops short of a tall, gutted building.

"What just happened!" Drake yells, unbuckling from his harness and standing to his feet. I do the same and immediately grab the harness to steady myself, my head still spinning. I listen to the howling wind outside as the wrecked hull rocks and creaks in the storm.

"Everyone okay?" I yell and move over to check on Shiloe, then Grish and Tripp. "No injuries?"

We all check ourselves. Miraculously, everyone is unscathed. But our skiff is a total loss. The entire console is missing. Only the internal wiring is visible as it sparks.

"What do you suppose happened?" Drake asks again.

"I imagine the skiff took a round, which means there's probably enemy in the area," Grish says. She looks around as if searching the cityscape beyond for enemy troops. Then she turns to me, along with the others.

I pull everyone together in a huddle. "Let's find some cover. This wreck will only draw attention to us. We're exposed if we stay put." I search the wreckage and find a bag that Lewin was carrying. Then we scramble out and into the storm as lightning crashes and thunder booms. The dark sky is unsettling, a blood-red hue from the burning fires, soaked through with a brownish-tan color from the blowing sand. as I look around the war-ravaged landscape. Nearby is the husked-out high-rise building we'd almost hit during our crash landing. With our group in a single file line, I lead the way across the pitted highway and into the building.

Once inside, the howl from the wind and rain diminishes. We do a quick search of the space, making sure it's secure, then we move to the interior and regroup.

In the corner of the one-room apartment is a table, and I clear it off. I search the bag I'd taken from the wrecked skiff. Rifling through it, I find a medic kit, some food rations and water, a bit of rope, and some sort of binoculars.

"Not much help," Vern says.

"No, it isn't," I reply and lay the homing device on the table. "Let's decide our next step. We went down just ten kilometers from the target site. We can either head back or continue on. According to this homing device, it's twice the distance if we turn and go back to base."

"We should go back," Grish says immediately. "I don't like this, Brin. Guinn, Lewin and the pilots…they're all dead. I doubt Commander Freemantle would be angry at us, given the situation."

"I'm probably in the minority here, but seems like we should press on," Shiloe says. "They were anxious to get us to the Eastern Theater. People are dying, Grish."

"Well, we almost died just now!" Grish snaps back, her voice raised. "Besides, we're not ready for this."

"Anyone else?" I ask. "Should we continue or turn back?"

"Brin," Vern says. "You decide. We're following you, man."

I look around at the others, and they give me a nod. "Alright. We continue on then. It's what we set out to do, and we're going through with it."

"They're probably sending out a rescue team, wouldn't you think?" Tripp says. "Shouldn't we stay close?"

"Our skiff was shot down," Shiloe says. "Staying in one spot is probably a mistake. We should keep moving."

"Yeah, I don't think there's anyone coming for us, Tripp," Vern says. "We're on our own now."

Grish looks at Vern and grips her arms a bit tighter. "Do you really want to go out into that storm? With all the sand and wind, we won't know which way is up or down. We'll be lost in minutes."

"We have the homing device to guide us," I say and grip her shoulder, hoping to give some confidence. "We'll use the rope to keep us from getting separated."

We quickly tie the rope around each other's waists, making sure it's tight, and then step out of the building and into the storm. Almost immediately I begin to reconsider, though. The gale-force wind takes my breath away, and I nearly topple over from the rush of it. But I lean into it and press forward as I lead the group. The ruined buildings around us are burning and provide little protection as a wind break. In fact, some areas seem to funnel the wind into hurricane-force gusts. The howling wind screams in my ears, and the dust sticks to the back of my throat. I can see old television screens still humming with static in the abandoned apartment buildings, somehow with enough electricity to run them.

I press onward, staying low in the trenches and craters, occasionally checking the tracker to set our course straight.

About two kilometers into the trek, I feel the line suddenly go taut and turn to see Tripp rolling on the ground. Everyone rushes over and huddles around him.

"What's wrong with him!" Drake yells.

"I don't know. He just dropped," Grish yells back.

I take a knee and check Tripp's vitals. His breathing is shallow, and I have no medical experience to diagnose his condition. I dive into the medic kit from Lewin's bag and locate a med-patch. The label on the package says *sedative*.

"He's in shock, I think," Shiloe hollers over the wind. "Something he breathed in, possibly?"

I can only shake my head. "Dunno, we need to get help." I lift Tripp's narrow body over my shoulder and continue on. The others fall in behind me without a word.

We march past a house as we reach suburban areas and stop to search the garage. We find a few wooden garden tools and a few blankets inside. We fashion a makeshift stretcher and lay Tripp on it.

We move on as lightning fills the sky and rain pelts down. With three kilometers left on the hike I hear something whiz past my head and immediately drop to the ground. I yank the rope, and everyone does the same and lies flat. I hold my hand out, motioning for everyone to lay low and I send them a thought.

...sniper

As I lay in the mud, I search the horizon, but there are so many places for a sniper to hide. It's impossible to guess where the shot was fired from. Thoughts run wild in my head. *What if one of us is shot, and we already have a person to carry? What if we're stranded here for too long?*

Then, I remember the camouflage ability of the helmet's visor. I pull it low and hear the hum as it activates. The others see me disappear and do the same. Vern reaches over and activates Tripp's visor, too.

I consider, laying low a bit longer as I search for the sniper. But in the back of my mind, I wonder why a sniper would even be out in this wasteland in the first place. We're still several kilometers from the front line, which is in the lower canyons. Up here on the surface is no-man's land. Regardless, my main goal is to reach the outpost, where we can get Tripp some medical attention. After a few minutes, I tug on the rope, and we continue through the trenches, hoping that our camouflage will conceal our movements enough to avoid attention.

It's slow going. We're forced to stop often, not wanting to move too fast in case we're seen. After a kilometer or so, we slow to another halt. Ahead of us is a partially dry riverbed. I creep forward to look, but the drop-off is tremendous. Repelling down it will likely be too treacherous, especially with snipers around. I look for a way across and notice a bridge. Its wrecked framework is at the bottom of the ravine, though. Unfortunately, what had once been an engineering marvel lay buried by overgrowth and vegetation. Still, we need to find a way across, and I'm not willing to give up so easily. But there's so much trash and debris clogging the steep shoreline of the river that I don't think we can traverse the slope, especially with Tripp.

I pause, trying to think over the storm and driving rain.

That's when I notice areas of beatdown reeds and underbrush. I see disturbed earth where rocks have been shifted and moved. In fact, I begin to make out the form of a pathway that I hadn't noticed at first. The trampled vegetation is from foot traffic through the area. I squint my eyes and follow the barely visible line as it crisscrosses and switches back down the hillside. Then it meanders down low and into the sandy bars of the riverbed.

I rifle through Lewin's bag again until I find the old pair of binoculars. Its green-light ability allows me to see with greater clarity, as if it's daytime and the sun is shining. It takes a few seconds, but eventually, I spot the trail at the river bottom. It weaves between the rusted-out cars and other flotsam.

I tug on the rope and send out a mental thought, letting the others know I've found a way across the dry riverbed. We begin to move again. Cautiously, I work my way down the hillside, stopping occasionally to check and make sure I haven't wandered off the trail. Once we reach the riverbed, I pause again to regain my bearings. I see how the rusted cars almost seem to align. The path winds between them but also provides some shelter from the elements.

Finally, we reach the opposite side, and I check the tracker. I send a message to the others.

...less than a kilometer to go.

As we near our target, I start to see cratered-out pavement and ruined structures ahead. This region of the city wasn't spared either, and it's in the same disarray. Ruined cars and blown-out storefronts stare back at us as we scramble up the hillside. I frantically look for cover as we enter an open street and hurry around the abandoned vehicles. In the distance, I see an entrance to what I assume is the city's underground system, perhaps an old subway.

But then something strange happens. I can't send thoughts to the others anymore.

It feels as though a brain fog has set in, and it's difficult to think. This hasn't happened to me before, and I feel an urgency to find cover now. I lead our group toward the underground entrance. We're soon sprinting and hopping over the burned-out cars. When we reach the entrance, we flood down the stairs.

Halfway down is when we're attacked.

I wheel around to face several bandits to my left. Vern and Drake are forced to set Tripp and his stretcher down to defend themselves. Grish and Shiloe back toward Drake and Vern and we form a protective circle around Tripp.

I guess that the group of bandits outnumber us ten to one. They're armed with clubs and knives and move in from all sides. Soon it seems there are hundreds more rushing from below. Dozens more seem to magically appear from the street, and our escape route is blocked. In short order, Shiloe is pinned by several bandits. Grish, Vern and Drake struggle with the masses of other attackers surrounding us.

I fight them with everything I've learned from my training. Strangely, I feel sluggish, like the brain fog has spread throughout my body now. I begin to wonder if I'm being affected by the same ailment that took Tripp. My muscles are slow to respond. I feel sedated.

But how can this be?

Only yesterday, I felt ready to take on an army. Yet these bandits are overwhelming our group with ease. All the training and meditation and sparring seem to be for nothing. I'm confused and angry with myself. I'd led my friends into a trap. And now it appears we might be killed by a simple group of bandits. The North's greatest hope—the Immortals who are destined to lead our entire coalition to glory—have failed. And it's all my fault.

Eventually, a bandit has Drake in a headlock and a knife to his throat. Vern, Shiloe and Grish are all pinned with dozens of bandits on top of them. I'm the only one left standing to face the horde of bandits.

"That's it, Brindall." A man who I assume is the leader steps to the front. "It's over. You're all coming with us now."

But I stand there, looking at the bandit leader. I glance around at the others, the surroundings and cars and burned-out buildings. Something isn't right, and I feel a strange tingling in my head. I begin to retrace the events leading up to this point. *Is this all one big charade?*

Have I really misled our group so easily?

Are we really that unprepared?

None of this feels right. None of this makes any sense.

Then I hear a barely audible voice in my thoughts.

...it's all a lie.

The strange voice is no more than a whisper. But it *feels* intuitive, like it's trying to guide me. I listen to it.

I step forward and remove my helmet. "Is there anything else you doubt, Commander Freemantle?"

Shiloe, Drake, Grish and Vern all stare at me in shock, along with the bandits.

I hear Vern chuckle, despite the situation. "Have you lost your mind, Brin?"

"Of course not," I respond and smile at them. "But then again, none of this is real, is it, Triton?"

Next to me, the bandit holding the knife to Drake's throat glitches, then turns to static and disappears. One by one, the other bandits fade away until our group is alone. The stairs, the city and our surroundings glitch and then also disappear.

The next thing I know, I'm standing in a white box. The simulation room is roughly a twenty-meter cube. Triton, Commander Freemantle, Lewin and Guinn stand in front of us.

"Well done, Brin," Freemantle says. "What tipped you off that it was a simulation?"

Vern looks at Freemantle in confusion, then chuckles. "Simulation?"

"What exactly is goin' on?" Grish asks, tugging at her ponytails.

"A test, I think," I reply and give Grish a clap on the shoulder.

"Well?" Vern says, holding his hands up and waiting for an explanation.

"Yes, this was a simulation," Triton says. "A test, to see how you would react in a crisis situation. More importantly, how you would *react* as a team. And Brin, you sly devil," Triton continues and wags a finger at me with a grin. "How did you figure it out?"

"It took me a minute, but there were several clues along the way. It didn't all come together until the subway, though."

"Go on," Freemantle says, holding his hands toward me and giving me the floor.

I cross my arms and think back to the beginning. "Well, the crash, for one. Not saying we wouldn't have survived, but not a scratch? Seems unlikely. Then the enemy shelling in the middle of nowhere? Buildings and cars were on fire. There hasn't been war on the surface in decades. The TVs still functioning with no source of power…the impeccable timing of Tripp's sudden emergency. We also had exactly what we needed in the bag. Towards the end, I couldn't communicate with the others, and the sudden loss of strength. Am I missing anything?"

Triton nods and places a hand on my shoulder. "Seems like you caught it all."

"There was more to this exercise than just teamwork," I say.

"Correct again," Freemantle says. "You need a leader, and I needed to see it. I think we're beginning to see each of your special abilities and how they might complement the team."

Vern chuckles at that. "Well, you coulda just asked us, man. We already knew who that was gonna be."

Triton smiles. "Perhaps. But we needed to see it in action, and so did you, even if you didn't realize it." Then he turns to face me. "So, what do you say, Brin?"

I tilt my head and lift the corner of my lip, considering. I don't like the attention as everyone stares at me and waits. "I'm not really the one to make that decision."

"Which is why I am asking you to consider it. But we can take a vote, if you prefer." Triton turns to the others and crosses his arms, patiently waiting.

Shiloe steps up next to me. She places a hand on my shoulder. "You've got my vote, Brin. You know you do."

Then the others step forward and also place their hands on my shoulder. First Vern, then Drake, Tripp and finally Grish.

"We're behind you, Brin," Shiloe says. "No matter what happens. That's if you're willing to take the lead, of course."

I look at them each in turn. I see a group of kids that are so different than just a few weeks ago. In only a short amount of time, we've developed into hardened soldiers, and I wonder if it's that inner light that Miss Henak often refers to. The transformation we've gone through seems to have impacted us in different ways. But I know one thing: we're a team now, and there's no doubt that I can trust these five with my life.

"Well, how can I say no to that?" I say and smile at them.

Triton gives us the rest of that day off.

"Enough action for one day. Please take some well-deserved rest," he says.

I'm beyond tired. Even though the test was a simulation, it drained all of us, and our nerves were on edge. Now that the adrenaline has worn off, I also sense that the others are ready for some rest and meditation.

Our living quarters are in the central district of the military borough known simply as Sigma. We're placed high up on a massive rock pillar that has a platter-shaped dais at the top. From here, we get a grand view of the surrounding borough. Situated around the edge are small apartments that create a barrier. Inside the apartments are modest living spaces, including a kitchen, restroom, bedroom, and den. There is some food in the cabinets, mostly canned goods and rations. It's the nicest living accommodations I've ever had.

After I change and take a quick shower—with warm water, no less—I meet Vern and Shiloe in the middle of the dais, which is more of a common area. We sit and talk softly under the large dome.

"You two couldn't sleep either?" I ask and sit down on a large rock.

"How anyone can sleep after today's events is beyond me," Vern says.

"Well, Drake, Tripp, and Grish seem to have found the peace of mind," Shiloe says. "Suppose we should be meditating, anyway."

Vern taps his thigh with a drumroll. "Already done mine. And yes, it helps."

Shiloe gives him a brief smile, then settles back on her elbows. "So, if today was a test, what's next? Because I'm not sure I trust this group after today. I'm feeling slightly hoodwinked at the moment."

That draws a chuckle from Vern. "That's a fair assessment."

"What do you think, Brin?" Shiloe kicks at my boot.

I give her a shrug. "Well, they kind of have a point. There's a lot riding on us working as a unit. I suppose I'd want to know the team's strengths and weaknesses, too. It's the logical thing to do."

"So, what did we learn about ourselves today?" she asks.

"That we work pretty well together." Vern doesn't hesitate when he says this, though I catch a slight hiccup in his voice. I sense that he's still a bit shaken by what happened during the simulation.

Shiloe gives Vern and me a knowing look and seems to read our thoughts. "But…Grish and Tripp both wanted to turn back."

Vern shrugs. "Can't say I blame 'em, honestly. The pressure was a bit intense, man."

I nod. "Yeah, it was intense. Freemantle and Triton really turned it on. They're prepping us, and today was a small taste of what we might see. That much, at least, isn't a simulation."

"I don't want to go into the next mission, or whatever, thinking it's all a simulation," Shiloe says. "I feel like we need a way to test our team in a real scenario."

I lean forward onto my knees and take a few seconds to consider. "I think we'll get that chance soon. Something tells me Triton and Freemantle have more planned for us. Still, I feel like we did alright today. There were several times we faced a real crisis in the simulation, and we didn't cave."

"Because of you," Shiloe says. "That's why you're leading the charge."

I frown, trying to ignore the compliment. "Guys, I have no training at this. I've never led anyone before—"

"Shut up, Brin," Vern says and gives me a playful shove that nearly topples me off the stone bench. "You're taking the gig, no questions."

I sit back and give them both a long glance. "Look, you two need to be prepared. They want everyone to rely on one person. That's fine until something happens to me or we get split up. That might be something they're planning. I don't think Grish, Drake or Tripp are up to leading this group. You two should be prepared, just in case."

"Grish doesn't seem to want any responsibility," Vern says, counting on his fingertips. "Drake has a savior complex, which I think sometimes clouds his judgment. Tripp is always thinking about fairness and equality, and he's a bit gun-shy to boot."

"Exactly," I say. "We all have our quirks. But still, you two need to be ready."

Shiloe crosses her arms and gives me a frown. "I just hate to think about us getting separated now that we finally know each other. They've been harping about us working as a team all along. Why would they separate us?"

"There may be a time when we have to work in smaller groups," I say. "Just be ready for it, if that does happen, okay? I don't want you two relying on just me."

Both Shiloe and Vern nod.

"Understood, boss," Vern says.

Then, Shiloe slaps me on the shoulder hard enough to leave a red mark. I yelp in mock pain but smile at her, then put her in a headlock and roll to the floor.

"Hey, hey now!" Vern hollers and piles onto both of us. He lands on my stomach, knocking the air from my lungs. I laugh and groan as the three of us roll around. The ruckus brings Drake and Grish outside.

"What's this?" Drake yawns, his curly, tight-knit hair pressed flat to one side of his head.

Shiloe, Vern and I stop and point at each other. Grish and Drake take a seat on the rocks. Soon, Tripp stumbles out of his apartment with a bowl of something that resembles dry oatmeal and sits down.

"You feeling okay, Tripp?" I ask as I stand and dust myself off.

Tripp rubs his forehead, brushing back the curls of his sandy-red hair. "Yeah, no lingering effects, I guess. That simulation was crazy. I couldn't talk or move, not sure how they did it. Sorry to give you such a scare like that. I wanted to help, but I had to just lay there while you all carried my lazy butt everywhere. It could've cost us, but…thanks for doin' it." He looks at everyone, then looks down at his gruel as if embarrassed.

I can sense the angst in him, just like with Vern. He's clearly still rattled by the events of that day, and I feel some sympathy for him. I can see the guilt in his expression and know I'd probably react the same way if everyone was sacrificing for me.

"Hey." I reach over and slapped him on the leg. "Don't worry about it. That's why we're a team. You'd have done the same for any of us. We're learning to work as a unit and trust in each other. That simulation was scary for all of us."

"I know," Tripp says. "I was always the youngest back home and got left out a lot. It wasn't fair. But today, I didn't carry my fair share. I'm sorry. Won't happen again. It wasn't a month ago I was working in an accounting office. Now look at me. I'm an Immortal, sittin' here in some fancy borough that I didn't know existed, and the entire Northern Coalition expects me to help win this war."

Vern chuckles. "Ridiculous, right?"

"Well, I, for one, am glad we all met," Shiloe says. "Under unfortunate conditions, granted. Maybe this was destiny. Anyone else feel that way?"

"Yeah," Drake says, rubbing the scars on his neck. "You know, I think the same. Can't explain it neither. But I'm here for a reason."

Grish finally speaks up. "Maybe it's the Vishmu? Didn't Miss Henak say we'd continue to grow the more we practiced?"

"I do feel more aware of my surroundings, now that you mention it," Vern says.

"Nothing to do but continue on," I say. "Things are about to speed up, I'm afraid."

"You sure?" Shiloe asks. "I didn't think that was possible after today."

I narrow my eyes at her and give each of them a long look. "I think we're about to start our next phase, and they won't take it easy on us. It's one day at a time now."

Early the next morning, Lieutenant Guinn rouses everyone. In my closet is a lightweight uniform that's sized to fit me perfectly. The material clings tight to my body, some sort of elastic fabric in a royal blue. My old clothing is incinerated. I have just enough time to choke down some of the dry gruel and get a quick session of Vishmu in before Guinn directs us out of our living complex.

The transit network in the Sigma Borough is sophisticated, with traffic moving in all directions. We take an elevated rail system that deposits our group dozens of levels below. In the lower bowels, the traffic fades to white noise. Guinn leads us by foot across several thoroughfares and dark stone-hewn passages, where we end our trek at what appears to be another training facility.

"You didn't really think Triton would just throw you all into the grinder like that, did you?" Guinn remarks as she turns to face us. "You were right all along, Brindall. You are not ready yet. Here begins the next stage of your training."

"Do you mean to say that the front line is still stable?" Tripp asks.

"Yes, for the moment," Guinn replies. "But we must ready you all. Our intel hints that the South is preparing their team of Immortals. It's a race now."

Triton stands in a large open bay inside the facility, waiting for us.

This training center, like the one Miss Henak led, feels much the same with its earthen walls and dusty stone floors. As with most spaces I've seen so far, this one, too, has a high, domed ceiling with a stasis field that soars overhead. Smooth rock walls, which are reinforced with steel plates, stretch upward in red and tan striations. I notice the same familiar venues: a sparring area, several meditation alcoves, and some study areas with racks of old books and charts.

"Congratulations." Triton holds out his arms and gestures to the space around us. "You've all leveled up. Now begins your next stage of training. First things first, though. We'll expand your fighting abilities. However, the mental training exercises you will continue on your own time, twice a day at minimum—morning and evening. Then, as much as you can beyond that. For your second phase you'll be introduced to some much more intense hand-to-hand combat. The third phase will be live-action. I'm talking about live-fire drills to reinforce your teamwork. This is the real deal, no more simulations. Give me two…Grish and Drake," Triton says and motions for them to step forward. "I want you to take me down."

Drake looks from Triton to us, then back. "Sir, no offense, but you're about sixty-five, right?"

"And there are two of you, both Immortals," Triton says, circling Drake and Grish. "Should be easy, no? Let's see what Henak has taught you."

Tyberius stands calmly in the middle of the sparring mat, his hands behind his back. Grishum and Drake look at each other uncertainly, then back to Tyberius.

"Well, what are you two waiting for?" Triton says, almost in a mocking tone. His hands are up now, and I can tell he's had some training just by his movements.

Grish walks in front with Drake circling around behind Triton. Vern, Tripp, Shiloe and I stand to the side and watch. I catch Guinn cupping her hand over her mouth to hide a smile. I can tell that this isn't the first time Triton's done this. He's no amateur, but can he best two Immortals? He might have more experience, but our enhanced speed, agility and strength would make up for any lack of training, at least I assume.

Grish leaps at Triton while Drake slides in low to take out his footing.

But somehow, Triton seems to guess their individual attacks and skips over Drake's leg sweep. Then Triton ducks under Grish's punch in one fluid motion. He rolls across the mat and almost magically materializes behind Drake before he can reset. Triton spins and pushes off of Grish. Drake immediately presses in from behind and leaps on Triton's back. But Triton rolls just as Drake is airborne. He flips to his feet, then sweeps Grish's legs out and takes her to the mat. Suddenly, Triton has managed to pin both Grish and Drake with each arm in a matter of seconds.

Shiloe, Vern, Tripp and I look on in shock. It's evident to us all—as powerful as we are, that even an Immortal can be bested by a well-trained fighter, even a sixty-year-old veteran.

Triton stands and helps Grish and Drake to their feet, then places his hands on his hips and faces us. "You both underestimated your opponent, that's mistake number one. Mistake number two: you didn't work as a team. In the next few weeks, I will teach you how to become a deadly warrior. You now have gifts—you're Immortals. But if you don't think on your feet, what good are those abilities? Even a mere mortal can defeat *and* potentially kill an Immortal. Never forget that. Never take your power for granted."

Drake and Grish dust themselves off and join the rest of us.

"Pair up, all of you," Triton says.

Shiloe and I face each other while Drake and Vern pair up, and Grish and Tripp take the far mat. I smile at Shiloe as she smiles back at me.

"Here we go again," I say and wink at her. "I owe you some payback from our last match, miss."

"Is that so?" Shiloe replies and blows me a kiss. "Let's see if you've learned anything then."

We begin to spar and ignore the others. It's as if no one else is there as we pace the floor, facing one another. Shiloe is quick, and I could swear that her strength has increased since our last fight. Even without physical training over the last several days, she's improved. It's evident that simply meditating with Vishmu has indeed enhanced her abilities in a short time. But I've also been meditating.

Time seems to pause as we spar. Shiloe manages to take me to the mat. But then I also bring her down. We go round after round, neither of us wanting to give up or stop. Her competitive nature rivals mine—Shiloe matches my ability in nearly every aspect.

Soon, I can sense the others have finished and are watching us. Even Triton and Guinn are watching us fight. Back and forth, we trade blows until I eventually make a mistake. I overcompensate and lunge too far. I try to correct and catch my balance, which allows Shiloe an opening, and she takes advantage. She grips me under my left arm and flips me into the air. On my way down, she times a perfectly executed roundhouse kick into the small of my back. I go flying through the air and hit the rock wall. I lay on the stone floor for several seconds, trying to catch my breath. I struggle to my feet to see Shiloe smiling at me with her arms crossed. The others are clapping and hooting. I hear Vern whistle in approval as I wince at my bruised ribs.

"That's two to nothing, Brin," Shiloe says, still grinning.

Triton guides me back to the sparring area. “Well, it looks like you two have something going. Let’s keep it good-natured, though.” He turns to face the others. “I can see that Shiloe and Brin have been meditating more than the rest of you. Please do not underestimate the importance of this; it may mean the difference between life and death. Vishmu is the lifeblood of your abilities.”

Triton motions for us to take a seat on the mats. “Out there, on the front lines, there is no mercy or break in the action. I won’t be there, and Henak cannot help you. You still have a lot to learn, and in a very short amount of time, I might add. You all have immense power, and your mind and body are sprinting to catch up. I can only show you the right way. The rest is up to the individual. You must continue to develop your unique ability, so this team can function properly. Let’s move on.”

We spend the rest of that day working on sparring. Triton shows us several more complex maneuvers. It’s obvious that he’s seen extensive combat and is a master in hand-to-hand fighting, even more so than Henak. After just one day of training with Triton, we’ve already moved up to the next level.

That night, after Triton dismisses us for the day, we shower, eat and go through our routine meditations. It helps recharge the energy we’ve spent during our training. We sit around in the common area of our living facility and rehash the events and what we’ve learned. I notice that the instructors no longer check to see if we’re sleeping or getting our evening meditations in. We’ve now earned their trust in that regard, it seems.

“You sore?” Vern asks me. “Because it looked like Shiloe got the best of you today.” He flashes his wide grin at me and pushes me playfully.

I smile back. It’s impossible not to with Vern. “Just my ribs. Shiloe, you need to take it easy on me. Otherwise, you’ll have to lead these hooligans.”

Shiloe chuckles but then frowns a bit. "This is a whole other level of training. Triton's a killer, you know? I can tell he's seen live combat."

"Without a doubt," Drake says. "He literally disappeared when I attacked him. I've never seen anyone move that quick."

Grish seems to wake up. She leans forward and wraps her arms around her knees. "It's getting' real. I didn't feel so rushed with Henak, but the intensity level here is a lot higher. We're not gonna get much of a break with Triton, I reckon."

Tripp leans back and stretches his short frame. "I imagine it's just like we've been hearing. The Northern Coalition is probably investing a lot in these instructors. We won't find better teachers than the ones we have right now. I just wonder how these people know so much about us."

"They've been training Immortals for a long time, I assume," Shiloe says.

"But who trained them?" Tripp asks.

"Maybe no one," Shiloe says. "Why can't these instructors just be professionals? They obviously have a lot of experience from the war."

But Tripp lays there with his arms crossed, shaking his head. "I dunno. I just get the sense there's more about these instructors. It just seems odd to me."

"We already know they're not telling us everything," Shiloe says.

"Yep. Still smells like a coverup," Grish whispers and leans in.

"Right," Tripp says. "And why is everyone calling this a game? I mean, we're fighting for territory, which equates to resources, primarily minerals and rare-earth. What's all that stuff really being used for? That big space station up there?"

"You don't think this fight for resources is real?" Drake asks.

"Oh, it's real," Tripp replies. "People are dying for this stuff. But they're saying there's not enough room for everyone on the Skylight System. Do you really believe that?"

"What're you getting at, Tripp?" Drake asks.

"It just seems like these Elites are burnin' through all their resources pretty quickly to win this contract. Remember, I do a lot of accounting. Numbers are my thing. I can tell something isn't adding up."

"By resources, you mean citizens?" Grish says and tugs at her iron collar, which elicits a warning buzz.

"And if we don't fight, our families will be sacrificed," Shiloe says. "It just doesn't seem like Henak and Triton, even Freemantle, would support such a thing."

"Who says they do?" I say. "Maybe they're just following orders. Maybe their families are in the same situation? Either way, do you really want to take that risk? I don't."

"That's admirable, Brin," Grish says, a hint of sarcasm evident. "But not everyone is built like you. No one asked if I wanted this. This isn't my responsibility."

"Doesn't really matter what we think, right?" Vern chuckles. "We're in this, and we don't get an option."

"Maybe it's not a bad idea if we keep our eyes open, just a little bit, anyway," Shiloe says, more or less directing the comment at me. "Who knows? We might dig up something."

Everyone looks at me, waiting. I shrug and hold up my hands. "I suppose it can't hurt as long as it doesn't get in the way of our training. That's the most important goal right now."

"I'd argue the opposite," Grish says. Tripp and Drake nod. "If there's a conspiracy behind all of this, it might be more important than you think."

"Surviving what's ahead of us and protecting our families is more important, Grish."

"Easy for you to say. You have a family that cares for you. That's not the case for all of us."

I remember Grish, Tripp and Drake all saying they'd had family issues, glad to be away from them, actually. They'd lived through a fractured childhood. Am I being insensitive or focusing on my own desires too much? What if Grish is right, and there's a bigger picture to all of this? *Maybe all of our challenges aren't meant to be fought on the battlefield?*

I reach out to Grish and look at Tripp and Drake. "Look, I'm sorry. I know you all didn't have the greatest upbringing. But…I think we can do both. We'll keep our ears open, like Shiloe said. In the meantime, we continue to focus on the task at hand. Sound good?"

Shiloe yawns rather loudly, breaking the tension. "Sounds like a plan. Now, I need to get my beauty sleep, and based on what I saw from everyone's sparring today, I'd suggest you all do the same." She slaps me on the shoulder hard enough to leave a mark, then heads to her sleeping quarters.

One by one, the others say good night and leave. Soon, I'm alone, and I sit staring up at the dome, lost in thought. Something about our training today still bothers me.

Triton.

The way he moved…the way he seemed to almost read our thoughts. Something isn't right with that man. If Grish wants to find a conspiracy, perhaps we won't have to look very far to find it.

Do I trust Triton?

Maybe…or maybe not.

DINNER PARTY | CHAPTER 8

B E H Θ I M

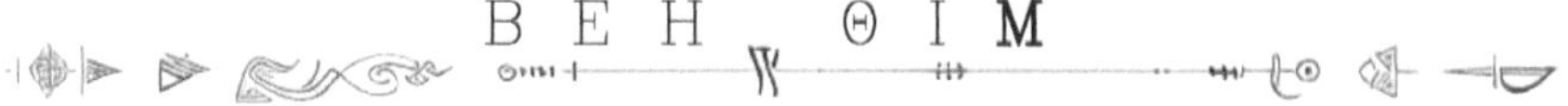

Once again, our entire group is up and at it early the next day. It's something that I acknowledge as a fixture in my new life, and I wonder if I'll ever get to sleep in again. Before all of this, I'd lived with a somewhat relaxed schedule, working long hours but able to come and go as I pleased. Those days are long gone.

We push through a rigorous physical training routine with Triton that day as he barks at us. I continue to study his moves and actions, though I'm still not sure what to think about him. Regardless of my uncertainty, Triton is showing us things we've never thought of when it comes to combat. The man seems to be a master at every type of fighting style, and on top of it all, he is a fantastic teacher. He's able to communicate with us in a way that seems so simple, even with some of the most technical maneuvers. He is indeed a master at his craft, and I'm thankful for that.

Day by day, I improve, and so does Shiloe. She's an amazing fighter and picks things up remarkably quickly. The others are also progressing, though not at Shiloe's pace. She is definitely our ace. Though I'm reluctant to admit it, I feel drawn to her more each day.

Every morning and evening, I meditate before breakfast and dinner. I can sense my inner light becoming more substantial, brighter and more powerful. I'm learning to enjoy the Vishmu sessions. What had once been disturbing and unsettling is now my favorite time of day, and it leaves me feeling rejuvenated. Though I still struggle to understand the things I witness, I continue to push beyond my comfort zone. Sometimes, I wonder if the things I see are from other planes of existence. Are these events in the past? The future? Am I seeing my own fate? I even begin to wonder if I can alter the things I see. I know one thing for certain—my bizarre journey over the last month is beyond comprehension. And as much as I've grown spiritually, I've also grown physically. My speed, strength and agility are well beyond a human's ability, and they continue to increase.

I spar with my newfound friends as we all continue to grow and develop under Triton's tutelage. We've reached another plateau in our journey. After leaving Miss Henak's facility, I didn't think we could get much stronger. I was wrong.

But soon, our time is nearing an end with Triton. On our final evening, he invites us to dinner to celebrate.

Triton's dwelling unit is much larger than ours and a bit more lavish than I expected. When we arrive, he gives us a tour around his home. Everything is pristine and seemingly untouched, as if he rarely spends time in it. I notice his sleeping quarters look undisturbed too, and I wonder if he ever rests.

The dining table is carved from rock, and it's loaded with food. The six of us, including Triton, gather around the table and sit down to eat. I've never really had a homecooked meal, and I can tell the others haven't either. This is a first for us all. I'm so used to gruel that I don't even recognize some of the food. But here, in this wealthy borough, it appears that Triton has access to many delicacies. I see some rare food types I'd only heard about: fruits, vegetables, and even some types of meat, which I'm told are processed in a special district. Even though we don't have many of the things the human race once had, there are plenty of necessities we can still manufacture here in the underground boroughs, including rare foods.

Triton watches us eat from the head of the table but doesn't partake in the festivities. Vern and Drake load up several plates and stuff their faces as the rest of us sit and enjoy the meal at a slower pace.

"I'm sad to see you go," Triton says. "You're all moving along nicely. I'm honored to have been a part of this journey with you."

I set my drink down and clear my throat. "Sir, I think I can speak for us all by saying thank you. But…is it okay if I ask you a question?"

"Please. I'm happy to answer whatever I can."

The others pause and wait. "You're obviously a very accomplished fighter. Where'd you learn it all?"

Triton sits back, as if drawing from some distant memory. "Well, let's see…I fought alongside Miss Henak many years ago. Those were the days before the North and South Coalitions. There was no frontline along the 37th parallel, the contract for Skylight didn't exist back then. I met Commander Gorgan decades ago and he recruited me into his service. When the Coalition split and the Frontline Wars began, I decided to share my knowledge and serve a higher purpose, which was training Immortals like you six."

"How did you end up here in the North?" I ask.

"I was born in the Northern territory. I suppose I could have left and gone anywhere, but I felt like my purpose was here. Plus, Commander Gorgan requested my help. He's not a man you say no to. He may seem harsh, but his spirit is kind."

"Speaking of coalitions, why are there differing priorities between the North and South?" Shiloe asks. "I mean, the Skylight System seems like a pretty big place. Maybe there's enough room for everyone. Why can't we work together?"

That elicits a chuckle from Triton. "I wish it were that easy, Shiloe. Once lines are drawn in the sand, it isn't so easy to erase them. Decades of fighting leave invisible scars. Unfortunately, there is no desire on either side to mend those scars, even if there is enough room for everyone on Skylight. Besides, living there in peace would be impossible. Bringing this war to the system would eventually destroy it as well. That said, only one side can win the right to settle there. I wish it wasn't so, and we could live in peace. But that time passed long ago."

"It's a shame. It all seems so petty," she says, her chin propped in her hands.

"Agreed," Triton says. "The Skylight System creators are up there working to finish it. They realize all of this as well, and thus the contract. The winning side is granted the right to populate the system as they see fit. It may seem petty or even cruel to leave so many people behind, but this is the way. What risk would you take, what sacrifice would you make, for your family and their future generations to have the chance to live in peace? An opportunity to live like our past generations, among nature as it once was. It's the chance of a lifetime."

Vern shakes his head. "But all the killing and fighting, sir…I just don't know. It doesn't feel right, man."

"Vern, you have a good heart. I would say don't lose that compassion. But at the same time, you will have to fight to save yourself and those you love. When you finally hit the battlefield, you must set those feelings aside. It won't be easy, but you must. All of you must do this."

As Triton speaks, I still wonder about his motives. But as I listen, I realize how genuine he is and that there's no doubt he's a good man. I detect no cruelty or malice in him.

"How do you know so much about us? About Immortals?" I ask.

Triton seems to consider, perhaps caught off guard by the question. "Well, there's plenty of documentation over the years. We've learned a lot about Immortals through prior generations. We continue to pass that information down."

"And what do you think of this?" Grish gives a quick, spiteful tug at her signature collar. "Do you believe we're still fighting for the 'right cause' while we have these around our necks?"

Triton holds her gaze for a long moment. I sense a split second of sadness in his expression. But it's quickly replaced by a clinical detachment, almost like a trained response to something he doesn't agree with but is forced to deal with anyway. "That I cannot answer. I am only here to help develop your abilities."

"Yet, you don't agree with our treatment, I can sense." Grish clenches her jaw in frustration. "You follow orders, and you'll not intervene on our behalf. I wonder, does Commander Freemantle feel the same?"

I reach across the table and place a hand over Grish's. "We've already talked about this. Let's just focus on what we have to do, at least for now."

Triton continues to hold her gaze, though, before speaking. I sense that he chooses his words very carefully. "If there was more that I could do at this moment, I would. Right now, the best I can offer is my teaching. Let us hope it will deliver you all through the ordeal to come, at least until a time when we can address more important matters."

That gets my attention, and I begin to wonder if there's something more he's insinuating.

"What should we expect now?" I ask. The others lean in and wait.

Triton's brow comes to a point, and he places his elbows on the table. "Once you hit the battlefield, an array of killer mech units. For starters, the TRI-SENTINELS, the South's most powerful unit. Then there's the V-ORPS, the giant niners, E-Class mechs—which can see into multiple spectrums—not to mention the enemy troops and the multitude of special units the South has at their disposal. All these mechs are designed for different purposes. The most numerous, and perhaps the deadliest, are the *Maulers*, or 'death hounds', which are smaller and more maneuverable mechs. They're fast, human-sized units that the South deploys to swarm the front lines. They utilize steel claws and teeth, can see in the dark and move as quickly as an immortal. Then you have the larger mechs, designed for different purposes. Some are heavy and slow, engineered for absorbing damage. Others are faster and designed to seek out our most valuable assets—immortals, like you six. There are a few units that can even hover over the battlefield, but we've figured out how to deal with those. We've heard rumors of subterranean mechs that can burrow beneath the battlefield, but there's been no sign of those yet."

"So, what you're sayin' is *watch our backs*," Vern says, a sarcastic grin on his broad face.

"What I'm saying is that you will face many challenges, not just dark immortals. I'm not trying to frighten you, but you need to know what it is that you will face. We will train you in how to approach the different types of units and how to identify them."

Everyone remains silent, letting the reality of it sink in.

Then, Triton drums his hands on the table. "What you can expect moving forward is the last phase of your training. At the end, you must face a very dangerous exercise."

Vern narrows his eyes and tilts his head. "Dangerous exercise, huh? This isn't another simulation, is it?"

"There will be no more simulations, that I can promise you. This will be the real thing."

"When and where?" Drake asks as he sits forward and balls his fist into his palm.

Triton lowers his gaze and crosses his arms. "You have one final instructor. If you pass beyond that level, then you'll face the final test. Death is a possibility, and no one will step in to help. You will be alone."

"Is this the same challenge previous Immortals have faced?" Tripp asks, his cheeks flushed. I can hear the nervous tension in his voice.

"It varies, depending on many things, mainly how well the team meshes," Triton says. "We evaluate your ability to work together, then we customize the challenge based on that. Your particular group is uniquely tightknit, something we haven't seen in a long time. It's not always that way. You should be proud of that. It makes you all stronger and more likely to succeed."

Despite the specter of death, we continue to talk with Triton, sharing background about our families and upbringing. Eventually, the ominous feeling of the final challenge fades. Vern works hard to get Triton to laugh, but only manages a brief smile. We chat late into the night, enjoying each other's company and the splendid food, which I'll probably never taste again.

Around eleven o'clock, we bid Triton goodnight, and we're escorted back to our living facility. I say goodnight to everyone, but Shiloe lingers as the others wander off to their sleeping quarters.

"About tomorrow," she says and sits down on one of the large rocks. "It'll be our last day here. It's silly to keep worrying about it, but I just wonder if they'll split us up."

I notice the hesitation in her movements, the slight shake of her hand. Shiloe is nervous.

"Triton did mention working as a team," I say. "That gives me some hope that they won't. Plus, he said something about a final phase of our training, which means we'll likely be together for that. Is there more that's bothering you?"

"I…just don't want to lose touch with you…and everyone else." She looks down and draws lines in the dirt with her foot. "Actually, there is something else, but I'm afraid to say it."

Shiloe holds my gaze, then places her right hand on her knee, palm up. The orange light pouring from the wound sparkles in the dim lighting. I can see the gossamer outline of her symbol of the letter 'B'.

I take a deep breath and reach out to her. I place my hand over hers. My turquoise glow and the symbol of the letter 'M' are noticeable. Our colors mix together, and I feel my hand and arm begin to tingle. Our colors seem to meld in the dark, the supernatural light from our wounds blend together: orange and turquoise. Her light enters my palm, mine does the same with hers. My chest heaves and I catch my breath. I feel a sudden longing I've never known before. My heart races as Shiloe looks into my eyes. I feel her squeeze my hand, and our fingers intertwine and lock together. Her eyelids drop slightly and her breath catches. I can barely keep myself from leaning in toward her.

"Wonder what we'll do?" Shiloe says, her voice a slow murmur in the darkness.

"I don't know," I whisper back. "We need each other. I feel like we've always needed each other, don't you?"

Shiloe only nods as she continues to hold my hand and look at me. She reaches out and takes my other hand and intertwines her fingers. For an instant, I feel so connected with her, as if we are one entity. The world around us seems to fall away, as if nothing else matters at that moment. I feel like I'm floating, like I'm meditating with Vishmu, and only Shiloe is there. It's familiar, like I've been here before, in this same moment with her, but eons ago. The surreal feeling lasts only a few seconds, but I feel a lifetime of longing flood through me.

I hear the groan of a door and see Vern step out of his apartment. He cups his hand over his eyes, searching the dark. Then he sees us and our hands interlocked.

I quickly release Shiloe's hands, and she does the same. We both stand and stumble around, flustered.

"Did I interrupt something?" Vern says, and there's a wide grin on his dark face. He walks over to stand opposite of us and crosses his arms.

Shiloe shakes her head and looks at me, her cheeks flushed. "No—uh, I was…just looking for something. Think I found it, though."

"Yeah," I say, and straighten my shirt. "Think we found it."

Then Shiloe waves and hurries off to her apartment, shutting the door behind her.

Vern follows her, then turns and gives me a quick wink. "Yeah. I'd say you found something too, Brin."

Triton goes easy on us the next morning. One last favor, maybe a sendoff gift, I think. Or perhaps he feels there's nothing more he can teach us. Either way, it's the most relaxed training day I've had yet.

That afternoon, we gather our items and wait in a large hangar bay with Triton. As we wait for the transport, he says goodbye to each of us. He stops in front of me last while everyone else boards the transport.

"Keep your calm, Brindall. They'll need that from you. Your leadership could mean the difference in this battle."

I'm caught by surprise and struggle to keep my voice calm and my hands steady. "I…I'll do my best. Thank you, again. I'll remember your lessons."

Our transport exits through an airlock and into the darkened tunnel. I don't mind the g-forces this time, and Tripp and Grish even catch a good nap as we zip toward our next stop, which still hasn't been revealed to us.

Our transit takes less than thirty minutes. I try to guess which way we're heading, but it's difficult to get my bearings. My instincts tell me we're heading east along the dividing line, though. We glide along the charged rail and past rough terrain. Suddenly, the tunnel opens up and I see another domed city along the horizon. This one is truly massive, though, and much larger than the first two military ports we've visited.

Our transport enters the enormous dome, along with thousands of other transits and ships, which move seamlessly through numerous airlocks. Hundreds of supply frigates exit the dome and ascend upward toward the Skylight System, which I assume are carrying supplies. We cruise into the dome and maneuver along busy traffic lanes.

Like the other port cities, below us are thousands of thin graphene thoroughfares, all layered at different elevations, spanning through the depths. This city is a series of rings interlocked together, unlike the others, which were just one massive loop. I can see citizens, workers and troops traversing the highways as our transport slows.

We finally dock at a lower hangar bay, and everyone hops off. Waiting for us is a group of soldiers led by a lady with silver hair. I notice an electric blue highlight down the middle of her bangs that shimmers in the light. She doesn't look to be much older than us, though I guess she's in her early thirties. Her dark skin is sinewy and ripples with muscle. She wears sleeveless military fatigues that match the earth strata around us. On her chest pocket are a few medals, and her rank is stitched into the fabric.

We march over to stand before her as our bags are unloaded and piled along one side. The soldiers stand at attention as the lady faces us, her hands behind her back.

"Welcome to the Belt Line Borough and your final training assignment," she says, bouncing on her tiptoes as she looks at each of us. I note the same stern but confident expression in her gaze as with Henak and Triton. There's no hesitation in her movement, no waver in her voice. "I trust that Henak and Triton have honed your abilities. If so, then you're in a good position to survive this final phase. My name is Kiff, and I'll be your last instructor. Follow me."

She leads us into a large steel structure built into the side of an enormous rock wall. Inside the space, I see a familiar style of architecture. Like the other facilities, this one has an open area that stretches the length of the building. There are multiple levels, which I assume separate the living quarters from the training facility.

Soon, we're sitting in another control room. But this one seems to have a more modern feel, thanks to the newer equipment. I assume there's a greater need for higher technology since this port is the closest to the front line. Of course, the Northern Coalition would want greater awareness, and the need for rapid response would be crucial here.

Kiff walks around the room, stopping at some of the terminals to examine the streaming data. She turns abruptly to face us, her hands tucked behind her back. "What you're seeing in this room is the most sensitive equipment in all the Northern Territory. Do any of you know why?"

Tripp lifts his hand, somewhat hesitantly. "We're pretty close to the front line."

Kiff nods and snaps a finger in his direction. "Correct. We need every edge we can get. We have to know when an area is falling below the fifty percent threshold so we can send immediate reinforcements. We keep rapid-response teams at the ready so we can scramble them in the event of imminent collapse. You six will be a part of this rapid-response team. This state-of-the-art equipment and facility will help us win the war."

Kiff walks over to the wall of displays and points at the three-dimensional holograms stretching the length of the room. It shows an enhanced satellite graphic of three large areas which I know now as the 37th parallel line. Commander Freemantle had referred to them as the Eastern, Western, and Central Theaters.

"Here," Kiff continues, pointing at the display. "The blue-shaded regions represent areas currently under our control and safe. Red indicates Southern control. The blue areas with red stripes are Northern territories at risk: areas that are susceptible to surprise attacks. Note the percentage at the top of the display."

We all look at the display and the number, which is currently at a fraction of a percent above fifty. This number fluctuates constantly, though, as if it's being instantaneously updated with the live battle footage in the holograms. The percentage shifts from just a hundredth of a percent.

Kiff remains silent, as if letting the moment sink in.

From one angle, I see the fluctuating number while the battle footage shows the war raging and troops dying. The satellite image shows reds and blues constantly adjusting as territory is won, then lost. Through the control window, I see military personnel below rushing around and preparing for deployment. War frigates, tanks and other war vehicles are being loaded while garrisons march around the hangar bays. All the while, low concussive booms shake the room as heavy artillery rounds explode just kilometers beyond. I can even smell the acrid scent of the war.

Kiff finally breaks the silence. "This has been going on for decades without a break in the action. I'm sure Commander Freemantle mentioned the three theaters. Any guess why the contract is limited to just the three theaters?"

"Because they're the most accessible areas," I say.

"That's partially correct," Kiff nods and jabs a finger at me. "The cave systems between the north and the south along that 37th parallel are separated by those three canyons. The line is heavily guarded. We have outposts and sensors in place, as does the Southern Coalition."

Shiloe nods to the display. "So, why not just overload one of the theaters?"

"If the South were to send that many troops to one area, we'd know. Relocating that much equipment would send a signal. We would quickly overwhelm the other two theaters. Short answer—it would be game over for the South. So, the framers of this contract limited the war to just the three theaters. Now, this is where you six might come into play."

Vern raises one eyebrow. “You expect that six people can sway that much territory?”

“I believe that six Immortals can, yes.” Kiff crosses her arms. “That’s what your final training will prepare you for.”

But Vern shakes his head and lets out a low chuckle. “I just don’t see how.”

“No?” Kiff says. “Then pay close attention to what I teach you. If you finish my training and still don’t believe, then nothing can save you.”

“How many other Immortals have you trained?” Shiloe says.

Kiff gives Shiloe a quick smile, the corner of her lips curling up in an impish sort of way. “Honest answer? More than I care to count.”

Vern begins to laugh. “Honesty for once. I like this lady.”

“What’s funny about that, Vern?” Grish says, gritting her jaw at him.

“I find no humor in this either,” Tripp chimes in, his cheeks suddenly flushed red.

“Hey, you have to appreciate her directness,” Vern continues. “I mean, would you rather have someone telling us more lies? Give me the brutal truth every time.” He holds up his hands defensively.

“What makes us any different than all the others?” I ask, turning the conversation back.

“Every time we instructors train an Immortal, we learn a bit more. Each Immortal passing gives us greater insight into your unique powers. That sounds a bit insensitive, I know. But you need to hear these things, some of them you won’t like. While it’s rare to find an Immortal in any given borough with such a large population in the North, we come across them more often than you might expect. But we haven’t had six of you at the same time for as long as I can recall. Your personas are all different. Our belief is that you’ll complement each other very well as a team. Bringing six Immortals into the fold at once may sway things in our favor, and at just the right time, too.”

Tripp starts to speak, then stops to reconsider and starts over. "What about the opposing Immortals? The ones fighting for the South have more experience, I would think."

Kiff tucks her hands behind her back. "We know they have several Immortals. We don't know how many. Of the three theaters, the fighting is the most intense here in the Central Theater." She points at the satellite map and the vast area of territory wedged between the right and left. "Whoever holds a majority of the central territory has a tactical advantage. That's most likely where the South will send all of their Immortals. We'll soon know more about them when you deploy there. We believe the South will show us their full assortment. As far as experience goes, yes. The opposing Immortals have seen more combat. But remember, you're a team. That's your key, and it's more important than experience. You'll get that soon enough."

"Are these three theaters equally split?" Tripp asks, showing a true interest. Then I remember that he was an accountant, and we're talking numbers now.

"Almost. The Central Theater holds slightly more territory. We hold the majority of that theater, which is currently the difference in the war. The other two theaters are essentially split equally between the North and the South. Holding the Central Theater is crucial. That's why you six will deploy there first. That's where you'll likely face the other Immortals and your greatest challenge."

THE VESSELS | **CHAPTER 9**

Kiff doesn't give us much time to unpack or catch our breath. As soon as we drop our bags off, Kiff asks that we change into our tactical gear. Then she leads us up to the training facility, which is on the highest level of the complex. From this vantage, I can actually hear the sizzling of the rain on the large stasis dome like static electricity. It feels like the storm outside might shatter the dome's protective shield and rain down lightning and hail onto our small group.

We start out on our meditation mats, clearing our minds with Vishmu. It's definitely something we all need, considering how hectic the morning has been. Along one side of the large open deck are rock walls and tiny cave openings, like the facility had been built around the natural formations. The other side opens out onto the decks below with metal guardrails surrounding the edge. Otherwise, the upper platform is mostly flat.

"This will be your first live exercise," Kiff says as we each pull from our meditative state. "Triton might have given you a heads up. Well, I hope you're prepared, because in those caves is a vessel. Your mission is to retrieve it. Don't worry, you'll know it when you see it. Be warned, you *will* face resistance. If you don't return with the vessel in thirty minutes' time, you've failed."

The six of us look around in confusion.

Vern holds his hand up and waits for permission to speak.

"Vern, put your hand down," Grish says and pulls on his arm.

"It's okay, Vern," Kiff says. "Just ask."

"Is that it?" he says. "That's all there is to this phase of training? Just one exercise?"

"Who said anything about that?" Kiff says curtly.

"I'm sorry," Grish snaps. "But where is the training part? You just said you'd be training—"

"Yes, but I didn't say when, did I?" Kiff says.

"What if we fail?" Shiloe asks.

"I guess we'll see, won't we? But I suggest that you don't, because it might be the last thing you do. Remember, you're a team." Kiff doesn't say anything else but snaps her fingers and a holographic timer begins ticking above the main cave's entrance. Then, a modulated voice starts the countdown.

"Let's move!" Kiff barks. She claps her hands and hurries around, slapping us on our backs.

I immediately turn and pull everyone together. "I'm guessing there're mech units in the caves. Remember your armor's camouflage. Stay hidden. There's probably a network of tunnels to slow us down. Let's split up into three groups. Vern and Tripp, take the left. Grish and Drake, go right. Shiloe and I will take the center. Use Vishmu to communicate. Take a deep breath and stay calm. Think. No panic! Let's move."

We move into the tunnel complex. Once inside, Shiloe and I take the central corridor. The rocky trails are mostly gravel and dirt, making it difficult to walk without causing a cascading echo down the narrow tunnels. We pause sometimes to listen, but after five or so minutes, we hear nothing. Occasionally, the modulated voice breaks the silence, and I begin to notice the time is announced every five minutes.

In my thoughts, I hear Shiloe wondering where the resistance is. I can only shrug as we move through vast chambers connected by the tunnel. The rock striations are lit with shale ferns. The bioluminescent plants infiltrate every nook and cranny, bathing the walls in a minty-green glow. The trail meanders down into the bottom of what looks like a natural spring, and the earthy fragrance hits my nostrils. On the far side, I can make out a narrow stone stairway. It cuts back and forth up the steep slope. The stairs lead my gaze up to the top, where a glowing crystal is perched on the edge of a cliff.

...there's our vessel. I send the thought to Shiloe.

...it's obviously a trap, she replies.

We remain crouched in the shadows, sharing thoughts on the best approach. Finally, we decide to split up. I send a thought to the other two teams, pinning our location. But the time is now past the halfway mark. With less than fifteen minutes, we don't have time to wait for the others.

I know as soon as we grab the vessel, we'll see this so-called resistance.

I ask Shiloe to wait by the chamber's entrance. My plan is to grab the vessel and then hand it off to her. I think I can throw it from above, which gives her a free path out of the chamber.

...no, Brin, Shiloe says. *I'm the better fighter. It makes sense for me to go first.*

...but you might get overwhelmed.

...no time to argue, Brin. Shiloe moves into the pit and begins racing up the narrow stairs.

I shake my head and mutter under my breath, but back toward the chamber entrance and wait.

Shiloe hops up the stairs, slipping and stumbling on a few occasions. I watch her, holding my breath as it seems to take her an eternity. But she finally reaches the summit and sprints over and lifts the vessel.

As soon as it's removed from the pedestal, the sides of the cave crumble, and at least a dozen mech units march out. I've never seen anything like these before. But then again, I've literally been living under a rock my entire life. I can see right away that these mechs are the latest technology in the Northern Coalition's arsenal. They stand upright on two legs, perhaps four meters in height. Each one has four arms and looks to be constructed of some strange metal.

Shiloe hurtles down the stairs as the mechs home in on the vessel. I watch with nervous tension, hoping she can make it to the bottom. In the dark chamber, the vessel looks like a floating star. The glowing green light strobes with each step she takes.

Then the mechs open fire on her.

She weaves between the rounds that pelt the ground around her. Several rounds hit her, but thankfully, the armor manages to protect her. Then there are more mechs, which seem to magically appear in front of her. Soon, there are so many that her path forward is blocked.

Still, I wait. It takes every ounce of my resolve to keep from rushing to Shiloe's aid. But I need to stick to the plan. I continue to wait by the entrance, finally losing track of the glowing vessel. I feel anxious when I lose sight of Shiloe beneath the pile of mech units.

Just when I'm about to rush to find her, I see several mechs go flying through the air. Then, the vessel is hurling toward me. I jump and catch it, tuck it under my arm and bolt from the chamber.

When I enter the tunnel, I hear the mech units' propulsion systems roar to life. The sound echoes down the tunnel as I sprint ahead. Soon I can hear the modulated voice sounding off the remaining time. I have less than five minutes to deliver the vessel.

But pouring into the tunnel ahead of me are more mechs. I see the glint of metal in the dim light, and the clicking sound of mechanical parts filters along the hardened walls. Somehow, the mechs have found a way to circumnavigate around me. They must have a detailed map of the tunnel system. I should have guessed that.

In a matter of seconds, the way forward is blocked, and I have no escape route. Behind me, the other mechs are approaching. My only option now is to fight. I'm about to find out if all my training was worth it.

The steel wave of mechs crashes into me. The blunt force of their rush pins me against the stone, and I feel their metal fingers reaching for the vessel. I twist up and rip back, surprised to see their arms pop off like toys. I'm so shocked by my own strength that I nearly drop the vessel. But before I can pat myself on the back, the next wave is crashing into me. I repeat the same maneuver, ripping arms and heads off of the mechs that venture too close.

I dismantle units by the dozens and watch them clatter to the stone floor. But soon, I realize I'm not moving toward the goal line, and time is running out. The mechs are simply stalling me now. All I can do is fight for my life and hope the others can pinpoint my location. I punch, kick, and slam units into the walls, and soon, the tunnel is filled with mechanical parts.

Then I hear a thought. It's Vern.

...push forward!

I focus all my energy, kneel, then lower my shoulder and heave forward. I feel one of the mechs dig its fingers into my shoulder and squeeze. The pain is excruciating, but I continue to push forward. Then, as if by magic, I see Vern's hand appear through the wall of mechs. I press the vessel into his hand and let go.

I feel spent. Using my abilities has weakened me, and I nearly drop to my knees with exhaustion. But I know I must prevent more mechs from chasing after Vern. I turn and engage the units, trying to get past me. But the mechs are so focused on the vessel that they ignore me. With the way blocked, they turn and began streaming out through an adjacent tunnel.

I follow the mechs, picking them off one at a time. Before long, I sense Shiloe's presence near me, and together, we're taking out the backlog of units.

I hear the modulated voice counting down from sixty seconds. It echoes down the tunnels as Shiloe and I finally punch through and onto the open training deck. At the opposite end, I can see the others surrounded by mechs. We sprint over and plow into the units from behind, clearing out a path.

"Go!" I yell to Grish. She leaps from the pile with the vessel in hand. Shiloe, Vern, Tripp, Drake and I set up a blockade between her and the mechs.

With just ten seconds left, Grish runs, trips and flops across the line in a cloud of dust.

The mechs immediately power down and stand still like gleaming statues. All is silent as the six of us wait and look around for Kiff. Then we hear someone clapping and turn to see Kiff standing near the vector accelerator. She beckons us over.

Grish picks herself up and dusts off the dirt. Together, we meet Kiff and stand in front of her. I glance around at everyone. It appears I'm the only one with an injury, and I wince as I lift my shoulder.

Grish hands the glowing vessel to Kiff. "I hope this thing's worth it."

Kiff takes the vessel and tucks it into her cloak. "I guess we'll see, won't we? The real question is how well did you perform as a team? Shiloe is your specialist, your group's most talented fighter. Tripp and Grish, you two move in ways that hint at subterfuge. Vern and Drake, you're the bruisers, it would seem. And Brin, you're well-rounded. You make good decisions under pressure and lead well. I think I have my answer. It looks like Henak and Triton have trained you well, which they always do. Let's move on."

I find myself still out of breath and hoping for a breather, though. Kiff seems to have read my mind as she leads us back down the vector accelerator and to the meditation levels.

"Vishmu. Two hours each," she says with a wink. "You need to decompress—you've earned that much. Then we spar. I know you're tired, but there is no rest in battle. Hop to it!"

I settle down cross-legged on one of the old rugs. I'm deep into meditation almost instantly. I'm surprised at how much energy I've expended. I need almost the entire two hours just to feel normal again. When I wake, my shoulder is much better, though it's still sore. The physical healing from just a few hours of Vishmu has done wonders.

But almost immediately, Kiff is pushing us into the sparring arena against each other. It's like there's an urgency with her I haven't felt with Henak or Triton. I wonder if she plans to keep this breakneck pace throughout our training.

My first pairing is against Drake, who I pin fairly easily. Then Vern, Grish and Tripp, all of whom I best, even with my sore shoulder. But when I face Shiloe, it's another story. We spar for what seems like hours until I misstep, and she quickly takes the advantage. I'm still unable to beat her, bad shoulder or not. It doesn't seem to matter.

At the end of the day, we're all breathing heavily and taking a knee. Kiff finally gathers us into a circle.

"You all did well today. I'm impressed," Kiff says with her arms crossed. She doesn't smile, though. Just like Henak and Triton, I imagine it's going to take time. But I find myself wondering if we'll get any smiles from Kiff, or breaks, for that matter.

"The live drills today put you as close to the real situation as possible," Kiff continues and paces between us. "I hope you are beginning to understand that this is your new reality. We're playing for keeps, and every opposing soldier will kill you without thinking twice. Are you prepared to do the same? It's a question you'll face very soon. Mechs are easy. You can disable them and think nothing more. But when you're looking into the eyes of another human…that's the hard part. You will face real humans, and you will decide their fate. Just remember, this is war."

I can barely get out of bed the next morning, thanks to Kiff's intense training session. My shoulder screams at me, and my muscles ache. I'm always surprised at this. I'd assumed being Immortal would prevent such things. Obviously, I'm wrong.

Now that our group has graduated to live drills, we face several more mech armies that day. However, these mechs are different units known as E-Class mechs. This time, the countdown is lowered by a few minutes, and additional units are added. The E-Class units are more powerful and quicker than the previous ones. Each time, our goal is to collect a single, colored vessel. After each live round, we're allowed time to meditate. But that time limit is also reduced.

The lack of conversation from Kiff is disappointing to me. Our first two instructors were happy to answer questions, almost excited. But Kiff is tightlipped, and I begin to wonder why. Perhaps she wants to keep us focused on the task at hand, now that we're so close to graduating? Whatever it is, I sense that the others feel the same way.

The third, fourth and fifth days are exactly the same, though with different types of units. We face increasing numbers, and each time, the mechs are tougher and more advanced than the previous version. Our time continues to decrease and the sessions of Vishmu that follow are almost non-existent, too. Kiff is pushing us to our limit. But we manage to survive, working as a team now. We've also collected our third, fourth and fifth glowing vessels.

On our sixth and final day of training, we follow Kiff up to the caves and wait for her.

"Well now, how do you all feel?" Kiff stands facing us, her hands tucked behind her back as usual.

"Like a sack of rocks, honestly," Vern chuckles, but then his smile fades. "Yeah. I'm tired. We're all tired, Kiff."

"Good," Kiff says. Then, she finally cracks a smile, which takes everyone by surprise.

I feel a bit nervous at her expression. It's then that I know our training today isn't going to be like the first five.

"This will be your final live mission. You'll be fighting me for the last vessel. You must reach and have control of it when the timer hits zero."

We all look at each other with confused expressions on our faces. Then everyone begins to talk at once.

Vern places his hands on his head. "Great, we're dead."

Grish holds out a hand to Kiff. "Wait, what?"

"That's not fair," Tripp says, practically yelling. "We're no match for—"

"For what!" Kiff snaps, and we all go silent. "What's not fair, Tripp? That you don't feel prepared? That you think I'm a tougher opponent? Is this what you'll say when you're facing your enemies on the battlefield?"

It's the first time I've heard Kiff raise her voice. Her normally calm, composed nature is sharp and cutting. Harsh.

Truthful.

"You heard me," Kiff says. She steps past us and crouches, placing herself between us and the glowing vessel beyond. "We fight now!"

The timer suddenly starts counting backward from five minutes. Kiff immediately turns and sweeps Drake to the ground. She slams her fist down, and he barely manages to roll away. I rush in and shove her in the back, but she sidesteps and flips as Grish misses with a roundhouse kick aimed at her head. Vern is there waiting for Kiff, but she twists and hauls him to the ground. The next thing I know, Grish is in a headlock, and I'm lying on the ground, my vision spinning.

And just like that, the fight is on. Six fresh-faced Immortals against one middle-aged instructor.

And she's beating the stuffing out of us.

...*GO!* I send the thought to Shiloe and Tripp.

They race for the vessel perched on the highest outcropping of the cliff some fifteen meters above. But Kiff is incredibly quick and leaps away from Vern, Drake, Grish, and me. We grab at her legs and try to pull her down, but no one can get a grip on her. Kiff manages to stay on her feet and sprints just a few meters behind Shiloe and Tripp.

When they reach the cliff, Kiff is practically on top of them. Shiloe jumps to the rock wall as Tripp turns to engage Kiff. I can see he's simply trying to slow her by sacrificing himself to give Shiloe more time. It's just long enough for the rest of us to reach them, and soon, it's five on one as Shiloe scales up the cliff wall.

But once again, Kiff proves too slippery for us. She brings Tripp, Vern and Drake to the ground, then leaps to the rock wall and starts climbing after Shiloe. We're immediately behind her, and it's a race to the top. I can see that Shiloe will make it just ahead of Kiff, but as soon as they get to the top, Shiloe will have to face Kiff alone.

I keep an eye on them as we hop, scramble, and climb the wall. I estimate we're several seconds behind Kiff. I can only hope that Shiloe will hold out long enough.

Once I reach the top of the flat rock, Shiloe is sparring with Kiff. She's somehow managed to hold her ground. We charge them and Kiff is forced to turn and face us. Vern, Tripp, and I engage Kiff while Drake, Shiloe, and Grish move behind her. During the fighting, Tripp stumbles and falls over the edge. A second later, Kiff sweeps Vern's legs out and he also tumbles out of sight. Kiff's arms and legs are a blur as she blocks and counters our attacks—she is tireless and simply too much for us.

We're down to just four when Grish takes an elbow to her ribs and goes flying over the cliff's edge. I'm still in shock at how Kiff is able to stand against all of us with seemingly no effort.

Then, Drake slips and falls. He's hanging from the ledge, and I slide across the gravel surface to grab his hand and hold him. This leaves Shiloe to battle Kiff alone, and it won't be long until she is overmatched.

"Let me go, Brin," Drake says. I can hear the exhaustion in his voice from the last several days of training. I can see the defeated look in his strained expression. "I'll be fine. Shiloe needs you."

I look from Drake to Shiloe and see that she's backed against the opposite side of the cliff now. Indecision grips me, and for the first time, I don't know what to do.

Then I feel Drake's hand begin to slip. I turn to see him pressing against the cliff face with his legs. He gives one last thrust, and he slides down the cliff and out of sight.

The timer chimes out: thirty seconds… twenty-nine seconds… twenty-eight seconds…

Shiloe is on one knee when I see my opening.

I stand, gather all my remaining energy and leap over Kiff and Shiloe. Kiff reaches for my ankle and barely misses. She corrects and moves after me as I sprint to the vessel. In the background, I can still hear the timer. Ten seconds.

Kiff is only inches from me.

Then, she finally makes a mistake and tumbles to the ground in a cloud of dust. From the corner of my eye, I see Shiloe roll on top of her and try to hold her down.

Now it's a race against the clock, and I use every bit of strength left in me.

As the time nears zero, I jump and grab at the vessel. But it slips from my sweaty hand and nearly hits the ground. I bobble it several times and finally grasp it just as the timer's alarm blares.

I hold the glowing vessel in my shaking hand as sweat pours down my forehead. I'm beyond spent, and I collapse to the ground and lay there, panting.

I look up to see Kiff reach down and grip my shoulder. Then she lifts me to my feet with a powerful slap on my back. Dust poofs out, and she waves it away good-naturedly. I see the smile on her face, almost in relief, it seems.

"Well done, Brin. Well done."

Behind Kiff, I see Shiloe step up, her face a sunset of bruises and cuts. I imagine my face looks the same. Together, we begin working our way back down the cliff to check on the others.

Vern, Tripp, Grish and Drake all sit on the ground in a circle talking softly. They stand when they see us approach and go immediately into a defensive stance. But Kiff laughs for the first time. It's a real laugh, one I've not heard from her, and I think perhaps it's because this part of our training is over. We've passed her test.

"Relax. It's over," Kiff says. "You've all done very well as a team."

It takes a few seconds, but everyone finally eases. I see Grish nursing her wrist, which looks to be badly sprained. Vern has several cuts on his face, and Tripp has a nasty scrape across his forehead. Overall, no major injuries, which is amazing to me, considering the beating we took from Kiff.

"Everyone all right?" I ask.

"We're good," Vern says. "You get the vessel in time?"

"Yeah, we got it, thanks to Shiloe." I give her a playful shake by her shoulders, and she groans.

Kiff stands behind us, still wearing a relaxed smile. "You're ready, all of you, in my book at least. I can see you all have unique abilities that complement each other. This is exactly what I'd hoped for. Sorry again about the physical part of this. Had to be done."

"Maybe we should just send *you* out to battle," Vern jokes. "How do you move like that?"

"Yeah, you're faster than us, much faster," Drake says and nods in agreement.

"When you've trained Immortals for as long as I have, you pick up a few tips along the way," Kiff replies, but I can hear the strain in her tone now, unlike before. There's a sadness, as if Kiff is finally letting her guard down, where in the beginning, she couldn't show that side of herself. I begin to wonder if she needed to see this result from us first.

We stand silently in a circle, arms crossed and waiting.

"I do have one last question, Kiff." I hold up the glowing vessel. Its pure white light bathes our faces and the cave walls. "What in the world are these things, and why did we fight so hard to get them?"

"It's known as a vessel, and there is one for each of you. They will be presented to you tonight during your graduation ceremony."

GRADUATION DAY | CHAPTER 10

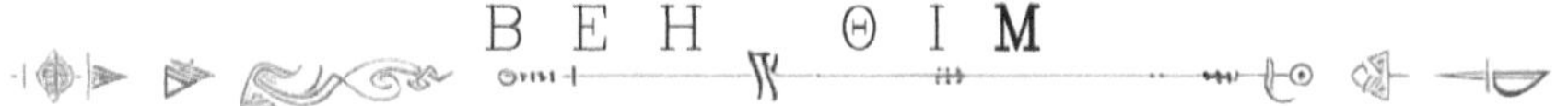

I shower and change into my best clothing, which is the royal blue uniform I'd been given earlier. To be honest, I'm not excited about tonight's graduation. What I really want to do is lay down and sleep for three days straight. Instead, we're attending some sort of special ceremony, where we'll be presented with the strange vessels we've won. Though I'm tired, I am curious to learn more about them.

I meet the others in the center of our complex, and together, we make our way down to the main thoroughfare. Once there, we're escorted by just two guards this time instead of the platoon that usually greets us. I wonder if it's possible that we've finally gained some trust.

We take the rail transit to Kiff's apartment, which is on the opposite side of the borough. If there's an upscale area in this military base, we must be in it. The stone buildings here are clad with marble, and the apartments have intricately carved doors. Some even have windows.

Inside Kiff's apartment is a spacious living area with high stone ceilings, and beyond is a long dining table loaded with food and other delicacies. Sitting on the back wall are the six vessels, each one glowing a different color.

Kiff greets each of us at the door with a handshake, then seats everyone at the table. I'd assumed I would never have another home-cooked meal again after Triton's dinner party. I was obviously wrong. I recognize some of the food on the table from before, but Kiff's dinner party is over the top, to say the least. There's enough food to feed twice as many people. It's an honor, I realize, to be served such a glorious feast, and it must have cost Kiff a small fortune. Normally, only dignitaries or celebrities are treated to such an experience.

"It's quite the spread," Shiloe says as she settles in.

"I'll admit, I am famished," Vern says, scooting his chair forward as his eyes rove over the table. "But this is way too much food, Kiff."

"Well, I took the liberty of inviting a few more guests," Kiff says.

As if on cue, someone knocks on the door. Kiff answers, and a middle-aged man and three women step inside.

"Triton?" I say and stand. "Miss Henak, Guinn…Lewin?"

The others stand, and we rush at the four of them with smiles on our faces. Then we're all hugging, along with a few tears perhaps.

"So nice to see you all," Henak says and gives Shiloe a hug. "Hope you're well, dear."

Vern and Drake nearly tackle Triton, and he chuckles as Grish and Tripp greet Lewin and Guinn. Shiloe and I talk with Henak and Kiff. It's the reunion I feel like we all needed after so many trials. I can't seem to wipe the smile off my face. It's then that I realize how close we've become with our instructors. The people who were tasked to train us have suddenly become our newfound family.

After several minutes, Kiff ushers everyone over to the table, and we dig in.

Vern and Drake's antics, along with Grish and Tripp's dry sense of humor, keep the party lively. Triton shares some background about his days fighting in the wars. We learn that Henak had also been on the front lines. Kiff finally begins to open up and shares that she'd once been a captain in the wars as well but seems reluctant to talk about it too much.

"I'm thankful that we had you all as our instructors," I say and push my plate back. "I don't know what we would've done without you."

Vern lets out a low belch and stretches his arms and arches his back. "Since we have you three together, can you share anything else? I mean, maybe a little more history or something? I've only heard rumors, most of them probably not true."

The rest of us stop and look at Triton.

He takes a drink and leans back in his chair, getting comfortable. "Now that you're all trained and ready, I don't see any issues sharing a bit more. Well over a century ago, the first war started with a simple disagreement. As with most wars, it escalated into a battle for underground territory, due to the storm called the Unbalance. As the storm grew worse, surface living became less sustainable, and more people began to relocate to the boroughs, the entire North American continent, in fact. Of course, everyone had to adapt to underground life. Great mining operations took place. Minerals, mainly the ones known as rare-earth, were sought after and fueled rumors about a great space station in the earth's atmosphere."

"The Skylight System?" Shiloe asks.

"That's correct. Eventually, a truce was placed along the 37th parallel line, which runs east to west along the Great Plains of North America. This was mainly to help reduce the conflicts over mining territory. Two factions eventually formed: the North and the South. Each stayed on their side of the line at first, and all was peaceful. But the demand for minerals gradually increased as the Skylight System became a reality, and the rush for minerals quickened, along with the desire for mining territory. Soon, the area along the 37th parallel was overmined and eventually caved in, creating three massive open pits, now known as the East, West and Central Theaters. Both the North and the South quickly realized the strategic importance of those locations. The three theaters were quickly fortified with troops and vehicles."

"The demand for minerals remained, though," Miss Henak says. "So, in return for minerals from both the North and South, the system creators drew up boundary lines and offered a contract. The side that held the most territory in the three theaters—and, by extension, more minerals—would be granted the right to settle and populate the Skylight System.

"Our history has been bloody," Kiff says and looks to Triton. "Immortals, once discovered, turned the tide of war. A new chapter began, and soon it was a race to locate people like yourselves. In the year 2080 A.D., the Great War began. Since then, it's been a never-ending series of battles. But there's a deadline. The Winter Solstice is coming."

Triton finally taps his hands on the table in a drumroll that draws our attention. "Tomorrow, you will begin in the Front Line Borough and the Central Theater."

This gathers in a wide-eyed look from us. Of course, I knew this day would come, but it still doesn't feel real when Triton says it.

"Will we be splitting up?" Shiloe asks.

Kiff folds her hands in front of her. "Not right now. But eventually, you may have to. The remaining time we have in this war will be crucial. Let us hope we can maintain what we have and perhaps tip the battle in our favor. Out there, on the front line, the situation is always fluid. You will be moved around quickly, sometimes with little notice."

Triton stands and motions to the vessels. "We have some gifts for you. As a reward for your success and perseverance throughout your training, you have rightfully earned these. Before you accept them, know this: each one is unique to you alone. What lies within is for you to discover, and no one can help you unlock its secrets. This has always been the tradition. Beyond that, I dare not say more, only that it is crucial that each of you do so."

Triton hands each of us one of the glowing crystals. I notice how they match the colorful light from our palms. However, mine is different. It's a pure white light instead of the turquoise color of my palm. The vessel is cradled in a strange metal, some sort of encasement perhaps. Each one is different in size and shape, and in the center is an object that's difficult to make out. I gaze into the depths of the crystal, trying to get a better glimpse. I feel my being begin to float, like I'm in a session of Vishmu or a dreamlike state. I lose myself in the glowing light, as if being drawn into a swirling vortex. In the background, I can hear whispers, some strange dialect or ancient language, I think. A long-forgotten tongue that steadily grows louder. The chanting fills my head as the light from the crystal becomes brighter and more intense. I feel a moment of paranoia until I finally see the object at the heart of the vessel.

But then I'm back, seated in my chair, head in my hands and shaking. I quickly glance around the room as the light seems to brighten, like storm clouds parting for the sun. Shiloe, Vern, Drake, Grish and Tripp all share the same stunned look on their faces too.

"Well," Triton says and claps his hands together to gain our attention. "You must spend more time on your own with your vessels. In the meantime, we have a few more trinkets to bestow upon you, ones that will prove invaluable in the war ahead."

He walks into a hallway beyond and disappears. When he returns, he's holding a wooden box. It's a medium-sized wood crate with dark weathered wood planks and a rusty latch on top. He sets it on the table and opens it.

We all lean in with anticipation as he pulls out six copper rings and hands them out. "These rings have been passed down from your predecessors who bore your class of symbol. They will provide valuable information on the battlefield. There's more," Triton says and pulls out six weathered cloaks and tosses one to each of us.

I catch mine and hold it up to the dim light. It's a dark material, though it feels somewhat wiry and a bit stiff. The cloak is lightweight and tattered in a few places, like it's been well-worn by someone else. It has a luster to it, reminding me of the sheen on a crow's feathers and shifts in the light from blue to green to purple. I also notice golden highlights, threads that seem to gracefully bind the fabric in a mystical way with geometric shapes interwoven, almost like a relic from a distant mythological fairytale. The golden lines are perhaps symbolic of the lifelines of previous Immortals, their story now connected with my own.

"Well. What are you waiting for?" Kiff snaps at us. "Try them on."

Each of us stand and slip into our cloaks. Mine fits perfectly. There's enough room to move freely, though it clings to my form.

"Draw the hood," Kiff says.

I do, along with the others. Then, something amazing happens.

We all vanish.

I hear the stunned yelp from Tripp and a gasp from Shiloe.

"What the…" Vern whispers next to me.

I look down and can't see my body. I'm standing there like some floating banshee, though I think I can see the others when they move too quickly. It's like a barely detectable mirage, although subtle. I pull the hood back, and suddenly, I'm visible again. The others do the same, and one by one, everyone is back with stunned looks on their faces.

"What just happened?" Grish says and brushes her red hair out of her wide eyes. I see the hint of a smirk on her face, though.

"These, too, have been handed down from your predecessors," Triton says. "I think you'll find them much better than your current armor."

"Armor? This?" Vern says, holding up the thin cloak.

Triton takes it. "This has graphene fibers woven into it. It may not look like much, but it is many times stronger than your other armor."

Vern looks at Triton cautiously. "You're not gonna shoot Brin again, are you?"

"No, of course not," Triton says, and pulls the cloak around Vern. "The way the fibers are woven bends light around your form. But you must be cautious. You're not completely hidden from other Immortals. Even though this offers much better camouflage than the armor, if you move too quickly, it could give you away."

A wide grin spreads across Vern's face. "Triton, I love you, man." He gives the middle-aged man a bear hug.

Triton claps him on the back and smiles. "Didn't think I'd leave you emptyhanded, did you? May these gifts serve and protect you. Master your immortal abilities. A storm is coming, one that threatens to sweep us away if we are not vigilant."

Kiff draws our attention again. "Prepare yourselves. We leave at first light."

"We?" I ask. "Are you going with us?"

"Of course," Miss Henak says. "We wouldn't leave you all alone, at least not yet."

Shiloe rushes over and throws her arms around Miss Henak. For a split second, I swear I see a tear on Miss Henak's cheek.

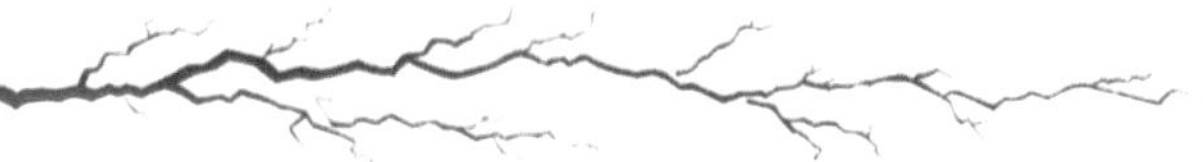

Kiff arranges for us to talk to our families that night. Patching us through the network is difficult, though, since most of the civilian communications are held for the war effort. Only a few minutes can be spared for each of us. I haven't really prepared what I plan to say, and even feel a bit nervous. I want to reassure Ben and my ma that I'm fine. I only hope they won't know that I'm lying.

That night, I sit in my cot and stare into the hologram. Ben grins back at me, though I can see his eyes are red and puffy, just like mom's. I try to hold a straight face, but my hands are shaking throughout our conversation.

"How is Grior treating you two?" I ask.

"It's fine, Brin," Ma says. I can tell she isn't being honest with me either. I see Ben start to sniffle. Then he begins to sob. It's soft, and I can barely hear him through the static. I watch him try to put on a straight face, try to impress me.

"It's okay, Benji," I say. "It's okay to cry. Get it out of the way, then when you wake up tomorrow, you move on. Alright? You have to stay strong. We're counting on you."

Ben wipes his eyes with his worn sleeves but nods. I see an older kid in that instant. It's like he's already growing up, even in the short time I've been away. His face seems leaner and hardened, his stature a bit taller, I think.

"Brin," my mom says. "We'll be fine here waiting for you. Come back safely to us, won't you?"

"Of course. You know I will. They can't get rid of me that easily," I joke, though it falls flat.

"Then they'll take that collar off, right?" she says. Tears suddenly stream down her cheeks as she holds my gaze through the hologram.

"Don't think about it," I say. "It'll be fine."

"I just can't believe they're doing this to you. It seems so…*barbaric!* You're risking everything, and they stick a collar around your neck like some prisoner. It makes me so—"

"Stop it," I say and lower my gaze at her. "You have to focus on each other so that I don't have to worry."

She nods, then grabs Ben and hugs him. "We will. Promise me you'll do what you know is right—"

The timer cuts her off, and the screen goes blank.

I continue to stare at the static for a few more minutes before laying back in my cot, my arms behind my head. I gaze up at the rock-hewn ceiling, thinking about my mom and brother. Most of what I'd told them wasn't true: I probably wouldn't return. The facts don't lie. I know most Immortals don't survive very long. I guess that my 'shelf life' is perhaps a few weeks, maybe a month, if I'm lucky. Grish had been right all along—we're just pawns being pushed around the battlefield. *Cannon fodder for the Elites.* If the war doesn't kill me, then the people I fight for will never free me. They can't afford to.

Controlling an Immortal is a power no one willingly gives up. I know this without a doubt. If I ever want my freedom, I'll have to find a way on my own. But first, I need to survive the war or 'game' as Gorgan Freemantle had so eloquently put it. But I know this isn't so much a game as it is a charade of lies, ones that I need to figure out, and quickly.

I spend the rest of the night studying the strange vessel. Triton hadn't gone into much detail about it, stating only that it was up to each Immortal to 'unlock' its secrets. Its compact, metal casing has a strange feel, almost warm to the touch. *Handed down from your predecessor*, Triton had said. Odd that he'd not given any guidance, though. It feels like an important artifact. *If we Immortals are so crucial to this war, then why wouldn't our instructors want us to have every advantage? Why risk us never figuring this thing out?*

The way the vessel glows in the dark haunts me, though. As I stare into the crystal's white light, I fall into the same trance again. Like at the dinner party, I seem to be caught in a bizarre session of Vishmu. I feel my ethereal being drawn into the white light. It tugs at my inner core, and I feel unsettled by the whispers I hear. Like thousands of beings, it chants my name, and I begin to see the object again at the heart of the light. It solidifies as I move closer. Finally, it takes shape in the swirling stardust.

What I see is the outline of a skull.

Vacant eye sockets and chattering teeth stare back at me. I hear the thing call my name in a mocking voice.

My eyes snap open, and I drop the vessel. It clatters to the stone floor, and I let it lay there, afraid to touch it now. The white light pulses at me like a heartbeat. *My heartbeat.*

I quickly pick it up and stuff it under my pillow, then take a deep breath. I try to relax and not think about it, but the skull is burned into my vision.

Eventually, I manage to drift off.

Nightmares fill my restless sleep. I think of my family, stranded on an island in the middle of a tumultuous sea. Waves crash around them as lightning fills the inky sky. Thousands of mech units fall from the heavens, crowding the shore and overwhelming my family. When I reach the rocky shore, the stones transform into skulls, like the one in the vessel. I pick one up, and it turns into a pure white light. In my mind, I hear a familiar voice speaking in a strange dialect. It's one I've heard more just recently, though I don't understand it. Still, I can feel its meaning, like some intuitive voice guiding me. I wield the glowing skull and fight my way toward my family. But I'm too slow, and they are soon engulfed by the mechs. The last thing I see is Ben's tiny hand reaching for me before it disappears beneath the flood of mech units.

PART TWO:

STORM STRIKE

The storm of crows is an ominous spectacle
because I know it means death is near.
—Brindall Harper

A STORM OF CROWS | **CHAPTER 11**

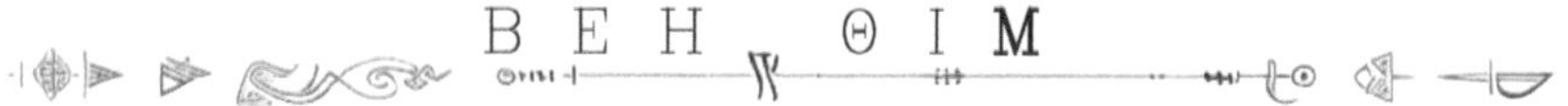

I awake with a start when someone hammers on my door.

"It's time," Kiff says and waits in my living area as I dress and gather my items.

We meet the others in the central courtyard of our complex. Shiloe and Vern are bleary-eyed. I imagine the few minutes they had with their families last night were just as difficult. Drake, Grish and Tripp seem to be fine, though, and I wonder if they even talked to their families.

"You okay?" I ask Shiloe as we follow Kiff out of our living complex, probably for the last time. She gives me a terse nod but hides her gaze from me. I don't need to see her face to know she's upset. "We have each other to lean on, Shiloe. That's what friends are for." I nudge her with my elbow, trying to make her smile.

She finally gives me a side-glance. I can see the pain and uncertainty in her expression. Her eyes are still red, and they start to well up with tears. She flares her nose and quickly turns away. I want to give her a hug and tell her we'll be fine. But I know that won't do. Such an action would probably embarrass her even more. Besides, I shouldn't show more attention to her than the others. Doing so would undermine everything we've built so far.

But the real reason I want to console her is…

…because I care for her.

We finally make it to the terminal. It's much deeper than any other station we've been to, and we're the only ones there. I get the sense this is a secret rail, one that very few people know of. A few minutes later, a bullet-shaped transport slides into the low bay and stops with a hiss. It's about twenty meters in length and tubular shaped with a shiny metallic skin. It barely clears the stone tunnel walls by half a meter.

"This is the transport I mentioned last night," Kiff says. "This secret rail will ferry our elite teams from each theater quickly. On we go, come on!"

Our small group boards the transport. Once our bags are packed inside, the train makes a loud whooshing sound, as if a charged turbine is gearing up. Then it hisses and shoots off with a thunderclap.

I grip the arms of my seat as the g-forces press me back. It's like riding a rocket, and indeed I was. The small round window next to me shows the tunnel outside passing by at a tremendous speed. Things begin to blur in my vision. It's neither relaxing nor enjoyable. Within fifteen minutes we slow to a stop.

I step onto the gangway, and the train bolts off. Around us is more activity now, people running from buildings, yelling and barking orders. A loudspeaker mumbles in the background, giving coordinates and schedules, arrivals and departures. The buildings in this district are sturdy bunkers, nothing fancy here. I realize we're at the final port city on the edge of the Frontline War now. This is the closest I've ever been to the 37th parallel.

"Welcome to the Front Line Borough. You have thirty minutes to prepare," Kiff barks.

In the background, I can hear the sounds of war with much greater clarity. Low booms shake the earth in massive tremors that rattle my teeth. I can smell smoke and other burning materials in the air. The cavern system is dimly lit by the minty green shale ferns. Occasionally, dust flutters down from the top of the cave, clouding the area in a fine haze.

We follow our guide at a brisk jog as the ground continues to reverberate. Some walls are cracked, and a few passages have completely collapsed from all the shelling.

We turn down a large causeway that spans across a canyon, then into a smaller passageway. The tunnel branches off and eventually stops at a dead-end.

"These are your living quarters," the guide says. "Unpack and gear up. You have five minutes."

I feel my heart leap into my throat just hearing that.

Five minutes...

Just five minutes until we're thrown into the Frontline War. My life is now on the line.

I don't know what to expect as I slip into my armor. Finally, I drape the worn cloak over my shoulders, the one handed down to me from all the previous Immortals of my own class—the symbol of the M. As I do this, I feel a calm settle over me though. It's a strange feeling, like the combined effort of all those previous Immortals is woven into the glossy fabric. That thought gives me a sense of pride. Next, I place the copper ring on my right index finger. The last thing I do is hide the vessel in my pocket. *Just in case*, I tell myself.

Before long, our guide is leading us along a narrow trail. The walls become more fractured the higher we go, and the sounds of war grow louder. The ground beneath our feet trembles nonstop now.

Minutes later, we're standing in an enormous, open canyon that spans beyond my sight. The earthen walls stretch up and breach the dark sky above. We're exposed to the elements here, and rain and lightning pour down. Rivers of water have formed from the years of precipitation. The constant downpours have created large ravines in the ground. I see vast lakes in a few areas and even some vegetation that's somehow managed to flourish, though it's beaten down and trampled from the war. The sound of battle rages in a full-throated roar, and my head spins from the explosions. But even through all the noise, I hear the squawking of carrion crows beyond. Thousands of them clot the horizon, their glossy black coats vivid through the storm clouds and lightning. I wasn't even aware that anything had survived the Unbalance besides humans. The storm of crows is an ominous spectacle because I know it means death is near.

I stand in shock, looking around me in a dreamlike state of disbelief. We're finally here, a place we shouldn't be.

Off to one side, I see Gorgan Freemantle with his top generals. They stand around a makeshift table with a tentlike structure overhead, which provides some shelter from the wind and rain.

Our guide turns and sprints off as Shiloe and the others turn to look at me.

"Well?" Shiloe says and holds up her hands.

"C'mon," I say and march over to Commander Freemantle.

We stop short of the tent and peer inside. The group is conferencing into a three-dimensional hologram with two other commanders. In the sidebar I can see their titles, which appear to be the leaders of the Eastern and Western Theaters: Commander Herron and Commander Taun. We wait outside in the rain and listen in to their intense conversation.

"…you can't expect them to have an immediate impact," Freemantle is yelling.

"It'll take time, I agree," Commander Taun replies. "But we need to start regaining some of our territory. If we fall too far below the halfway mark, we may never regain it. You know how this works, Gorgan. They have at least four Immortals on the battlefield right now, and they have more experience. Even though we have six, their inexperience worries me—"

Freemantle pauses the discussion when he sees me and the others standing outside. He motions to us. "Please, come inside."

I step into the tent but continue to wait silently, not sure what to say. My stomach is suddenly doing flips, and I struggle to steady my hands.

"You must excuse the manner of our blunt conversation," Freemantle says. "We have much to discuss before you all are ready to engage the enemy."

"How do you plan to use us?" I finally say.

"Like lightning strikes," Freemantle replies without hesitation.

"Excuse me?" Vern practically yells from behind me. "You're just gonna stick us in the front and march us through the enemy? Hey, I don't know about this, man!"

"Forgive my analogy, Vern. It's not meant as a literal tactic, think of it more as a hit-and-run approach. Remember that your new cloaks are a much better camouflage than the armor. Come stand here, do you see this area?" Freemantle points at the center of the holographic map.

I see the thin line, the one referred to as the 37th parallel, running directly through the middle of the Central Theater. On the south is a red swath of color, and to the north is a blue swath. There are hundreds of areas along that line that are constantly switching from red to blue. In fact, they flicker so quickly that it's almost purple in color.

"Those little areas are where the fighting is the most intense," Freemantle says and draws the six of us closer and lowers his voice. "Even though it doesn't look like much, when you add it all up, those small pieces equate to a very valuable percentage of territory. Multiply that by three for each of the theaters, and it covers roughly one percent of the territory. That would make the difference in this war right now. We are down, and it may take months to gain it back. There's not much time left till the Winter Solstice, when the contract will be fulfilled. After decades of fighting, we are coming down to the final sprint, and we're struggling to keep up."

"So, what are you asking us to do?" I say.

"You six will start in this area." Gorgan points at the very center of the theater. "We need to see how you do there first, then we can reassess."

"So, we just walk in and…fight?" Drake says.

"You barge in and fight like hell," Commander Taun says through the static-laden hologram. "You make that line buckle. By the time they get reinforcements there, our troops will have flooded in and have barricades set up. When the South's reinforcements arrive, you six are already on to the next one. They'll be playing catch up, like chasing ghosts. So, it's hit-and-run."

"Won't they just retake the area when we leave?" Grish asks.

"Maybe we lose a few," Commander Herron says. "But it'll cost our enemy time and resources, which will cause disruption. That's what we're hoping for."

"Remember, once you take an area, our forces can shore up the barriers," Freemantle reiterates. "I think we can hold most of those areas if we're quick to set up. Eventually, the South may decide spending their troops and resources isn't worth it."

I see Taun sit forward in the hologram to address us again. "We'll be moving your team around constantly. It'll be quick strikes, and we may have to split you up eventually. But right now, you'll work together. We have several coordinated strikes planned, and we have the ability to quickly move troops where we need them."

I take a deep breath as the three commanders look at me. I feel a split second of nervousness in my stomach again. All of our effort is now coming to this moment. I turn to face my team. "Are we ready?" I ask. One by one, everyone looks me in the eyes and nods.

Shiloe stands next to me and claps me on the back. "Just like the last mission with Kiff, huh? We work together and use our thoughts to communicate."

"We're ready." I nod to the commanders.

"Very well," Commander Freemantle says. "The terrain ahead is too rough, impassable in some areas. We'll air lift you to the first site."

Not far from us is a small skiff hidden in a rocky cove. Its matt-black finish almost disappears in the shadows, the hull sleek and knife-like with angled faces for stealth. It hovers a meter above the mud, ready for us. I climb inside, along with the other five, and we buckle into our harnesses. Nervous glances stare back at me from the others. Shiloe and Vern sit next to me. Grish, Tripp and Drake are hunched on the opposite bench. The skiff lifts and hovers out of the cove, then cloaks. There is no warning as the craft rockets out across the pitted terrain beyond. The speed causes my head to spin and my stomach to drop. I'm hit with so many emotions at that instant: the unfamiliar feeling of flight, the rush of exhilaration as we speed along, the flood of adrenaline as we race toward battle. Soon, I'm seeing the war with my own eyes, and my heart races.

Below is something straight out of a nightmare. The ground looks like the surface of an alien moon. It's filled with massive craters and burning vehicles. I see fallen soldiers everywhere, mixed in with downed mech units. I notice all the different types of units Triton had mentioned: TRI-SENT's, serpent-like V-ORPS, giant niners, E-Class mechs. I see thousands of maulers, or *death hounds*, swarming the battlefield. Their gleaming skin reflects the light like tiny razor blades, and they scour every nook, searching for troops to rend.

The possibility that I may die in just a few minutes becomes a reality. But I continue to communicate with the others through my thoughts, and it calms me.

The wind pushes our skiff around like a toy. The concussive impact from shelling reverberates inside the cabin. I'm handed a pair of night vision binoculars. It shows a digital layout of the battlefield in three dimensions, pinpointing the boundaries of where we're expected to attack.

"Down there, near the middle," one of the soldiers says and points. Then he hands us all an earpiece. "The Commander will communicate through these."

I nod and give him a thumbs up, then place the binoculars in my cloak. I clap for the other's attention. "Follow me as soon as we hit the ground. Stay spread out and cloaked. We'll communicate using our thoughts."

Our skiff yaws through the thickening cloud of crows, then hovers about ten meters above a cratered field. We unbuckle and drop from the open bay door, cloaked and ready. The skiff jets off as we move into a smoking crater and assess our surroundings. I project my thoughts to the others so they get a clear visual of the battle plans.

They don't know we're here…let's move in.

I lead our group through the railgun fire and directly across the 37th parallel line. All around me is the brutality of war. It is fierce and unforgiving, the rhythm quick and unrelenting. I watch the death hounds race by, oblivious to our cloaked forms. I see their silvery coats up close with greater detail: sharp serrated scales like chain mail with tiny daggers pointing downward like steel fur. They look sinewy and almost muscular in the moonlight and move gracefully. Their red eyes rove the field, searching for enemy troops. They attack with abandon, like they're under some bloodlust spell.

Within seconds, we're in enemy territory. I sprint across the ruined ground, stopping occasionally to gain my bearings. The entire time, I force down the nervous anxiety threatening to distract me. Adrenaline flows in my veins, helping me forget the imminent danger. Still, I recall Triton's words to stay calm. *They'll need that from you.*

We move from crater to crater, passing enemy soldiers as we press deeper into enemy territory. Tracer rounds whiz past, and explosions erupt nearby. Then, the incoming fire stops. It's the sign we're waiting for. Freemantle is diverting artillery out of the area to avoid harming us. The enemy troops look around with stunned expressions as the area grows hauntingly silent.

Then I send the command to the others.

Rain hell down!

We all leap to action.

Shiloe and I move in from the side and topple one of the transports. Vern and Drake attack several platoons from the front, throwing enemy troops into the air by the dozens. Grish and Tripp sneak around the flank and push from behind. The coordinated attack sends the enemy into a frenzy of confusion. We begin working our way back toward the front line, continuing to take out enemy troops and vehicles. Behind, we leave a wake of smoking ruin. All the while, we're still cloaked and invisible.

Then the enemy reinforcements arrive.

Towering giant niners step over the troops and zero in on us. I realize then that the giants must have a specialized targeting system that can spot our cloaks. What's worse is they seem to be relaying the information to the smaller death hounds, which quickly turn and encircle us.

We all freeze, and there's a momentary standoff. I look around, a bit surprised, though. There are maybe a dozen of the hounds and three of the niners. I had expected more mechs and find myself wondering why there are so few in this particular area.

Then, like the start of a race, the hounds launch at us. The six of us back against each other and brace for the onslaught.

I raise my arm and let the first hound latch onto it. My armor, shrouded by my cloak, takes the brunt of it. The hound's bite force is tremendous, though its sharp teeth still can't penetrate my cloak's fabric. I lift my arm, then ball my other fist and swing it up and into the underside of the hound. Though its steel armor protects it, the blow sends it soaring through the air and out of sight. I refocus on the next hound, which also launches at me. I use the same tactic, bringing my arm up as a shield, then fling the hound away and check on the others.

I pull a few hounds off Grish. Tripp, and Vern seem to be doing okay while Drake and Shiloe work together. But the hounds return quickly and swarm us from all sides. The battle seems to be a stalemate when I realize that we need to take out the giant niners. Without their tracking system, the hounds will be blind.

I send the message, telling the others to focus on the giants. Shiloe and Tripp take the one on the left. Grish and I take the one in the middle, while Vern and Drake take the one on the right.

I dodge past the hounds and leap to the niner's chest. Its armor is mostly seamless, but there are creases at its joints, which I use to climb up. The giant mech is slow, swatting at me with one massive hand. I duck and flip on top of its head while Grish tries to distract it from below. I plant my feet, reach down and grip the area near its eyes, then pull with all my strength.

The top of it peels back like a can. Revealed inside is its control system. Grish is suddenly there, and she hops into the opening. Her arms are a blur as she rips wiring and gears out, tossing them aside. The giant mech powers down and collapses to the ground, crushing a few of the hounds beneath it.

I step aside and look over to see the other two mechs power down and crash to the surface in a plume of sand and dust.

The remaining hounds pause, no longer able to see our cloaks.

Then I begin to see some Northern heavy mech units move in, and the enemy line suddenly collapses. Seconds later, thousands of Northern Coalition troops are flooding in like a tidal wave, overwhelming the enemy. The Southern forces turn and run in full retreat.

"Let's move out," I holler.

We race to the 37th parallel and back into Northern territory. I can hear a rousing cheer rip through the ranks of our soldiers. Almost immediately, barricades are being set up to section off and defend the reclaimed area. Though it's relatively small and doesn't put much of a dent in what we need, it's a moral victory for everyone, including the six of us. At first, I'd had no idea what would happen. The specter of death had felt inevitable and instead the exhilaration of battle has completely overtaken me. I feel alive, but I temper that feeling, knowing things are just getting started and we have a long day ahead of us.

We stay just long enough to make sure the barriers are in place, then we hurry to the extraction point. The same skiff uncloaks, and we board.

I watch through the open bay door as Southern forces bear down on the area with heavy mechs and armored vehicles. But the area is already fortified and our artillery resumes, pummeling the Southern forces that are surging in.

The skiff picks up speed, and I hear Freemantle through my earpiece. He gives me intel about our next target. I scan the battlefield with the night vision binoculars, which highlight the data I'm receiving through the earpiece. I see the target, the borders, the troops in bright greens and reds on the binocular's display.

Within seconds, our team is going through the same drill.

Just like Freemantle predicted, once we overtake an area, the Southern Coalition rushes in to try and recapture the territory. But each time, our troops are ready and have barriers set up, which in turn funnels the enemy into a trap where they're pulverized by artillery.

Like a special ops team, we strike with quick and deadly precision. The skiff continues to drop us in, and we cloak our way behind enemy lines. Throughout the day, we work together like a well-oiled machine, pouring destruction and chaos on the Southern Coalition. Sometimes, the enemy troops are able to regain the lost areas. But largely, the coordinated attacks are successful.

With each mission, we grow in confidence while speaking through our thoughts and attacking as a team. Like the glossy crows I'd seen looming over the battlefield—our cloaks symbolic of the death that follows us—we're in and out before the enemy knows what hit them. I listen to Fremantle's instructions, relay the orders to the others, then we attack. I lose count of how many times we go through this exercise. By the end of the day, it's burned into my thoughts—the explosions, the lightning crashing in the background…the screams of men and women dying.

That night, after our debrief, we sit at our living facility in an open courtyard in the center of the complex. It's more of a cave, hollowed out by some massive machine. The smooth walls rise up high and are topped with a stasis dome. Even though there's a large living area with an old couch, we prefer the less confined space outside. There are no information displays, no news feeds or other devices. I think the Northern Coalition is probably trying to isolate us. But I don't care. The last thing I want to see is more recordings of war and death.

Through the stasis dome, we get glimpses of the stormy sky above. In the background is the sustained sound of war. The low explosions and cawing crows go ignored though. I feel like we're all shell-shocked from the day's events.

Vern starts a fire, and we circle around it on the rocky outcropping. It's cooler that night, and I can see my breath puffing out. I kick back and pull off my tactical boots, which were covered in mud and blood. I ignore the large blisters and close my eyes and lean back, trying to relax.

"Anyone else's ears still ringing?" Tripp says, breaking the silence. "All I can hear are those annoying crows. I mean, how are they even still around?"

"They've found a way to survive, just like us. Hell, we are those crows, we even look like them in our cloaks," Vern says and reaches over to slap my shoulder, causing me to wince. "You did good today. I wanted to say thanks for that. You kept us pretty calm."

The others chime in, too.

"Please, stop," I say and wave it away. "We did it, just like in our practice runs. We worked as a team."

"How do you do it?" Shiloe asks.

I shake my head, not really in the mood to talk about it. "Can't we just relax a bit? We gotta go through this again tomorrow, and the next. When we get time to relax, we probably need to take it."

"It's not that easy, Brin," Shiloe continues. "People died today at our hands. And you don't want to talk about it—"

"No, I don't!" I say, raising my voice and sitting forward. "We don't need to talk about it right now."

The five of them stare at me. I can see the shocked expressions on their faces: brows furrowed and eyes averted.

Then I sigh and draw in a steady breath. "Look, guys. I'm sorry. We all have to find a way of dealing with this. I know it makes sense to talk about it. I just need time to let it sink in. We can talk about anything else, just not that, okay? Maybe later, I'll be ready."

Vern nods and grips my shoulder. "I know you had a lot on your plate today. Take your time. When you're ready to talk, we're here for you, man."

There's a quiet moment. We sit and watch the fire with our legs pulled up and hands stretched out for warmth. I steal quick glances at the others, feeling somewhat guilty for not wanting to talk about what we just experienced that day. I see Grish holding back tears. I see Tripp's ashen face, Drake's pursed lips. Shiloe's downcast gaze.

But I'm just not ready to talk because…

…I'm afraid I'll break down if I do.

I can't allow that to happen, not on our first day. Maybe later, it'll be okay to let those feelings come crashing out. But not today. I must stay strong for the others, just like I did for Ben.

Drake sits forward and kicks at some rocks. He glances sidelong at me. "Sorry, but I gotta ask the question. Why were there so few mechs today? Where are these other Immortals?"

"That's a good point," Vern says and leans forward and points at Drake. "Honestly, I was worried we'd run into more resistance. It was mostly just troops and vehicles. Hardly any mechs. If I was a guessing man, I'd say they dropped us in areas they knew we'd face minimal resistance."

"That does make sense," Shiloe says. "They wouldn't want us to face defeat right away. They're trying to build our confidence before we hit the tougher assignments."

"I wonder how tough these other Immortals will be, once we do face them?" Tripp asks.

I shake my head. "No sense in worrying about it right now. Let's enjoy the small victories while we can."

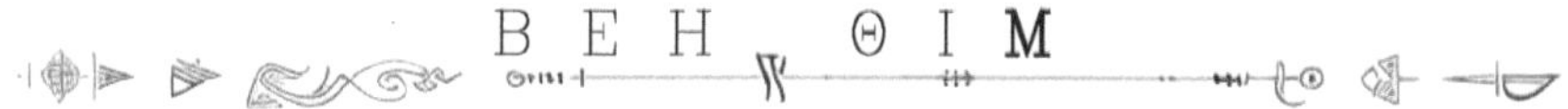

I spend the rest of that evening meditating and ask that the others do the same. At this stage in our journey, I know we're all capable of preparing ourselves in our own way: none of the others need my prodding. Still, I feel that it helps them to hear it from me.

That night, my dreams are filled with war. I see the faces of the men and women who died, many by my own hands. Bright slashes of red and yellow strobe across the hellish landscape as bombs explode and flesh is rent. I see the carrion crows feasting on the dead. I'm constantly running through mud and craters, struggling to find the others. In the background, I can hear Benji's voice calling for me to come home.

I rise early on my first morning in the Frontline Borough. I roll out of my lumpy cot, feeling sore and tired from the previous day's missions. The cold shower water is bracing and harsh. In the background is the sound of nonstop explosions that funnel into my small apartment.

I meet Shiloe, Vern and Drake in the courtyard for some cold gruel. We sit at the stone table and talk softly, avoiding any discussion about yesterday's events. We all know that today will be more of the same. Eventually, Tripp and Grish join us, and we wait for the military police, otherwise known as MPs, to arrive and escort us to the battlefield.

We go through the same exercise that day, skiff hopping along behind enemy lines and allowing the Northern troops time to secure the territory. The next day we repeat it all over again, and then the next day is more of the same. I find myself wondering when the South will move to counter our tactic. Surely by now they've formulated a way to prevent it. Yet, they make no move to bring in more mech units or other Immortals.

At our debrief on the seventh day, I ask Commander Freemantle about it.

"They're waiting till the last minute," he says, as he busies himself with couriers and aides hurrying around the makeshift tent. I can't decide if he's busy or simply dodging my question.

"We know that most of their mechs are in the Eastern Theater," he continues. "We've heard rumors that the South's Immortals are in the west, though we think there might be a few here. But that hasn't been confirmed, yet."

"You're trying to coax them out, aren't you?" I say as Shiloe and Vern gather near and listen in. "You want to lure them to the Central Theater, and you're using us as the bait."

"Yeah," Vern huffs. "But they're not biting, man."

"You're playing us, aren't you?" I say. "How long have you been planning this?"

Freemantle wrinkles his brow as he looks us over. Then he lowers his piercing blue eyes at me. I feel as though he's peering into my soul then, trying to read my thoughts.

"You're sharp for a miner," Freemantle says. "The ARC Borough, isn't it?"

"My father taught me a thing or two before he was drafted," I say. "We're nothing more than assets to you people."

"Extremely valuable assets, Brindall. Pardon me for sounding insensitive, but that's war."

"I understand the position you're in," I say and lean in a bit closer to Freemantle. "I wonder, though. Would you warn us if you knew the opposing Immortals were making a move into our area?"

Freemantle crosses his arms. "That's classified information, Brindall. I could be court-martialed for such a thing."

"Yeah, but it'd sure be nice to know."

"And how do you propose I forewarn you?" Freemantle says and lowers his voice. Then he gives me a barely perceptible wink.

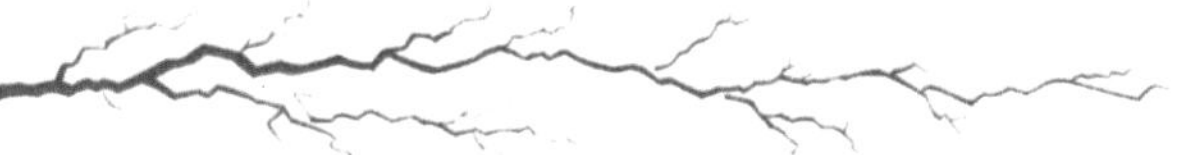

That night, around the firepit, Vern says the one thing that's been on my mind. "Don't pretend you all didn't see that from Freemantle."

"Oh, we saw it," Shiloe says.

I hunch forward, resting my elbows on my knees. "Tomorrow will be a whole new ballgame, I think. The South's had time to get their assets in place. They won't let us take any more territory. They'll be prepared. We're being marched into a trap."

"And how do you think that's going to work out?" Grish snips. She's got her boots kicked up on a rock, and I can tell she's in a grumpy mood.

"Do you really think the South would just give away all that territory?" Tripp says in a low voice. He balls his tiny fists against his sides. "They've been preparing for this. Losing a bit of territory is a worthy tradeoff if you can take out the opposition's entire team of Immortals!"

I nod and point to Tripp. "That's also been bothering me this entire time. Now it makes sense. This *is* a trap. I sense the South's going to have everything there, waiting to greet us."

Shiloe holds up her hands. "Hold on a minute. How could they possibly know? There are thousands of locations along the 37th. It'd be impossible to guess the right spot unless—"

"Unless someone's tipped them off," Grish finishes for her. "There's a spy around, but I think we already knew that. This level of information is top secret. It must be someone in the upper ranks."

"Commander Freemantle?" Drake asks.

I think for a moment but lift my shoulders. "I don't know. We're not going to figure this out tonight. We need to be ready for anything. If we make it through tomorrow, I'm guessing they'll ship us off to another theater."

"You think they want to keep doing this hit-and-run rubbish, but on a larger scale?" Tripp asks.

"Yes. They'll expand beyond the Central Theater."

Everyone goes silent as I consider the implications. Yesterday had been hectic, and my head is still spinning from all the activity. Multiply that by three, and I'm uncertain how long any of us can survive that much battle.

"I'm worried that these other Immortals will be more experienced," Grish says, breaking the silence.

"Maybe." Vern crosses his arms and gives us a worried look. "Except Freemantle said there might only be a few of them."

"He also said that hasn't been verified," I say. "Guys. Our routine hasn't failed us yet." But I say this halfheartedly, because I know that sooner or later, something will break.

The next morning, while I'm eating breakfast with Drake, Tripp and Shiloe, we receive a message. The Northern Coalition is sending in more experienced troops with us during our mission today. The elite soldiers are known as *recon*. Apparently, they are the top-trained soldiers the North has to offer. I'm surprised they're sending soldiers with us instead of the more powerful mech units, and it makes me suspicious. I also learn that fighter skiffs will be used as backup. It's a risky maneuver, considering all the anti-air rockets on both sides.

At 7 a.m., we stand in the rocky hangar bay and wait. It's a brisk morning, and I pull my cloak tight to fight off the chill. The six of us are quiet, preparing ourselves mentally. Just outside the cave, rain pours down, and the ever-persistent sound of cawing crows echoes off the canyon walls beyond. I feel a slight foreboding in my gut, more so than the previous days. Something isn't right.

Finally, I hear Freemantle in my earpiece, and I relay it to the others. We board our skiff, and seconds later, we're zooming across the battlefield. I see troops begin to mobilize, and large vehicles are positioning near our area. The recon units are already dug in as our skiff hovers and deposits us. We hit the ground, cloaked and ready. Our own troops and vehicles move past us, unaware of our presence.

Right now, we should be rushing behind enemy lines and causing disruption. But I can sense that something is out of place. That intuitive voice in the back of my mind is warning me to hold tight.

...what are you doing? Vern sends the thought to me.

...listening to my instincts, I respond and continue to hold our group back.

Finally, my earpiece beeps. Freemantle is asking about our position and why we've paused. But I ignore him and wait.

A few minutes pass when I see the explosions hit the location where we were supposed to be.

"They set a trap!" Tripp hisses. "Just like you said, Brin."

"Quiet!" I whisper.

Ahead of us and near the front line, something approaches. It's blurry, like a mirage on a hot day, and it moves quickly between the line of recon soldiers unnoticed.

"What is it?" Shiloe mutters, and I hear the uncertainty in her voice.

"It's another Immortal," I say. "It knows we're here, too. Spread out, now!"

Shiloe stays near me as Tripp and Vern move left and out of sight. Grish and Drake take the opposite side. But the approaching Immortal moves directly at me, not slowing.

I take a defensive position and ready myself for battle.

The Immortal barrels down on me with some sort of mace or club in its left hand. It glows a bright purple that matches the glow from its palm. The weapon reminds me of the vessels Triton gifted us. *Is there a connection?*

It lashes out with the mace but misses and strikes the ground. The impact leaves a small crater. Then we're rolling on the ground and through the mud. I struggle to defend myself but can't help wondering how in the world this Immortal knew my exact location. Even though we're all cloaked, it seemed to know how to find us.

I clear my mind, knowing I'm dead if I don't focus. This Immortal is fast, quicker than any of us. I manage to scramble to my feet and dodge the scepter again. I sense Shiloe is near, and she calls the others for help. Then she's on its back, trying to pry the club free. I grip its arm from the front, and between us, we barely manage to hold the Immortal still. During the struggle, I pull its hood back to reveal a young man of perhaps seventeen. He's as tall and broad as me, with cropped blond hair and a long beard that's caked in mud. He lets loose a guttural growl, and his attack is relentless.

Just when we have him completely immobilized, a second Immortal appears. It catches us both by surprise. The Immortal grabs Shiloe by her cloak and flings her to the side. Then it's on top of her almost instantly. I watch from the corner of my eye as it attacks her with a similar glowing mace.

The blond-haired boy brings a knee up and into my stomach. I drop to the ground but still manage to dodge the glowing mace. But as I stumble backward, I realize I'm losing this fight. When I glance at Shiloe, I see she's also in a fight for her life. I can see the other Immortal now. The girl is younger, maybe Tripp's age. She has black hair, pale skin and dark blue eyes that match the azure glow from her mace. The look on her face is like some crazed lunatic, howling at Shiloe as she attacks.

Finally, Vern and Tripp are there. Vern hops on top of the boy while Tripp brings a hard left hook under his chin that lifts him off the ground. As the boy lies in the mud, Vern slams his boot onto his collarbone. I hear a sickening crack as bones snap, and the boy yells in pain. He rolls and vanishes.

I flip to my feet and run to Shiloe's aid. I grab the dark-haired girl and hurl her into the side of the crater wall. Just then, Grish and Drake burst over the edge of the crater's lip and stand next to Vern and Tripp.

"Brin, you hear that?" Tripp screams and points toward the horizon. "Inbound mech units!"

I help Shiloe to her feet, and we join the others. I search the crater for the Immortals and see them on the opposite side now. The girl is holding the boy, and they look directly at us but don't flee.

We have the advantage, and I try to decide if we should engage them. However, what I really want is to talk to them and learn more. But I sense the enemy mechs are just seconds away. Still, I linger, indecision biting at me. This might be our best chance at communicating with the other Immortals.

Then the air is filled with the sound of mech units. Their onboard targeting system pinpoints us, and railgun fire erupts. We use our cloaks to shield our bodies as the mechs open fire from above. We're pinned, unable to move.

Suddenly, artillery rounds explode from the opposite side of the large crater. Our recon troops take up positions along the edge and return fire. Seconds later, the enemy mechs land and charge toward us.

When I turn to search for the enemy Immortals, the blond-haired boy is gone. I see only the dark-haired girl. She stares directly at me and sends a single thought.

...it's all a lie!

Back at base camp, we gather with Commander Freemantle for our typical debrief. We recount the battle to him as he sits at a small desk. The makeshift tent is dark, with only a dim light hanging above us, swaying in the breeze. Mud and rain are everywhere as troops march by, the distant sounds of war reverberating through the space.

"There were only two enemy Immortals that I could see," I say.

"They were fast," Shiloe chimes in. "Quicker than any of us. If it had been just Brin and me, we'd both be dead right now."

"Did they say anything to you?" Freemantle asks and lowers his piercing gaze at us. His voice is raised slightly and sounds anxious to me.

I glance at the others and wonder if I should tell him the truth. "No. They said nothing."

"Are you certain?" Freemantle holds my gaze, as if he knows there's more.

"That's it, Commander. Just the fighting, nothing else."

There's a moment of silence as Freemantle taps his lips.

"Commander," Vern says. "They *knew* we were coming."

"Yes, I know. What concerns me more is that they knew your exact location."

A medic enters the tent and moves over to examine Shiloe, but her injuries are already healing. Freemantle dismisses the medic and waits until the tent is clear.

"What are you thinking, Commander?" I ask. "How close is this spy?"

Freemantle lowers his voice. "Very close, it would appear."

"Who else would know our battle plans?" Tripp asks. "That's a very small group, I reckon."

"Are you sure it's a spy?" Shiloe asks. "Maybe our comm links are tapped?"

"That's unlikely. We have very advanced technology that scrambles all communications."

"Commander," I say. "Had we followed orders today and moved into position, we would have been shredded by friendly fire. Your entire group of Immortals would be dead right now. That should concern you."

Freemantle leans back against the table and crosses his arms. "Now it's my turn to ask. How did you know, Brindall? If there was no indication of a trap, how did you know?"

I want to tell him the truth, but I'm not sure how. Trying to explain some strange voice or premonition doesn't sound like a good idea at the moment. Though that *subtle whisper* had been responsible for the warning, Freemantle might think I'm shellshocked or delirious from battle. But as I stand there in front of him, I begin to grow more suspicious. Should I trust anyone? *The trap, the location, the enemy immortals…*

Although I sense that Commander Freemantle is a good man, and probably someone we can trust, I feel better about saying nothing.

"Sir, I guess it was just a hunch."

He holds my gaze, his arms still crossed as he leans on the table. His eyes probe mine again, and I get the sense he knows I'm lying. But he stands and claps me on the shoulder. "Well, that's some quick thinking on the battlefield. You saved the lives of your company. Maybe the entire war. But you also disobeyed a direct order."

I hadn't considered that.

"Then why keep us all grouped together, sir?" I ask. "As much as I don't want our group split up, strategically, it makes some sense. If we're caught in the middle of an artillery round, we're dead, and the South wins."

That strange intuitive voice begins to whisper to me again. The wheels are turning in my head: conspiracy theories and lies about who we really are. Am I truly an Immortal? Or is that too a lie? I need time to think, to meditate. Perhaps then I'll find some answers.

Freemantle finally stands. "Tomorrow, you're all being relocated to the Eastern Theater. You're dismissed." He turns and leaves the tent without looking back.

That night, outside of our apartments and circled around the firepit, we talk softly to each other. The popping and hissing of the fire does little to settle my nerves, though. Our new living complex is perched on the edge of a cliff that overlooks the battleground beyond. Why we're given this particular view is beyond me. The last thing any of us want to see is more war. But I begin to think that's the real reason behind it. The commanders don't want us getting too comfy. At least the sound of battle, along with the thunder and crows in the background, gives me some solace that our conversations will go unheard. The one thing on my mind is tomorrow's relocation to the Eastern Theater. We're being moved again, and I know the others are worried as well.

As I listen to my friends talk, I realize how important our time in the evenings has become. Though the subject matter is often grim, our discussions have strengthened our bond. It's almost like our own little 'debrief' about the day's events, but without the formalities the commanders expect. Besides, it's something we all need. Talking about it helps us deal with the trauma. I'm quickly learning that witnessing such violence shouldn't be held inside. The scary thing is that we're all becoming accustomed to the horrors of battle, almost desensitized to it, in fact. I can hear it in the way we talk now. What had once been almost taboo to speak of is brushed off casually—and we're only a little over a week into our campaign. In that short time, I can see how much we've changed, too. We're no longer innocent kids from different boroughs. We've been transformed into hardened soldiers, at least on the battlefield.

"What's on your mind, Brin?" Shiloe asks and nudges me with her shoulder. She sits with her knees drawn to her chest and her cloak wrapped around her. I see her breath in the cool evening air.

I shake my head and speak in a low voice. "Today. When I disobeyed Freemantle's orders."

"What about it?" Vern asks. He's busy picking dried mud from his curly black hair.

I glance around the circle, then lean forward onto my knees. "I…have any of you been hearing voices?" No one answers at first and I begin to regret speaking about it. "Yeah, forget I asked that. Maybe I got hit on the head or something—"

Shiloe interrupts me by grasping my arm and shaking me. "No, Brin. You're not alone. I thought I heard it too."

"Okay," Tripp says. "I'll admit that I've heard something, not quite a voice but more like thoughts."

"What did yours say, Brin?" Drake asks.

"It was like an inner voice, intuitive may be a better description," I say. "It was a warning. That's what kept me from attacking today."

"Inner voice," Grish says. "So, that's what we're callin' it, huh?"

I shrug my shoulders. "Sure, why not? It's the best way I can explain it. Sounds like everyone here has heard it, too."

"Yeah. More or less since we've been here in the Central Theater, come to think of it," Vern says. "But I'm with Brin. It's subtle. I have to really pay attention."

"Could it be from using Vishmu?" Shiloe asks. "I think Henak said something about it. A side effect of meditation."

Tripp leans in and whispers. "Guys. Should we be talkin' 'bout this? I mean, what if our rooms are tapped and they find out about more of our secrets? They may use it against us."

Vern settles back on his elbows. "Nah. We can trust Freemantle, right?"

"I think we're okay out here, Tripp," I say and give his flushed cheek a playful pat. "As far as who we can trust, I think deep down the answer is yes. I don't get any malicious vibes from Freemantle. Still, there's something—"

"That dark-haired girl today," Drake says. "What was it she said?"

"It's all a lie," Grish says. "Whatever that's supposed to mean."

"It's pretty apparent, isn't it?" Shiloe whispers. "We all know there's more going on than just this war."

"Wait a minute." Drake holds out his hands. "What do you mean, something more? You talking about the so-called spy again?"

"That's the only way the enemy could've known our battle plans and location," I say. "Only the highest ranks are privy to that information."

"I dunno what's happening around here, but I'm glad you held us back today, Brin," Vern says with a smile and grabs my knee. "Guardian angels? Intuitive voices? Whatever it is, I like it. Otherwise, we're not here right now."

"We know that someone's trying to sabotage us," I say. "We have to be more careful. I don't like being grouped together, for one. A single explosive round could take us all out. Freemantle's smarter than that. I'm guessing someone else is calling the shots, someone higher up, maybe."

"So, stay spread out and disobey orders?" Grish says. She raises an eyebrow. "We keep doin' that and someone's gonna notice."

"What're they going to do? Throw us in jail?" Tripp says. "They still need us. I say we do whatever we want."

"Maybe," I say. "But I don't want to give anything away just yet. Right now, no one thinks we know about the spy, except Freemantle, perhaps."

"There's something else we need to discuss," Shiloe says.

"Right," Vern chuckles. "What the hell were those Immortals using today, man?"

"You mean that glowing mace?" Tripp says. "It's obvious, ain't it?"

"The vessels Triton gave us," I say and give him a nod. "They're a weapon. Based on how difficult it was to fend off just two of those Dark Immortals, we need to figure out how to unlock them soon, or we're going to be in trouble."

HELL'S GATE | **CHAPTER 13**

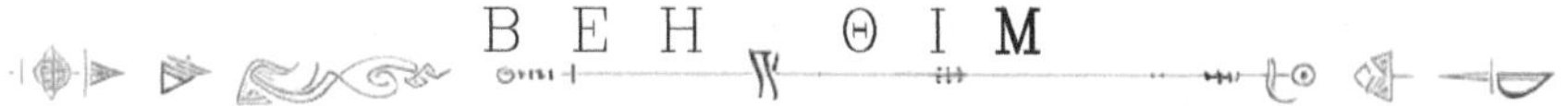

Early the next morning we're rounded up and loaded onto the transit. Less than an hour later, we reach the Eastern Theater. The supercharged transport deposits us at the terminal, then reverses and rockets back down the rail and toward the Central Theater with a new group of passengers.

Commander Taun meets us on the boarding platform. Surprisingly, he grants us a few days off. I imagine the look of shock on my face is one of comical confusion. I actually begin to think it's some cruel prank, and it doesn't sink in until about an hour later. Regardless, it gives us all a much-needed breather and time to settle in and recoup. Shiloe and I branch off from the others and explore the new underground borough known as Hell's Gate.

Though the city is covered with a stasis dome, the constant rain has carved a large river into the landscape and snakes down the defunct mines and empties somewhere below. Similar to the Central Theater, we can't seem to escape the sounds of war and the smell of smoke. We stroll along the city's large rim wall. Beyond the edge, we see the lower canyon that stretches for kilometers along this portion of the 37th parallel. From our higher vantage, we can see the battlefield with explosions and the distant sounds of war.

Behind and below the protective canyon wall, the city is divided into multiple districts, which provides support for the war effort. The districts meander down into the lower reaches below. Near the upper rim, we see training facilities, barracks, and hangar bays. But deeper are the markets and entertainment. We don't linger for very long, not wanting to think about the war and follow the thoroughfares into the lower levels until the sounds of war grow distant. I'm surprised at how lively the lower areas are as we discover busy shops, markets and malls. They line the vast chambers, and the noise of trading fills the air. The deeper we go the more vibrant the activity is.

Shiloe and I finally step into a secluded café and order some food and drink. There are a few citizens inside with some soft music playing in the background. I order some sort of pastry and a warm, brownish-colored water that smells like roasted nuts. Shiloe does the same. We find a corner booth and strike up a quiet conversation. Through the side window, we watch the people hurry by, and I feel suddenly awkward sitting with her. It's the first time we've been out and away from the others.

"It's a date," I say, half-jokingly. "I've heard people talk about it, never been on one, though."

She laughs at that, then smiles. "Well, you're not wrong, I suppose, but I never agreed to it."

It makes me chuckle. "So, should I ask then? Would that help?"

Shiloe taps her index finger to her lips with her eyes trained on the ceiling in mock consideration. She lets out a dramatic sigh. "Fine…it's a date, I guess." She places a hand on my forearm and squeezes. "It seems so strange, doesn't it? I mean, here we are, hundreds of kilometers away from our homes, in some lonely café, having a casual bite to eat, no less and…"

"…and war is just around the corner," I say, finishing the sentence for her.

She turns to face me, then looks out the dirty window at the busy thoroughfare beyond. "It's unfortunate that we can't enjoy one night together without thinking about it. I feel guilty just having a quiet moment of happiness. Don't you?"

"Yeah, I know how you feel. But we needed this. You, Vern, all of us. Just a moment to catch our breath. I'd say we've earned it. We need to enjoy it because we may not get another break anytime soon."

We sit there for a moment, silent and staring out the window as citizens hurry by. I look down at her hand, which is still on my arm.

"What about us, Shiloe?"

The question catches her off guard. I watch her expression as she turns to look at me. "Us?" She shakes her head.

I place a hand over hers now and give it a gentle squeeze. "We've been through a lot together already. Hell, we've almost died together a few times and yet, I feel like I barely know you."

Once again, the look on her face is one of confusion. She lifts the corner of her mouth and turns her gaze back to the window. I can see she's uncertain how to answer the question.

"What would you like to know?" she finally asks and looks into my eyes.

But it feels different now. It's like we're meeting for the first time, like starting over again. Two strangers in a café instead of a few kids forced into a war against our own will. I stare back at her, noticing the gold flecks in her hazel eyes, the way she tilts her head when she listens, the way her mouth turns up when she's being sassy. Shiloe is that ray of sunshine in a dark room. She's strong-willed, capable, and steadfast, yet kind and softhearted and caring. It's at that moment I realize I've fallen in love and hadn't even noticed until now. I feel breathless as the realization takes me by surprise, and she notices it.

"What's wrong?" she asks in a cheeky way, then winks at me.

"I…I dunno," I say, trying to think now, which is a bit difficult all of a sudden.

"About those questions," she continues with a quick smile.

I draw in a breath and straighten in the booth. "Oh…right. Well. what's your family like? What's your favorite color? You said something about painting? What do you like to paint—"

"Hold on," she chuckles and holds up her hands.

I find myself laughing along with her. "Sorry. That all just came out at once, didn't it?"

"Yeah. That's a lot to unpack."

"It is," I say and feel my skin flush. "Maybe we should start with something simple, like your childhood then?"

"Not sure that's so simple, honestly." She shakes her head and settles back. "My father was a load master, or balancer. He taught me everything I know. Mother died from Absentia Disease. Her immune system was weakened, and we couldn't afford time in the light booths. Then, when Father got drafted, it was up to me. I took over, and it was just me and my little brother, but he was too young to work. We moved in with my Uncle Rin in upper Hammer Fall. I started working with the Northern Airlift Division. Pay wasn't bad. Then, came my Day of the Nail. Well," she holds up her hands, "here I am. Guess that's the summarized version of it, anyway."

"Do you miss your brother?"

"More than anything. He's all I have left now. His name's Deacon. He's a good kid. I tried to show him everything I could before I left. I just hope Uncle Rin will look after him until I get back, whenever that is. I…I try not to think about him, but it's hard. He's young but sharp. I think he'll be fine." Shiloe grips my hand a bit tighter, and I can tell she's trying to calm herself more than she's trying to convince me. "So, what about you, Brin? I'm just as curious about your story."

I give her a brief smile. "There's nothing exciting to tell, to be honest."

"I don't care. I want to hear it."

I stare into her hazel eyes, considering how much more I want to share, not because I don't trust her, but because I don't trust my own voice. "I have a younger brother named Ben, and my Ma, Grace. I was their primary provider after my father was drafted into the Coffin Wars. I tried to fill in for him, so I worked as a miner and part-time in the local militia. Ben likes to sit on the porch, draw little pictures in the dirt. He'd wait for me to get home each day. It's tough, you know? Of course, we want the best for our families. I wanted to buy him a drafting board, somewhere to sit and draw his pictures. It broke my heart to see him sitting in the dirt and using his finger. But it took everything I could earn in the mines to cover our basic living expenses. Ma did some work on the side, knitting and repatching militia uniforms. It's just that I don't trust the man who made the promise to me. Grior, the governor, he's…I'm just anxious to get home, that's all." I pause, trying to think what else to say.

"You became their father figure."

"Yes, I suppose so. Didn't really want to, but my family needed me."

"So, that's why," Shiloe mutters.

"What?"

"That's why," she says again. "I was wondering why you feel the need to watch over everyone."

I narrow one eye at her. "I'm not sure about that."

"Well, I am. You just can't see it. Everyone else does, including our instructors."

I shrug. "If you say so."

"Doesn't matter," she continues. "We all play a part in this, Brin."

"Okay. And what part do you play?"

Shiloe sits back and gives me a long look. "You tell me."

"Come on, Shiloe."

"I can't share everything with you, at least not tonight."

I lift one shoulder at her. "Why not? I just did."

Shiloe holds her smile for a brief second, then it slowly fades. "Because I'm afraid to."

I grip her hand. "Why?"

Shiloe seems to cycle through several emotions then. Her face contorts into a grimace, and she looks away and tries to pull her hand back, but I don't let go.

"What if you die, Brin? What if any of us die? I have friends now: Vern, Drake, Tripp, Grish, and you. I just don't know how I'll handle that. If you and I go any farther…I just don't know."

"So, you think keeping your distance will make a difference? I feel like we're past that, Shiloe. I understand your fear. You don't want to lose this new family you've found. Neither do I."

She shakes her head at our interlocked fingers. "Brin. I can't make this decision about us right now. If you're asking whether I like you, then the answer is yes, of course. But I need time to open up to those feelings. That's fair, don't you think?"

I sit back, still holding onto her hand. "Yeah. I'm sorry. I just…there's something…and, well, I don't want to lose that. I just want to know you a little better, that's all."

"I feel it, too, Brin. But you may end up somewhere else, in another theater, who knows. We may never see each other again and…these blasted collars—" She gives it a tug, then lets her hand drop. "We aren't free to just do whatever we want. I don't know if we'll ever be."

I give her a wry smile and tug at my own collar. "Yeah, these things kinda kill the mood, right?"

That draws a laugh, and her eyes well up with tears. "None of it seems fair."

I sit forward and move closer until our faces are nearly touching. I feel her breath on my cheek, and it quickens, like my heartbeat. I want to wrap my arms around her and leave this place. I want to take her away from this war and death and suffering.

"Somehow, Shiloe, we'll make it happen. We'll be free of this."

"I'd like that."

With our fingers intertwined, sitting in the quiet café, miles away from our homes and families, I feel suddenly helpless. Doubt creeps in. *What if I can't help her or my other friends?* And then my thoughts turn to my family and Benji. I finally let go of her hand and sit back.

"Anyway," I say and try to keep my voice steady. But somehow, I know that Shiloe hears the heartache in it. "About that favorite color of yours."

She smiles, then laughs, and I join her. Shiloe finally wipes her eyes with the back of her hand. "It's green," she says.

We sit next to each other in the corner booth until the café closes. Even though it's late, neither of us is ready to go back to our living complex. So, we spend the rest of the evening walking the thoroughfares of the large Eastern Theater Borough.

Never before have I felt so drawn to a girl. Being near her makes the war feel distant, if not bearable, at least. Occasionally, our hands brush, and it sets my heart fluttering. I catch her looking at me with quick side glances. I know she's struggling with her feelings, too. Shiloe's concern about what might happen to us is something neither of us wants to think about. I understand her concern: an affair in the middle of this war could be costly. We need to stay focused on our missions. If we don't, it could mean death. Still, I can't help letting my imagination run wild thinking about her. What would it be like to leave this war behind and spend our lives together on the Skylight System? Though it's nothing more than a dream, I cling to it and hope someday it might become a reality. Subduing my desires won't be easy. I sense there's a silent agreement between us to set aside our feelings for each other and focus on the war, at least for the time being.

SECRET ASSIGNMENT | CHAPTER 14

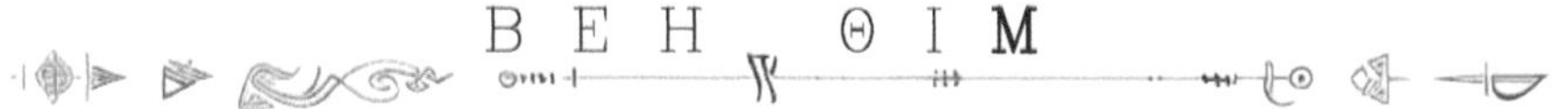

When dawn breaks on the third day, we're summoned to Commander Taun's quarters. I'm surprised to hear that our new assignment is something completely different than what I'm used to.

"Reconnaissance?" I ask, looking from Commander Taun to the others, my brow furrowed. My fists clench involuntarily by my sides.

"That's right," Taun says. He's a tall, slender man in his fifties. His blond hair is turning gray at the temples, and his prominent nose juts out like the blade of a knife. "You may use your cloak as needed. You're perfectly suited for this type of mission."

I give him a quick nod. "That may be, sir. Still, we've had no training in that area."

"You have all the tools you need to accomplish this task." Commander Taun waves my concern away and sits back in his plush chair in the otherwise drab office. Except for his ornate chair, the rest of the furniture is basic, simple, and unadorned. His high-brow attitude and upturned gaze seem out of place for the position he fills. I can envision him sitting more comfortably in a politician's office with aides buzzing around at his command.

"What is it we're looking for, sir?" Vern asks.

Taun picks at his nail and doesn't look up. "Just information." He stands and walks over to a display, scrolls through a map of the Eastern Theater and points to an area south of the 37th parallel. "See this? It's about ten levels below a factory building. We believe that's the HQ for the entire Eastern Theater. The Southern Coalition thinks they're clever. A lot of information is stored there on hundreds of holopads." He holds up a small device about the size of his hand and gives it a shake as if presenting something to a toddler. "Holopad, yes? Anyway, your mission is to take as many as you can get."

I give the others a sidelong frown, then face Taun. "Yes, we know what a holopad is, sir. But we're not spies. We're troops. I'm afraid we'll be spotted quickly."

"Uh, fish out of water, Commander," Vern pipes in. "I think that's what Brin is trying to say."

But Taun ignores Vern and focuses on me. "We've been wanting to infiltrate their HQ for ages. Many of our top spies have tried and failed. Now that we have a group of Immortals, we have to take a shot. It's worth the potential sacrifice."

I glance back at the others again. "Does Freemantle know about this?"

"It's none of his concern. You're in the Eastern Theater now, son. It's my call."

Shiloe shakes her head and crosses her arms. "I think Vern's right, sir. If you send us in, there's a good chance we'll get caught. We're as good as dead if that happens. You're willing to sacrifice us to gain information?"

But Taun stands and paces the room. I can see he's getting worked up. "Again, you have the cloaks, and you're Immortals. That makes you as qualified as anyone else! How many times do I need to say it?"

"What about the E-Class mechs?" I say. "I hear they can see our cloaked forms."

"They are still limited in that," Taun replies. "I suggest you be careful."

I hold up my hands, then place them on my hips. "What's the plan?"

"I'm sending you and Vern. We'll increase fire on the opposite side to draw attention away from you two, so listen for it. Shiloe will lead Drake, Grish, and Tripp along the front line. Brin. Vern. You're going in tonight. I'm giving you eight hours to collect as many holopads as you can."

I slowly shake my head. This all seems wrong, too fast... *forced.* But there's little point in arguing with Commander Taun. I can see he's dug in. "What's on these holopads that's so important?"

Taun walks over and holds the door open. "The rest of you are dismissed. Wait in your quarters for instructions."

Vern and I sit through some briefings. We study maps and download information about the South, in particular, the areas we'll be infiltrating. After an hour or so, I feel we're as prepared as can be expected. Yet, Taun gives us no indication of what's on the holopads. As we leave, I hear Taun give the order to send Shiloe and the others to the front line.

Back at our complex, I sit with Vern on the 'front porch,' which is the name we've bestowed on the gathering area. Perched on the rock outcropping and high above the battlefield, I look down and wonder where Shiloe and the others are.

"They're out there, fighting without us," I say.

Vern chuckles and claps me on the back. "She'll be fine, Brin. You know, if anyone can lead our group besides you, it's Shiloe."

"Yeah," I say and kick at a rock. I watch it tumble down the cliff and echo into silence as low booms fill the cave.

"What do ya think about our little mission?" Vern asks.

"Not really sure yet. Taun seems determined to get that information, though."

"I'd say so. Willing to risk two of his Immortals to get it."

"That's what worries me."

"This a trap, Brin?" Vern asks. I hear the nervous hitch in his tone, which is something rare.

I sit there, gazing beyond the edge of the tunnel and at the lightning and explosions in the distance. "Well, we're about to find out. You going to be okay?"

"Yeah, of course, man." But his voice is unsteady. I sense his nervous tension.

"We'll be fine."

"I know. I've been accepted into our group. As long as I have that, I'm good."

This takes me a bit by surprise. "What do you mean by that?"

Vern shrugs. "Just never thought I'd be accepted outside of my family. And yet, here I am with a group of strangers with different backgrounds from all over. And you guys have taken me in. That means a lot. That's all I ever wanted, really."

I reach over and grip Vern's shoulder and give him a shake. "Hey. Look at me, Vern."

I wait for him to face me. He's struggling to keep a straight face, and I feel my own eyes begin to sting.

"We're brothers now. Nothing will change that, got it? We're going to look after each other, I promise."

Vern wipes the back of his hand across his cheek and gives me a hug. "Yeah, got it. Thanks, Brin."

An hour later, Vern and I are led down dozens of levels below the main thoroughfares and into the dark bowels of the Eastern Theater. Military police surround us as we board a black bullet train that I didn't know existed.

Once aboard, I'm shoved into a forward-facing chair and harnessed in. The ride is bumpy and unsettling, and I sense we're heading even further downward. The confidence I had built up over the last several missions suddenly falls away as we plummet. I have no idea what to expect or how to lead this particular mission. Even with the briefing, there's little direction given, almost like Taun is purposely trying to confuse us.

Minutes later, the train stops with a jolt, throwing me into my harness. Vern and I step onto a small boarding platform, and I get the sense that very few people know about this place. It's dark and silent, and I hear only the soft pitter-patter of dripping water. Even the sounds of war are missing at this depth. None of the military police stand to help us or say anything. The doors hiss shut, the train seems to magically reassemble on the rail, then shoots off in the direction it came from with a thunderclap.

Vern lets out a long sigh, one eyebrow raised, with his typical grin plastered on his face. He holds out a hand. "After you."

I locate the handheld tracking device Taun had given me and study the menu. It shows a three-dimensional map highlighting our destination. We follow the imaginary path, making our way across the pits and husked-out caverns. I can only assume we've been dropped in a spot well below the main battlefield of the 37th parallel—*a secret backdoor*. We trek through small caves and tiny chambers that are linked together to form a natural channel. The rock formations appear to have been created by subterranean waterflow from ages past. But the way forward is difficult. Some of the chambers are small, and there is no light, though the tracker provides some guidance through our night vision visors.

Vern and I press on. Occasionally, we have to help each other over stalactites and other formations, getting turned around several times, even with the tracker. Hours pass as we labor across the uneven terrain. Eventually, the light level increases, and I sense we're moving closer to the battlefield. The cave walls cast jagged, strobing shadows, like dragon's teeth, playing tricks on my vision. I feel a paranoia moment, wondering if this *is* actually the trap. *What if we're simply being led in circles? What if Taun plans to strand us here to wander until we run out of food and water?* That feeling worsens when I think about Shiloe and the others, left to fight alone. Being away from them, especially Shiloe, makes me anxious.

Suddenly, we stumble across a worn path. I pause and take a knee to catch my breath. Vern is doubled over, breathing heavily. Beyond, the trail leads through a barely noticeable void in the canyon wall with occasional openings in the side. Otherwise, it's completely hidden, like an optical illusion in the flashes of lightning and explosions beyond. Rain pours down around us, though the path in the wall is mostly dry and protected. In the background, I hear the familiar sounds of war underpinned by the cawing crows. Low booms shake the ground beneath our feet. I hold the tracker up and see the path leading us through the hidden pass and toward the southern port city called the York Borough. In the far distance, I see a cliff rising up to a high canyon rim wall.

I pull at Vern and lead him toward the passage. "I think we've crossed the 37th. We're in enemy territory now. You going to make it?"

Vern gives me a disapproving look, his eyes narrowed and waves the question away, though I can see he's still struggling.

I give him a firm shake and a heavy clap on his back. "Remember. If we use our thoughts to communicate, another Immortal might hear us, so go sparingly. If they're out there on the battlefield, we need to be careful. Stay cloaked, move with random movements, pause occasionally, shield your thoughts. Off we go."

I see Vern take a deep breath, and he clenches his jaw. He finally nods.

We cloak and move into the canyon passage and toward the York Borough.

YORK | CHAPTER 15

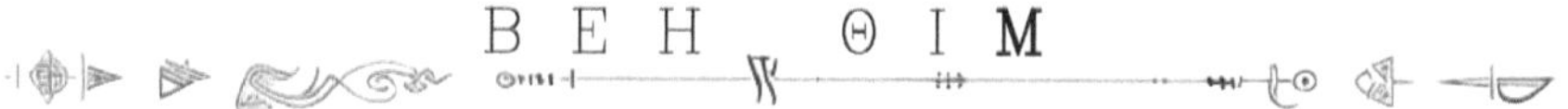

Vern and I make our way through the hidden canyon pass. In less than an hour, we're working our way up the steep cliff without incident. I estimate it's about fifty meters tall, where the lip spills over onto the front edge and into the Southern Coalition's York Borough. I can still hear the sounds of battle and crows beyond, but we're deep into enemy territory and kilometers behind the 37th parallel now. As we near the rim wall's summit, I begin to hear the sounds of city life. It's faint but distinct, with loudspeakers barking information. The top of the rim wall is heavily fortified with scouts, patrol units and detection equipment. I can see troops from about halfway up and motion to Vern for caution. Thanks to our cloaks, we're well hidden from even the highest-tech surveillance. Still, we keep an eye out for other Immortals and move in slowly.

After what seems like an eternity, we finally reach the top and wait for a break in the patrol's shift. Then we're over the cliff edge and across the rampart. Seconds later, we're scaling down and moving into the York Borough.

Wide elevated streets run perpendicular to the cliff edge. The thoroughfares form a grid about ten meters high and gradually slope down to street level. I can see patrols marching along them. Spanning over the huge city is a stasis dome, which is very similar to the Northern Boroughs.

Vern and I leap between the elevated streets and avoid the patrolling troops. When we finally reach ground level, we crouch in the shadows and take in our surroundings. I can see the city is much the same as ours: layered thoroughfares and open pits below. Steel structures are built right into the cave walls, and the pits drop into nothingness below.

I pull out the tracker and study the map. According to the display, we're about halfway to the factory quadrant.

"Hope this is worth the effort," Vern whispers.

"Yeah, but I'm starting to get more suspicious," I reply.

Vern pulls at my arm. "Hey, you sure we should go through with this?"

"What do you mean? You think we should just abandon the mission?"

"You know this is a trap, Brin. Why we doin' this?"

I consider for only a brief second. "If we don't go through with this, that gives Taun all the ammo he needs. We'd be disobeying a direct order. He'd court-marshal us on the spot."

"You really think they'd court-marshal us, though? They need us."

"Let's don't give them that reason," I say in a low whisper. "Besides, they might use Drake, Shiloe, Grish and Tripp as leverage, or our families. I'm not taking that chance."

"You really think it's Taun, though?"

"Right now's not the time, Vern. Come on. We gotta go through with this."

Vern looks at me, still uncertain. "What's our backup plan?"

"Working on it. Just remember that those E-Class mechs can see our cloaked forms if we move too quickly," I say and give him a slap on the back. "Let's just hope we don't see any."

Vern follows me, and we stay cloaked in the shadows. We stop occasionally as we make our way from the elevated roadways and into the city alleyways.

...five more kilometers. I send the thought to Vern as we move deeper into the city and toward our target.

As we dart between buildings, I go over our options. I start to wonder if we should just pay a quick visit to the site, then leave. Maybe Vern is right. *Why are we doing this if we know it's a trap?* But we need to bring back some proof, something that shows we made the effort. Then I think about the last trap we'd almost fallen into while grouped together.

We need to split up.

I send the thought to Vern.

In the distance, I can see the warehouse, just as Taun had described it. It's built into the rock walls and faces an empty street. There's barely any lighting inside or out. The main façade has numerous windows. A few are broken out. But I know that's just a distraction. I assume this building is made to look abandoned. If there's a trap, it's waiting inside for us.

Vern moves left along the alleyway as I flank the opposite side.

I notice more detail the closer I get. The warehouse is framed by the canyon walls with red striations of earth and rock running diagonally behind it. The structure is made of the same sandstone blocks, which are dry stacked in a running bond pattern. It's about a dozen stories tall, but the footprint is spread out over several city blocks. All is quiet in this area, and the distant sounds of city life are barely detectable.

As I kneel from across the intersection and in the shadows, I have no doubt now that this is a trap. I can hear that familiar voice begin to whisper—a warning, I think. Going through the main entrance makes me nervous, yet I see only one way inside. But overhead, there are multiple catwalks near the top floors. I decide it'll be safer to enter from an upper story. I backtrack and scale up an adjacent building to one of the catwalks and cross over. I locate a broken-out window and enter the warehouse at the highest level.

Once inside, I crouch in a dark corner and assess my surroundings. There are thousands of old shelves aligned into rows on each level and a thick layer of dust blankets everything. Outdated equipment lines the perimeter walls in what I assume was once a control center. The lighting is dim, the only illumination spilling from the street-side windows. I glide silently between the racks, find a few holopads and browse through them. It's mainly standard issue instructions that give no tactical information about the Southern Coalition. I read through the articles but see nothing about 'top secret' data. I place a few of them inside my cloak as proof. That's when I notice fresh footprints in the dust. I kneel to get a better look, but they aren't like any prints I've seen before.

A strange feeling overtakes me then, one that causes the hair to rise on the back of my neck. The intuitive voice in my head begins to whisper again.

I crane my neck to look above me.

In the darkness, I make out dozens of large metal trusses spanning the length of the roof. The ceiling seems to shift, and at first, I think my eyes are playing tricks on me. But then my heart skips a beat when I realize what it is. There are hundreds of E-Class mech units looking down at me.

I immediately send a psychic message to Vern. *RUN!*

I race between the racks as mechs begin to drop and hit the floor around me. Some crash down onto the racks, knocking them over and spilling holopads everywhere. I sprint just ahead of the surge, weaving and crashing my way toward the window. At five meters, I dive through it and onto the catwalk just as several mechs crash through behind me. Within seconds, there's a horde of them chasing me across the catwalk. I feel it bounce and sway under the weight. When I near the halfway point, the catwalk groans, then collapses.

Due to my momentum, I hit the adjacent building's wall with enough force to crack the sandstone blocks. But I grip the stone jamb of a window and manage to stop my fall. The mechs on the catwalk plunge to the street below with a crash, scattering mechanical parts everywhere. The remaining mechs inside the warehouse reverse course and flood down the warehouse stairs and toward the ground entrance.

I hop down the building façade two stories at a time and reach the street level quicker though. Standing near the intersection is Vern, cloaked and hidden. He doesn't ask any questions as we race back through the inner-city alleyways. I look over my shoulder to see the mechs surging through the warehouse entry below.

Vern and I sprint through darkened alleyways, searching for the path back to the canyon rim wall. In our haste, we get turned around a few times and then separated. When I turn, Vern is gone. I backtrack and eventually find him engaged by several units. I rush over and pull a mech off Vern's back. I focus some energy and rip it in half. Vern slips and falls to his knees as two other mechs move in. I block one, then sweep the other one to the ground. Vern regains his footing and hammers a fist through the downed mech's visor. But we're quickly outnumbered as the mechs continue to pour into the alleyway. I feel myself slipping as we fight: my energy is fading. Vern is struggling too, and I begin to think this might be our last fight together. We struggle to keep our footing among the parts and pieces around us, but their numbers seem endless. If we turn and flee, the mechs will eventually run us down. The thought suddenly hits me that we're not making it out alive.

Then I feel a presence near me.

In my mind, it seems familiar, like someone I'd recently met.

It's the presence of another Immortal.

I feel my heart drop. Whatever hope I had left fizzles away. There are dozens of mechs still bearing down on us, and now we're facing an enemy Immortal. I prepare myself for a final stand.

I can see the Immortal barreling toward us. But it stops short and doesn't move to attack. Instead, it does something that shocks me.

It begins fighting the E-Class mech units.

The Immortal is powerful. It uses the same glowing scepter I'd seen the others use. The scepter pulses with energy and cuts through the mechs with ease. The Immortal wades into the middle of the units and splits their ranks as they reorient on it. But any mech caught near the Immortal's scepter is quickly pulverized. In a final move, the Immortal hammers the ground with its scepter, and a shockwave sends the mechs flying in all directions.

Vern and I stand our ground, poised and ready to fight. But the Immortal makes no move to engage us. Instead, it lowers its hood. A tall girl stares at us. Her bleached white hair is dyed turquoise at the tips, and her pale skin seems to glow in the dull light. Her nose and eyes are fair and pixie-like. She appears to be about my age of eighteen with an athletic frame.

"Why?" I ask.

The girl slowly raises her left hand and holds her palm outward. I see the glow now, a brilliant turquoise color. It shimmers in the dark, pulsing slowly to match her heart rate.

I let out a gasp and look down at my hand. The color matches almost exactly. When I look at her again, I notice the letter 'N' hovering inside the light from her palm. I squint my eyes, thinking of the chart. Her symbol is next to mine, at least from what I remember.

"You're an enemy Immortal," I say. "We're on opposite sides. Why did you save us?"

Vern tugs on my cloak. "Brin, we gotta go, man!"

But I ignore him and step closer to the girl. "What's your name?"

...*Varance,* she says with her thoughts.

I don't understand, I respond. *What are you trying to tell me?*

...*it's all a lie!* Her voice is nearly a scream inside my head. It echoes and reverberates. Her voice seems to stick in my thoughts. It feels different than when I talk with my friends. Her tone is angry, belligerent. *Dark.*

"What's a lie?" I whisper to her. "Just tell me."

"Figure it out!" she hisses at me and bares her teeth like serpent fangs.

I sense her mood change, and she turns to leave.

"Wait!" I say and leap after her. I grip her arm and hold her. "Who's trying to kill us?"

The girl named Varance faces me. "Who's trying to kill you…*OR*…who's trying to kill *Immortals?*"

Varance discretely slips a small metallic case into my hand. "Now's not the time," she whispers, then she pulls the hood of her cloak over her head and disappears.

A STRANGE GIFT | CHAPTER 16

I hear shouts in the alleyway next to ours. I place the small case inside my cloak, then sprint after Vern. We flee the area just as Southern Coalition troops begin flooding in.

My head spins with questions as we search for the right alleyways back to the canyon wall. Is it just a coincidence that two different enemy Immortals have told me the same thing now? And why had this girl, Varance, saved us? Was she really offering helpful advice, or is it an elaborate hoax? I'm beginning to wonder if it's wise to go down this rabbit hole. But these Immortals don't seem deceptive, as far as I can tell. Then again, the first two had tried to kill us.

Now's not the time! Varance had said. Was that meant as an invitation? Something to be continued later?

I feel for the case as I run. I'm dying to open it and see what's inside but push the desire away so I can focus on getting the hell out of the York Borough alive. Getting across enemy lines with Vern is priority one right now.

We climb the side of a building and leap across the rooftops, trying to get a better view of the maze of alleyways. Then I nearly smack my head. In our haste, I'd forgotten about the tracker device, and I fish it out.

Vern stops next to me and leans his head on my shoulder to catch his breath. "Brin. We've been runnin' for an hour straight! I don't know how much longer I can go, man."

I feel the same way, like I could lay down and go to sleep right there on the rooftop.

I check the tracker's time and location. "We've got three hours till extraction. You can sleep all day tomorrow."

"Assumin' Taun doesn't send us straight to the front line," he says.

We follow the tracker, communicating through our thoughts. Below us, there's more activity in the alleyways. Luckily, the buildings are clustered together so densely that we're able to stay above the turmoil, cloaked and undetected. Soon, I see the canyon wall, and ten minutes later, we're scaling over it and down the cliff face. Eventually, we're far enough away from the city to take a quick break.

I slump down and lean against Vern. Once again, my searching hands find the metal case Varance had given me, and I want to open it. But then I check the time and see we have about two hours to make it back. Vern is nearly asleep as I stand and pull him up. "Come on, Vern. Stay close."

The way back through the caves seems easier this time since we're moving downward. Though my energy is drained, I feel anxious to get home. The tracker keeps us on the right path, and soon, we're crawling out of the caves and into the open chamber, where we sit and wait for the transport.

It seems like hours later when the rail finally arrives. I see the military police hop out and help us onboard. I can barely buckle in after plopping down into my seat. I doze off several times on the ride back. My thoughts are in a haze the entire time, with Varance's voice in my head, speaking riddles and strange languages.

Taun is waiting for us at the boarding platform, hands on hips and his nose turned up like he's annoyed to be there. The MPs escort us off the transport and march us up the trail behind Taun.

I'm hoping we'll be allowed to go to our quarters, but instead, we're taken straight to Taun's office and seated at his desk. A group of high-ranking officers are already there, waiting expectantly.

"Well?" Taun asks and shuts the door. "Let's see what you've got."

I pull out the three dusty holopads and slide them across his desk. "I don't think there's anything of worth on these holopads. I'm not sure what data you were hoping for, but it would seem that your intel was wrong. By the way, we were ambushed when we got there."

"Ambushed?" Taun barks. "That's not possible unless you were seen going into the borough. Were you cloaked?"

I glance sidelong at Vern, who's looking straight ahead in a trance, probably trying to keep from screaming at Taun. "Of course we were cloaked," I say. "There was a horde of mechs in that warehouse, waiting. Thought you said it would be vacant? They were expecting us—"

"Anything else to report?" he says and looks at us down his long nose.

Immediately I think of Varance and the case she'd slipped me. I can feel it wedged against my thigh. But I hold Taun's gaze and shake my head. "No. Nothing."

Somehow, I can sense that he knows I'm lying.

In that instant, I feel the need to talk to Triton or Henak. Maybe I can get word to Kiff or, better yet, Freemantle. Either way, I know if we don't get out of the Eastern Theater soon, we'll all end up dead.

"We'll look into this so-called 'ambush,'" Taun says with a dismissive wave.

But I already know he won't. In fact, I sense that he'll make sure that no one does. I sit back and close my eyes. I know now there's no useful data on the holopads we stole, and there never was. Commander Taun knows it too. Bringing back the holopads has simply bought us some more time. Soon, we'll be sent on another foolish mission. And another. Until one by one, we're all dead. And if we refuse, we'll be court-martialed and likely executed, along with our families. If Taun isn't the spy, he's at least involved.

After the long debrief with Taun and his top brass, we're finally allowed to return to our quarters. We meet Shiloe and the crew standing atop the overlook, waiting. Shiloe runs to us and wraps her arms around our necks. The others are right behind her, and soon, we're all hugging each other. I feel my eyes sting as we embrace. I feel a warmth in my chest at seeing all of my friends alive.

Then, everyone is talking and asking questions all at once.

I hold up my hands. "Showers first, then dinner. After that, assuming we're still awake, we can talk."

After my cold shower and some lukewarm gruel, I catch a second wind. Despite the events of that day, I'm wide awake now. Everyone meets around the fire pit overlooking the cliff. We sit in a circle with the familiar sounds of war echoing through the cave. Surprisingly, the sound sets me at ease. That realization frightens me, though. I'm becoming even more desensitized to this whole ordeal.

Shiloe kicks at the dirt and pats the stone next to her. "Sit here, Brin."

I move over and plop down and stretch my legs.

"So?" Grish says. "What the hell happened?"

"Top secret. Sorry," Vern jokes and sprawls out next to Grish, giving her a playful shove.

"Come on," Drake says. "Let's hear it."

I tilt my head at Vern. "Where should we start?"

But before I can even begin, Vern leans in and blurts out, "We saw another Immortal!"

I quickly pull him back. "Quiet!" I hiss.

Now, everyone is leaning in. We huddle around the fire.

Shiloe lowers her voice. "Was it that same girl as before? Ooh, I don't like her."

"What did the Immortal say?" Drake asks.

"Did you fight it?" Tripp asks.

I hold up my hands and wave. "Whoa, hold on. We'll get there. Just relax. First, the mission."

Vern nods. "Right. Go on, Brin."

"So, Taun sends us to some abandoned warehouse in the York Borough," I begin. "He gives very little information, just that it's supposed to be empty—"

Vern pounds his fist in anger. "I knew it was a trap."

"Vern, you mind?" I say.

"Sorry, go on." He pats me on my back, then crosses his arms.

I drop my voice even lower, and it's nearly drowned out by the crackling fire. "Like Vern said, we suspected a trap, so we split up. I entered the warehouse at the top level and grabbed a few holopads. Then I get this feeling we're not alone. I look up and see all these mechs in the ceiling rafters. They'd been waiting to ambush us."

"You still think someone on the inside?" Grish asks.

"Yeah, without a doubt. This mission proves it. Well, then we escape the warehouse. But eventually, the mechs catch up and we're in a fight for our lives. Right when I think we're done for, this enemy Immortal shows up with one of those glowing scepters."

"Guys," Vern says and leans forward. His fists are balled, and his forehead is strained. "You wouldn't believe how powerful this Immortal was. And with that scepter…" Vern trails off, shaking his head.

"For some reason, it helped fight off the mechs," I continue. "By itself, it destroyed more than the two of us combined."

"Why would it do that?" Shiloe asks. "The other two just tried to kill us. I thought the Immortals fighting for the South wanted us all dead?"

"So we've been told," Grish adds. "But consider the source. Is it not potentially the same group that wants us all dead?"

Tripp shrugs his narrow shoulders. "Still begs the question. Why?"

I shake my head. "I don't know. Her name was Varance. She seemed to be warning us, just like the last one. She said it's all a lie."

"Wonder what it means?" Drake asks.

"Pretty obvious, Drake," Grish says with a huff. "She must be talkin' about this war, or game, as they call it. This charade."

Which means the Southern Coalition Immortals know more than we do," Tripp says. "They've figured somethin' out."

"Was there anything else, Brin?" Shiloe asks.

"Yes." I rub my chin, considering for a second. "Something that Varance said. It sounded like an invitation. She said, *now's not the time*. I think she wants to meet with us. We should probably keep this to ourselves, at least until we know more."

"These missions are getting more dangerous," Shiloe says. "Someone wants us out of the way. Don't you think they're just going to keep sending us on these crazy fool's errands?"

Vern grunts. "Here-here. And I'm betting this 'someone' wants us out of the picture before the Winter Solstice."

Everyone sits quietly around the fire. I think about Vern's last comment. The Winter Solstice isn't far off, a handful of months or so. With everyone looking at me for answers, I feel that pressure to lead again, something I really don't want, especially right now.

"Let's get some rest," I say and clap my hands. "Maybe tomorrow will bring something new."

Everyone stands and makes their way to their sleeping quarters. I wait a second longer and pull at Shiloe. She turns as the others leave. Then she sits down again.

"What's wrong?" she asks.

I look into her hazel eyes, and I want to wrap my arms around her. I want to tell her how much I missed her. But I know it isn't the right time. “I just wanted to hear how things went for you while Vern and I were gone.”

She returns my gaze, considering for a few seconds. “Just another battle on the front line. No sign of the enemy Immortals.”

She tries to brush it off, but I can tell she’s rattled.

“You led the others alright then?” I ask.

She blinks a few times, then waves it away. “Yeah, it was fine. A bit stressful, but I managed. We all made it back, and that’s what’s important.”

“That’s good to hear,” I say and place a hand on her shoulder but quickly remove it.

Shiloe tilts her head, her arms crossed. “Brin, what’s up? Something else is on your mind.”

I look around the cave, making sure we’re alone. Then I pull out the metal case from my cloak and hold it out. “The Immortal, Varance, gave me this. I just didn’t want to mention it to everyone yet.”

Shiloe takes the box. “Wonder what’s inside?”

I shrug. “I don’t know, haven’t opened it yet. Look, this Varance girl is an older Immortal and obviously has more knowledge. She’s probably been in this war longer than any of us. What if she’s trying to pass some of that knowledge along?”

Shiloe flips the metal case over and holds it up to the firelight. “No marks or anything. So strange.” She hands it back to me. “But why? They’re our enemy. It just doesn’t make any sense. Maybe it’s another trap?”

“I don’t think so. She could have killed Vern and me or just let the mechs overwhelm us. I think she knows what this is all about. I sense that she wants an alliance.”

Shiloe’s eyes go wide at that. Her mouth opens a few times, trying to respond, but nothing comes out.

"Yeah, I know, Shiloe. It sounds ridiculous. But when I spoke with her through Vishmu, I heard that intuitive voice again. The more I think about it, the more it kind of makes sense."

Shiloe takes a deep breath. "If that's what you really think, then we need to be careful."

"Agreed. Which is why I haven't said anything to the others yet."

"Okay," she says. "Well, let me know when you figure something out. Maybe it'll answer some of our questions. Is there anything else you noticed about this girl?"

"Her symbol was the letter 'N'. The color of her palm matched mine almost exactly."

Shiloe's reaction is a bit suspicious at first, and she furrows her brow but doesn't say anything.

I lean in close and hold her gaze. "Those glowing scepters the Immortals use are a game-changer. If we don't figure out how they got them, we'll all be dead before the Winter Solstice."

Despite how tired I am, I flop onto the meditation rug as soon as I walk into my room. I spend the rest of that night in Vishmu. There, I seem to find little moments of clarity. I let my 'inner light' run free and recharge. When I do, epiphanies seem to flitter in and out of my consciousness. I think about Shiloe. I think about the box and what it might mean. I think about Varance and the mystical scepters, the war, the danger we're in, and how I'm going to lead my friends out of this mess. I wonder if I should contact Miss Henak, Triton, Kiff or even Commander Freemantle. I search for answers as I float in my subconscious state, amongst the stars and galaxies and multiverses.

But no answers come to me that night.

When I finally lie in my bed, I hold the metal case. I flip it over and over, searching for signs. But there are no buttons or markings.

Just smooth pieces of metal. Whatever message Varance is trying to send me is connected to the strange metal box.

The following morning, I have a quick bite with Tripp and Grish at our rickety dining table. The cool air down in the caves has continued to drop as the year wears on. Winter is coming, the solstice is just around the corner. The chilly temperatures are driven from the wind howling in from the canyon beyond, carrying the sounds of war and death with it. That chill seems to bite right through my cloak and armor, more so than just a week ago. The more I try to ignore it, the worse it gets, here in the Eastern Theater. And with the Winter Solstice just a few months away, I'm more aware of the time we have left. It seems to tick inside my head, a constant reminder of our impending danger. I feel more anxious. There's an urgency to find a solution to Varance's message.

I'm barely aware that Tripp and Grish's conversation has turned to me. They stare at me, waiting.

"Sorry, what was that?" I ask.

"They said we have to fight till the end," Tripp says. "which would be the day of the Winter Solstice. That's just a few months away."

"We've been over this a thousand times, Tripp." Grish grits her teeth, and I can sense the frustration in her tone. She tugs irritably at her red ponytails. "Get it through your thick skull. That doesn't mean the war's gonna end. What do you think will happen when one side is declared winner? You think the other side will just 'peacefully' step aside?"

Tripp sets his fork down and turns to face Grish. He balls his tiny fists and sets his jaw.

I place a hand on their shoulders. "Easy. Both of you."

But Tripp raises his shoulder and pulls away from me. "Go on, Grish. Say it."

"Why should I?" Grish says, her nostrils flared, and skin flushed now.

"Yeah, well, remind me again," Tripp bristles.

I stand and place myself between them. "Calm down. We've got a long day ahead—"

But Grish is already trying to push past my larger frame and insert herself in front of Tripp again.

"Tell him, Brin," Grish continues. "This isn't gonna end on the solstice. They'll make us fight forever. We'll never be free again. These things aren't comin' off, Tripp!" Grish tugs at her collar.

"They can't do that…it's not fair!" Tripp yells.

Shiloe and Vern step out of their rooms, followed by Drake.

Vern rubs his eyes. "What's all the bickering about?"

"Need some help here," I say, trying to hold the two apart.

Shiloe and Drake stand by Grish while Vern pulls on Tripp.

"Let it go, guys," Shiloe says. "We gotta get our heads straight."

Tripp looks at us, then shakes his head. He tugs at his red, curly hair and juts his chin out at Grish. "You know this isn't right!"

"Never said it was, Tripp," Grish fires back. "Just pointing out the facts. You really upset at me, or is this more about what's fair and what isn't? Things ain't always fair so grow up!"

"Oh, you're one to talk," Tripp yells back. "How about you accept some responsibility for once in your life? Why are you hiding from it? Is it the easy road for you again?"

"Relax!" I roar, trying to contain my own frustration now. I place a hand on Grish and Tripp's shoulders and guide them into the living area. Grish sits on one side of the old sofa, and Tripp on the other. Shiloe sits next to me while Vern and Drake sit on the dusty floor.

There's a quiet moment and everyone looks at me.

"Listen, all of you. We're about to hit the front line. We all know someone's trying to take us out of the picture. They want us divided. We can't have all this arguing right now. I don't know what'll happen on the solstice, no one does. That's out of our control, which means we need to stick together. Don't forget our promise to each other. I'm holding everyone to that."

Grish looks at Tripp. She shakes her head at him but shrugs and lifts a hand in a 'whatever' type of gesture. When I look at Tripp, I see his neck veins bulging and can tell he's still upset. But he brings his hands together in a peaceful motion, though it's forced and a bit sarcastic.

I grip them both on the shoulder again. "Alright. So, let's regroup, maybe do some meditation. Families will fight, but we have to look after each other. We'll hold no grudges around here." I pull them closer and into a hug.

"Yeah…okay," Tripp says and smiles wryly when I tussle his red hair. Vern moves in and lifts Grish over his shoulder and starts running around the apartment, hooting and hollering. Of course, it's hard for any of us to remain upset with Vern around, and soon, we're all laughing.

But eventually, things calm down, and Tripp takes a seat. "Sorry, Grish. You're right, I just want to believe that things are always fair. I know they're not. Shouldn't have yelled at you."

Grish gives him a rare smile. "It's fine, Tripp. No worries."

Tripp continues to shake his head though and sniffles.

"Hey, what is it?" I say. "What's wrong?"

He looks up at me, and for the first time since I've known him, I see real fear in his expression. He reaches out and grabs my arm with his small hands. "I don't wanna be here anymore. I want to go home."

Grish moves over and sits next to him and wraps her arm around his tiny frame. "Hey, it's gonna be alright. We're here with you, Tripp." She pulls him closer and presses his head against her shoulder.

It's a moment that I haven't seen from Grish before either. She's normally so secluded and wrapped in her own world. Grish rarely shows any emotion toward others. But I can see that it's genuine, and I feel a split second of pride. Even Grish is maturing.

Tripp buries his face in her cloak. "I can't take it…I just want out."

I sit next to Tripp as the others gather around. "Listen, Tripp. As long as I'm here, I'll look after you, I promise. You hear me? You'll be fine. We're all going to be fine."

I say this with as much conviction as I can muster. But I know I'm not fooling anyone. I know that my promise is nothing more than a lie.

The others know it, too.

THE SECRET GATHERING | **CHAPTER 17**

That day, Vern and I battle next to each other. Shiloe and Drake are grouped to my right while Grish and Tripp are placed on the left. The fighting is fierce, and I witness more death. There's the typical mass of crows looming overhead. Like some ominous thunderhead, they wait patiently for the fighting to move on before feasting on the dead. The men and women around me battle bravely, sacrificing life and limb, all in the name of territory. I try to save as many as I can. I want to help these people…these mortals. But that word resonates in my thoughts like some foreign notion. It has a strange ring to it, one that I'm still not ready to fully accept. Though I try not to look down at the dead or dying citizens, it's impossible to avoid.

The things I see from that day prevent me from finding restful sleep. I realize that I'm spending more time in Vishmu to cope with the trauma. I know the others are struggling as well. Not long ago, I thought I had overcome the horrors of war. But it's something that I know will never leave me now.

Varance's words continue to echo in my dreams that night. At times, I wake and look at the metal box, trying to figure out how to open it. The anxious desire to crack the code is constantly on my mind, but I'm no closer now than the day she'd given it to me.

In the following days, I go through the same routine. I fight during the day and try to find solace at night. Our group remains in the Eastern Theater, though we see no sign of the enemy Immortals. We also manage to stay separated, careful not to group ourselves too closely during the battles, despite orders from Taun. Some days, we're sent behind enemy lines to fight forward, like we'd done in the beginning. On other days, we're simply leading the charge into enemy fire. I feel an impending dread throughout our eastern campaign, as if something bad awaits us just around the corner.

I continue to chat with Shiloe through it all. We stay up late in the evenings, neither of us wanting to go to bed, like we're afraid to close our eyes. Our new ritual at the end of each day is dinner at the overlook. Our entire group gathers around the firepit and chats about the day. We share our lessons and things we've witnessed on the battlefield. Dreams, nightmares…fears. Sometimes, we laugh, and many times, we cry or console each other.

"So, you can sense something's coming?" Shiloe asks. "Is it something bad?"

We sit at the overlook, the night air cool and breezy. Low booms underpin the ominous mood of late. We'd finished our dinner, and the others had already gone to bed. In the distance, the typical lightning and explosions strobe along the canyon walls. Our breath puffs out as we warm our hands by the crackling fire. I sit next to Shiloe, huddled in my cloak and she leans against me, gripping my arm.

"Yeah, well…I don't know," I say. I rock forward, then blow into my hands. "It's a feeling I'm getting. Things have been quiet for too long, don't you think?"

"I wouldn't say it's been quiet, really," Shiloe huffs.

"You know what I mean. No one's been pushing us. No attempts have been made on our lives like before. No sign of the other Immortals. It just seems like the calm before the storm."

I feel Shiloe nod her head against my shoulder, but I continue to look into the fire as I pull the metal box from my cloak and hold it at arm's length. "I'm also feeling anxious about this."

"What about it?" she asks.

"I'm still confused why Varance gave it to me. Can't sleep, can't focus. I've got to figure it out soon, or I'll go crazy."

Shiloe grips my arm. "This is all tied together, isn't it?"

"Why else would she have warned me, warned us?" I give Shiloe a side glance and let out a long breath as I flip the box over thoughtfully. "Truth be told, I sense I'm close to figuring it out. I felt something after my meditation the other night—"

Shiloe sits forward and turns to face me. "I knew it!"

I raise one brow and give her a look of surprise. "Something you want to share?"

"I sometimes feel things after my meditations too. After using Vishmu. I thought it may be a side effect, though Miss Henak never mentioned it. She did say we'd gain more powers. I was wondering if it was just me."

I give her shoulder a nudge and watch the dancing fire in her hazel eyes. "The more I use Vishmu, the more I feel these little epiphanies, I think."

"So, what do you think?" Shiloe nods to the box.

I toss it up in the air and catch it. "There's no physical way to open it."

"Okay. So, what's your epiphany then?"

I smile and tap my forehead. "I think it uses a mental signature, like these collars." I give mine a tug. The cold steel brushes against my neck and sends goosebumps up my arms.

She leans on her elbows, silent for a moment. "Well, that would make sense. You think only an Immortal can unlock it, then?"

"No. I think only I can unlock it. My theory is that Varance set the signature for me."

"You seem to have good instincts, Brin. Follow them."

"I just hope my instincts hurry up," I chuckle in spite of the situation.

Shiloe gives a subtle laugh, then stifles a yawn. "We should try to get some sleep."

"Apparently, being an Immortal doesn't get you out of that, huh? Too bad."

"These days, yeah." Shiloe leans back and stretches her legs. "Trying to find sleep is the worst part of my day."

"I'm starting to feel the same way."

"You see them, don't you?" she asks. Then turns away and stares into the fire. I sense her retreat a bit as she hugs her knees tighter.

"If you're talking about the men and women, then yes."

I can sense her emotions without seeing her face. When she finally speaks, I hear the strain in her voice.

"I remember every one of their faces, Brin. Many were too young to see such brutality. It's…just not fair." Shiloe clears her throat, and I hear the emotion in her voice.

I place my arm around her and pull her closer. I halfway expect her to push away, but she leans in. "I feel the same way, Shiloe. I see their faces, the broken bodies. Their lifeless stares. No…it isn't fair, for anyone. Not even the Southern citizens. I wish I could help them all."

"I wish that too. More than anything else."

We sit there, holding each other in the cold, the fire hissing and popping, the bombs exploding in the background. I breathe in the aroma of her hair as it brushes against the stubble of my cheek. It smells of smoke and earth in the brisk night air. I wish we could sit like this forever, at least until the morning comes, regardless of the cold and fatigue and aching muscles. I know she doesn't want to say goodnight either: that she doesn't want to face the night alone.

"There's something else, Shiloe," I whisper.

She places her hand on my chest and pushes away to get a better look at me. "What is it?"

"We shouldn't fight the enemy Immortals when we see them."

She narrows her eyes. "What are you talking about? You saw what happened last time. They nearly killed us. We'd be dead right now if the others hadn't shown up. How can you be sure they won't do it again?"

"Because I think they're ready to talk to us."

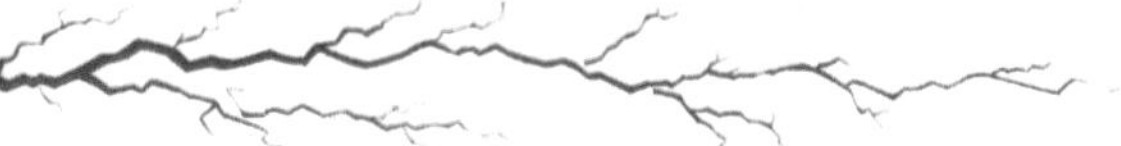

Days pass, and nothing happens. I can only assume that those plotting against us are playing a game of attrition. Perhaps assuming the rigors of battle will take its course and someone in our group might be killed. But the longer we're on the battlefield, the higher the odds that one of us might die. A stray bomb, a random mortar, a lucky bullet. Furthermore, we're all being pushed to our limit. It's nonstop war from the crack of dawn till late in the evening, and we're given no breaks. Day after day, with hardly any rest. Only Vishmu seems to keep us going. We rely on each other and grow closer with each passing day. Our friendship is rock-solid now. I realize that these five kids are like siblings to me, and I feel the need to protect them. Though we're all capable, I can't shake the desire to watch over them, especially Shiloe and Tripp. With Shiloe, it's a different feeling—she's more than just a friend. But with Tripp, I've come to think of him as a slightly older version of Ben. When I look at him, I can almost see my younger brother looking back at me. I want to keep Tripp close, but I know that's not always possible.

With each completed mission, I feel my power growing, too. And perhaps this is one aspect that 'they' didn't plan on. I can feel my presence emanating on the battlefield, like some magical aura. Troops fold before me as if some unseen flame or forcefield surrounds me. I seem to know where to go and where I shouldn't. It's like that inner voice is growing more intuitive, guiding me, warning me. Sometimes, I have only seconds to react. Other times, I feel it days in advance. Pitfalls that would wound or kill me I avoid in a way that I cannot explain. Shiloe, Vern, Drake, Grish, and Tripp feel it too.

Thanks to our efforts, the North is gaining territory back. We've managed to outmaneuver the South. It's odd that the North keeps us stationary, though. When this all began, we'd been moved around constantly. Stranger still, the South seems reluctant to push into areas or challenge us for lost territory. It makes me nervous.

On the second week back from my mission to the York Borough, we receive orders to return to the Central Theater's Front Line Borough. When we arrive, we're warned that we might finally meet some resistance. In that morning's briefing, I sense some uneasiness among the commanders. Freemantle stands front and center of the war room. His top commanders, Herron and Taun appear beside him in a three-dimensional hologram. A map of the Central Theater floats over the large conference table. I watch Freemantle closely, trying to detect any hesitation.

"This is where you must focus today," Freemantle says, indicating an area just past the front line. "There will likely be resistance, but you're to stay in this area. Understood?"

I look to the others and notice Shiloe's concern. I see Grish about to blurt something out, and I hold up a hand to stop her.

"Sir. Can you give us more data?" I ask.

Commander Herron's image enlarges. "Look closely." He brings the map to full screen, and we see real-time battle footage now. I see the troops moving around, tanks and other vehicles populate the battlefield as explosions rock the ground. The terrain is pitted, which is no surprise. Otherwise, all seems as it should.

"What are we supposed to be looking for?" I ask.

"This is an artificial intelligence engine, an A.I. think tank," Herron says. "We let our computer simulation run through millions of scenarios, and it averages out to a single predicted outcome. It's not always right, of course, but it gives us a good interpretation so we can strategize. Watch closely."

I watch the A.I. battle play out, wondering why they'd never shared this with us before. The others watch the screen with interest too as the battle is waged using artificial intelligence. I see troops and vehicles, which are highlighted in blue or red. The troops and smaller vehicles are represented by thousands of tiny pinpoints of light. The larger blips represent more powerful units, like tanks or mech units. Soon, I see six massive blue dots moving across the field.

"Those are you six," Herron says, nodding to the screen.

The battle plays out, and soon, four massive red blips appear. But these are much larger in size than any other piece on the field.

"These four red dots represent the Southern Coalition Immortals," Herron says. "We've been trying to track them over the last several months, using the data from the prior battles to estimate their power and movements."

Taun speaks up, his image enlarging in place of Herron's. "Based on the simulation, we think the South is planning to send them into your area. They want that territory back, it seems. You'll finally meet all four of them on the field today."

Grish looks around nervously. "Your simulation shows them as more powerful units. Are they, and why?"

"Yes, they appear to be more powerful," Freemantle says. He scratches at his gray scruff, and I notice the worn look on his face. His deep-set eyes are like caves, and his normally blue piercing gaze is red and bloodshot. "We know two of the members are older, more experienced than any of you. The other two are much less experienced, though."

"Then why do they show as stronger in your simulation?" Drake asks.

Herron's image takes over the hologram again. "Unknown, Drake. My apologies. What we do know is this: today will be your first true test against them. Your training as a team will be your strength, and there are six of you compared to just four of them."

"You're purposely pitting us against them," Shiloe says, but I hear the barely controlled disgust in her tone. I watch her fists clench as she stares through the hologram at Taun. "This *can* be avoided."

"Are we simply to hand over that territory then?" Taun asks. He speaks with his nose upturned, gazing down at us. "We are willing to take the collateral damage."

"Pawns," Vern chuckles, then claps his leg. "See Brin. What'd I tell you, man?"

Taun waves a hand dismissively, then looks at his nails, picking at his index finger. "Nevertheless, you will all be there, and we'll be watching."

"I'm afraid we cannot ignore this particular conflict," Herron says. "In the past months, we would've moved you around to avoid them. We didn't feel you were ready. I don't believe that is the case now. If you hope to survive today, then you must rely on your abilities as a team. Vern and Drake up front, Grish and Tripp working from behind. Shiloe and Brin calling the shots and attacking from the side."

Vern leans back in his chair and kicks his boots up. He knocks some mud onto the expensive-looking conference table and places his hands behind his head. "Doesn't sound very smart to me. We're doing pretty well as is. Why mess that up? Is there something else you want to say?"

Taun looks at Vern through the hologram, as if he wants to slap his boots off the table. But he crosses his arms instead. "Regardless, you'll do as ordered. No questions from any of you."

I look at Freemantle, hoping he might offer some help. But he looks at the map and avoids my gaze.

"Is this what you really want, Commander Freemantle?" I ask.

He finally turns to look at me, then eyes the rest of us. "It's two votes to one, Brin. I'm sorry."

"But that's not fair…you're the Supreme Commander!" Tripp erupts.

At that, we all stand and begin pointing at Taun and Herron. Shiloe holds out her hands in a plea to Freemantle. Tripp is hopping up and down, and Drake paces behind the table, shaking his head.

"That's enough!" Freemantle finally says, his voice raised. I see his hand shaking as he gives us a stern look. He lowers his gaze, his eyes narrowed to slits. "I've done all I can for you. He stares at Shiloe last, then drops his head and shakes it. "I'm sorry. I can do nothing more at the moment."

The MPs move into the war room and begin corralling us toward the exit. But I stop and turn to Freemantle.

"Sir, you never finished telling us what the simulation predicted."

Freemantle continues to avoid looking at any of us. "They're…just simulations, Brin. Nothing more—"

Shiloe steps forward, pulling her arm from one of the MPs. "Freemantle, please. It's the least you can do."

He looks directly into Shiloe's eyes, and I detect a moment of weakness. Perhaps it's my Vishmu training, or some trick of my eyes. But I sense a connection, something between them. I feel a sadness in my heart as I watch Freemantle.

"Look after each other, please," Freemantle finally says, and the MPs drag us from the room.

I look up to Taun's holographic image and see him holding the controller to our collars. He's tapping it with a grin on his face as I leave the war room.

The six of us are marched toward the boarding platform. No one speaks as the familiar sounds of war greet us when we near the station. We load onto the transport and buckle in. As we zoom away, I begin to wonder if it's for the last time.

Once the transport arrives, we're led up the trail. Soon, we're standing inside the makeshift tent. We're given one last check, then everyone is pushed outside. Ahead of me, the battlefield opens to the vast canyon. The clouds above choke out the sunlight, and the rain falls in heavy sheets. The driving wind nearly topples us as lightning crashes in the background.

I stand with the others and prepare myself, just like I have every day of this godforsaken war. Yet, something feels different this time. I push aside my concerns and connect with the others through Vishmu. I implore them to forget about Taun, Herron, and Freemantle and focus on the battle ahead.

...let's move out! I send the thought, and we cloak and make our way toward the front line. There's no airlift this time, and we begin our trudge through the mud.

Tripp falls in behind me with Shiloe and Grish to my left and Drake and Vern to my right. It doesn't take long before shrapnel and mortar rounds are hurling past us. We spread out and look for troops that need help as we move forward. When areas of the line buckle, a few of us fall in and reinforce it. We keep our eyes open and continue onward.

It feels like hours pass as we trek forward, slowed by the fighting. The ominous feel of battle permeates the air. Lightning crashes down, the smell of smoke, and the non-stop rain soaks us to the bone. The flickering of the crow's feathers in the bomb blasts is burned into my vision.

The North counters the South's mechs with their own powerful units. The Niners, Maulers and V-ORPs clash with us, and we take many of them out as we lead the way. I witness more bloodshed and loss of life. I see bodies and blood and the wounded, but I manage to block out the worst of it. I let my mind traverse in another plane of existence, as if it's hovering over the death and destruction. The disconnected experience helps me cope with the brutality of the battle. The voice I hear guides me, keeping me out of harm's way as I lead the others.

Then, something odd catches my attention. It feels like a hiccup of sorts, a ripple on a pond, perhaps. I can sense those ripples like little vibrations on the air and move toward them. When I near the source, I stop. Across the battlefield, I count four shimmering objects. In my trance, I'd led us to an offshoot or hidden ravine of sorts. I work my way down the ravine, which soon turns into a tiny cave. It's dry inside, and the sounds of battle grow distant. The cave shelters us from the elements, and it's dim inside, with only a few shale ferns there to light the space. There's no fighting in the area, just the shimmering figures, which I know now to be the Southern Immortals.

I watch as they uncloak. The shimmering mirages solidify from across the cave but hold their ground. I know we're in danger. Any two of these immortals could probably wipe us out in a fight. We're supposed to meet on the battlefield, yet I feel we've been led here for a reason. It's obvious that a fight is not what they want. Shiloe, Tripp, Grish, Drake and Vern lower their hoods, and we wait.

The four opposing Immortals face us, each holding one of the deadly glowing scepters. In front of them is the girl from the warehouse—Varance, who I assume now is their leader. Her long blonde hair and dainty features look cold and grim in the dull light. Next to her is the tall boy we'd fought in our first encounter. His broken collarbone, issued by Vern's boot, is fully healed. The younger dark-haired girl of fifteen stands next to a dark-skinned boy about the same age.

I give the others a quick side-glance, "Stay calm," I say and step forward. "What's this about?" I ask, my voice echoing off the stone walls.

Varance holds up her left hand immediately, then faces her palm out, bathing the cave in a turquoise light. She taps her forehead. She wants to communicate with thoughts. Fine, I think. I nod to her and open my mind, inviting her in. I feel the others do the same.

...we must use our thoughts for now, otherwise they will hear us. Varance says.

...I don't understand what you want.

...we must be quick! she warns. *I lead the Southern Immortals. With me are Isotere, Soto and Roan.*

As I noticed before, Varance's thoughts feel different. They seem to seep into my brain and chill me to the core.

...I'm Brindall. This is Shiloe, Tripp, Grish, Drake and Vern...what is it you want with us?

An earth-shattering boom rocks the cave, and I nearly tumble to the ground. I start to feel nervous and turn back to Varance.

...this is not what you think. I hear an urgency in her voice now*...have you opened the box I gave you?*

...I don't know how.

...yes, you do. You must before we meet next—

There's another loud boom.

...figure it out, Brin...our lives may depend on it.

The four Immortals cloak and speed from the chamber.

I turn and pull Tripp and Grish, cloaking as we flee in the opposite direction. Just as we exit through a small tunnel, the entire ceiling shatters and caves in right behind us. Moving along the ravine are multiple heavy mechs with large, mounted howitzers. They pulverize the surrounding cliffs with their cannons, and eventually, the entire hillside collapses.

We race to the frontline as quickly as possible. I feel the urge to converse with the others, a desire to hear their thoughts. But doing so right now is too risky. In the back of my mind, I can sense the presence of the Southern Immortals nearby. But we manage to maintain our distance, and I find myself hoping that the 'powers-that-be' don't suspect anything. Also tumbling around in the back of my mind is how I'm going to explain the 'box' to the others.

It's late when we're finally relieved from the battlefield. I'm too weary to shower or change. I go and make some dinner and meet the others around the firepit and eat. We talk in hushed tones about the day's events, especially our meeting with the other Immortals.

"So, when were you gonna tell us about this box thingy?" Vern says, getting straight to the point.

I'm starving, but suddenly, the cold gruel seems unappealing, and I set my spoon down and look at the others. "Yeah, sorry about that. I didn't know what to do with it at first and thought I should keep it a secret until I knew more."

Vern crosses his arms and continues to hold my gaze. I can see he's upset at me and wants to say so but seems to be holding his frustration in for the moment. "Well, let's see it," he says.

I take a deep breath, sigh and pull out the metal box. I hold it up to the firelight and point it at Vern. "This is what that girl Varance was talking about. And I still have no idea how to open it."

Vern reaches across and takes it. He flips it over a few times, then hands it around to the others. Tripp snatches it away from Grish and begins analyzing it.

"So?" Grish asks. "Sounds like another riddle we need to figure out, and quick. I think this Varance girl said our lives may depend on it, if you can believe our enemy. Any idea what she meant by that?"

We all shake our heads.

Tripp finally leans in. "They didn't want to fight us today, though I'm sure they'd been ordered to do so."

"And we've been ordered to do the same," Shiloe says. "Do we see a pattern here?"

"Is it possible that the same person wants all of us Immortals dead?" Drake asks.

"It's pretty obvious, isn't it?" Tripp says. He sits back and wraps his cloak tighter around his narrow frame, his cheeks flushed red in the cold air.

"Well, I guess the real question is, should we trust these Immortals?" Shiloe grits her teeth when she says this, the line of muscle along her jaw taut. "I, for one, am not so sure. I mean, they tried to kill us the first time."

"Well, if they wanted that, they could've done it today, right?" Vern says. "They're obviously more powerful, especially with those 'clubs-of-doom.' And by the way, how did they get those? Anyone else askin' that same question?"

Tripp clears his throat. "Well, if you noticed on the simulation today, they are shown as more powerful units on the battlefield. Pretty sure that's why. I mean, maybe this Varance and her boyfriend are older and more experienced, but certainly not the younger two."

"So again, how do we get our hands on those scepters?" Vern asks. "Cause I really want one."

I start thinking about the vessel again and how their light matches our palms. "What was it Triton said about the vessels he gave us?"

"Think he said something like, these would serve us well?" Shiloe muses, narrowing her eyes.

"We all know it's the vessels," Tripp says, sitting forward. I can see some excitement in his expression, and his eyes light up.

"Well, let's take another look," Drake says and pulls a fist-sized crystal from his cloak. "I carry it with me, always. I don't know why, maybe because it's comforting. Actually, soothing might be a better description." He tosses it across the firepit, and I catch it in one hand.

I hold the vessel up to the firelight. "I've noticed that each one of these is different. The shape, size and look are unique. If you look closer, there's something in the center. I think each of these represent who we are. See, the light even matches the color from our palms."

"That's gotta be it," Vern says and takes the vessel from me. "Obviously, these are somehow connected to the weapons we've seen. But how do we unlock it? The Southern Immortals seem to have figured it out."

"I just don't understand why Triton, or Kiff wouldn't tell us, if they knew something." Shiloe looks at the vessel, her chin propped in her hands.

I give Shiloe a pat on the back. "They've always pushed us to find our own way. We were never spoon-fed information. We had to earn it. Either way, it's our responsibility to figure it out now. I'm working on it, guys."

"While you're at it, better work on this box too," Tripp says and tosses it back to me. "At the moment, it sounds just as important."

I take a deep breath and nod. "I'll take another look tonight when I meditate."

"Sounded like the other Immortals want to meet again," Shiloe says. "If I didn't know any better, I'd say we're dangerously close to an alliance with our enemy counterparts."

"We need to tread lightly," Tripp says. "I don't trust those people."

"But they weren't the ones who gave our position away tonight," Grish says.

"No, they didn't," Shiloe says. "Whoever it is tried to take the cave out with us in it. Interesting that nothing was said in our debrief, huh? None of the commanders asked why we were in that cave to begin with. Even Freemantle said nothing. We'd better have our stories straight in the morning, Brin."

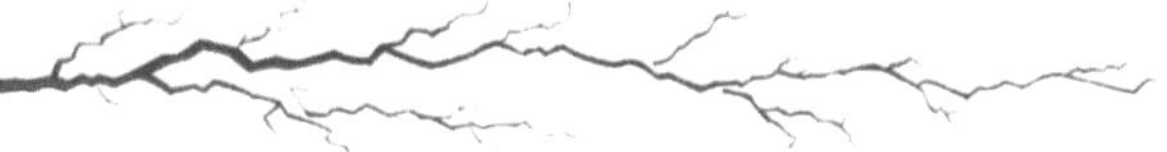

Later that night, I lay in my cot with the metal box pressed to my chest. I go over all the different scenarios in my head again. The intuitive voice begins to speak as I drift in and out of Vishmu. I hear it whispering in my ear, leaving me feeling cold and unsettled. Like some cosmic wind, that ghostly voice chills me to my core.

...*meditate,* it says.

And that was the answer, of course.

I wanted to kick myself.

The solution had been right in front of me the entire time.

I roll from my cot and sit cross-legged on my meditation mat. I fall quickly into a trance and feel my inner light transported away. I let it run free while I follow…

…and I wait.

I watch and observe as it races off, like a child at play. Space and time seem to slip away, and reality feels distant. Still, I let it roam and recharge. What seems like hours later, I finally rein it in. Slowly—*reluctantly*—my inner light returns to me. Then the transition begins. That odd, lengthening out feeling, as if my body is stretched light years beneath me.

Thoughts. Patterns. Symbols.

Then my eyes snap open.

I know how to unlock the box.

A TRUTH REVEALED | CHAPTER 18

I lurch to my feet, steady myself, then race over to my cot and pull the small metallic box from beneath my pillow.

It's the chart. The same one in Grior's prison. The one in Miss Henak's training facility…the one I've somehow known my entire life.

I let my mind scan over the patterns that make it up. In my mind's eye, I notice the Greek symbols aligned with the twenty-four Roman numerals. It's like a clock, the way they represent the twelve hours of daylight on the right side and the twelve hours of night on the left. Varance had created a mental signature pattern in the symbols themselves, specifically for me to discover. I'd known that was the key to unlocking the box. Now, it was a matter of cracking the code.

Excited, I try several combinations. Eventually, I narrow it down to just ten Greek symbols. Beta, Epsilon, Eta, Theta, Iota and Mu, which happen to be the six of us representing the Northern Immortals. The other four are Nu, Xi, Pi and Sigma, which are the four Immortals in the South. I have to remember the color of the Southern Immortals palms, which align with their symbols. After several tries, I finally figure it out. It starts with the most senior members on their team—I have to guess at their ages—followed by our symbols in the North, sorted by our ages.

As if by magic, I hear the box click open. I tip it over, and six small discs tumble onto my meditation rug. They're slightly larger than my thumbnail and black in color. I pick one up and hold it to the dull light in my room.

I move to the edge of my cot and sit there, looking in wonder at the strange discs. There are no instructions in the box. I have nothing to go by.

Eventually, I place the discs back in the box, seal it, and place it under my pillow. It's late, and I lay back, trying to think what they might be. I finally decide to sleep on it, hoping something might come to me. I'm tired and worn from the day, and at some point, I doze off in a fitful sleep.

That night, I dream about the Skylight System. I feel a hope in my chest of bringing my family there, of living a normal life without the signature collar. A life without fear and war and death. I experience a joy that I didn't know existed. I can almost feel the sunshine on my face, a gentle summer breeze or a spring rain shower. The sound of crickets at night, a waterfall crashing in the distance, birds singing in the trees. I've never considered how special it might be to one day experience such things. But in my dream, I finally feel the desire awaken within my soul. I know then that making it to the Skylight System has been my goal all along. Saving my family only works if I can take them away from this dystopian nightmare. Here, on this ruined earth, there will never be any joy or peace. Taking them to the Skylight System is something worth dying for. But in order to achieve that, I have to gain my own freedom first.

I sit up in bed, wide awake, my breathing heavy and sweat on my forehead. One word is stuck in my thoughts.

Freedom.

Varance has given us freedom.

The following morning, I meet the others for breakfast at the overlook. I can see by the red eyes and long faces that everyone's still worn out from the prior day's events. *What's new?* I chuckle to myself. But clearly, there's still some concern about yesterday. Their wounds and scratches have already healed, but the mental anguish isn't something that can be fixed so easily. I'm nearly bursting to share the news about the box, but I decide to wait until we've finished breakfast.

The temperature that morning is noticeably cooler as we sit silently around the fire, trying to mentally prepare for the day. I feel the news will help cheer them up and finally set my bowl of gruel down and clear my throat.

"I have it," I say in a low whisper.

"What?" Shiloe says and leans in. "You got it to open?"

I give her a side smile as she grips my shoulder. "I did, and I think I know what it's for."

The others look at me. I notice the confusion and skepticism on their faces. Vern squints at me through one eye. Tripp and Grish hold spoons halfway to their mouths while Drake stares with arms crossed.

"Are you foolin' around with us, Brin?" Vern says, lowering his gaze. "You've cracked the code in one night?"

"I'm mildly offended, Vern," I say, but with a slight upturn at the corner of my lips. "What? You didn't have faith I could do it?"

Vern places a hand over his chest. "Forgive me. I never should have doubted you."

Shiloe claps my shoulder. "Well? Let's see what we have."

I stand and stretch my legs. "Follow me."

We all walk back to our apartment, trying to contain our excitement. Everyone huddles in my room as I lift my pillow and hold up one of the tiny discs.

Shiloe takes it and holds it on her index finger, her brows knitted together. "Alright. What exactly is it?"

I take it back and lead them out of the apartment again and back to the overlook. I wait for them to gather around. The sound of the crooning breeze and fire help drown out our voices. I kneel and whisper to them. "I believe this device will scramble our collars' signal. There are six of them."

They all stare at me in disbelief.

Vern shakes his head. "No way!" he whispers.

"You're joking, right?" Shiloe says in a low voice.

"I don't think so," I say. "I believe the coalition can't track us when we use these. But the problem is timing. We have to be careful when we use them. Too long, and they might catch on to us."

"How do you know this?" Tripp asks.

"It's a hunch," I say. "My guess is that these send a ghost signal to the collar, essentially giving us stealth mode, for a brief time anyway."

Tripp claps his hands. "So that's how the other Immortals were able to meet with us without detection?"

I nod, trying to contain my enthusiasm, but a smile creases my face. "Yeah, I think so, and at the warehouse, too. We now have some semblance of freedom, though limited." I hand each of them one of the small devices. "Promise that you won't use these without talking to everyone first. Deal? We have to be on the same page."

They all take the device, then tuck them inside their cloaks.

"Keep them secret. Keep them safe," I say. "The next time we meet the other Immortals on the battlefield, we'll need them."

"Brin, thanks." Shiloe gives me a hug, and I feel the others gather around, and we all embrace.

"We're going to figure this all out, a bit at a time," I say.

"And what about the vessels?" Vern asks. "If you can figure those out, I'll cook a nice dinner for you, honey."

That makes us all laugh. I give Vern a serious look, though. "Nothing yet on the vessels, but I'll figure it out soon. I promise."

The following day, we receive word that we're being sent to the Western Theater. Freemantle notifies us of a massing of Southern troops along the 37th parallel. *We mean to tamp it down*, he tells us. *There'll be no uprising*. But I know this also means we'll encounter 'resistance', a.k.a., the opposing Immortals. We'll soon get our chance at that extended discussion. I like to think that my discovery of the black discs' true purpose has given us some hope. These blockers, as I'm referring to them now, have opened up new possibilities, if we're cautious.

I spend some time with Shiloe around the firepit on the eve of our departure. It's late, and the others have already gone to bed. I notice some hesitation in her movements, which isn't like her. Something's on her mind.

"We'll be on the train out first thing," Shiloe says, pulling some dried mud from her braided hair. "What do you think the Western Theater will be like?"

"Dunno. I assume more of the same, but maybe we'll get lucky and have a better view." I motion sarcastically out to the canyon beyond and the sound of war.

"I'm sure you're right," she says. "Dirty caves, a drafty breeze…these ghoulish shale ferns. Not to mention the constant sound of war. Nothing seems to drown it out. I can't wait for all of this to end. I want to be away from this nightmare, Brin. Have you ever wanted something so badly before?"

I sit next to her, thinking about that. Of course, I want my family with me, I want freedom. I want her.

I reach over and take her hand. "I…had a dream the other night. You know what's funny? I've never really bought into this whole Skylight thing until that dream."

She leans back and looks at me. I see the longing in her gaze, and I feel the shared desire.

"I know it was just a dream, but it felt so real," I say. "It was beautiful, in my dream. I could feel the breeze on my face, the sunshine, the warmth. I could hear the birds and nature. It hit me then, how much all of that would mean for us, for our families and those who've suffered through this war. I realized that we owe it to these people, Shiloe. I feel a duty almost, one that I hadn't considered before."

"And now we have the ability to give them that," she says. "Do you ever think that's why we were chosen? Is that why we have this power?"

"Maybe. I don't know. Henak did say the inner light selects those who reflect its persona."

"If you could walk away from it, would you?"

I chuckle at that. "It's a tough question. But…I don't think so. Maybe at first, I could have, but not now. I want to help the others, and not just my family. These people have suffered too."

Shiloe gives me a quick smile, then turns away. She grips my arm and squeezes. "Wouldn't it be nice to make it there someday? To the Skylight System where we can live among the stars?"

"With the ones that I love?" I give her another long look. "Yes, I want that. I want that more than anything. And if I can't bring my loved ones with me, then I don't want to go."

Shiloe slides over and wraps her arms around me. "Don't worry, your family will be fine. Mine too. We'll make it through this. Together."

I take in a long, steady breath. "I feel the pace picking up, don't you? It's like a war drum beating in the distance. I swear I can feel it in the air, the ground…the walls around me."

Shiloe grips my arm tighter, and I know she feels it, too.

"The Winter Solstice is coming," she says. "I don't know what'll happen next. Just that we need to stick together."

"They'll try to separate us, Shiloe. They know our strength is when we're together. We've managed to survive their missions. Separating us will be their last attempt, and it may not be so subtle as the solstice gets closer."

She leans back and looks at the storm beyond. The sounds of war fill the silence between us.

I find myself hoping that our next meeting with the other Immortals will answer some questions. I know that it might be our last chance to figure this out.

Early the next morning, the six of us are on the train out of the Central Theater. The trip to the Western Theater and the Sun Breach Borough takes less than an hour. As I step onto the boarding platform, I feel nothing—no butterflies, no fear, no anxiety. I glance at the others and see the same stoic expression and realize that we've become so used to this now that it barely registers.

This theater is Commander Herron's territory. Though I've never met him in person, he seems to handle himself with a bit more control and perhaps humility than his counterpart, Commander Taun. When we step into the war room, I take in my surroundings. Much like the other war rooms, this one, too, has the latest technology and equipment. Holographic displays fill the air, and officers rush around, barking at each other.

I take a seat in one of the plush chairs. The others settle in, while Vern and Drake continue to stand at the back of the room. Herron's tall, lanky frame seems to reach to the ceiling. His silver hair is matted flat to one side, indicating he probably doesn't sleep much. And if that wasn't evidence enough, the dark circles under his eyes underscore that fact. His craggy face seems to be carved from granite with carelines and deep, inset eyes with no bottom. Ashen skin from his years of sitting in a room, while typical with most citizens, seems more pronounced in the dull light. His persona is skittish and somewhat nervous, though I sense anger and a quick temper.

Herron looks us over, nodding and humming to himself. An officer hands him a tracker and points at an area on the war map, which I assume is our target. He flips the tracker around and points at it. "You'll wait here," he says, his tone light and airy for his build. "You're not allowed to move until we give the order. Understood?"

I look to the others, then nod to him.

Herron snaps and then holds up five fingers. "We move out in this many." He hands me the tracker and walks away, then he stops and turns. "Sorry, I'm usually not this direct. Just trying to set the tone. Cheerio!"

A few seconds later, the MPs are marching us out of the war room and toward the front line.

The Western Theater is nearly identical to the other two. Its large canyon walls stretch kilometers before disappearing. I see the strata here is slightly darker, but otherwise, it's the same hellish landscape. The sky above opens to the Unbalance, which is mostly clogged with the carrion crows massing in areas where the battle is the worst. Lightning crashes, and rain courses down, creating rivers of muddy water. In the darkness, I've already lost track of what time it is.

We stand on a small hill and look out as the war rages beyond. The MPs seem to keep their distance, as if afraid to give us commands or press us. Then a transport lands nearby, and I hear Herron in my earpiece. "Let's get a move on, chop-chop!"

We climb aboard and buckle into the harness. The skiff lifts, then rockets toward the front line, hugging the ground just meters above the mud and rocky terrain. I sit quietly, conversing with the others mentally.

...stay spread apart...Shiloe near me. Vern, Drake, take left...Tripp and Grish to the right.

Our transport drops to the ground with a jolt, and we're instantly out and moving. We stay cloaked and invisible as the skiff lifts off. Before it can rotate, a missile strikes its hull. The small transport is literally vaporized as we watch in horror. The blast knocks us to the ground, and I nearly tumble into a platoon of Northern troops. I manage to roll away and hop instantly to my feet. I wipe mud and rain from my eyes and check myself for injuries.

Before I can check on the others, a mortar round lands near me. I have just enough time to roll and pull my cloak around me. The explosion rips through the platoon of soldiers, sending them flying in different directions. There's nothing left where the mortar hit but a smoking crater.

I hear the intuitive voice screaming at me to flee the area. I send a mental signal to the others as I run.

Within seconds, the entire area erupts in fire. Heavy artillery rounds pummel the ground as I scramble over the cratered battlefield. I lose track of the others, thanks to the ringing in my head and ears. I manage to clear the area, barely avoiding the next wave of incoming artillery. I place the blocker device on my collar, hoping I'm correct and that it will scramble my location. If it truly does work, then I'm now off the grid. I pray that the others are able to do the same.

I follow my instinct, that 'intuitive voice,' as it leads me across the battlefield. I zigzag and weave between smoking craters, sometimes tumbling down into the bottoms, where I wait and listen for artillery. Soon, I'm headed toward an outcropping of rock. I enter a small opening and pause to catch my breath. I feel an instant reprieve from the rain and lightning and artillery.

My eyes adjust as I take in my surroundings. The rock walls are lit in the typical bioluminescent glow of shale ferns. Explosions still rock the ground, and some flashes strobe through small openings above. Rainwater streams down the rock in silvery rivulets, the soft pitter-patter a stark contrast to the raging war beyond. Otherwise, all is silent.

Ten meters from me, I see the glow from another Immortal's palm. Then another, and another. All four of the opposing Immortals are here.

And I'm alone.

There's no sense in trying to flee. But I know they're not here to fight. I take a deep breath, then walk over to meet them.

"You're so clever, Brindall Harper," Varance says. The obvious sarcasm is hard to miss in her tone.

I tap my collar and give her a quick nod. "Would've been easier if you'd just told me about the discs."

She lifts one corner of her mouth in a mischievous grin. "Where's the fun in that?"

The tall, blond-haired boy named Isotere steps forward. "We don't have long. Where are the others?"

"I'm not sure. We deployed right in the middle of an artillery barrage. We were separated."

"Figures," Varance says. "They've done that to us many times."

I want to wait for the others, but I realize how important this meeting is, and there's not a second to lose. "What can you tell me about that? No more riddles, just straight talk."

Varance turns to Isotere, and the tall boy gives her a nod while still holding my gaze.

"Soto and Roan?" he asks, and the other two Immortals nod as if agreeing on some secret. "It's time, Varance," Isotere continues.

Varance grimaces, then gives me another crooked smile. "Let me be clear. I don't care for any of you. We're enemies, you know this. But as you've already guessed, we're being targeted. All Immortals, since the very beginning. What they tell you about these missions are lies. They don't care about gaining data."

"I don't understand. Thought this was war? Wouldn't that make gaining information a critical factor?"

"Oh, it's war," Varance chides, "without a doubt. People are dying. Innocent people who don't know the truth."

"And what is the truth?" I stand in front of the four of them, waiting expectantly. But inside, my heart is racing, and my hands are shaking. I grip the sides of my cloak, trying to hide my nervousness. I wonder if I'm about to learn the real reason behind this decades-long war.

Varance smirks and lifts her chin at me. "Well, unfortunately, we're not entirely sure just yet. We're getting closer to figuring it all out, but the Winter Solstice is near, too."

"But you do know something?" I say, a bit disappointed. "Don't tell me this is all a lie, then leave me with nothing. Let's hear what you do know."

Isotere places a hand on Varance's shoulder as if to say, *it's okay.*

Varance lets out a long sigh. "The war will be won by the North or the South, so they say."

I tilt my head, hearing the sarcasm. "Right. The side that holds the most territory wins the contract—"

Varance slaps the side of the cave, and the echo resonates down the tunnel. "Wrong! Do you believe everything they tell you? If you're gonna survive, you need to challenge everything. Think! The Skylight System is almost complete and soon, the ferries will begin transporting people. Why do the territories even need to produce more ore, minerals and rare-earth?"

"Maybe they'll need supplies for the buildings?"

Isotere chuckles. "Surely they will, but couldn't either the North or the South supply that afterward?"

I feel a cold chill run through me as I listen. Things are starting to come together in my head, and I'm not sure I like it. "What you're suggesting would create overpopulation. The North and the South can't all fit on the system—"

"Says who?" Varance interrupts, her arms still crossed. "Consider the source of that data."

I look from her to Isotere, and that's when I know she's not lying. Even though I barely know these Immortals, I know they're telling me the truth. After all, they've been around longer and have had more time to work things out. There's no reason for them to mislead me in this. But…that doesn't mean they're telling me everything they know, either.

Varance walks over to stand directly in front of me. In her hand is the glowing scepter, its turquoise glow a perfect match to her palm. She could kill me with one blow of that scepter.

Varance walks behind me and stops. "Sounds like the Skylight System would be a glorious place to live." Her mouth lingers near my ear and her voice is nearly a whisper. "A utopian dream come true for higher-class citizens. Wealthy citizens, people who don't care to be around rubbish like us. It's not such a stretch to assume they might not want to share such a place with us. They can have it all for themselves and their future generations. Why not just leave the filth down here?"

The realization of what Varance is telling me hits like a bomb.

The lie I've been told. The lie everyone's been told.

"You think they're trying to kill us off?" I can hear the disbelief in my own voice, even though I know it's true. "Who are these people?"

"We don't know that yet," Isotere says. "What we do know is the only people that can stop them are standing here, in this cave, wearing signature collars. Now do you understand why they want us dead?"

"Then why don't they just do it?" I ask. "Why the pretense of war?"

Before Isotere or Varance can answer, I feel the presence of someone enter the cave. Shiloe uncloaks and rushes over to stand next to me. Then Vern, Grish and Drake are there.

I hold up a hand. "Stay calm, guys." Then I turn back to Varance. "What is it you want with us?"

"Isn't it obvious?" Isotere says, a smug grin on his face.

I can sense that Shiloe and the others are nervous, but I continue to hold them back. "You want us to work together? To defeat these people?"

Varance gives a mocking curtsey, holding out her hands in a grand gesture.

"How are we supposed to do that if we're wearing these?" Vern roars.

Suddenly, the cave rattles from a violent impact. I feel the ground turn to putty, like a giant is stomping on top of the cave. I look at Varance, Isotere and the other two Immortals just as they vanish.

I draw my hood and also disappear, then sprint from the cave with the others close behind.

When we exit, I see the source of the impacts. A gigantic mech unit stands near the cave, its fists hammering down. The cave finally collapses, and the giant kicks the rocks aside and begins rummaging through the debris.

We spread out and flee the battlefield.

Soon, we're all standing in a huddle not far from the cave where the mech continues to sift through the rubble.

"Where's Tripp?" I have to yell over the explosions to be heard.

Everyone looks around, surprised that he isn't with us. In my excitement, chatting with the other Immortals, I hadn't even noticed. Apparently, neither had the others. Instant panic hits me.

"Fan out," I say. "Let's find him!"

Without another word, I'm racing across the battlefield. I listen to my intuitive voice and let it guide me between the fighting troops, explosions and burned-out vehicles. It doesn't take long before I feel an impulse and follow it. I hear the others in my thoughts, and soon, we all converge on an area that's taken heavy artillery. Bodies are strewn everywhere. In the center of the area, I see Tripp fighting for his life.

He's surrounded by several dozen death hounds. The silvery sheen from their razor-sharp armor glistens in the moonlight, and their red glowing eyes dot the surrounding area like floating orbs. He's managed to take out ten or eleven of them, and they lay at his feet in a jumble of wreckage. But the remaining pack of hounds has shredded his armor, though his cloak remains intact. Tripp's face and hands are bloody, and he's holding his side where I can see a deep gash.

We all race to him, still cloaked, and attack the hounds.

I pick several up and hurl them into the air. Shiloe, Grish, Vern and Drake do the same. The hounds can't see us, though, and focus on Tripp. As if they're communicating with one another, the hounds mount a concentrated attack, and soon Tripp disappears beneath their frenzied swarm. We drive into the chaos, pulling the hounds off him, and I manage to rip a few of them in half, cutting my hands in the process.

Eventually, we take enough of them out, and the remaining hounds flee.

I finally drop to my knees and place a hand on Tripp's thin shoulder. Then Shiloe, Drake, Grish and Vern are there, kneeling in the mud. When I look down, I see one of the hound's large claws protruding from Tripp's abdomen. Coating the claw is some sort of greenish residue, which I know now is poison.

Tripp opens his eyes and grips my arm. His mouth twists in anguish, and he gasps for breath. I feel a moment of panic as everyone looks to me, as if I can do something for him. But I already know he's down to his last few breaths, and the poison is quickly setting in.

Tripp tries to smile at me, "Sorry, Brin. I…I fell behind. They must've tracked me."

I feel tears sting my eyes but manage to keep my voice steady. "Why weren't you cloaked?"

Tripp turns away, avoiding the question. His cheeks are flushed, and I brush his sandy-red hair from his brow. I think about the first time we met, how he seemed so shy and standoffish. The youngest in our group, and too young to be involved in this war. Too young to be lying here in this muddy pit and certainly too young to bear the weight of the Northern Coalition's fate on his shoulders. In that instant, I see my younger brother, Ben. He's lying there in the mud, pain gripping his small body. He's shivering, with fear in his eyes and a confused expression on his face.

Then, Tripp begins to cry.

It's a low moan full of pain—*full of fear*. His tiny frame begins to convulse.

"I don't want to die, Brin…I don't. But I can't take this anymore. I don't want this life, not this way. Can you understand?"

"Tripp. Just hold on." I stand and try to lift him, but he pushes my hands away.

"Stop it. I'm not comin' back. Where's Grish?"

Grish moves closer, her hand is over her mouth, and tears are flowing down her cheeks. "I'm here, Tripp," she says, choking back sobs and rocking back and forth.

"You were right, Grish." Tripp's voice trails off in a whisper. "Things aren't fair for me. They never were. People like us were always meant to suffer."

Amidst the bombs and explosions, the rain and thunder, we kneel silently around Tripp's broken body. I forget about the raging war surrounding me as the youngest member of our group dies. The light from his palm fades to a lighter green, then it extinguishes.

During our debriefing, Herron demands to know what happened. He's furious about the incident, about losing an Immortal. He berates us as we all sit in the conference room. I can only stare at my cut and bruised hands, which are covered in Tripp's blood. All I think about at that moment is how I failed him. Tripp had placed his trust in me, and I'd let him down. Apparently, he had been dealing with more stress than he'd let on, and I had missed the signs. Why else would he have gone into battle uncloaked? He was too sharp to make such a mistake.

A defeated feeling takes hold of me. Herron's droning voice becomes white noise in the background, and his yells no longer register. But it's obvious to us all that he's the only one in the room who's pretending to care about Tripp's death.

Later that night, we move our things into our new living quarters. The Eastern Theater is a bit different than the other two theaters. The stone rooms are more cramped, though the cots and furniture are the same: dirty, lumpy and worn out. In front of our apartments, we have a clear view to the battlefield. It seems we can never get away from that backdrop. It's as if the commanders want to keep us connected to the sounds of battle and never let us get too comfortable.

Once again, Vern and Drake create a fire pit, and we sit outside in the cool breeze, quietly listening to the war beyond. It's difficult for me to believe that Tripp is really gone. I'm still struggling with my feelings of failure. I want to apologize to the others, but I know this isn't what they want to hear from me. It takes several minutes before I trust my voice enough to say something.

"Everyone okay?" I say, but it's barely audible over the crooning breeze.

Shiloe wipes the back of her hand across her cheek. "Tripp wasn't cloaked today. But that doesn't sound like him. He was always so cautious and calculated."

Grish glares at Shiloe from across the firepit. The dancing firelight sparkles in her dark eyes. "What're you tryin' to say?"

"It's obvious, ain't it?" Vern says. "Tripp couldn't take it, so he fought those hounds without cloaking." Vern holds up a tiny black disc on his fingertip. "Besides, he didn't even bring his blocker disc. I found it in his rucksack. He fought those death hounds uncloaked because he wanted this to happen."

"Shut up!" Grish says, and she stands. For a split second I think she's about to launch herself at Vern.

Vern holds up his hands. "Hey, take it easy, Grish."

"Tripp *didn't* want this to happen!" Grish says, still standing.

"Fine…okay," Vern says, still holding his hands up. "Doesn't mean anything less, either way."

Grish continues to look around at everyone as if challenging us to say something more. Then she turns and walks into her apartment.

I lean forward onto my knees and let out a long sigh. Everyone else remains quiet for several seconds.

"I don't want to talk about it anymore," Shiloe finally says. "Not tonight. Okay?"

"What about the other Immortals then?" Vern says.

"Well…what they said is in the realm of possibility," I say. The others look at me with wide eyes. "It aligns with what we already know. If these people remove us from the picture, who's left to fight them or defend the citizens?"

"Yeah, it does make sense," Drake says. "I believe there's enough room on Skylight for everyone."

"Still, those Immortals aren't telling us everything," Shiloe says. "Though, what they did tell us, I tend to believe."

"So?" I say. "Should we entertain joining them?"

"Why do they even need us?" Vern says. "With those magic scepters, they don't seem to need anyone's help."

"Maybe," Drake says. "But imagine if we also had our own scepters. That's a pretty formidable force."

"Yeah, except we don't have them." Everyone turns to see Grish. She stands at the edge of the fire pit, kicking at the dirt. "Sorry. I didn't mean to yell at you guys. Last thing I need is to have another argument. It's not what Tripp would want."

Vern stands and playfully tugs at Grish's red ponytails. "It's alright. Come on, have a seat."

"What should we do now?" Grish asks as she sits on a large rock. "I mean, if those Immortals are correct, then who can we trust?"

Vern shakes his head. "Don't know. I reckon we should continue doing the same thing, maybe?"

"And how far has that gotten us?" Grish snaps but immediately holds up a hand. "Sorry. But Tripp's gone, and we're still stuck fighting in this war. We're no closer to getting answers. I think we need a change. I vote we join the Southern Immortals."

Everyone looks at me, waiting for an answer. But I continued to stare into the fire. I know we need a better plan, but right then, I feel like a failure. All I can think about is Tripp and how I will feel if anyone else dies.

"Brin?" Shiloe says and touches my arm. "You alright?"

I look up, grimace and nod. "Yeah. I'm okay."

"You know it's not your fault, right?" Shiloe continues.

I nod but avoid her gaze.

"Did the other Immortals say anything else?" Vern asks. "We missed a lot of the conversation, man."

I try to think through my brain fog. That entire sequence feels distant and hard to recall, like my memory is trying to forget the entire night's events. "Just what we've already discussed. They think the whole war is a big lie designed to kill off as many citizens as possible, including us. Their theory is that only the wealthy, upper-class citizens should inhabit Skylight. It's all an elaborate conspiracy, this contract. They want us to help them find out who's behind it and defeat them."

"Isn't it odd that no one's ever suspected it, though?" Drake says.

"Maybe someone has, and they're not around anymore," Grish says with a heavy hint of sarcasm and grits her teeth. "Other Immortals like us, that is. Seems like they'd want to bend us more to their will than kill us, though."

"They're already doing that," I say. "Look. I think Grish is right. We need to change things up. I say we join these other Immortals. I don't feel so bad about it now that we know we're facing the same challenge as them."

"Just remember, they weren't telling us the whole story. You know that, right?" Shiloe says.

"Yeah, I got that," I say.

"We don't even know what their offer is," Shiloe continues. "You think it's wise?"

I shrug. "We can at least hear what they have to say. Besides, I'm ready for a change. I feel like we need this, especially after what happened tonight."

"But when and how?" Vern says. "You saw how hard it was just to get a few minutes alone with them."

"I don't know," I say and grab his shoulder, then I pull the others in close and lower my voice. "We have the blocker discs now. That gives me some hope. Call it fate, I don't know. But somehow, this is going to play out as it should. At the very least, we need to hear what they have to offer."

Later, I sit in my room with my legs crossed and begin a meditation that lasts early into the morning hours. Before sunrise, I shower away all the blood and gore of battle. But the cold water can't wash away the screams that haunt my thoughts. Soon, I'm thinking about my friends, and Tripp, most of all. I feel the tears sting my eyes. This time, I let them fall. There, in the shower, where the others can't see me cry, I finally let go. The flood of emotions pours out like a tidal wave. I've held myself together since the Day of the Nail because I can't afford to let my friends see my moment of weakness. For their good, for their well-being, I've held it all in. But this is something I need, and I finally give myself permission and break down.

FALLEN ONES | CHAPTER 19

I feel weak and slightly nauseous the next morning. But I roll out of my cot—having managed just a few hours of sleep—and eat a silent breakfast with the others before we hit the battlefield. As before, we carry the discs hidden in our cloaks, but we're careful when to use them.

In the back of my mind, I can't help but think about Tripp. What happened to him is a grim reminder that even though we're Immortals, we still have to remain alert. *Let the voice guide you!* I remind myself. I only hope that today will reveal something new. Perhaps a clue, a sign…anything. Time is running out, and we all know it.

We immediately spread out when we hit the front line that day. I follow behind some Northern troops, keeping a protective eye on them. But I decide to back off, realizing that my close proximity might place them in danger. I send a mental thought for the others to keep an eye out for signs of the Southern Immortals.

It isn't long before I feel their presence from across the battlefield. I see the telltale blurry figure, then another. I send a mental signature to Shiloe and the others to move parallel to them and follow their lead. A few minutes later, we're placing the blocker discs on our collars, prepared.

The other four Immortals continue to an area where there's less activity and stop. This time, we all remained cloaked on the battlefield. I don't like that we're out in the open. We can't even talk over the sound of battle, but I can still read their thoughts at this distance.

...we're listening to what you have to offer.

...very good, Brindall. You learn quickly.

I can sense her sarcasm even through the telepathy.

...what is your plan? I ask.

...to die.

I'm stunned at that and begin to feel nervous. *...what exactly do you mean? Have you found a way to fake our deaths?*

...if you and the others in your group will swear allegiance to us first, then we will help you out of this war.

I nearly explode in laughter. Then I feel anger rise up *...why would we swear allegiance to you, Varance?*

...do you want out of this misery or not? she continues *...we can save you and the others.*

...out of one prison, only to fall into another? But despite the absurdity of the thought, I find myself considering it. What would I give to free myself and my friends? My family?

...what's it going to be, Brindall?

...you need our help, Varance. If so, why make such a ridiculous request?

...that's our offer, and it expires tonight.

I stand there in the mud and rain, with war raging nearby. I can sense that the others are nervous, too. They know as well that this proposal is a double-edged sword. I'm not even sure Varance's plan will work, since I still haven't heard it. Yet, the allure of getting out of this is so enticing that I feel I'm on the verge of agreeing to it.

But before I can answer, I hear whistling in the air and know immediately that it's the sound of incoming artillery.

Suddenly, we're all scattering in different directions. The scene unfolds in slow motion, gradually gaining speed until things are flying by me full blast. I shroud myself in my cloak and feel shrapnel pepper my backside. It threatens to bite through the graphene-reinforced fiber and end my life. Booms reverberate and rattle my brain. Those heavy concussions rock the ground I stand on. Mud, dirt, and gore hurtle through the air and cake my face. At that instant, I know I'd take Varance's offer. *Anything to get away from this!*

I see Shiloe in the distance. Through the haze, she's fighting a platoon of troops, her mirage visible only to my eyes. Beyond are Drake and Grish, helping a platoon of Northern soldiers to retreat. Vern is nowhere to be seen, and that feeling of unease takes me. We've only just lost Tripp. I can't bear the thought of losing Vern, too.

I decide to run to Shiloe, unable to find Vern. I can help her at least, then look for Vern after. I stand next to her and lift a large vehicle. It's smoking and ruined, the burning chassis still on fire. Together we move it to help block incoming fire. Shiloe's winded already, her breathing is labored. She gives me a thankful but worn look. I watch her face strain as we move the vehicle, her delicate brow caked with mud and grime.

The rain pours down around us in heavy sheets that turn the earth into ponds of standing water. Railgun fire whizzes past. It carries the sound of death with it. I can hear the rounds pelting the burned-out vehicle's carcass as we gather soldiers near us, but many of them fall despite our efforts.

I see an enemy platoon nearby, and Shiloe nods her head in that direction. "If we want to save our troops, we need to take out that platoon."

"Around the ends," I say. "Hurry!"

We drop the vehicle and run, our cloaks taking the brunt of the incoming fire. I focus ahead, one foot after the other, hunching low and sliding down craters and through the mud. Finally, we top the crater and attack.

It's at that moment that I feel remorse.

Though I've been through this hundreds of times now, I can't seem to block out the enemy's faces this time. I can't suspend my guilt. Maybe it's the loss of Tripp or maybe the conversation we had with the other Immortals. I know these Southern troops really aren't the enemy. They are fathers and mothers, brothers and daughters. What I'm doing seems unforgivable now that I know the truth. But I have no choice and do what I've been trained to do. I see the fear on their faces when I attack. Their confusion and pain stick in my mind. I know this moment will haunt me tonight, in my dreams and meditation. It's so much more pronounced now because I know about the lie.

I make a silent vow to them and to their families. Somehow, I will repay their sacrifice.

Then, it's over.

The entire platoon is gone. Wiped out by Shiloe and me. I watch the leftovers flee, carrying their wounded. I find Shiloe, grip her shoulder. Then give her a hug. Because I know she feels the same way I do.

"Come on," I say and tug at her. "We need to find Vern and the others."

We split up and search the battlefield. Minutes pass, and I begin to worry. The thunder and lightning crash above us in angry flashes as the wind and rain drum down. The ground continues to gyrate with mortar rounds and artillery. I splash through the mud and pitted terrain while scanning for the others. At times, I have to pause and wait for flashes of lightning to see.

Then a mental thought floats into my head. It's Shiloe.

I race to her location, using the mental signature to find her, like a homing beacon. It's not hard to find, based on the gathering of crows I see in that area.

Kneeling in the bottom of a crater with her arms around Vern is Shiloe. She's trying to lift him. I breathe a sigh of relief when I see him moving and race to help. I grab Vern's other arm and drape him over my shoulder. Together, we scurry for shelter. Soon, Grish and

Drake are there, and we gather in the burned-out hull of another large transport.

We circle and check Vern.

"What happened?" I kneel and hold the light of my palm to his eyes. His dark face is caked in mud. Blood runs freely down his forehead but has already started to clot above his thick brow.

Vern shakes his head. He sits up and rubs his sleeve across his forehead. "I was helping some troops. Then…there were mechs, a lot of them. They focused on me and let the others go free. I had to run. Took several out, but they kept coming for me and ignored everyone else. Never seen them do that."

Shiloe gives me a look, her brows arching upward. "You think they're starting to single us out?" Her voice echoes inside the transport as the others look to me and wait.

I shake my head. "I don't know. Maybe they're starting to learn?"

"So, they know how to track us now?" Shiloe asks. "Did you not use the blocker?"

Vern lets his head drop to the side of the metal hull. "I took mine off. I felt I'd had it on too long and didn't want Herron getting suspicious." Vern looks at us, his hands held up. "Hey, we talked about this, remember? Use the blocker for brief periods. You mean, y'all are still wearing yours?"

Realization hits me then. Vern is still being tracked.

"We gotta move, now!" I say and pull Shiloe with me. "Get out. Go!"

We all race from the wrecked transport. Just as we exit, the metal hull heats up, then erupts in fire. It takes a direct hit from a heavy howitzer round. Shrapnel flies through the air as the hull literally disintegrates. I feel my body floating like I'm weightless. For a moment, time seems to slow down as I summersault over the battlefield. In my vision, there are colorful blasts of light. Explosions like fireworks fill the sky. Shiloe, Grish, Vern and Drake are flung in opposite directions. I feel my ears begin to ring, and everything around me is muted and dull. Then I hit the ground and feel my shoulder sink into the mud. My vision grows blurry, and I think I'm on the verge of passing out.

But I will myself to stand and find the others. When I do, I tumble back to the mud, my legs still numb and tingly. I know more artillery could be heading our way and begin to panic.

They mean to finish us off.

Yet, my body feels numb, and I wonder if I'm wounded, or perhaps this is what being dead feels like. Sluggish. Out-of-body. Nonresponsive.

It takes all my will and focus, but I finally pull myself from the mud and stand. I wobble, a bit disoriented, and hold my hands out to gain my balance. The rain washes down, rinsing the mud from my vision—then I realize it's blood…*my blood.* I taste the coppery blend with the grit of dirt and mud and spit it out.

Get it together! I scream to myself.

Heavy tremors bring me to my senses. Something nearby is hammering the ground repeatedly. I scan the battlefield for the source.

Then I see Drake.

He's standing in front of a large mech unit, one that I recall from our training with Triton. The TRI-SENT, one of the South's largest and most formidable mech units, something we have not yet faced.

The massive mech stands over him, its three legs slamming down, trying to crush him. Each impact shakes the ground like an earthquake. The twenty-meter-tall unit continues to slam the ground as Drake dodges it. He stares up at the mech and screams into the night. We hear his war cry and hurry over to help. But before we can get there, the TRI-SENT finally hits home.

Drake moves just a second too late and barely manages to raise his arms to slow the blow. The force of the strike drives him into the mud. But amazingly, Drake holds his ground.

I watch in horror as we race toward him. The mech's blow would have been enough to crush any armored vehicle, yet Drake is somehow holding it back.

But the giant robot continues to press down onto Drake. I hear him begin to scream. The strain in his voice is evident, and he's sinking further into the mud. Soon, he's up to his waist, then his chest, then neck. Drake finally collapses, and the full weight of the mech crashes down. Drake disappears in the mud, and his roar goes silent.

The massive TRI-SENT reorients on Shiloe, Vern, Grish and me. It's then that I notice the markings on its hull: a bright red triangle with the number 717.

The only thing left of Drake is his right hand. From beneath the unit's clawed foot, the orange-colored light from Drake's palm fades and goes dark.

But instead of attacking us, the giant TRI-SENT turns and races off, the impact from its clawed feet creating tremors as it leaves us alone in the crater.

"No! *NO!*" Vern screams and sprints into the crater after Drake.

He reaches the bottom and tugs at Drake's hand, trying to drag his body from the mud. We slide after Vern and kneel beside him.

"Why didn't the mech attack?" Grish says, barely containing the emotion in her voice.

But almost instantly, we have our answer.

The sound of artillery fills the stormy night air again. I see tracers streaking toward our location.

"Incoming!" Grish yells and points to the dark sky.

I pull on Vern but struggle to find footing in the cone-shaped crater. I dig into the mud with one hand as I lift Vern with me. I feel the others pulling him, too.

"Vern. Let him go!" I scream.

Shiloe somehow finds Vern's blocker and places it on his collar. We finally manage to pull Vern from the crater and drag him across the field. He falls limp, almost resigned now as we reach another husked-out vehicle.

We look on just as howitzer rounds pummel the crater where Drake's body lies. Concussive waves rock the ground, and the crater is obliterated. I watch as the scene unfolds like a stop-motion movie. The lightning strikes a perfect freeze-frame of spattering mud and metal parts that fly a dozen meters into the night sky. Then the sound of the mud hitting the earth around us fills the air.

I wait for a few seconds, then pull the others to their feet. "Keep moving!" I say and pull Vern to his feet.

I lead the way back toward the front line and past our own troops. I zigzag and weave, running full speed and dragging Vern along. Soon, I can see Northern soldiers with their blue insignias. We hop an earthen barricade and finally collapse.

I lean against Shiloe, feeling her body heave with exhaustion and grief. I see the tears on her cheeks, and she looks away from me. As I watch her, I remember when we first met—the girl with hazel eyes and a friendly face. A smile that welcomes a person in, like a ray of sunshine. How all that has changed now. The horrors we've seen. We will never be the same.

Vern slumps against the dirt wall as rain washes down across his dark face. Grish looks up at the night sky. Lightning flashes, and I can see the tears in her eyes, too. Then I feel the sting in my own eyes.

I sit up and face them. "Look at me, all of you!" I try not to yell, but it sounds harsh anyway. I take a deep breath and calm myself before I continue. "We can't stop now. Remember. We have unfinished business."

Vern looks at me, and for a split second, I think he might try to hit me. "They just killed Drake. They murdered him!"

"They're trying to split us," I say. "That's what they do. It's how they'll win, if we let them. It's always been their strategy. That's why Henak, Triton and Kiff pushed us to stick together. I know that now."

"I don't know if I can go on, Brin." Grish looks at me. Her eyes are wide with dark circles beneath, and she wrings her hands, then shakes them as if fighting off a sudden panic attack. Shiloe has an uncertain look on her face for the first time. I can see Vern's already resigned. Our entire group is on the verge of a breakdown.

I start to feel anger well up inside me at seeing them in this state. I want to yell at them, but I know that's my emotions talking from the loss of Drake. Triton's words come to me suddenly—*remain calm, they'll need that from you, Brindall.*

I grab Vern by his cloak and shake him, then face Shiloe and Grish. "Listen to me. I know the feeling. I want to give up, too. But I'm not going to let them win this way. Look, let's just make it through the night. A few hours, then we can talk this over." I take Shiloe's hand, grip Vern's shoulder and nod to Grish. "Come on, guys. We can do this. We have to make it through their game if we want to win. Do this for me, and I will find a way out. I promise you."

Then Shiloe squeezes my hand. "I trust you, Brin." She stands and pulls Vern with her. She grips his shoulder, then holds out a hand to Grish, pulls her to her feet. We all hug. Among the sounds of war and death and destruction, we hold on to each other for several minutes before I finally push away.

"Put it from your thoughts, for the moment," I say. "I know it hurts. Think about each other now. This is your family. We need everyone. Pull from that thought, and let it push you through."

We fight through the rest of the night in a haze. I don't know which way is up. I struggle to go through the paces. Like the other days, I use Vishmu to guide me. The voice in my mind is strong, and I let it take control.

We finally finish and soon we're on the transport back to headquarters.

In the debriefing, Commander Herron demands to know what happened. It's like Deja vu all over again. I notice how he once again feigns dismay at the loss of yet another Immortal. I think I even see him holding back a grin on a few occasions. The thought crosses my mind to strangle him. I feel the urge to reach out, grasp his throat and squeeze the life from his lying soul. I know full well that would be the last thing I do, though. The mental signature collar would activate instantly. I would die, my family right behind me. As satisfying as the thought of taking Herron to hell with me is, I let the thought go. I remain slouched in the chair as he berates me.

We're finally allowed to leave and make the long trek back to our quarters. Once there, I throw my cloak in the dryer vault, strip down, and shower. The cold water purges the mud and blood away. I stay in the shower until I can't feel my fingers. I dress and make a quick meal, then place the blocker disc under my pillow.

Afterward, I gather with the others at the firepit. I hold my hands out to the heat and thaw my fingers. The smell of it hits my nostrils, and the crackle sets my soul to ease for a moment.

Shiloe sits on a rock, her knees pulled to her chest, her dainty chin on her hands. "Drake…I can't believe he's…I can't—"

Everyone waits for her to finish the sentence, but she can't seem to say the words. No one else offers to help as the fire mixes with the sounds of battle and thunder outside the cave.

Vern sits slumped, his cloak wrapped around him like a blanket. Only his eyes are visible in the dark, the glint of fire reflected in them. "If they want us dead, why don't they just do it?"

"They have to make it look realistic," I say. "You know that. We're supposed to die in war. If they kill us on the battlefield, no one asks questions. If it's a public execution, there may be an uprising. They won't risk that. They still need these people to finish the Skylight System."

"When the hell did you figure this out?" Grish asks.

"After my last talk with Varance," I say. "That's when it finally hit me."

"It's how all the past Immortals have died," Shiloe says. "It all makes sense now."

"It's my fault," Vern says. "Had I not been an idiot and taken my blocker disc off today, Drake would be here now!"

Shiloe places her arm around Vern's shoulders. "It's as much mine as yours. I was there when it happened. I saw Drake. I could've helped him, but I hesitated. I…I knew. But I hesitated because I was afraid. I had a split second, and I didn't do it."

I kneel before the three of them. "Look. That's over now. If we don't pull through this, Tripp and Drake's sacrifice means nothing! We have to take this a day at a time now."

"For how long?" Grish asks. "Because I can't do this forever."

"Till I can figure this out," I whisper back. "I promised I would, and I'm not going to let you guys down."

CHAPTER 20

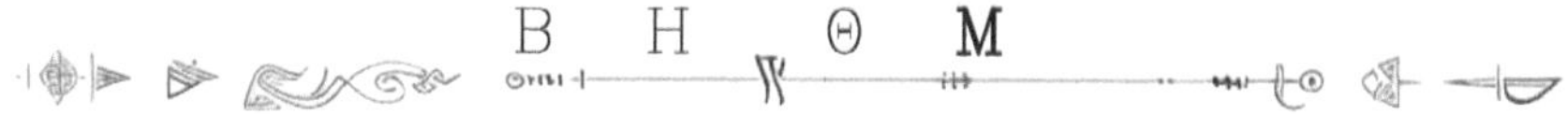

As usual, sleep doesn't find me that night. Instead, I seek solace in meditation and Vishmu. I grieve for Drake and Tripp. That empty, bottomless feeling in the pit of my soul lingers, refusing to let go. Though I grieve, my inner light remains hopeful that I will find a way out of this and keep my promise to my other friends.

During meditation, my inner light races off, and I follow it. I watch it play and frolic, amazed again at how quickly it seems to rejuvenate from the loss. Soon, there are other lights, other immortals that join it. I think of younglings, evergreen saplings of some ancient tree—youthful sprites perhaps, traveling through the ages. When I look closer, I think I see Drake's light, then Tripp's. I can sense their presence, as though they're whispering to me on cosmic winds, asking to be set free.

...it's okay, Brindall...you can let go now...

I snap awake and wipe the tears from my eyes.

I sit cross-legged in my room, breathing in gasps and slowly easing back into reality. It's then that I understand. Tripp and Drake aren't asking for forgiveness; they're asking me to set them free. In order to do that, I must first forgive myself.

The sunless dawn breaks, and we make our way to the war room for our daily briefing. It's the typical group: Herron and his top brass, along with Taun in holographic fashion from his theater in the east. But we're all shocked to see Commander Freemantle standing in the back of the room. I notice his quick glances in my direction and wonder what would bring the Supreme Commander to the Western Theater.

"Morning to you all." Freemantle holds his hands behind his back as he talks. His typical shorn grey hair has grown out a bit, his beard slightly bushier than before. Though I sense he is frazzled, his air of command is still undeniable. Yet, I detect the subtle hesitation in his movements. "First, let me convey my sincere condolences. I know that Drake and Tripp were close friends and valuable assets to our team."

I clear my throat, and everyone faces me. "I'd like to know why there was so much friendly fire in our area yesterday, sir."

The look on Freemantle's face tells me that he knows we were being targeted. I'm half tempted to say as much, but I sit back, arms crossed.

"That was a mistake on our part," Taun interjects, not giving Freemantle a chance to speak. "I have to remind you that friendly fire is sometimes an unfortunate part of war."

I don't respond and the others remain silent as well. But I can see Grish is barely holding back. Vern's fists are clenched, and Shiloe is glaring at Taun through the hologram.

"I have a new assignment for you today," Freemantle continues, as if everything is back to normal. "However, this mission is for you, Brindall."

I sit forward slightly and meet his gaze. I feel a nervous chill race through me.

Fremantle looks directly at me. "You're being moved back to the Central Theater. Alone."

Shiloe, Grish and Vern stand immediately and began pointing fingers at Freemantle and Herron. Their raised voices echo around the control room as the two commanders hold their ground. MPs enter the space, hands on their railguns and nervous looks on their faces. But Freemantle remains calm and expressionless as he ignores the others and holds my gaze.

"It's okay," I say to the others and turn to face them. I place a hand on Shiloe's shoulder and pull her in front of me. I stare into her hazel eyes. "It's alright, Shiloe." Then I pull the other two into a huddle. "Vern, Grish. I'll be fine."

"What's happenin'?" Grish asks, and I can see she's on the verge of a breakdown again. I pull her closer, along with Vern and Shiloe. I speak to them with my thoughts, trying my best to calm them.

But inside, I'm screaming, *this isn't supposed to happen yet!*

"They're splitting us, Brin," Shiloe mutters through her tears. She grips my cloak and pulls at me, not wanting to let go. "You know it! If they take you, we don't stand a chance."

"You have to remain strong for them, Shiloe," I whisper. "It's what you have to do now."

Then, the MPs pull us away from each other. I see Herron's hand hovering over the holopad that controls our mental signature collars. His finger twitches, and I can see he's nervous. A simple press of the button, and we're all dead.

I sense Shiloe's frustration, Vern's anger, and Grish's anxiety. I know they're on the verge of launching into the guards. And yet, I want to break free with them and flee this war and misery. But that would be the end of all four of us. I send one last thought to them—

...hold it together...for me, please.

Shiloe is the last to let go of my hand. She looks up, and her hazel eyes brimming with tears.

Then I'm escorted out of the control room and given five minutes to pack while the MPs wait at my apartment door. In my rucksack I place my clothing, a few trinkets and the vessel: pretty much all I have to my name. I glance at the guards and quickly reach beneath my pillow and stow the blocker disc inside my cloak. Then, I march to the front door and follow the guards.

I stand at the boarding platform, a queasy feeling in my stomach. I should be heading to the front line with the others. Instead, I'm being forced onto the rail transport and heading back to the Central Theater with no reason given. Varance's voice is stuck in my head. But at the same time, I feel like this might be my last train ride. Freemantle's unnerving gaze still stares into my soul.

I know that he knows we've figured out the lie, which means the other commanders do as well. With that in mind, they've decided to eliminate me and take the leader from our group. Shiloe is right. With me gone, our group will likely fall apart. They know their best chance to dismantle us is by separating our group. It's what they'd been trying to do all along, but in a more subtle approach. Now, I can sense their desperation in this blatant move as the Winter Solstice grows near. Still, I wonder if Shiloe can hold our group together now. I pray that she can stay strong, that her resolve will grow into what I know it can be. One thing I'm certain of: I'm not really heading back to the Central Theater. I'll be dead before I get there.

As I'm buckled into my harness, I glance around. There are ten guards, and they sit around me making light conversation but avoiding eye contact. I feel like a prisoner, now more than ever. I start to wonder for the first time what is really happening and how much longer I'll live.

The bullet train rattles and clanks as it hits cruising speed, and soon, we disappear into the side of the cliff wall. The darkness of the tunnel consumes us. I sit, hands on my legs, and feel the bounce rattle through me. I close my eyes and begin to meditate, trying to calm my nerves and relax. In the background of my mind, thoughts swirl out of control, though. I see Freemantle, his eyes boring down into my soul, searching for answers, plucking at my secrets. Shiloe looking to me, pleading for me not to leave her. Grish and Vern with uncertain expressions on their faces. And to top it all off, the realization that I have broken my promise to my friends. I will never find a way out for us now.

Certainly not Drake and Tripp!

The failure of that broken promise rips through my soul like a bomb: a constant reminder of my lie to them. I feel small, inadequate…a failure.

Suddenly, the train jolts to one side, and I pry my eyes open. I reach out to steady myself as the lights above flicker and go dark. The train continues to move forward, but I feel it beginning to slow, like it's lost power. Then it stops with a jarring halt that throws all of us forward. My harness strains against my chest. Then, an explosion rips through the front of the cabin. I'm completely disoriented from the sudden impact. Light flashes, and smoke billows to the top of the cab as it's violently ripped apart. The sound of rending steel and screams fill the cabin.

I unbuckle and stand, wobble, then steady myself in the dark. I feel around for the guards, but everyone is gone now. I'm alone in the cabin and use the glow from my hand to light the path in front of me. There's a sudden pressure on my neck, and I reach up. I place my hands on the graphene collar, and the pressure becomes so intense that I see lights dance in my vision. Everything is turning red, like blood rushing to my eyes, and I struggle to breathe. I grasp the collar and pull at it. I'm forced to my knees. The metal spikes inside the collar begin to bite into the skin of my neck. I feel it constrict tighter.

Just before I lose consciousness, I realize that this is how it ends for me. Alone and away from my friends and family…on a train to nowhere.

PART THREE:

STORM BREAK

"Face the storms in your life,
not alone but together,
so that you may lean on each other for strength."
—Christian Albright

B H Θ M
A Δ Z K

I'm in a dark place.

Lights from the final explosions still flash like glowing balls of red and orange in my mind. I hear people rushing toward me and the sound of railgun slugs pelting the side of the transport's cabin. I try to open my eyes, try to see what's happening, but I can't move my body. Someone lifts me and carries me, maybe there are multiple people. I hear screams and the sound of more explosions—the acrid scent of smoke as my body floats. Time seems to slow to a crawl, and I slip in and out of consciousness. Minutes? hours? *Days?* All I know is that I'm immobilized but alive, unless this is what purgatory feels like.

I continued to slip in and out of consciousness: awake, though my eyes won't seem to focus. Eventually, I sense that I'm being loaded into another transport vehicle, perhaps another train. I feel the rattle and bump of the vehicle, then I'm being lifted again by several people before finally blacking out.

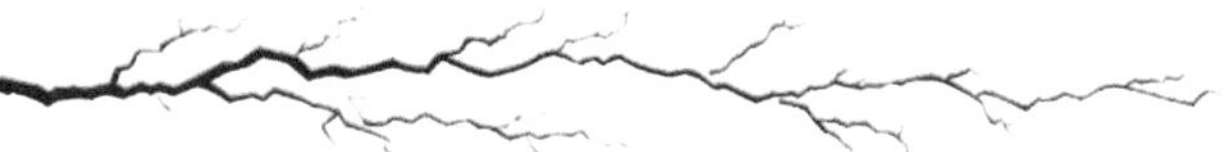

When I wake, I lie still and listen. The room is quiet and dark, with only a dim light from a countertop opposite me. The cot cradles my body and prevents me from rolling over. Around me is the familiar rough-hewn surface of stone, setting me at ease. The striations are tones of gray, telling me we're further north and away from the typical reddish clays of the Central Theater. I don't hear any sounds other than the soft beeping of some equipment in the background. I feel bruised, especially on my left side, where the explosion ripped through the transport.

After a few moments, I kick my legs over the cot and feel the cool stone floor on my bare feet. I'm wearing a stained, white gown of sorts, maybe a hospital gown, I think. I grip the edge of the cot, feel strength return to my arms and crane my back, stretching out the kinks. When I reach up to rub my neck, I notice something is missing.

I leap to my feet in shock when I realize the collar is gone. I pace around the small stone holding cell, hardly believing it.

"Is this a dream?" I mutter. "Am I dead!" I yell into the dark room, feeling a moment of panic.

From the opposite side I see a light pulse, maybe a digital device or some equipment. It enlarges into a three-dimensional hologram, casting some light around the room. Sitting in a chair in the corner is a man that I recognize, at least I think I do. I rub my forehead, trying to think through the haze.

I know this man's presence…because my inner light knows his presence.

But his physical appearance is different somehow. The short, gray hair is longer, more silver. His cropped beard, usually so neatly trimmed, is bushy. Those eyes, though. They hold the same piercing blue gaze.

"Commander…*Freemantle?*" I ask slowly, cupping a hand over my squinted eyes to see him in the dark. "It's you. I know it is, yet…you're different. How?"

Freemantle sits in a relaxed position, one leg draped over the other, his hands resting gently on one knee. Then, he steeples his fingers in front of his face. There's a digital pad resting on his lap, a holopad, I think. He wears the same strata-patterned military fatigues as always, though. It *is* Fremantle, I have no doubt.

He gives me a warm smile. "We have much to discuss, Brindall. Right now, I ask that you have some patience. Can you give me that?"

"Sure…okay," I stutter. Dirt still cakes the back of my throat, and it sounds more like a croak in the quiet room. "I'm just a bit confused about how you removed my signature collar."

"As you should be. More on that later. This has been quite an adventure for you, I have no doubt." Freemantle speaks in a more measured tone than before, perhaps now that he's not in front of the other two commanders. Still, his voice demands my attention. Nothing will change that.

Freemantle stands and places the holopad inside his jacket. He points to the cabinets under the countertop. "Inside, you'll find some clothes. Please put them on. I'll wait outside."

I dress quickly into some old cargo pants, a bit worn and used, of course, and a long-sleeved government-issued tactical shirt and boots. I follow Freemantle down tunnel-like corridors and through a subterranean complex. Like all the other facilities, this one expands as we traverse from the smaller private tunnels into more public thoroughfares. The level of personnel increases, too, and soon, we're working our way through throngs of people. They're all dressed in similar fatigues with high-ranking medallions adorning their uniforms.

"Where are we?" I ask. "Can you at least tell me the location?"

"Somewhere north of the God's Grace Borough, but more on that in a minute. Your questions will be answered soon." Freemantle doesn't slow or stop, and I hurry to keep up.

We take a few vector accelerators up long empty silos, like vertical tunnels, and eventually stop in front of a basic control room. When I step into the room, I gasp in disbelief. Sitting around a table are several familiar people. Yet, I get the same confused feeling looking at them as I had with Freemantle. Though I know these people—rather, their *essence*, I suppose—I still don't quite recognize their physical appearance. It feels like a dream, one where I know the person next to me, though I can't quite see their face.

Before me are my former instructors. One by one, they stand and walk over to greet me. First Miss Henak, then Triton and Kiff last. The three of them gather around me and I struggle to maintain my emotions. I shake Triton's hand, give Henak a hug and nod to Kiff.

"What is this? What's happening?" I ask in a voice thick with emotion.

"I suggest you take a seat." Freemantle nods to one chair in particular. It's then that I notice the rickety table which looks to be thousands of years old. It's large and round and the perimeter is cracked and checked, but otherwise whole. Carved around the edge are twenty-four symbols, which I recognize immediately.

"The chart!" I look side-long at the table and walk around it, touching all the symbols, which are roughly carved into its wooden surface. When I reach my own, situated behind the letter 'M', I hold out my hand to see that the symbol matches it exactly.

"This is the old chart, isn't it?" I say. "But…what is this table?"

"That's a different story for another time. Sit there, if you don't mind." Freemantle nods to the chair positioned behind the letter M.

I walk over and slide the chair out. When I sit, something odd happens to me—what I've heard some people call an out-of-body experience. I seem to hover over my physical form. Unlike the meditation sessions, though, this is different. I'm still awake but thoughts fill my mind from ages past, perhaps the former lives of the 'M' class symbol. Those memories fly past too quickly to interpret, though. I guess there are hundreds, maybe thousands of years of memories. Little glimpses of ancient eras, even other worlds that I sense, which are all wedged into that small glimpse. It's enough to make me dizzy, and I almost lose consciousness.

But just as quickly, I'm back, seated in my chair behind the wooden table and panting.

"A glimpse," Freemantle says. "Very fascinating. A look into your past lives, and not just in this realm, I should add. Something you'll grow accustomed to over time." Freemantle pushes in his chair and paces around the table. Henak, Triton and Kiff all sit in different chairs around the table and wait silently. "You know me as Gorgan Freemantle. But my real name is one that you may have heard before. I am Christian Albright."

I chuckle softly at first. But when I look around, no one else smiles or laughs. I realize that Freemantle is serious. Though I'm tired and rattled by the last several hours, I know this man is telling the truth. Whoever he is, I can sense that he's honest, if nothing else.

I take a moment, trying to think clearly. My brain fog is mostly gone now that the collar's been removed. I feel like a new person, and the exhilaration floods through my body at the thought that I'm finally free. I can hardly believe it, and the concept is almost too much to handle. I find it nearly impossible to focus on the others in the room.

I find my voice after several seconds. "I'm…sorry, but it's just a bit shocking. I'm free of the signature collar, sitting here with you. I mean, I've heard the rumors, but I didn't think Christian Albright really existed." I sit up in my chair, drum my fingers on the table and cross my legs, trying to get comfortable. "Well, I'm not sure what to say, other than I feel a bit confused."

Albright pauses behind a chair near the twelve o'clock position of the table and sits down. "Brindall, I imagine you're wondering several things. Let me start by introducing some people you already 'think' you know. Everyone seated around this table is actually an Immortal."

I sit back in shock. My mouth drops open, and all I can do is shake my head. The surprises of this day just keep coming. But then it all makes sense. I recall their movements, their battle techniques and the speed at which each of them had moved during our training. It's glaringly obvious now, and I want to kick myself for not figuring it out sooner.

Henak stands and gives me a wide smile, like a professor might to a student who had finally graduated. She holds out her right palm to me, showing the wound, almost as if offering a peace gift. The color is a bright, glowing blend of orange and yellow. The symbol matches the letter Z. "My name is Harriet Sanders. It's good to finally meet you."

She sits, and Triton stands next. He holds out his right palm and it shines in a brilliant reddish-orange color, like a tangerine sunset. His symbol is that of a triangle. He bows to me with a quick smile. "Glad to have you back, Brin. My real name is Tyberius Alexander."

Next is Kiff. She stands and holds out her right palm for me to see. Her light glows Yellow, and the symbol is the letter K. "My true name is Kleegan Yewell. You are a welcome addition to our team, Brindall. I hope you will consider joining us."

Lastly, Albright holds out his right hand. I see the bright red glow and the symbol of the letter A. "Together, the four of us make up the core of an ancient group known as the *Lucem*—we are children of the *Light*. More on that in a minute. Let's get to the most pressing question first, which is why you're here." Albright places the digital pad-like device he's been carrying onto the old table. The display enlarges and shows an area of North America.

"The Great Plains," I say.

"Correct, at least, as it once was long ago," Albright says. "You've heard people refer to this war as a game, or a contract, yes?"

I nod. "More of a charade or a lie, I'd say. But yeah, a contract for territory, as it's been explained to me." I think back to my conversation with Varance. She had proclaimed that this 'so-called' competition was nothing more than a scheme pushed by wealthy elites. I'm about to find out if what she'd told me was true.

"Well, I can tell you that most of what you know *is* a lie." Albright crosses his arms and stares at me as if he'd just read my thoughts.

And there it was. Varance hadn't been lying, at least not about that part.

Albright leans in and steeples his fingers in front of his face. "Our group, along with another faction known as the *Atrum*, or the children of the *Dark*, form an ancient race known as the *Heliographi*. We are twenty-four individuals whose inner light has traveled through time. Yes, we are Immortals, and it is true that we do not age, once converted. Over the millennia, the Lucem and the Atrum have mostly been at odds with each other. The Atrum are simply known as the Southern Immortals, and one might say we don't get along very well. Our moral beliefs are different from their darker mindset. As you can see, the left side of the table is empty. The twelve symbols that belong to the Atrum are on that side, some of them I believe you've already met."

"We've been used as pawns, haven't we?" I phrase the question tentatively, not wanting to give away what I already know. I want to hear the full story from Albright himself.

"This entire war has been under the pretense of a 'contract,' which will be awarded to the side who holds the most land when the clock strikes midnight on the Winter Solstice. This charade of lies has been created by the wealthy elite, upper-class citizens, in other words. They view the Skylight System as a utopian world fit for only the finest citizens. They've managed to force millions of people into battles in hopes of whittling the population down. Their plan is to leave them behind, the ones that survive, anyway. The fewer the citizens, the less resistance there will be when they finally learn the truth. Oh, Brindall, there is *plenty* of room for all people on the Skylight System. But we've seen this before. Throughout mankind's history, some of the worst atrocities were driven by this sort of 'culling' of the human race. We mustn't allow this to happen again."

"But you created the Skylight System. Don't *you* make the rules?"

Albright chuckles, and I sense the pain within. His forehead wrinkles, his brow coming to a point. Even his laugh holds no joy. "Yes, I created the system. I lead the development. I'm currently heading up the final touches as we speak. But with something this large, and so much of our resources invested, the backers have the final say. An Elite by the name of Horvin. Unfortunately, he feels that we should sacrifice the many for the few. It is as it always has been. Now it's up to us to ensure that does not come to fruition."

"And what happens when you pull us Immortals out? Won't the war get out of control, or the South take too much territory?"

"Actually, the Atrum have just pulled their Immortals out, too. But I will keep a close eye on it. If things do get out of control, we may have to intervene."

"So, your plan is to eventually stop this by challenging Horvin and his Elites?" I say, and look around the room, noting the grim looks on everyone's faces. "Who are these people?"

"They are leaders in high positions, mostly," Albright says. He pulls up a hologram showing a dozen men and women. I read their names and titles.

"Governors, senators, and generals. Even the president, Horvin," he continues. "They have deep pockets and hold sway over the boroughs' political systems. Corruption took root long ago. We cannot defeat them through that avenue. Subterfuge may be our best approach for now. Eventually, we may have to use force."

"But how will you stop them? We have no army."

Albright stands and places his hands on the table. "We have no army, *yet*."

I narrow my eyes suspiciously. "What exactly are you saying?"

"We are going to set these people free."

"You mean the Northern and the Southern citizens?"

"Yes."

"All of them?"

"Hopefully. And we'd like you to help us, assuming you want in on this plan."

"Do I have a choice?"

"If you decline our offer, you're free to go."

I consider that. I'm free, but my friends aren't, and neither is my family. I remember the faces of the dead citizens on the battlefield, many by my own hand. I recall my silent promise to them…to Tripp and Drake and their families. Besides, where exactly would I go? Certainly not home to the ARC Borough. I realize then that I have no home.

It's not something I consider for more than a few seconds, though. Of course I will join Albright, if for no other reason than to set my friends and family free. I won't leave them behind or the millions of others. I feel a fire beginning to burn within me. Knowing that these Elites, with their misaligned intent, have managed to deceive so many people. It enrages me. *So many lives lost over greed!* I grip the edge of the table and feel the splinters pierce my fingers.

"When do we begin?"

Albright gives me a knowing look and lowers his gaze. "We start as soon as possible. I must warn you. Once you make this decision, there is no turning back."

I stand and hold out my hand. "I would have it no other way."

Albright walks over and grips my hand and smiles. Then Tyberius, Harriet and Kleegan are there, clapping me on the back and grinning.

"Though we don't have an army, exactly, we do have the semblance of one called *The Agency*." Albright nods toward the doors of the room and the complex beyond. "Out there is the beginning of a secret organization that I hope will one day become the protector of the Skylight System. For the greater good of humanity. This hidden base is well north of the 37th parallel. From here, we will make our plans and free these people. We will expose the truth, and we must do it before the Winter Solstice."

Albright places his hands behind his back and strolls around the room. "When I began work on the Skylight System, my wish was that it be shared with all people, regardless of status, religion, or race. It was a gift to everyone, knowing what we'd lost because of the great storm, The Unbalance. I wanted to give some hope back. Now I'm forced to work undercover until we can resolve this issue."

"How are you able to stay so well hidden? I mean, I barely recognize you all."

"With this." Tyberius shows me the plain-looking ring on his hand, then points to the one I'm wearing. "The ring that we gifted you is one that's been passed down from generations of your symbol."

I take my ring off and hold it up to the light. Its copper hue is dull, somewhat patinaed, and there are no other markings on it.

Tyberius takes it and taps the top. Then he pulls up a menu I'd not noticed before. "This nifty trinket has a pre-programmed alias designed specifically for you. Handy for uniform changes. Go ahead, try it out."

I slide the ring on my index finger and then look down at myself. I'm completely different now. I'm still the same height with broad shoulders and an athletic build. But my eye color is brown, my skin is much darker, and my hair is longer with colored beads woven in. The hole in my hand seems to magically mend with no sign of the glowing light.

I look at Tyberius in shock, and he chuckles.

"That's amazing!" I blurt.

"Yes," he says. "Your new alias. I took the liberty of programming it myself. These aliases will allow us to accomplish our missions."

"But why just one alias to select from?"

"We're working to develop more. Maybe soon we'll have additional options. Just be sure your alias isn't compromised."

I slide the ring off and place it in my pocket. "When you say missions, are you talking about the five of us?" I ask and sit down again.

"Well, not just us," Tyberius says. "There are many others involved and several are out there, on assignments as we speak."

"Like who?" I ask, wondering if I'd ever met any.

"There are hundreds working as spies, like Commander Taun and Herron," Albright says.

"What!" I say and nearly leap out of my chair. "They're the ones that sent us into those messes! They were trying to kill us."

"Well, that's not entirely accurate," Albright replies. "Orders come from higher up. Much of that is out of our control. Whether you realized it or not, Taun and Herron were working behind the scenes to save your life. But they have to appear adversarial. I apologize for that."

I nod, feeling a bit guilty then. "I think I understand why the Elites don't just kill us Immortals—I mean, Heliographi. They want to make it look real, but only on the battlefield. They want to avoid upsetting all the citizens. Is that right?"

"That's correct," Harriet says, speaking up for the first time. "With the Heliographi out of the way, there will be even less resistance at the Winter Solstice. The Elites can't just hold public executions. That would enrage the public, and they fear an uprising. People view us as heroes on both sides. Instead, the Elites have to kill us in a believable fashion, like war accidents or friendly fire."

I stand and walk around, trying to make sense of what I'm hearing. I once felt that the Day of the Nail was the most shocking thing I'd ever experienced. Now I realize how wrong I was.

"I do agree that the Day of the Nail is a barbaric ritual. I grant you that, Brindall," Albright says.

I look at him in surprise, and he gives me a quick, knowing smile. I could swear he'd just read my thoughts this time.

"Had you not been identified before your twenty-fourth birthday, you would have died, though," he continues. "The Heliographi, which is that inner light inside of you, would have move on to another host. It's what makes us an Immortal."

"Everything you've been told about Immortals is still true for the Heliographi," Kleegan says. "Immortal is just another name. You'll continue to grow more powerful throughout your life. As you practice, you will learn new things."

"Immortal…yet, human," I say. "We will live forever, yet we can still be killed, like Tripp and Drake. It sounds like another charade to me."

Albright purses his lips and takes a long, steady breath. "As you've witnessed, we are still flesh and bone and can be killed. If that happens, the Heliographi finds another person that matches its liking and starts over. Again, I am sorry about your friends Tripp and Drake."

"If we're so powerful, how come the mental signature collars are so effective?" I ask. "And how did you manage to unlock it without killing me?"

Albright holds up a small disc similar to the ones I'd been given by Varance. "I recently invented this device. It took a while, and it was a race to complete it. After we lost Drake and Tripp, we sensed that the Elites were finally making their move. I knew they were coming after you, so I chose not to wait any longer. Last night, we took the gamble, and thankfully it worked. You're now a free person."

I give him and the others a long look. "Thank you, I am grateful. I'm heartbroken about Tripp and Drake, but I'm still worried about my other friends. They won't last long if we don't do something."

Albright looks around the room at Tyberius, Kleegan and Harriet. "We brought you in as planned. It was all made to look like an accident. I believe the Elites will wash their hands of it and move on. We did the job well. Brindall, you are officially off the grid. You no longer exist in their minds."

Kleegan gives me a devilish grin. "This gives you the freedom to do things we desperately need help with. You can move around under the radar. We'll free your friends very soon."

"And my family? They'll be in danger without me now. Grior said he'd protect them even if I died in battle. But I don't trust that man."

"If you can wait a bit longer, we will free your family, too," Albright says. "I can use my authority to protect them for the time being. At the moment, we need to focus on your friends. The road ahead will be difficult as we move into the next phase of our plan. We will face challenges, but I think you're ready, Brindall. We need you, that's why you're here. We must solve this before the Winter Solstice, and you'll play a key part."

I hold Albright's gaze. I can see that he's on the verge of finally letting me in on something that not many people know about.

"What is your plan?" I ask.

Albright looks at the others again, then leans forward. "We plan to use a mass deactivation code on the citizens' collars, and I'm almost there. I only need a few more things, and that's what you're going to help me with. Right after you rescue your friends, that is."

THE SHADOW AGENT | CHAPTER 22

I sleep better that night than I have in a long time, perhaps my entire life. Having answers to many of the questions swirling in my mind sets me at ease, for the moment, anyway. But now I have new questions, primarily about my new mission to rescue my friends. What will my primary role be in this new organization, the Agency? How will I get to my friends, and can I help them in time?

But the thought that my first mission will be to rescue Shiloe, Vern and Grish gives me hope. Albright hadn't gone over any details yet, just that going undercover would be dangerous. But that does little to dissuade me. My friends' safety is all that matters, and the longer they spend on the battlefield, the greater their risk of dying. I feel an urgency pressing me forward. But in the back of my mind is my family, too. Being asked to wait before I can seek them out also worries me. Though I trust Albright now, I'm still anxious to bring them to safety.

The next morning, I'm greeted by Christian Albright in the mess hall. We sit and eat breakfast together, which is more of the dry vitamin-infused gruel and watered-down coffee. At least it's warm, though. Surrounding us are hundreds of other agents and Agency staff.

"You must wait until they're on the battlefield." Albright sets his coffee aside and holds my attention. I still struggle with the fact that I'm looking at an ally now, not the cold and calculating Gorgan Freemantle. "Your first target will be Shiloe," he continues. "Bring her home safely. I will be commanding the battlefield during that time. I'll give you as much cover as I can."

I think for a moment while fiddling with my mug. "How am I supposed to do this?"

"You'll have your new alias, of course, which is a high-ranking officer in the North's Elite Recon Brigade. I recommend you wear your cloak beneath your clothing for protection and quick access. That way, you'll have it handy in case you need it."

"That's going to be a tight fit in these fatigues." I look down at the military cargo pants and shirt I'm wearing. The reddish-gray striations woven into its fabric are meant to give some camouflage, though in truth, I know the garish pattern will be covered with mud in short order.

"It'll work. Trust me, I know." Albright gives me a wink, and I can only assume he's been through this same situation before. "You must find Shiloe on the battlefield. Make contact with her through Vishmu first, but only her. Then, use this device on her collar." Albright hands me the small disc he'd used to free me.

"I'm familiar with these, actually." I take the tiny disc and hold it up to the light.

Albright scrunches his gray eyebrows. "Oh, how so?" he asks with genuine interest.

"One of the enemy Immortals named Varance gave us several of them. We used them to sneak around without detection. Some sort of stealth technology, I think."

The perplexed look he gives me is one I haven't seen from him.

"She offered you a disruption disc?" he says.

"Is that what you call it?" I shrug. "Well, I guess so. It's much smaller and, I assume, less powerful than the one you used."

"Disruption discs are very hard to come by, very illegal too. I wonder how she was able to get her hands on so many. What were her terms, out of curiosity?"

"She wanted our group to swear fealty to her before she would free us. I said no."

"Interesting," Albright says. "I imagine her tune has changed, now that they've been freed by the Atrum. Don't expect any sympathy next time you meet her."

"I understand."

"Regardless, I will order a strike in the area. You must remove Shiloe's collar during that time, but only after you place the unlock disc. A decoy body must be used to cover our tracks. There's a lot to do in a short amount of time. This will be dangerous due to the live fire. Can you handle this mission?"

I place the unlock disc in my jacket. "Live fire I'm used to. I can handle it. What about Vern and Grish?"

"One at a time, Brindall. Otherwise, we risk failure."

"And it's also a risk to leave them on the battlefield too long," I say.

Christian grips my shoulder and gives it a squeeze. "I understand this. But we must stick to the plan. I have ways of protecting the others for a brief time, at least."

I give Albright a quick nod, then tilt my head. "Out of curiosity, why Shiloe first?" I sense something in Albright, something hidden in his voice, in his body language.

"We deem her the most important Heliographi of the three," Albright says, but he looks away as he says this. I catch a split second of guilt, I think.

I hold that thought for a moment, thinking it a bit morbid to place one person above another. But deep down, I'm glad it's Shiloe. "Assuming I succeed, how do we return?"

Albright pulls out the small holopad and brings up a three-dimensional map. He zooms in on an area and points to it. "Located here is a hidden passage. Your ring will open it. Just look for the symbol."

"Huh," I mutter and shake my head. "Hidden passages, cloaks, rings, symbols," I chuckle. "What's next?"

"It's there, Brindall. It'll lead you to the boarding platform. Keep Shiloe safe and I will meet you there. We're counting on you."

I sit back, starting to feel a bit overwhelmed now as I stare at Albright. More concerns begin to flitter into my thoughts, but the biggest one is my family, mainly Ben. "I know you say my family will be safe, but I won't wait long. Promise me you'll look after them till I finish these missions."

Albright raises his hands and clasps them together. "You have my promise. I will personally see to their safety. But first, you must save your friends if you want to help your family."

A few hours later, I board the highspeed train, wearing my new alias. I'm now a shadow agent on a mission. On board are several other soldiers, also wearing an alias and traveling to other missions. Along this back channel, our rail transport makes a few more stops, and before long, it's half full of men, women, and teenagers. Everyone is wearing the same uniform—red and gray striated fatigues, mostly as mid-level ranked officers. Some of the younger spies and privates who wear the lowest ranks likely won't make it through the day. I find myself wondering if they know this before I realize that I'm in the same situation.

As the train enters public thoroughfares, normal citizens finally begin to board. I'm now in enemy territory—even though I'm still in the North. Now that I know the Elites are running both sides, there's no difference between the North or South anymore, though the citizens don't know that.

The rest of the transport begins to fill with real troops, citizens who are being forced to fight. I hear wails and cries from loved ones saying goodbye, and I try to block it out. Families wish safety and hope to their loved ones as they're ferried off to one of the three theaters for battle. It's difficult to see the mothers leaving their families and the young teenage kids sitting alone, wide-eyed with uncertain looks. These kids are not soldiers and certainly aren't ready for war. Seeing this, and knowing the truth now, reinforces what I'm doing. Though my current mission is to free just one Heliographi at a time, I feel it's the first step toward a tipping point. I've never felt more resolve than I do right now.

The train stops several more times along the winding route between the Fault Line and the Belt Line Boroughs, and each time we pick up more troops. As we rocket toward the Front Line Borough, I see occasional breaks in the cave's ceiling, showing ominous flashes of lightning. Raindrops hammer the top of the speeding train, adding to the tension in my chest.

A few hours later, we arrive at the main boarding station for the Central Theater. Thousands of new troops are being brought in by the hour and I blend in with them, making my way up to the barrack districts.

I glance at my watch and review my orders. They are directions given directly from the 'higher-ups,' and I know Albright had a hand in it. I'm to report to Burn Battalion, J-Group at 0700 hours, first thing in the morning. The platoon leader is also a captain, and I'm to report directly to him. I'll be leading one of the platoons. One of the troops in that platoon just happens to be an Immortal by the name of Shiloe Van Saint. I already know that a trap has been set for J-Group that day on the battlefield.

I go over the assignment in my head for the tenth time that morning. First, I'll make the connection with Shiloe, then use the unlock disc provided by Albright. But this must be done just before the shelling starts. That's my signal, which will come from Albright himself. *You'll know it when you see it*, he'd told me that morning.

I've been given a decoy cloak. But the real trick is finding the body of a dead soldier, preferably one about the same height and weight, and getting it into the area of incoming fire *before* I engage the unlock disc for Shiloe's collar.

Sounds easy, right? I joke to myself in a Vern-like chuckle.

I'm at the barracks within the hour. I find my bunk and quarters—captains have their own room—and sit at a small, square desk. I'm anxious, like I'm about to start this whole thing all over again. Bad memories come flooding back in a rush, and I have to force them down. I've been through this routine so many times, but it feels different now. In the morning, I'll be back on the battlefield, only this time I'll be saving the life of my good friend, Shiloe.

Early the next morning, I meet Burn Battalion in the barracks courtyard and wait for our platoon captain. He's a younger man, probably not much older than me. He's short and squatty with a low center of gravity. His jaw is set with a jutting chin, and his skin color is dark, with matching hair and scruff. He speaks to us in short, barking commands. He glances around at the troops, his eyes finally settling on me.

"Captain Burris, that you?" He eyes me sharply, scrutinizing my stature, then gives a quick salute. The rest of the troops wait in the yard, silently staring at us. I acknowledge him with my own awkward salute.

"I'm platoon leader Haff. They said you'd be here." Haff pulls some orders from his vest pocket, turns them around a few times, trying to focus on the text. "Says you're leadin' J-Group. That sound right?"

I give him a nod, wondering if he has any idea that he's leading these people into a trap. I feel the sudden urge to warn him. I know that most of these troops will be dead in less than an hour.

"Good, stay to my left flank," Haff barks. He waves to the troops in the back, and we start marching.

Along the way, we meet up with several other platoons. I'm greeted by the sounds of war in the distance. There's a light rain as we leave the covered shelter of the caves and enter the open canyon pit. Captain Haff orders everyone onto the transport, and I help get the soldiers lined up. I continue to scan the crowd for Shiloe, but I see no sign of her.

The transport ride is bumpy, as concussive explosions rock the air. It pushes our skiff up and down, causing several troops to look ill. I close my eyes and search the nearby transports for any mental signatures from other Immortals, but still, I sense nothing.

My hand brushes across the unlock disc in my pocket, and I go over the plan yet again. I've memorized the motions and know them forward and backward. Now I just hope I can locate Shiloe and time everything just right.

Our transport comes to a halt, then lowers and settles down. I order troops from the craft immediately and lead J-Group to the battlefield, where we hold our position and wait. The command comes through my earpiece with orders to maintain the line till further instructions. I face my lieutenant and give him the command. Then I turn and leave.

I run behind the platoon as the anticipation of battle increases. The sound of artillery can be heard in the distance: deep booms that shake the mud beneath my boots. I can sense panic setting in with the nearby troops. I know they're on edge; most of them are new to this war. All it will take is a single nearby explosion, and they'll scatter in fear. I must find Shiloe.

I march through the ranks of soldiers, sending out messages with my thoughts. I begin to wonder if I've misread Albright's directions. I'm about to turn and go over to the next platoon when I hear the high-pitched whistling of incoming fire. I'm forced to dive and roll as explosions hit the ground near me. Then, I'm running for my life.

As I sprint through the mud and rain, I feel a mental signature tug at me. I come to a full stop, sliding in the mud and nearly tumble onto my backside. I sense another Immortal nearby, then another. But they're beyond the front line and in enemy territory.

This wasn't part of the plan.

I'm forced to improvise now. I feel for my cloak and brush across it tucked under my fatigues. I strip away my uniform and reach for the hood, and pull it over my head, instantly vanishing. I race to the front line, leaping over soldiers and across pitted craters—straight into enemy territory. I follow the mental signature, my intuitive voice guiding me around the artillery and certain death.

Soon, I'm nearing the signal and slow to look for signs of Shiloe. When I top the edge of a smoking crater, I stumble into a platoon of Southern troops. Beyond, I see an Immortal pinned by the troops with heavy vehicles bearing down. Railgun fire saturates the air around me, and I use my cloak to block the rounds. I can also see an opposing Immortal mixed in with the Southern troops. I move behind the heavy vehicles and ram my shoulder into the leading tank and overturn it, causing immediate chaos.

The area begins to clear as I cut a swath through the enemy ranks. With most of the enemy troops fleeing, I scan the field for the Immortals. I see Grish and Vern, then I see Shiloe engaged in combat with the other Immortal. I don't have to see who it is—I can already sense that it's Varance. She has an arm wrapped around Shiloe. Then she swings her glowing scepter and hits Shiloe on the forehead. Shiloe slumps to the ground, unconscious.

Then, they both disappear.

The incoming artillery continues. It peppers the area where Shiloe and Varance had been standing. Chunks of mud and earth rise up as the rounds pulverizes the ground. With Shiloe gone, I decide to go after Vern instead. I race toward him and tackle him to the ground.

"Vern! It's me!" I yell to him.

He looks at me in confusion at first, since my disguise is still engaged. But then his eyes grow wide in shock and disbelief. "How! They said you died. We got the news just—"

"No time to explain. We have to move!" I lift him to his feet and place the unlock disc on his collar. The signature collar instantly drops away, and I can see he wants to ask questions. But I hold up my hand. "Draw your cloak and follow me!"

Together, we sprint from the area, dodging between blasts until I locate a downed soldier. I kneel and examine the body. It's roughly the same size as Vern, with matching dark skin but badly mangled. I rip the old collar off of it, then replace it with Vern's collar. Then I pull the decoy cloak out and wrap the body. I throw it over my shoulder and plow onward. The voice guides me, and I follow it. I stop and listen for incoming fire, knowing I must get the body as close to ground zero as possible. Otherwise, the remains might be identified.

Seconds before the ground erupts, I hoist the body off my shoulder then we race away. When the artillery strike hits home, everything is pulverized, nearly vaporized in fact.

We run a good distance and find a quiet spot in a crater. I pull the tracker from my belt as Vern bumps me with his elbow. "You wanna tell me what this is all about!" he hollers. "Where exactly are we goin'?"

I turn to face him. "Just trust me, alright?"

It begins to rain down in heavy sheets as I follow the tracker. We slip and tumble across the cratered battlefield until I locate a chasm that seems to have been cut out of the cliff face. I notice a strange

symbol roughly carved into the rock and I can barely make it out between the lightning flashes. I press my ring into the etched symbol, and it lights up. The rock separates, and a passage seems to magically appear from thin air. I shove Vern inside and follow as the rock seals shut behind us.

The sounds of battle are muffled now, and the cave walls seem to press in on us. It makes me feel a bit uneasy as if I'm being smothered.

"Stay close and keep quiet," I whisper.

Some areas of the passage are so narrow that we're forced to crawl. The path tilts and veers downward as we creep along. I stop occasionally to listen, but only the low croon of a haunting breeze interrupts the distant sounds of war.

Some thirty minutes later, we approach a larger chamber, and I see some firelight ahead. Vern and I approach cautiously and stop. Before us is a group of five people. Harriet, Kleegan and Tyberius are flanked by two Agency troops.

"Timeout," Vern finally says and pulls at my arm. "I think I deserve an explanation, man. I've been quiet, I've followed you. It's time to talk, Brin. Who are these people, and where are we goin'?"

Tyberius steps forward and puts his ring on. Vern's eyes light up with recognition. Then Harriet and Kleegan do the same. Standing before us are our old instructors: Miss Henak, Triton and Kiff.

The three instructors move forward and greet Vern with a smile and a clap on his back.

Tyberius faces Vern. "I wish we could stay and explain everything right here, but now isn't the time. This isn't a safe zone. We should move on."

"What do you mean?" I ask. "Who else would know about this passage, let alone be able to access it?"

"The Atrum," Tyberius says as he starts walking.

Vern and I follow behind Kiff as we begin to trot along the path. It continues to undulate as we move. It feels like hours later when we finally near a cliff wall and stop. Tyberius locates a hidden keypad and punches in a code. We enter a metallic corridor and move through a series of stairs and vector accelerators until finally arriving at the Agency war room.

Inside is Albright, waiting. His hands are steepled in front of his face as he sits hunched over a monitor, watching it intently. He stands immediately to face us, takes one look at Vern and then glances at me. "What happened?"

I sense the split second of panic in his expression, but it's quickly replaced with his normally calm demeanor.

"Varance got to Shiloe before I could," I begin and wring my hands under Albright's steady gaze. "She managed to subdue her with the scepter. I'm sorry, Albright. I…things just didn't go as planned. No one was where they were supposed to be. I found Vern and decided to free him instead. I didn't want to come back empty-handed."

"Can someone help me understand what's happening?" Vern says and holds up his hands and places them on his head. "Did you just say Albright? Is this Christian Albright?"

"This was a rescue mission for Shiloe," I say. "Sorry, Vern. No offense, but we're doing this one person at a time. What do you know about her? What did I miss?"

Vern shrugs. "I didn't notice much. I was too busy runnin' for my life!" He sits down with a huff and leans forward, placing his head in his hands. He tugs at his dark, curly hair nervously.

I walk over and place both hands on his shoulders. "Hey. It's good to see you again, Vern. I'm sorry about all this. I just couldn't explain at the time."

"Well, maybe you can make it up to me by explaining how you're still alive," Vern chuckles.

"I'll let the others fill you in on that. Right now, what you need to know is that you're a free person."

Vern turns to face the others, but his eyes linger on Albright, as if he knows he's the ringleader. Vern holds his arms up, then rests his hands behind his neck. "Alright, let's hear it. Who are you and what is this place?"

"This is called the Agency. It's a secret group sworn to protect the human race. My name is Christian Albright, but you might remember me as Supreme Commander Gorgan Freemantle."

Vern holds Albright's gaze. "I don't know whether to laugh or take you all seriously. You're *the* Christian Albright? Is this a joke? Man, my head is spinning."

Albright gives Vern a quick nod. "I'm sorry for my shortness right now. We're glad you're here, and we'll fill you in momentarily. I need to know what else you saw today. Are you certain there's nothing more to tell regarding Shiloe?"

Vern rubs his chin, considering. "Like I said, it was Varance. She was the only enemy Immortal I saw on the battlefield today."

Albright starts pacing the room with his hands behind his back.

"What're you thinking?" I ask him and look around at the others.

Harriet, Tyberius and Kleegan remain silent and wait for Albright to speak.

Albright eventually stops pacing and turns to face us. "I believe the Atrum kidnapped Shiloe and are holding her for ransom."

I watch Vern's reaction as Albright tells him the full truth about the wars. Although we'd already guessed most of it, Vern is still furious. It takes all of us to keep him from rushing out and tracking down the people responsible.

Eventually, Vern is shown to his quarters after the debrief. But I stay in the control room, wanting a few more words with Albright.

"How do you manage to conceal the Agency? Seems like these Elites would have some idea of its existence."

"There are some rumors floating around. I've managed to keep our group below their radar, so to speak. The Elites' main goal is to eliminate all Immortals—the Heliographi, that is. I have spies in place to keep an eye on them."

"Which would mean they do too?" I ask.

"Probably."

"Here in the Agency?"

"Perhaps."

I wonder what might happen if the full might of the Northern and Southern Coalitions came down on the Agency, though. What if the Elites discovered the Agency and turned their combined might against it?

"Are you concerned that the Atrum might have spies too?" I ask.

"Yes. However, I'm almost certain the Atrum aren't working with the Elites." Albright pauses for a moment, then straightens his back. "What is it you really want to ask me, Brindall?"

I take a few seconds to compose myself, hoping I don't offend him with the question I'm about to ask. "You…seem to be insistent on finding Shiloe. More so than Vern and Grish. Why?" I sense the same split second of hesitation in him again. It's brief, but it's there.

"Because I believe that Shiloe has a larger role in the future of our race, the Heliographi. Maybe even the future of humankind."

"Is there more to her that you're not telling me?" I ask.

I watch him closely, and I can tell there is indeed more. Though I believe this man is honest, there's obviously something about Shiloe he isn't telling me.

Albright squares his shoulders, then tugs at his fatigues. “It’s of no concern at the moment. We need to get her back, and that is our main priority right now.”

“But how? We have no idea where to look for her.”

“I have a back channel with the Atrum.”

I narrow my eyes, then tilt my head. “That sounds dangerous. Why didn’t you say so before?”

“Because you didn’t need to know, and yes, it is dangerous. I only use that channel in dire need, and now is such a time.”

“Who is your contact?”

“A lady by the name of Riven Sybold, the leader of their group. She is a very powerful and cunning Atrum. We must proceed with caution.”

CHAPTER 23

I sit with Vern in our living quarters later that evening. I can still see the shock on his face, the disbelief in his expression. That was me just a few days ago. But in the back of my mind, I can't stop thinking of Shiloe. More specifically, the way Albright had seemed to prioritize her over Vern and Grish. And now, I wonder about this powerful Atrum named Sybold, who has apparently kidnapped Shiloe.

"How is this even possible?" Vern asks and I turn my attention to him. "I never thought we'd be free of that lovely collar," he continues. "I just didn't expect it to happen like this, so soon and all. Now I'm free…except I'm not, I guess. Does this group expect us to pay off this debt?"

"There's no catch, as far as I can tell. They offered to let me go free if I wanted. I just couldn't leave you all behind, or my family. I mean, where would I go? Besides, the more I thought about what this organization is doing, the more I want to be a part of it. The Agency seems to be a good group of people. They've taken a vow to protect and shepherd the human race. Sounds like something we should get on board with, right?"

"Yeah," Vern chuckles and rubs at the missing collar. "I guess…me too. I want to make those Elites pay for what they've done to us." Vern tugs at his curly hair, though I noticed the distant look on his face.

I sit back and hold up my hands and give him a quick smile. "What is it? You tired of looking at me or something?" Then I give him a more serious look. "We're back together. We're family, Vern.

And we need to bring our girls home safe. You and I are going after Grish tomorrow."

"Yeah, I know...*I know*." Vern pushes back in his seat. "I'm just struggling to understand all of this. You know me, I'd never leave our girls behind."

I give him another smile, then a slap on the shoulder. "Good, because I need you. Albright has plans for us."

"Albright..." Vern says and lets the thought taper off. "Wow. The legend, right here among us. It's kinda shocking, knowing he was, *is*, Freemantle. And Triton, Kiff and Henak too? My mind is blown, man."

"You'll have time to grovel later. Right now, we need to focus on Grish. Get some rest."

"Hold on, Brin. I have to ask about our families. How long do we wait?" Vern's stare doesn't waver, and I can see his fingertips dig into his large biceps as he holds my gaze.

"Albright has promised to protect them for the moment, until we can free Shiloe and Grish. They need us, Vern. The Agency needs our help to free these millions of citizens. We can save so many lives from this war by getting the truth out there."

"And what happens if this *Agency* decides not to let us go after our families?" Vern retorts, and I see the doubt in his eyes. "We've been lied to so much—I don't know if I can trust anyone right now."

"I hear you, Vern." I reach over and grip his arm. "But I think we can trust Albright and the Agency. Apparently, we're part of some ancient race, a family of sorts. Albright, Tyberius, Kleegan and Harriet are part of that family. I sense they'll look out for us."

"I trust you, Brin. And if you trust them, then so do I."

"Good," I say. "We'll go after our families soon, I promise. At the moment, we have to take Albright's word that he can protect them." I reach out and shake Vern's hand, then I give him a hug. "I'm really glad you're back."

Vern and I are up early the next morning. After a quick briefing, we're out the door. It feels good to have him around again. His cheerful nature sets me at ease as we head back into the Central Theater to recover Grish.

The plan is much the same as yesterday—find Grish, use the unlock disc on her collar, then find a downed soldier to replace her. Thanks to Albright's inside informant, we know there'll be another ambush today. The goal is to position ourselves close to Grish and wait. When we get the signal, we make our move. But as I focus on Grish, Shiloe is still on my mind.

According to Albright, the Atrum will continue to hold Shiloe but won't harm her. In a strange way, she's safe in our enemies' hands, if one were to consider the Atrum our enemy now. But I don't like it. They've obviously gone to great lengths to capture her by using an unlock disc on her collar and placing a body on the battlefield. It means that Shiloe is now free from this war, too. But I question why the Atrum would take such an aggressive step now. I sense that Albright knows but won't say.

But despite his secretive nature, I like Albright. I feel compelled to do great things when near him. He seems to inspire those around him in a way I can't explain. His accomplishments are legendary already, and the Skylight System isn't even complete. He is a leader, one that demands respect, though he doesn't ask for any.

Vern's alias is clever. He's now a light-skinned male with long dark hair, similar to my true appearance in fact. *We just swapped places*, he jokes and slaps me on the back. We both have a good laugh as we prepare for that morning's mission.

We go through the same routine: donning our cloaks beneath our armor and uniform. Once again, the rail transport ferries us through the different boroughs, gathering up new recruits and soldiers. Once we make it to the Central Theater, we sit in a tent near our platoon and wait for our captain to arrive. I can tell by the blank expression on Vern's face that he's experiencing the same thing I had just recently. Being on the other side of this war is a strange feeling.

"Just stay close until we can locate Grish," I whisper to him with a nudge.

When our captain arrives, we snap to attention and move into place. It's like a carbon copy of the day before as we go through the motions and board the transport. No matter how many times I go through this exercise, my stomach churns. But I wonder if it's because I'm worried for the other troops around me now. I sense that Vern feels the same, though his expression is solemn.

We hit the ground running as soon as the transport lands. The shelling explodes all around us, leaving our troops little time to set up behind the earth berms. Vern and I race behind the lines as railgun fire whizzes overhead. We stay low and scan the battlefield with our thoughts, hoping to find signs of Grish. Vern grabs my arm and juts his chin in a southerly direction.

We find a quiet area and slip our hoods on and vanish. Soon, we're racing across the battlefield, slipping through the mud and rain. We pause occasionally to gain our bearings, then wait for a lightning strike or a bomb blast as we move across enemy lines.

I feel gun-shy, as they say, and keep expecting something bad to happen. My muscles are tense, as if in preparation. It's a horrible feeling and I try to push it from my thoughts.

We sprint deeper into enemy territory, past platoons of Southern troops and heavy mechs. I continue to reach out for Grish and wonder why she's so far behind enemy lines. *Had the Elites sent her on a suicide mission we didn't know about?*

Then suddenly, I see her.

Grish is sitting alone, her legs pulled up to her chest and rocking back-and-forth as explosions erupt around her. Vern hollers as we slide in the mud next to her. I grab her by the shoulders and look into her eyes, but she doesn't seem to notice me. I can sense that she's lost her focus, that she's closed herself off.

"She's lost it, man," Vern says with concern in his voice.

I shake my head and pull her closer to me. "Grish! Snap out of it!"

"We gotta move, Brin!" Vern yells. "Artillery's gettin' closer!"

"Wait, the timing has to be perfect, Vern! Remember, this has to be done right."

I start counting the seconds between artillery rounds. "Vern, see if you can find a body. We need to have a decoy ready."

Vern races off as I place the unlock disc on her collar. It beeps and snaps open. I pick Grish up and carry her away as the shelling grows closer. A few seconds later, Vern slides through the mud with a downed soldier. I immediately replace the collar on the downed soldier with Grish's. Then, Vern heaves the body into a nearby crater and I throw the decoy cloak in behind it. We dive and roll out of the area as explosions hit the ground and vaporize everything. I pull the tracker out and locate the hidden cave portal. We race to the cliff face where I press my ring into the symbol. It slides open, and we're tumbling into the cave, out of breath. The portal door slams shut behind us.

We lay there, breathing heavily and not saying anything in the dark.

When I roll over to check on Grish, her skin is white and cold to the touch. "I think she's in shock."

"What's that mean?" Vern asks. "Can we fix it?"

I prop Grish against the cave wall. "Maybe we can reach her with Vishmu. It's the only thing I can think of."

Vern and I sit cross-legged across from her in the dark tunnel, the sound of war just beyond. I take her right hand, and Vern takes her left hand. Then Vern and I join hands as I drop into meditation. I focus my thoughts, calling out to her. I hear Vern do the same.

At first, I sense only emptiness. Grish seems lost and in a dark place. It's like I can see her inner light floating alone in space. Losing everyone has taken a toll on her. She's on the edge, like her will is empty. I'm afraid that I won't be able to reach her, that she's already given up. But if I can just let her know the truth that Vern, Shiloe and I are still alive…throw her a lifeline—a psychic rope to pull her back. I can see her. *She's here!* I reach out, calling her name and letting her know we're okay.

Together, Vern and I continue. Minutes pass, and it feels like eons as we wait for her to respond. Finally, I reach her and lead her away from the darkness and back to the light.

Then suddenly, the three of us are awake, and sitting in the dark cave. Grish finally opens her eyes and takes a long, shuddering breath. She looks at Vern, then at me. Her eyes well with tears and she leaps at Vern, then me. Grish hugs us both in racking sobs.

After several minutes, she lets go. "I…I was gone. I've never been that afraid."

Vern chuckles, then wipes his own eyes with the back of his hand. "Yeah, it's good to see you, Grish. Thought we'd lost you there for a second."

I ruffle her red hair and then playfully tug at her ponytails. "Welcome back, Grish."

We sit there on the cavern floor, caked in mud and staring at each other. Grish finally laughs, a light trill that fills the small cave. It's something I've never heard from her before. "Thank you, Brin…Vern. Thanks—"

For what seems like the first time since I've known her, I don't hear that familiar, spiteful tone in her voice. Instead, there's a true joy, a happiness that I had felt when my collar had been removed.

Grish scoops up a handful of mud and flings it at Vern, and it sticks to his cheek. Then she does the same to me, and soon, we're flinging mud and laughing.

Even though I know we need to move, I let the mudslinging and laughing go on for a few minutes before pulling Vern and Grish to their feet.

"Are you going to tell me 'bout this?" she asks as she stands. "How is it you're both alive, and my collar's gone?"

"When we get to base, I'll explain everything," I say and lead the way down the passage.

After several wrong turns—and a few dead ends—we eventually find the secret transit rail and board it. A few hours later, we're walking up to the Agency headquarters. I breathe a sigh of relief when we hit the control center. Waiting there is Harriet, Kleegan and Tyberius, but they're all wearing their disguises. They immediately pull us in and check for injuries.

"I'm good," I say. "But Grish might need some attention—"

"I'm fine," she replies, "Thanks to Brin and Vern, I'm okay. I owe you both. Thanks for coming after me."

"Aw, hush up, Grish," Vern says and grips her narrow shoulders. "You know you'd have done the same."

She leans against the wall and slides down into a sitting position. Her skin is still paler than normal. "Can you please explain all of this now?" She motions around the room, then points at her neck and the missing collar. "And how did you three get here? I take it you're all more than instructors?"

"As of now, Grish, you're off the grid, just like the rest of us," Tyberius says. "The Elites think we're dead, and we've taken great care over the years to ensure that illusion remains intact."

"That was their goal anyway," I say. "They want all Immortals dead."

"And we're going after our families next," Vern says.

"I could care less 'bout them," Grish says. "I'm just interested in why I'm here, along with our old instructors."

Tyberius holds up his hands. "In good time, we will see to your families soon. For now, we have a few items to take care of first. We're asking you three to trust us."

"Do you think the Atrum might make an attempt at our families, like they did with Shiloe?" I ask.

"No, I don't think so," Tyberius says. "They'd have to infiltrate behind hundreds of miles of enemy lines. Besides, the Atrum don't care about such things. They have more valuable targets, no offense, of course. Your family is of little concern to them. Whatever they're up to, it doesn't involve family members."

Vern and I sit and listen to the same spiel as before. Tyberius, Harriet and Kleegan reveal their true identities and explain the Agency and its mission to Grish. She listens wide-eyed when hearing the truth behind the Frontline War. I can sense her anger and know it won't take much to convince Grish to join the Agency.

Thirty minutes later, I'm back in my quarters. I shower and change, then I gather with Grish and Vern in an outdoor commons area. It's much quieter than any other living complex we've lived in. There is no smoke in the air, no exploding bombs or sounds of war. I feel uncomfortable, oddly enough. The stillness doesn't feel right after being engaged in battle for so long.

I glance at the other two. Vern sits uncomfortably on a stone bench, his head bowed and hands gripping the stone so tight I can see the white flush of his fingers. Grish sits opposite of me with her cloak wrapped tight and rocking back and forth.

"We're not done yet," I say.

"Yeah, I know," Vern says. "I was hoping to get some rest. But we're not leaving Shiloe out there."

"So, we're goin' after her, I take it?" Grish says.

"Soon," I say. "We're bringing her home and you're coming along."

The next morning, we're all back in the command center, sitting around the old wooden table with Tyberius. It's early, but there's still plenty of activity around the Agency base. Staff and personnel rush around, and I wonder if some of these people ever sleep.

"I don't understand why Varance tried to help us, then kidnapped Shiloe," Grish says.

Tyberius taps an index finger to his lower lip as he sits back and considers. "The Atrum can be very deceptive. We've learned that much over the centuries. There's usually an ulterior motive in everything they do, which makes it difficult to trust them. But Varance made her offer before she was freed. Thanks to Albright's high rank, he has learned that the Atrum have decided to bring their Immortals in as well. What was her offer?"

"She would free us if we swore allegiance to her," I say.

"Preposterous, huh?" Vern chimes in.

"The audacity," Grish says.

Tyberius gives a few nods. "It's unfortunate that the Atrum have such dark motives. Otherwise, they'd make a good ally. We've been at odds with them for millennia now, and I don't think that will ever change."

The door opens, and Christian Albright strides into the room. He's still wearing his disguise as the Supreme Commander, Gorgan Freemantle. He stops in front of Grish and extends his hand. She stands awkwardly and greets him. I can see her shell-shocked expression—her eyes are wide and her hands fidget.

She stumbles through her greeting. "I…It's nice to meet you, Christian, or is it Mister Albright?"

"Please, just Albright will do," he says and removes the ring, causing his appearance to revert back to his slightly younger age with cropped hair and piercing blue eyes. "Have a seat."

We settle in, waiting to hear his plan. I feel anxious again, like I'm going through yet another battle briefing.

"First, let me say that we're glad you're all here and safe. It's been our plan for some time to free you and bring you into the Agency. Unfortunately, we didn't get the unlock discs finished in time to save Tripp and Drake. But it's crucial that we free Shiloe now."

"Are we officially part of the Agency, then?" Vern asks. "I mean, no swearing in or ritual?"

Albright smiles and places a hand on Vern's shoulder. "As long as we're all clear on our main goal, which is helping other citizens, then there's no need for any formalities. Do each of you understand this?"

I watch Grish and Vern, but neither says a word.

"Good," Albright says. "Then we need say no more. Now, about Shiloe and the Atrum. Though we're not entirely sure what their full motive is, we do have some ideas. We've scheduled a special meeting. Are you prepared for this?"

I look at Grish and Vern again.

"Yes," I say. "we're committed to whatever it takes to get Shiloe back."

"Excellent," Albright says. He gives the three of us a long look. His piercing blue eyes seem to search my soul, as if trying to verify our commitment to the Agency. "You must keep your thoughts closed. The Atrum will try to pry and steal any secrets they can. Where we're going, no one can be trusted. Understood?"

"What are they after?" Grish asks.

Albright places his hands behind his back and pauses for a second. "We'll know very soon. We leave within the hour. Brindall. Please stay for a moment. I'd like to discuss our plans with you alone."

RESCUE MISSION | CHAPTER 24

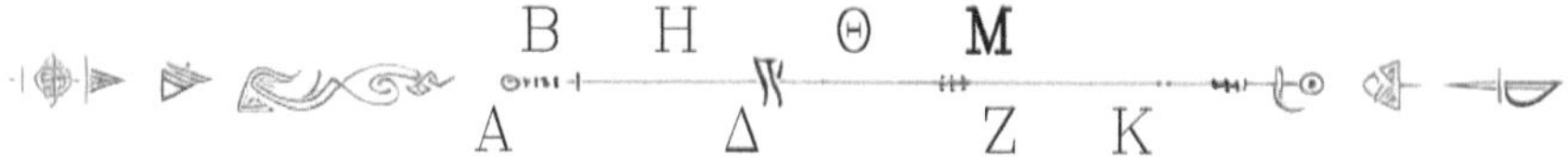

I hang back as the others file out of the control room. Once everyone is gone, Albright shuts the door and sits down at the large round table and motions for me to have a seat. I find my chair behind the symbol of the 'M' and settle in apprehensively.

"Is there something wrong?" I ask.

Albright steeples his fingers in front of his face and holds my gaze. "I have a plan in place, but I didn't want to discuss it in front of the others just yet."

I fidget with my cloak, feeling a bit nervous. "What is it?"

"The Atrum want our vessels. All of them."

"In return for Shiloe?"

"That's right."

"I assume that's out of the question?"

"Yes. This is something I cannot do, even as much as I want Shiloe back safe and sound, we cannot give up this much."

"Speaking of the vessels, what are they exactly?"

Albright stands and pushes in his chair. "Let's just say they are not of this world. Each one is imbued with the essence of a celestial being. They have been gifted to the Heliographi to guide and protect us."

I'm not sure what to say at that. I'd known they were special, but this takes me by surprise. I'd heard the voices, and now it makes sense. But a paranormal artifact?

"Tyberius told us that we had to figure out how to unlock them on our own," I say.

"That much is true. I cannot help you in this. The sooner, the better, I might add."

A soft chuckle escapes my lips, and I find myself wondering why this clan's rules are so strict. "Can you give me a hint at least?"

"I would not dare do such a thing in this plane of existence anyway. You must take matters into your own hands, Brindall." Albright gives me a wink. "Regarding our plan, I have a proposal for you, one that I hope you will consider."

I sit forward expectantly. "Let's hear it."

"I believe that all your training has brought you to this point. What I propose is that you lead your group into the Atrum's base and rescue Shiloe, while Tyberius, Kleegan, Harriet and I distract them."

"But…they'll be expecting all of us."

"Perhaps not," Albright says, a mischievous grin on his weathered face. "As of now, you three are officially deceased. What if that's all they know? The Atrum might suspect something, but I believe we can keep them occupied."

I can see now that Albright has been planning this approach for a while. It appears that he wants me to lead this mission without him. I take only a few seconds to consider, then quickly stand. "Of course, we'll do it. I know Grish and Vern wouldn't walk away from Shiloe either. We'll bring her home."

Albright stands and strides over to shake my hand. "Excellent. Now, let's discuss the specifics of this plan."

After my talk with Albright, I meet Grish and Vern at our apartment.

"He wants the three of us to go into the Atrum base alone?" Grish whispers. She sits forward in the rickety chair at my dining table.

"I dunno," Vern says. "Sounds pretty risky. Don't you think?"

"I sit back, arms crossed, and give them a reproachful look. "So, you'd both rather leave Shiloe there?"

"Come on, man," Vern says. "I never said that. Of course not. Just…sounds pretty aggressive."

"Look." I scoot my chair forward. "We're ready for this. We've been through a lot worse. It's like Albright said, this is what we've been trained for. We have to bring Shiloe back. If he thinks it'll work, then who are we to argue?"

Grish chews at her lip. Then she holds up her hands. "To hell with it. Just tell me what to do."

I give Vern a look, and he shrugs. "Works for me."

I give them each a clap on the back, then pull out a tracker device Albright had given me, and I set it on the table. "This is the location of the Atrum's base. It's in the York Borough, below the rim wall of the canyon. We'll take the hidden rail as far as we can, then we're on foot. Tyberius says there's a secret passage below the Hell's Gate Borough that they've been working on. It'll take us close to the Atrum base. Supposedly, Albright will start bartering with the Atrum around noon in another location. We have till then to figure out how to break Shiloe out."

"And that's where Albright thinks they're holding her?" Vern asks, nodding at the dot highlighted on the holographic map.

"Yes, and we can't use Vishmu to track her or speak to each other. Otherwise, the Atrum might hear us."

"Perfect," Grish says. "That should make things interesting. By the way, what did the Atrum want for Shiloe?"

"Our vessels," I say. "All of them."

"Why not," Grish huffs. "We can't figure 'em out anyway."

I hold up a hand. "Actually, I have something to say about that."

"What? Did Albright decide to tell you?" Vern jokes.

"Not exactly. But what he did tell me sounded like a riddle."

"Which was what?" Grish asks.

"Just that he wouldn't dare tell me in this plane of existence. He also said I have to take matters into my own hands."

Both Grish and Vern look at each other, then back to me with blank expressions.

I shake my head at them. "Just bring your vessels with you in case I figure it out."

We gather in one of the lower chambers of the Agency base. Kleegan, Harriet, Tyberius and Albright are all there waiting when we arrive. All seven of us are wearing our Lucem cloaks, since there's no need for Northern Coalition garb for this mission.

I'm beginning to learn how vast the network of tunnels is when Tyberius pulls up a holographic map. Below the main battlefield of each theater, I see hundreds of tunnels snaking out and covering hundreds of kilometers. It's apparent the Agency had been busy over the last few decades developing the hidden passage system.

"So, we're splitting up when we hit this point?" I ask Tyberius and point at a network of tunnels just outside the Atrum base.

"Yes. We'll take our own rail system as far as we can. Then we're on foot from there."

Albright moves ahead of us, leading the way and holding his hand aloft to light the tunnel. I notice the striations of the walls are a mix of velvet red clay and gray shale. The green glow from the shale ferns casts a gentle light on the puddles of water that seep from the walls. The sound of dripping water echoes down the tunnels, and an earthy scent hits my nose.

We board the rail. It's small with just one personnel cabin. The transport shudders, then begins to glide forward. I sit near Grish and Vern, but my gaze never leaves Albright. He shuts his eyes, and I can tell he's in a session of Vishmu. I glance at Vern and Grish, then close my eyes and do the same.

Time seems to pass slowly. Though we're only fifty or so kilometers from the Northern Boroughs and the Front Line Borough, it seems to take hours to get there. But eventually, the rail transport slows to a stop, and we all hop out somewhere below the Hell's Gate Borough.

We start our trek with Albright leading the way, then Grish, Vern, and me, followed by Harriet and Kleegan, with Tyberius bringing up the rear. It isn't long before I hear muffled thunderclaps in the distance, mixed with artillery, as we approach the frontline. Occasionally, the ground quivers from a blast, reminding me that the war above continues to steal innocent lives.

I'm constantly glancing at my tracker to get a sense of where we're heading, which is directly toward the York Borough. Areas of the passage pinch down to just a meter in some spots, and the trail undulates up and down like a wave. We work our way deeper into the bowels of the tunnel system. On more than one occasion, the path splits, and soon, I'm turned around, even with the tracking device. Every time Albright comes to a fork, he doesn't hesitate. Occasionally, he stops to use his ring to open another passage. Eventually, we're deep enough that the sounds of war are gone, and I wonder how much deeper Albright plans to take us.

Finally, we slow to a stop. Albright turns to gather everyone around him. He holds his hand aloft, the red burning glow from his palm lights the area in an eerie way. "Here we are. The point of no return. Are you three prepared? Once we begin, we are committed."

I glance at Grish and Vern, then at the tracker and the red dot where Shiloe is supposed to be. I give Albright a nod.

He grips my shoulder. "Remember. Keep your minds closed. The Atrum will be listening. Some of them are older, and their essence has been around for a long time. They are powerful entities. Don't let your guard down."

Albright turns and continues down a side tunnel followed by Tyberius, Harriet and Kleegan.

I let a few quiet seconds pass before turning back to Grish and Vern. "We ready?"

Grish chews at her lip nervously and Vern doesn't look me in the eyes.

"Come on, you two. We need to focus." I stride past them, shaking my head, and lead the way down the passage.

After several twists—and twenty or so minutes later—I slow and take a knee to observe the path ahead. The passage we're on opens up into a series of large chambers. The trail continues out and into the drum-shaped rooms that measure perhaps fifty or so meters in diameter. Above are stasis domes and hundreds of pod-like structures that cantilever out from the curved walls. The trail weaves through the string of chambers and out of sight.

I turn to the others and pull them close. "According to this tracker, Shiloe is somewhere down there. If we get separated for some reason, make your way back to this spot. Think you two can remember this location?"

Grish shrugs. "Sure…maybe."

"Vern?" I ask.

"Yeah, got it. But we're not gonna get separated."

"Probably not, but just in case." I give him a playful shove and smile at Grish. "Okay. Let's move. Stay close."

We cloak and blend into the dim surroundings. I lead the way onto the open path and follow it. The trail is about three meters wide and spirals down into the darkness below. When I get closer, I can see large pools of stagnant water at the bottom. Once we make it to the ground level, the stench hits my nostrils. I cup a hand over my nose but keep moving.

At the bottom, I pause to gain my bearings. There are a few shale ferns giving off some turquoise light. They reflect off the large pools, which are calm with only the occasional drip from a sidewall. I glance at the tracker and maneuver around the pools, clinging to the rock walls where the trail is too narrow.

"We're close," I whisper to the others.

The passage in front of me snakes through tightening walls, and a cool breeze gushes out, along with an earthy scent of stale mildew. Our cloaked forms glide through the darkness like wraiths, and we finally emerge into a dead-end chamber. It's small, like a holding cell. In the center is a holopad.

I stay near the back, glancing around in the darkness.

The holopad is powered on and blinking.

I can sense the tension between Grish and Vern, probably thinking the same thing as me: this feels like a trap.

But…where is Shiloe?

We'd followed the pinned location on the tracker only to wind up in a dead-end.

I wait a few seconds longer, then move to the center and check the display of the holopad. There's a single message on it.

…it's all a lie.

I know immediately that Varance had left the message for me specifically. After all, she was the one who had taken Shiloe. It's obvious that she's working with the other Atrum.

I step back into the shadows and look at Vern and Grish. Then I lead the way out of the dead-end chamber, a bit unsettled. I don't like the feeling of being trapped in the cavern. We hurry back the way we'd come, no one asking questions. Minutes later, we're approaching the canyon's rim and the upper trail.

I finally slow and lower my hood. Vern and Grish do the same.

"What the hell just happened in there?" Grish asks.

"Yeah," Vern whispers. "I mean, we followed Albright's directions exactly. So, where's Shiloe?"

I can only shake my head as I sit down on the dusty trail and cross my legs. "There's just one thing I can think to do."

"But…won't that give away our location?" Grish asks.

"Probably. But obviously, things aren't going as planned. Besides, that was Varance who left the message, so it's apparent they already knew we were coming."

"Yeah, I guess that makes sense," Vern says and sits down across from me along with Grish.

"Come on," I say, and grip Vern's hand. Grish reaches out, and the three of us drop instantly into Vishmu.

Soon, I feel myself floating, wandering the cosmos. I see Vern and Grish's Heliographi also racing off. I free my inner light to search for Shiloe, and I follow behind it. As I do, I hear a voice speak to me. It's from a great distance, and I can't seem to make out the words, mainly because they're in a language I don't understand. Yet, I can feel emotions within the phrases. I get a sense that it's not from this plane but some alternate universe: an ancient being, perhaps. Then I recall Albright's description of the vessels and think about his words again—*I wouldn't dare in this plane.* And…here I am in another plane, at least while I'm in Vishmu. But what was the second thing he'd said? Something about me taking the matter into my own hands, I think. I glance down at the vessel hanging around my neck. The pure white light glows and pulses, almost as if it's willing me to take it…

…into my own hands.

A moment of clarity hits me as my Heliographi continues to search for Shiloe. Suddenly, I think I understand Albright's riddle.

But my epiphany is interrupted by Grish's thoughts.

She's located Shiloe's Heliographi.

All three of us snap out of our meditation.

We sit across from each other, still holding hands and blinking.

"I know where she is," Grish says. "They've taken her back to the battlefield."

I stand and pull Grish to her feet. She brushes her red ponytails back and takes a deep breath. I pull her around to face me and look into her wide eyes. "Lead the way, Grish."

Grish turns and races off. Vern and I fall in behind her, cloaking as we sprint. The trail meanders through the series of chambers. Soon, I can hear the familiar sounds of war. As we gradually rise upward, the ground begins to vibrate from the shelling. Artillery impacts cause dust and rocks to shower down. I begin to see lightning flashes beyond, and the ground grows damp from rain.

Seconds later, we burst from the tunnel and through the side of a craggy outcropping.

"She's that way," Grish says. "We need to hurry."

Grish sprints off with Vern and me right behind her. Soon, we're weaving between artillery blasts and husked-out vehicles. But just as we crest the rim of a crater, we stumble right into a swarm of death hounds, half a dozen niners and one of the massive TRI-SENT mech units. The markings on the TRI-SENT match the one that murdered Drake: a red triangle with the number 717. My fists tighten, and I feel adrenaline surge through my veins.

But as much as I want justice for Drake, I immediately know we're not likely to fend off this many mechs. On top of that, we can't afford the delay. I feel suddenly at a loss and uncertainty floods my thoughts as Vern and Grish look to me for direction.

I close my eyes.

I think about Albright's words again.

A sudden moment of clarity hits me. As I stand there on the torn battlefield, with a host of death hounds facing me, an intuitive voice whispers to me.

I know how to solve Albright's riddle.

Only in Vishmu can I unlock the clue he'd given me.

I quickly drop into a conscious meditative state and feel for the white vessel around my neck. I place my right hand's cauterized wound directly over it, and the white light from the crystal-shaped vessel pulses when it nears the turquoise light. It increases, matching my heartbeat. In my head, I finally make out the strange voice, the one I'd heard from the celestial being Albright had mentioned. It speaks a single word.

...finally...

The vessel transforms in my grip. It extends to a length of about a meter, and a steel haft elongates from the bottom. The steel is bright silver in the dull light and flashes like a star. The surface is pitted and worn, like an ancient patina has graced it. When I look down, I'm holding a glowing scepter. It's hefty, almost like it belongs to some larger-than-life being. But despite its oversized nature, it's also light and simmers with energy.

I hold the scepter up, and it pulses. A low moan emanates from it, some ethereal voice that speaks some strange, perhaps ancient dialect. I know one thing at that moment. This sentient weapon is somehow alive now.

Vern and Grish look at each other in surprise. I witness the curl of Vern's lips as he reaches for his own vessel and places it in his right hand and grips it tight. He closes his eyes, going into a quick session of Vishmu. A second later, his own vessel transforms into a scepter. Grish does the same.

The three of us launch into the death hounds in one synchronized attack. With the new scepters, we scatter the hounds with ease. Vern leaps into the middle, slamming his scepter into the mud and a fireball erupts, sending dozens of hounds into the night sky. Grish sneaks around behind, using Vern's distraction, and sweeps the back ranks away in a wave of fury. I sprint to the side and swing my mace into their flank, shattering the hounds with crushing blows. Their razor-sharp armor is no match for my scepter, and it folds like tin foil under the ethereal force of the club. With each strike, energy is discharged into the hounds' bodies, causing many of them to freeze or convulse.

But my focus is on the larger units, even as the unrelenting hounds charge and try to rip through my cloak and armor. I'm able to shrug them off as I charge through them and toward the niners and the TRI-SENT.

Like a wedge, Vern, Grish, and I soon break through the hounds and stand before the feet of the larger units. Vern and Grish continue to handle the hounds and the niners while I stand before the towering TRI-SENT mech. Its three legs slam into the ground while its head slowly orients on me. I look up at the giant, some twenty meters high, barely able to see its glowing red eyes in the smoke and dust.

Then, its large howitzers and chain guns lock on me and fire. I use my cloak to absorb some of the rounds while I sprint under its legs. I leap up the side of it, circling around the thing as it tries to reorient on me. Upward I climb until I reach its face. I wedge my legs into a crease near the neckline. The giant's cannons and guns target me. At this close range, I doubt I'd be able to survive. But I shove the end of the scepter's glowing jewel into the face of the TRI-SENT. An electric pulse shoots out and lances directly through its head, exiting the back like a missile. I gaze through the opening as a smile eases across my face.

Then the thing drops. Like a collapsing building, its giant legs fold. The wrecked body comes down quickly in a cloud of dust. I leap from it just as the head crashes down. I roll and stand to my feet, looking at the scepter in amazement. Just yesterday, had I seen a TRI-SENT, I would have turned and fled. Finally, having the might of the scepter, I feel a renewed enthusiasm and confidence.

"For Drake!" Vern yells and raises his scepter into the air.

"Yes!" Grish roars. "That one's for Tripp!"

We give each other a quick hug, but I abruptly pull away.

"Come on, guys. We need to move."

I can hear troops yelling on the horizon, and I see the blurry mirage of several Immortals. They shimmer in the explosions and lightning strikes. The three of us struggle across the rugged terrain, sliding around in the mud. A few seconds later, we're standing atop the hill, facing the blurry mirages.

They lower their hoods, and I see Varance, Isotere, Soto and Roan. Behind them is Shiloe. She looks groggy and is barely able to stand.

"Well, well," Varance says. She glares at us and twirls her glowing scepter. "I knew you'd figure it out, Brin. We were determined to get you here, one way or another, away from Albright. Of course, you couldn't just leave miss priss all alone."

I give Varance a side glance, then look down at her deadly scepter. The other three Atrum also brandish theirs amidst the lightning strikes and explosions. Upon the sundered hilltop, I know now that Vern, Grish and I will face our most challenging mission yet. If we want to save Shiloe, we must defeat these four Atrum with their glowing scepters. But now that we have our own scepters, I feel much better about our chances.

"Looks like things are a bit more even now, Varance," I say and step forward and point the tip of the vessel at her.

Varance's eyes go wide, but her shocked expression is quickly replaced by a snarl. "Are you certain?" She looks over her shoulder.

Vern, Grish and I turn to see several more Immortals materialize. They step forward and stand next to her.

"Well," Vern chuckles, "things *were* looking good for a second or two."

The four new Immortals are the Atrum that Albright had mentioned. Two men and two women. The one that draws my attention, though, is the lady standing in front, who must be the Atrum leader named Riven Sybold.

The woman looks to be in her early forties. She's short with a square jaw and a sharp brow that seems to cast a mysterious shadow over her features. Her skin is fair, her hair and lashes dark. But it's strange, when I glance at her, I can't seem to get a good look at her face, though when I tilt my head to one side, I can see her clearly. Her attitude is noncaring and disturbingly calm. I get the sense of immense power. An ancient energy radiates from her being, an aura of evil. Just looking at her makes me uncomfortable. It's a similar feeling I get from Albright, though his persona is inspiring, encouraging and safe. This woman's aura feels dark and foreboding and dangerous.

Sybold holds her glowing scepter loosely. It's made of the same strange metal, but there seems to be a black, tarlike substance coating it with snakelike tendrils circling the haft. Strangely, the red glow from her hand does not match the glow from the vessel. It's pitch black, and inside the faceted jewel, I can see a shape that resembles a black serpent. Its sinewy body writhes and twists with hate as it claws at the walls of the vessel to get out.

As I face Sybold, my scepter roars at hers. It's a war cry I hear in my mind. I can also hear the other scepters doing the same, like ancient beings who oppose each other. I sense they have been at war for ages, not unlike the Lucem and the Atrum.

Then Sybold speaks to me. I also hear her in my thoughts like multiple voices speaking at once, all in different octaves. It makes my skin crawl, and I can barely control my emotions.

"You are out of your league, Brindall," Sybold says. "Did you think we'd let you walk out with Shiloe so easily? Oh, we knew we could lure you in by using her."

"What have you done with the others?" I ask.

"I've sent them on a little adventure," Sybold says with a dismissive wave. "Christian always was a fool, placing others' feelings above his own common sense. It has forever been his weakness. I'm afraid they won't be joining you. They'll have their hands full, especially where they're going. Besides, it's you I was after all along, Brindall. But since I have all of you here, well…I suppose we might as well clean up this little mess—"

The outline of four cloaked figures interrupts Sybold in mid-sentence.

Everyone turns to watch the figures step onto the hilltop and materialize. I smile when I see Albright, Tyberius, Harriet and Kleegan.

THE WAR-TORN HILLTOP | CHAPTER 25

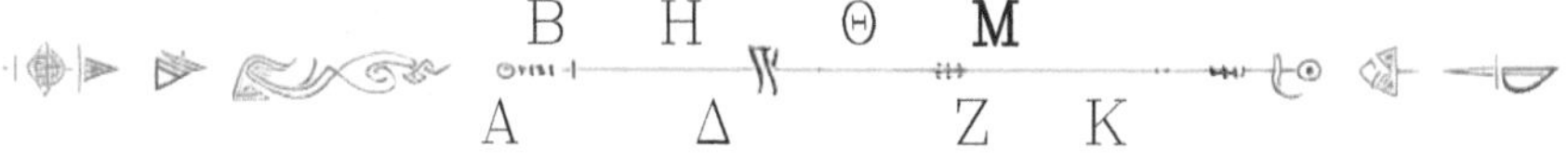

"How kind of you to bring your entire group, Riven." Albright stands in front of Sybold with his hands behind his back. He speaks clearly with no hesitation and his calm demeanor sets me at ease.

As the two leaders stand facing each other atop the war-torn hilltop, I take a quick glance at the other Atrum. The ones from Varance's group I'd already met: Isotere, Soto and Roan. But the other three look to be senior members. Two of them—a young man and a tall woman—both appear to be just a few years older than me. But the way they move and carry themselves tells me they're more skilled and experienced, though. I know that aging ceases once a Heliographi is converted, so there's no telling their actual age. However, the third member, I can sense, is much older and wiser. The glow from his left hand is a deep indigo so dark that it almost matches his skin color. His dark beard is long, and his head is shaved in an intricate pattern on one side. Just his presence sets me on edge, and I avoid his gaze.

Sybold raises the corner of her lip. "So courteous, Christian, as always. I should have known you wouldn't fall for my trap." Her voice rings with sarcasm. I feel the melodic tone tug at me, trying to lull me to a place I dare not go—a place I may not return from if I allow it inside.

She smiles, turning her gaze toward me. I feel my heart race as her dark eyes seem to bore into my soul. My head swims in confusion, and time seems to slow to a crawl. But then she turns back to Albright and suddenly I can think again.

"I see you've managed to pull your Atrum out of the conflict," Albright says, and I can tell that he's trying to keep Sybold's attention focused on him.

She shrugs, a quick lift of her slight shoulder beneath her dark cloak. "And…of course you've done the same. Except for this one." She steps aside and motions to the figure behind them, as if presenting a prize to be won in battle.

Varance shoves Shiloe to the front. She blinks, as if trying to focus through the strobing lightning and explosions. Once again, I can see she's under some sort of influence.

Albright gestures with one hand, though his other rests within his cloak. Like some gunslinger waiting for his opponent to make their move. "Let's not waste more time, Riven. What are you proposing? A request for our vessels is off the table."

"I do have an offer, now that you mention it. I know you value Shiloe, Christian. I know your plan revolves around her…" Sybold lets the comment trail off in a way that makes me wonder what that plan might be. "We are all in the same situation—hunted by the Elitists. They want the Heliographi eliminated. The Elites hold great influence over the South *and* the North. They know we frequent the lower thoroughfares, though they dare not venture down there yet. But how long will that last?"

"I am aware of that."

"So, why should we live in hiding, Christian? Why should we allow them to corral us into such 'unsavory' places? Are we not superior to them?"

"If we place ourselves above them, then we will eventually become them. I will not risk further harm to innocent citizens if I can help it. Besides, our interference may cause more suffering for the citizens if we don't time everything properly. You know about the mass deactivation code. The Lucem will handle the North. The Atrum must take the South. This was agreed upon long ago."

"So…we will simply continue this charade?"

"For just a while longer, yes." Albright crosses his arms and locks his eyes on Sybold. "It's the only way, Riven, if you want to defeat the Elites. I know your desire for revenge is strong."

"As is your love for these pathetic people you call citizens," Sybold says with a dismissive wave of her hand. "Of course, I will ensure the South is handled. This does not make us allies."

Albright chuckles and nods to Shiloe. "I see that you will not change. You still wish to go through with this barter, even knowing that we need each other to defeat the Elites?"

"We are talking about two separate issues, Christian. If you will not give me your vessels, then I offer one last proposal. A Lucem for a Lucem. Give me Brindall in Shiloe's place."

Albright flinches at that. I can sense he's considering the proposal. It's then that I realize how important Shiloe must be to him. Again, I wonder why. What plan is she a part of? *What could be so important that he would even consider such a barter?*

Without warning, Albright steps forward. He moves with blinding speed. In one swift motion, he removes his hand from his cloak. I see a blur of red from his glowing scepter as it comes to the ground like a lightning strike. The surface of the hilltop explodes, and a massive shockwave rocks the ground. A crater opens in the mud, followed by a thunderclap. In the next instant, I feel my body cartwheeling through the air. Albright's surprise strike catches everyone off guard. I see every Heliographi floating in different directions. Dizziness takes my vision, and for a few seconds, I can't tell which way is up or down. All I can see is a bright red light from Albright's scepter as it pulses in the night sky.

Then I land in the mud and lie there, stunned. When I pry myself free, I see Albright and Sybold standing atop the hill, doing battle. Her black mace slashes, and his red mace counters. I see the other Atrum race toward the hilltop, followed by Tyberius and Harriet.

Kleegan stands at the base of the hill and battles one of the other Atrum. I scan the area for Vern and Grish. Near me, half buried in the muck, is a cloaked figure that isn't moving. I rush over to find Shiloe, but she's unconscious. I reach over and place her vessel in her hand and close her fingers around it. Just as I'm reaching down to feel her forehead, someone barrels into my back, and I topple face first into the mud.

"I don't think so!" Varance screams at me.

I quickly flip to my feet and bring my scepter up defensively. We both circle Shiloe's unconscious form. In the distance, I can hear Grish shouting and Vern cursing as they engage in combat. But I keep my focus on Varance; otherwise, I know I'm dead.

"Just relax," I say and hold out my other hand.

"I will play this charade no longer," she says through clenched teeth. "I will kill these humans. They deserve death for what they've done to us, Brindall. You're in my way, which makes you no better."

"You just helped us. Now you want to kill us?" I say. Varance doesn't answer, though I can see her thinking things through. "Not all of these people are bad," I continue and sense a second of confusion in her. It almost seems like Varance is under some sort of influence.

"Maybe there are," she hisses. "But I don't have time to sort them out."

"What if you need us later? This fighting one another isn't going to help our cause."

"It's no longer my call, Brindall. I'm following orders."

Varance leaps, and I barely manage to bring my scepter up in time. Her mace strikes mine and sends off a shower of sparks. The embers light up the surrounding area. I lean into it as she presses back. Our two weapons begin to whisper. I hear their ancient language, filled with a hatred that goes back eons.

Thunder rolls in the distance as I finally force Varance back, and we begin circling each other again. I know that she has more experience than me, especially with her weapon. But I feel confident now, just holding the scepter. It almost feels like something familiar, like I've used it in a past life. That experience floods through me, like the glimpse I'd had recently. I can feel centuries of prior Lucem who bore my symbol pouring from the weapon.

The look on Varance's face tells me she knows that things are even now.

She hurls herself at me again. This time, I roll and kick as she lands, which sends her flying to the ground. But she's up instantly, and we're fighting again. She swings her scepter relentlessly, and I parry each blow. Each time our maces strike, sparks fly like some unearthly forge. Amidst the lightning and artillery and explosions, I face Varance as everything around us seems to fade away. I see only her scepter and its turquoise light as it clashes against my scepter and its pure white light.

Our battle seems to last hours, neither of us giving up ground. Then, I feel the presence of someone beside me. I see a reddish-orange glow that falls from above. The strike hits Varance on the shoulder and blows her backward and into the mud. She lies still, unconscious.

I turn to see Shiloe standing with her scepter in hand. She drops to her knees.

"Shiloe!" I rush to her side and catch her.

She smiles, then nods. "Go. Find the others. I'm alright, just need to catch my breath."

I give her another hug, then race toward the hilltop.

I can see the other Heliographi fighting. Reds, blues and greens flash as sparks fly. The epic battle atop the hill is in full swing. When I arrive, Vern is sparring with Isotere and Roan while Grish and Soto are circling each other and hurling obscenities. Tyberius is fighting the indigo Atrum, while Kleegan and Harriet do battle with the other two. In the center is Albright and Sybold. Their scepters light up the surrounding area with bright flashes.

I race to Vern's aid and circle behind Isotere and take out his legs. Roan turns in surprise, allowing Vern the advantage. He brings his mace down on Isotere's arm. I hear the sound of cracking bones and Isotere screams in pain. Roan looks at us, his eyes wide. Then he cloaks and races off. Vern stands over Isotere, and for a split second, I think he's about to finish him off. I stand to stop him, but before I can say anything, Vern lifts Isotere and tosses him off the hill.

Together, we rush to find Grish. She's on the ground, her scepter held above her as Soto presses down with her mace, trying to crush Grish's throat. Vern launches himself into Soto's side and knocks her to the mud. Grish stands immediately and brings her knee down on Soto's forehead and instantly knocks her unconscious.

At that same instant, I hear a loud whistling sound, and it's growing louder. I know the sound well.

"Incoming artillery!" I scream. I grab Grish and Vern and shove them down the hill. "Go! Get to Shiloe. I'll see you back at base."

I turn and search for the others. I see Harriet on the ground, she isn't moving. Tyberius is now fighting two Atrum while Albright and Sybold are still doing battle.

Then the ground erupts just a dozen meters away. The artillery impact causes mud to shower down and cover all of us. I smell smoke from the fresh craters, but I know there's more artillery coming.

I rush to Tyberius's side and engage the Atrum girl. With the sound of artillery getting closer, I plead with her.

"If we keep this up, we'll all be dead!" I yell.

It feels like we're playing a game of chicken, and the first one to flinch is the loser…only, in this game, everyone dies if we stay. I sense her concern, though, as her strikes land with less aggression. Then she stops and pulls her hood over her head and vanishes. The indigo Atrum facing Tyberius runs to pick up Soto, then vanishes, too. Soon, it's just Albright and Sybold.

Despite the approaching artillery, the two leaders show no intent of stopping. Sybold's hatred matches Albright's disdain. Their scepters roar within my mind as angry sparks fly. It looks to be a standoff, like the two titans might fight like this forever. A stalemate with no winner, except for the incoming artillery.

Tyberius and I approach Sybold. She senses our presence and slows, then takes a step back. The look she gives me is one I will never forget. In the flashing light—for just a split second—I see a massive serpent glaring back at me. Then…she's gone.

As soon as we enter the hidden passage, I turn to face Vern and Grish. "I thought I told you two to get back to base," I say, trying to keep my voice calm.

Vern bats his eyes in my direction. "Well, geez! We weren't going to leave you there, man."

"Yeah," Grish chimes in. "No need to act so heroic. You'd have done the same thing."

And I realize she's right. I wouldn't have left my friends either.

"How's Shiloe doing?" I say, changing the topic.

Vern has one arm around her waist and Grish the same on the opposite side. "She's out like a light," Vern says. "Wonder what they did to her? She seems really weak."

"Dunno, but she's alive, and that's all that matters," I say and guide them down the tunnel.

Our group hurries through the hidden passages. Albright leads the way, nearly sprinting as we struggle to keep up. Harriet is with us, though there's a gash along her brow, and she's limping badly.

Somewhere along the way, Shiloe wakes and pushes away from Grish and Vern. "Stop it, I'm fine," she says when Vern tries to hold her.

"Hey, take it easy, Shiloe," Vern says.

I walk next to her and can tell she's still somewhat rattled. Her steps are confident, but her shoulders slouch as she glances around, still groggy.

"What happened, Shiloe?" I ask, and Vern and Grish step up behind us to listen.

"Shiloe's eyes go wide when she sees my face. "Brin! It's you!" She wraps her arms around me. "I…I thought you were dead. They said—"

"Shiloe," I say and hold her at arm's length. "I'll explain all of this later. Tell me what happened."

"It was Varance," Shiloe says. "She, uh…she attacked me. I wasn't prepared. I just thought…well, she hadn't done anything like that the first two times we met. I let my guard down. The next thing I know, I'm waking up in a dark room. Somehow, they'd removed my collar. Now, I'm just worried about my family—"

I grip her shoulder and give her a gentle shake. "Don't worry. Albright has a way of protecting them, for a while, anyway."

"Albright?" she says and rubs her forehead. "What? So, it *is* him! And…how'd they get those blasted collars off?"

Vern sticks his head between us. "Some sort of new disruption disc Albright's developed. Fools the sensors into thinking an Atrum or a Lucem is dead."

Shiloe slows and turns to face him. "A what? Who are you talking about?"

"Oh, you mean the Atrum and the Lucem?" Vern says.

"Don't you mean Immortals?" Shiloe continues.

I hold up a hand and whisper. "Let's talk about it later." I pull on Shiloe's arm to keep pace with Albright and the others.

Shiloe continues walking next to me in a trance, though.

"Albright…I can't believe it's actually him!" she whispers back at me. She shakes her head and brings a hand to her brow. "There's something about him, don't you think? Something odd, like I know him from somewhere. But I'm positive we've never met before."

"Well, he *is* an Immortal—I mean, a Lucem, like us," I say.

"Right. But there's something else..." Shiloe's voice tapers off.

Vern sticks his head in between us again. "Just ask him when we get back. He seems pretty honest, though he talks in riddles a lot. You notice that, Brin?"

"Yeah," I say in a low voice. "Probably because he doesn't trust anyone. And if we want more information, we're going to have to gain his trust."

When we get back to the Agency base, it's late. I want to go straight to bed, and I can tell by Shiloe's shuffling gait that she does, too. She can barely keep her head up and focused on me when I speak to her. But Albright insists on talking to her. *A quick 'debrief' about her time with the Atrum*, he says. Albright bids the rest of us a goodnight and practically slams the door in our faces. The last thing I see is Shiloe's dazed expression.

The three of us find an open space in the cavernous headquarters near our barracks and build a fire. *For old times' sake*, Vern says. We sit up late into the evening and wait for Shiloe's return. The antechamber in front of our barracks is large with high ceilings. But unlike our last few barracks, we're deep below the surface and can see no hint of the stormy skies beyond. Occasionally, we can hear low rumbles from the artillery, though it's barely audible and sounds more like background noise.

"Did she say what happened to her?" Vern asks.

I pull my gaze from the fire and shake my head. "Not really. She just sounded tired and disoriented. She wasn't herself, though I don't think they hurt her."

"Wonder what Albright wants with her?" Grish says.

"He probably just wants to know if she remembers anything," I say. But in the back of my mind, I keep thinking about how Albright seemed so interested in Shiloe. Some sort of special plan, Sybold had said.

Vern props his head in one hand, scratching his curly scruff and pulling dried mud from it. "I wanna believe what they're tellin' us. It's just hard not to worry 'bout my family, you know? I can't stop thinking about my sister and my mother. I imagine they've gotten word about me being killed. Or would they even bother to notify our families about that?"

I heave a sigh as I sit on the cold stone floor and shuffle my feet. Just as I'm about to answer, I see someone approaching. I recognize the confident strides of Shiloe. Vern, Grish and I run to greet her. I wrap her in a bear hug and lift her off her feet. Vern smiles and pats her back as Grish ruffles her hair.

"Why are you three still up?" she asks, her voice a bit hoarse.

"We weren't going anywhere until you got back, honey," Vern says with a chuckle.

Shiloe rubs her eyes. "We've got a lot to catch up on, but I'm beyond tired. Can we do this in the morning? I'm about to fall over."

"Hold on," Vern says and turns to face me. "Brin, you didn't answer my question."

Shiloe yawns and scratches her head. "What question?"

Vern places his hands on his hips. "How long should we wait before we go after our families?"

Grish, Vern and Shiloe look at me expectantly. Yet, I struggle with that question. An internal voice argues for sooner, while another, calmer voice urges me to wait and trust Albright.

"I just don't know," I finally mutter. "Part of me wants to abandon this whole circus as soon as possible and get back to our families. But then I have to ask the question, what then?" I pause and give them each a long look. “Even if we could somehow get back to our families unnoticed, where would we take them? How would we get them out of our boroughs unseen? And, if we flee this group, the Agency, then we belong to no one. I think our best bet now is to trust Albright and see where it leads us. I don’t think he’s lying to us. If we truly are considered dead, then I see no reason why the leaders of our boroughs would harm our families. What good would that do?”

Vern looks at me, then the others. “I hope you’re right, Brin. I just don’t want to wait too long.”

I grip his shoulders. “Neither do I. But I don’t see many options at the moment. Let’s take it a day at a time. Maybe something will work out sooner than we think.”

THE NEXT PHASE | CHAPTER 26

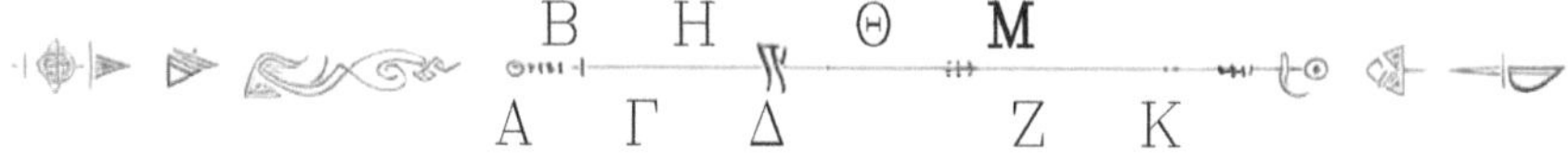

I'm awakened by the sound of laughter. I dress and walk into the common room of our apartment. Vern and Grish sit at the dinner table telling jokes, and I smile at them. I fix some gruel—it's warmer and tastes tons better than any that I've had to this point—and sit next to them. I watch them make fun of each other and smile. It's good to see Grish back to her normal, sarcastic self. Vern has a way of doing that to people.

Soon, Shiloe joins us, and we sit at the small square table and chat, just like old times. We bring her up to speed on everything we know: the collars, the real purpose behind the war—at least according to Albright—and his plan to free the citizens.

"So, what happened last night?" Vern asks. "What did Albright want to know?"

Shiloe gives us a long look. "I…I'm not supposed to talk about it…" She trails off and gives us an apologetic look, then shrugs and holds her hands up. "I'm sorry, guys. I know we share everything, and maybe soon I can tell you. He just made me promise. I mean, it's Christian Albright. What am I supposed to say? But hey, I want to hear more about this Agency. What do you guys think?"

I look at the others and shrug. "Yeah, well, Albright created it to protect the human race. I think we can agree he's a good person, so that probably means the Agency is too. They removed our collars and freed us. Unless this is some elaborate hoax, I think we're in a much better place, thanks to him. Tyberius, Harriet, and Kleegan are also part of this group. They're our old instructors and we trusted them. They seem genuine."

"What do you guys think of the other Immortals, I mean, Atrum?" Shiloe asks. "Did I say that right?"

"Yeah, A-trum," Vern replies. "And we're called the Lu-cem. That's Latin for the *dark* and the *light*."

"The term Immortal is what other people use," I chime in. "But that's because they don't know about our group, the Heliographi. I assume Albright prefers it that way to avoid attention."

Grish pulls her cloak around her as if fighting off a sudden chill. "I guess the Atrum have their own secret operation, too. That Sybold character worries me, though. Something's wrong with that lady."

"She is scary," Shiloe says and shivers. "I couldn't seem to talk or look directly at her. Something about her presence that made me feel so uncomfortable, like she wasn't really there. I don't want to talk about her, honestly. Can we move on?"

I reach over and take Shiloe's hand. "I'm just glad you're alright and we're back together."

"Yeah, me too." Vern pats Shiloe on the back. "Now that we are back together, what do we think about the Skylight System?"

Grish leans back on her elbows and stares at the ceiling, like she's trying to see through it. "Well, it would seem there's enough room for everyone, according to Albright. Apparently, the Elites want the entire system to themselves, and they're trying to kill off all the citizens with this war."

"Right," Vern says and smacks his fist into his hand. "Less people for them to fight off once they find out they're not coming along."

"If the secret about this war gets out, people will riot," Shiloe says. "So, why *wouldn't* the Elites just use the collars to kill everyone right now?"

"That's why Albright and the Agency are on the inside," I say. "My guess is they're trying to prevent a riot, at least for the moment."

"Then why wouldn't he just tell us that?" Grish says.

I shake my head. "Maybe he doesn't want us to worry about our families. Then again, if the Elites just killed everyone, there'd be no one to mine the minerals or finish building the Skylight System. They don't want that either. Whatever the case, if we make a move too soon, the Elites might be forced to use the collars. Albright won't risk that."

"If we can pull off Albright's plan, then we'll have a place for our families and every citizen, too," Shiloe says. "It's worth a shot, right?"

"With the hope that I could live on Skylight, with my family?" Vern chuckles. "Yeah, count me in."

"This isn't going to be easy," I say. "But these people deserve to know the truth. It's our responsibility to let them in on it, when the time is right."

"What if it doesn't work out?" Grish asks. "Sorry, I don't mean to be negative, but what if?"

At first, none of us answer. After several seconds, I speak up. "Then I think Albright will never allow the Skylight System to be completed. He must have a backup plan, a doomsday scenario. He'd probably destroy the whole thing rather than let the Elites live there alone."

"Then we need to make sure they don't win," Vern bellows and grabs Shiloe and Grish and pulls them in close. "For our families. For the citizens. You guys in?"

"For Drake and Tripp," Grish says, her voice a bit unsteady."

"Yes," Shiloe says and grips Grish tighter. "Nothing's changed. I won't forget about them. We're still a family. As long as we have each other, I feel like we can accomplish anything."

I smile at them, then I hold my right hand out. Vern grins back and places his hand over mine. Then Grish does the same and finally Shiloe. I look down to see the colors from our palms intertwined, our symbols overlayed. The colors mix together, and I feel a sense of pride course through me. The bond between us is stronger than ever.

"For Drake. For Tripp. I swear to protect these citizens and each other," Shiloe says, and we all repeat it. Then Vern lets out a long howl, stands on the table and starts dancing around until Grish pulls him down. They start wrestling on the ground while Shiloe and I stand there and watch them, laughing our heads off.

An hour later, we're summoned to the control center.

Tyberius, Kleegan, Harriet and Albright are seated around the old table, behind their symbols. Sitting near Shiloe at the two o'clock position is a young lady I've not met before.

Albright motions to us. "Please, have a seat, all of you."

I settle into my chair, still trying to get familiar with the new surroundings. I'm a free person now, and it feels odd to think that I can do whatever I choose. But the feeling hasn't completely sunk in.

Albright finally stands and holds out his hands. "Let me formally welcome you four to the Agency. I believe this is the first time in a very long while that we've had this many Lucem around the table. I know you've all been waiting to hear our plans. Today, I will reveal them. But you must all swear to keep them secret."

Albright looks around the room with his piercing blue eyes. He gives each of us a meaningful glance before continuing.

"Very well," he says and slides his chair in. "First, we have a truce in place with the Atrum, one that Riven and I agreed to long ago."

I gaze at the others, then clear my throat. "Do you think that's a good idea, sir?"

"Yeah," Vern chimes in. "She just tried to kill us. How can we trust them?"

Albright holds up a hand. "At the moment, the Atrum have as much reason to fight the Elites as we do. Who else would watch over the Southern Coalition? It certainly can't be us. If things go as planned, hopefully we won't even need to interact with them."

I glance at the other Lucem and see them shaking their heads doubtfully. I get the sense this isn't the first time the matter has been discussed. Clearly, Tyberius, Harriet and Kleegan don't seem comfortable. But I can see Albright's point. No one is better situated to secretly watch over the Southern Coalition than the Atrum.

Albright continues. "Despite our mistrust in each other, the truce between the Lucem and the Atrum must last until the Winter Solstice. This will allow us to focus on the North."

"They seem to like bargains," Grish says. "What did they want in return for watching over the South?"

Albright tries to brush the question aside. "It does not matter at this point—"

"Sir," I say. "If we're to be a part of this group, then we should be aware of everything."

Albright pauses for a few seconds, then purses his lips. "If you must know, I have promised them some territory on the Skylight System. The ninth belt, to be exact."

I see Tyberius continue to shake his head, though he says nothing.

Albright pauses again, then nods to the new lady. "Let's move on. I would like to introduce Daylon Terne. She is also a Lucem and has been undercover for a while now. She has been a part of the Agency for nearly half a century. She's here to discuss the next phase with you."

Albright takes a seat as the lady stands and leans on her chair. The symbol from her palm is the shape of a lowercase letter **r**. Her hair is cropped short and dyed pink on one side, with a few colorful beads woven into her blonde dreadlocks. Her skin is dark, her stature tall with broad shoulders, hinting at the fact that she might have originally come from the mines. If so, I wonder what borough and how long ago.

"I'm honored to meet you all," she says, and I notice a slight accent in her voice. "Albright's correct. I've been undercover for nearly fifty years now. I have infiltrated some mid-rank positions in the three theaters. Taun and Herron have been instrumental in this. They'll work with us to pass information along when the time comes."

Vern looks around at us, then raises his hand.

Grish slaps at him. "Just ask your question, Vern."

"Ah, right. I think it's time we hear this plan."

"We're going to overthrow the Elites," Albright says without hesitation, and the four of us sit forward in our seats.

I feel a surge of adrenaline rush through me, and I grip the edge of the weathered table. Though I'd assumed fighting the Elites would be part of the plan, it was still a shock to hear him say it. As of yesterday, I'd only heard that we would free all the citizens. Fighting the Elites is new to me.

"How?" I ask. "They have greater numbers and mech units, not to mention their superior equipment."

"It won't be easy," Albright nods in agreement. "It will take time, and we must be careful not to show our hand too early. We will work in secrecy, using our alias. There are three steps to my plan."

He turns and pulls up a large holographic display with several sub-maps. I can see the Eastern, Western, and Central Theaters. Highlighted deep within the Northern and Southern districts are several green dots, which I assume to be our targets. Though the

Atrum are supposedly handling the southern marks, I find myself wondering if we'll be required to assist them at some point.

"Step one," Albright says and folds his hands into his cloak. "The citizens *must* know the truth about this war. They need to be alerted that an uprising is coming. More importantly, they must know what to do when that time arrives. We will not alert everyone, though. Only the highest-ranking officers will know the truth about this war. They will hold that information until the time is right."

"It'll be risky, giving that information out," I say. "Just one slip and the whole plan backfires."

"Indeed," Albright says. "But no one wants freedom for themselves and loved ones more than these people. It's a secret I imagine they're willing to take to their grave. These trusted informants know the risk."

That draws a nod from around the room, and I can't argue with Albright's rationale.

"Step two," Albright continues. "As I mentioned earlier, I'm working on a virus that will disrupt the collars' signal. But in order for me to complete the disruption code, there are a few things I still need. Let's just call them ingredients. Some of the information is stored on very valuable devices, which lie deep within the Elites' strongholds. We'll need to infiltrate and attain these items."

"Sounds dangerous," Vern says. "I like it."

"What kind of devices are these?" Grish asks.

"We believe they are specialized holopads," Albright says. "Which will require a special operator. We'll need that person as well."

"Are you saying we'll have to kidnap someone?" I say.

"Yes, and I cannot do this part. As Supreme Commander, I can't go missing for that long. Neither can Tyberius, Kleegan, or Harriet. However, you four don't have a high-profile alias, which puts you in the perfect position for this mission."

I look around the room, somewhat shell-shocked. I've only just joined the Agency, and I'm already being given a critical mission.

"So, this entire plan hinges on us getting these special devices?" Vern asks.

"Yes. Daylon will work with you," Albright says. "She's an accomplished operative and knows her way around the different theaters and boroughs. She will train you."

Daylon stands and walks to the display map. "There are six total devices, yeah? Three of 'em are in the South along with their operators, which the Atrum will acquire. The other three devices and operators are in the North, which we believe are indicated here." Daylon points out the green dots on the holographic map. "There're roughly thirty districts on each side. That's a lot of ground to cover. Your journey will be through the boroughs. You'll need your alias to infiltrate each of them. Once you attain the devices, you must return as quickly as possible. Albright'll need them to finalize his disruption code."

Tyberius motions at all three theaters. "While you're searching for the devices, you'll need to alert operatives in the different boroughs. They will begin spreading the word down through our lower informants and eventually to the citizens when the time is right."

Albright crosses his arms. "Once I have the disruptor ready, I should be able to override the master controller to the signature collars. I can free every citizen with the press of a button. That alone is worth the effort we're about to put forth. If you five achieve your goal, millions will be spared. You can save the human race."

Vern chuckles and then starts to laugh. We all stare at him in surprise.

"Oh, no worries, man," he says over his laughs. "No pressure. Are you hearing this? Here we are, being asked to go on a mission to save the human race!"

Albright bows his head. “I realize what we’re asking doesn’t seem fair. Just remember, you’re fighting for your families as well. Let that thought strengthen your resolve. Your training has prepared you for this mission.”

“And what about our families?” Vern continues. “Thought we would be allowed to go after them. Is that not true?”

“I said I will protect your families, and I will,” Albright says. “For now, you’ll have to trust me and focus on your new mission.”

“We will split you into teams for this mission,” Tyberius says. “We feel that Brindall and Shiloe should go as team one. Vern and Grish as team two. Daylon will go alone as team three. We need three miracles to pull this off and hope that Sybold and the Atrum can do the same. You will leave in one day. Take that time to prepare yourself and study up. We don’t have much time left.” Tyberius hands each of us a holopad.

“Albright,” I say and wait for him to face me. “What is the third phase of your plan?”

Albright lowers his gaze at me before answering. “We go to war.”

Following the meeting, I grab a quick bite to eat with Grish, Vern, Shiloe and the Lucem named Daylon. We gather at a food court, which is located in the central district. Like the other places, this chamber is carved of stone with shale ferns lighting the tables and chairs. A serving line dishes up the lumpy gruel I’ve grown so accustomed to, though there are some assorted flavors available. Surrounding us are hundreds of officers, troops, and agents of all types. I find myself growing more impressed with this outfit that Albright’s cobbled together. I can sense the pride and determination in these people. Every operative here has sworn an oath to protect the human race and will die for that cause.

As we sit and eat, I watch Daylon closely. The glow from her hand is a light orange, similar in color to Tyberius. Her demeanor is straightforward, and she speaks in direct terms, which I assume is from years of working as a spy. There's no hesitation in her movements either, likely from being in dangerous situations so often. I begin to wonder how I'll hold up. It's going to be an adjustment from the battlefield.

"You'll need to shift gears," Daylon says as she scoops up some of the soupy gruel. She points her spoon at us. "You're all trained killers on the battlefield, but that'll be of little use where we're headed. You need to sink into your role. Live it. Breathe it. You're someone else now, and you must be convincing."

"Is that how you manage it?" Grish asks. "Being undercover for that long would seem nerve-racking to me."

"Well, that's what the Agency is asking you to do." Daylon looks at Grish and juts her chin out. Then she turns and squints one eye at me. "It's Brin, yeah? You and Vern have been through this already."

I nod to her. "Yes, in the York Borough. But it's not quite the same, Daylon."

"You'll do fine, all of you," she continues, spooning more gruel into her mouth. "It'll start to come naturally after a while. Just stay focused. Mentally place yourself in tough situations. That's how I prepare. The more often, the better."

"So, exactly how long have you been doing this?" Vern asks.

Daylon stops eating and twirls her spoon. "Oh…let's see. I've lost count. Over fifty years? I haven't seen much combat during that time. I've been wrapped up in this charade for so long. It's a game of illusion, one might say."

I glance over at Shiloe and the others and sense their relief at finally leaving the battlefield behind, though. But I also feel a new kind of dread just thinking about the life of a spy.

"You all know the truth now," Daylon continues. "Our fellow citizens deserve to know the truth as well. That's what compels me. After my family was murdered, the Agency adopted me, I guess. It's become a mission, the hope of delivering the truth to these citizens, that is. Maybe I can save someone's father, mother, or child. I've slowly been spreading the word to the informants, building connections with them across the boroughs. It's been a slow process, though."

"Sorry, but that's a lot to take in," Shiloe replies.

Daylon sets her spoon aside and settles back into her seat. "What you four have been through—and survived, I might add—defies the odds. Thanks to your training, you've made it this far. Now, you'll have to survive this new chapter if you want to save these people, including your families. I trust Albright, and if he believes this plan will work, then so do I."

"And what about the Atrum?" Vern asks. "Do you trust them to keep their word?"

"According to Albright, they want revenge on the Elites. The best way to do that is wait for his disruption program and play along with us. The Atrum aren't stupid. They know that even they can't take on the Elite's forces by themselves. If they want their revenge, they need Albright's help. They see the Lucem as a necessary vehicle to achieve that goal. That's fine by me."

"What do you think of Albright's promise to gift them the ninth belt?" I ask. "Tyberius didn't seem to like the idea."

That draws a devious grin from Daylon. "Albright has a reason for every decision he makes. Don't worry yourself about that. We just need to focus on our mission. If we accomplish that, then everything else will fall into place."

"Well said." Vern leans back in his chair. "Any other words of wisdom?"

"Just pay attention," Daylon says. "I won't lie, there's only so much I can teach you with the time we have available. A lot of this you'll have to learn on the job."

"Like what?" Shiloe asks.

"For example, each borough has different governances and rules. Always watch the locals when you're in a new borough. I usually spend a day or so in the different districts just to get my bearings. The best places I've found are in the slum areas. In the more affluent regions, I learn the dialect—and yes, there's a difference in the accents. You'll need to practice that if you want to fit in."

"That'll take some time," Vern huffs. "I'm gonna stand out like a sore thumb, man."

"Speak less, then. Find creative ways if you're struggling in some boroughs. That's what I'm talking about. You *have* to think on the fly, improvise when you have to. It may mean the difference between this mission's success and failure."

Daylon plucks a holopad from her cloak and brings up a holographic menu. It projects over our table and shows the North and South regions with all the boroughs divided into colors. I notice their names for the first time and realize I've never taken the opportunity to learn them, especially the ones in the South. I count thirty on either side of the 37th parallel line.

Daylon draws our attention to the North. "Your first assignment is to learn…no. Scratch that," she corrects herself. "The assignment is to memorize every single borough. I want you all to study this map and know the shape, size, and population of each one. Know the demographics, rules, the way around it, the names of each governor—everything you can, like your life depends on it. It'll be an ongoing process because we don't have a lot of time. Now, we'll start at the far reaches of the North. For Brin and Shiloe, there are eleven, and they are dense. Your boroughs feed recruits into the Central Theater, which includes the ARC Borough and Hammer Fall. Vern and Grish, you two'll tackle the Western Theater. There are only nine boroughs, but they are spread out, lots of ground to cover." Daylon indicates them on the map. "You're both from those areas, Gruelough and Crater. So, you have an advantage. As for me, I'll cover the Eastern Theater. I'm very familiar with those ten boroughs."

"And the Atrum are handlin' our enemies to the south. Hope they get what's coming to them." Grish says this last part with a disgusted look on her face.

Daylon lowers her gaze at Grish, almost in a reproachful way. "You understand there's no enemy south of us, right? We've been taught to believe that some imaginary line makes us opponents. We must relearn everything we know, yeah?"

"Well, old habits die hard," Grish replies, though I catch some hesitation in her tone.

"Mind if I ask how you ended up here?" I ask.

Daylon seems reluctant to talk at first. For a second, I think she'll ignore the question. But her mood softens, and she sits back, letting her eyes roam the ceiling. "I haven't thought about it in a while. First, my father was drafted, followed by my three brothers. Finally, my Day of the Nail came. Imagine my surprise—we have an Immortal in the family."

I lower my eyes and look away. "Sorry. I didn't mean—"

"Naw. It's okay," Daylon says. "It helps to talk about it so that I don't forget why I do this. At any rate, my mother was left all alone when I was sent off. I got word she died soon after. Ever wonder if someone can die of a broken heart?" she pauses and shakes her head. "I somehow managed to survive the war, rescued by Albright—the collars were easier to remove back then. Fifty years later, here I am, still working with the Agency. I don't regret a single day either."

Apparently, Daylon had suffered as much as any of us. I suddenly have a new respect for her.

"We only have a few months until the Winter Solstice," I say. "I wonder how realistic this mission is."

"I've laid the groundwork in many areas," she says. "A lot of people are counting on us. Just be cautious, there's an underground network of spies for our enemy as well."

I tilt my head at her. "Seriously?"

I see the hint of a smile at the corner of her lips. "Do you *really* believe the Elites are that blind?"

"But Albright said—"

Daylon waves her hand. "The Elites know something's afoot, whether Albright admits it or not. They have their own informants and spies. That's the tricky thing, you see? We can't just waltz in and start talking to everyone. This'll be one of your biggest challenges. You must ultimately decide who you can and can't trust."

THE LAST TRAIN OUT | CHAPTER 27

B H Θ M
A Γ Δ Z K

We spend the rest of that evening and into the early morning hours chatting with Daylon. She is a wealth of information, having memorized every borough in the North and the South, even down to the dialect and laws.

Afterwards, Grish, Shiloe, Vern and I sit in our common room and talk. There's a shared uneasiness between us in this upcoming mission. War is pretty straightforward—dodge bullets. Now, there's an element of illusion, and a reliance on subterfuge. Instead of using a battering ram against our enemy, we'll need to use darts. Precision is key.

At daybreak, I meditate. I lose myself in Vishmu and let my Heliographi recharge. Like so many times before, I walk along an ethereal plane. The voice I hear speaks with greater clarity as my abilities grow. I hear it whispering in that same ancient dialect that, strangely enough, I am beginning to comprehend.

Later that morning, we meet Daylon in a secluded classroom. The space is roughly square, with earth-colored walls and a holographic board at the front.

We practice switching between uniforms quickly, using the menu on our rings. "Always wear your cloak below your uniform," Daylon reminds us. "The added protection and ability to disappear quickly is handy, though not comfy. You'll also have a decoy signature collar, which'll help you blend in. Don't forget, your cloak is your best friend. It can scramble almost any detection system, right?"

"Where do we sleep?" Grish asks.

"That's up to you," she says. "Your alias has been preprogrammed, and a job has been created for you. You can rent an apartment if you like. Honestly, I prefer the underground network. That's where you'll find the good informants. There're plenty of hostels to crash at, if you know what to look for. Many are friendly to our cause."

"So, what do we look for then?" Shiloe asks.

"The Lucem symbol, like the ones carved into the hidden passages," Daylon says. "The lowercase letter 'i' surrounded by twelve stars."

"Odd, don't you think?" Vern says. "You say underground network when we're literally underground."

"Just another way of saying 'illicit' areas," Daylon chuckles. "Get used to being in those places. You should spend plenty of time there."

"Sounds…interesting," Shiloe says and gives Daylon a frown.

"You don't have to look very far in most boroughs, trust me," Daylon says. "By day, you'll work the job we've assigned for you. At night is when you move through the underground markets. The quicker you pick it up, the better. You find clues. You get tips. You move on. Don't forget to clear your tracks as you leave each borough, yeah?"

"How will we do that?" Grish asks.

"The Central Department." Daylon shows us an area on the map in one particular borough. "Most are in the heart of each borough. Use your ring, and you can reset your credentials there. Just make sure you do it before you move on. The main rail system is the quickest way between the boroughs. There are some hidden tunnels, but that takes time. Use your best judgment."

"So, we may not have to visit every borough?" Vern asks.

"Well, you might get lucky and locate the device right away. But don't bet on that. I've been looking for a while now with no luck."

"So, what's the first thing we should do?" Shiloe asks.

"Get established and set up a homebase—living quarters. Then, check in with your primary job. Once you've settled in, find clues about the devices."

I shake my head and sit back. The amount of information is overwhelming. Daylon notices our concerned looks.

"You'll do fine," she says. "Just blend in, lay low when needed, right? Most importantly, use your instinct. I know it sounds like a lot, but you've faced tougher challenges than this. There's really not much more I can share. Get some sleep, we're leaving first thing in the morning."

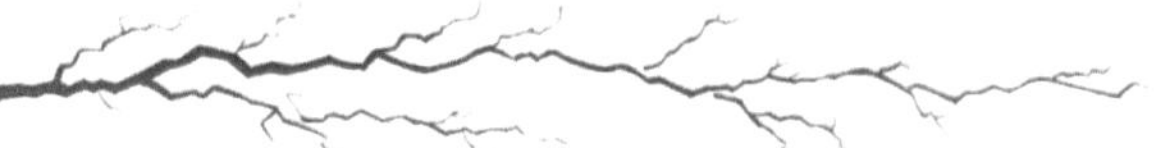

We're greeted by everyone early the next day. I'm expecting more training from Daylon, but instead breakfast is provided as we sit and talk. It's not the lukewarm gruel I'm used to, but a feast with toast, biscuits, fruits and vegetables.

We all laugh as Vern recalls some of his adventures. I smile as he recounts some of our early days together. We try not to talk about Tripp and Drake, but it's difficult, and eventually the mood changes.

It isn't long until Tyberius is ushering us out the door, along with Harriet, Kleegan and Daylon. We eventually pack our things. We're instructed to travel light, taking only a few personal items. Most essentials we'll have to find along the way. Tyberius asks if we all have our vessels with us. *Keep them close*, he says. *There is more to them than you know*.

As we stand before the main tunnel passage, Albright greets us. He speaks in a low voice. First to Shiloe, then Grish and Vern. Lastly, he stands before me and pulls me aside.

"We're counting on you, Brin," he says. "Do me a favor and watch over Shiloe, won't you?"

I hear the subtle concern in his voice. "Yes, of course." I pause, wondering if I should ask the next question. Part of me wants to wait until we have more time. But then I wonder when that might be. I may be undercover until the Winter Solstice or…I may never return.

"Sir, can I ask you something about Shiloe?"

Albright raises an eyebrow but nods for me to continue.

"Sybold mentioned something about your plan and how it includes Shiloe. What did she mean by that?"

For the first time since I've known Christian Albright, I sense a genuine uncertainty. He hesitates, fidgeting with his hands before placing them behind his back. "Brindall. Now isn't the time to talk about it—"

"Please, Albright," I say. "Before I leave, I feel that I deserve to know the truth about your plan…about Shiloe."

After another long pause, Albright lets out a sigh. "It's something very important, even more than what we face with the Elites. That is all I can say for the moment. I apologize."

The others look at us, waiting. I turn back to Albright and nod. "One more thing, sir. You knew that the Atrum set that trap for us. They wanted to separate me from you for that final battle. Why did you allow it?"

"Because you needed that in order to unlock the vessel. You work better under pressure, just in case you haven't noticed." He gives me a wink.

That makes me grin. "Fair enough."

Albright grips my shoulders and holds my gaze. "Face the storms in your life, not alone but together, so that you may lean on each other for strength. Promise me that."

"I promise," I reply. "I will look after Shiloe."

"Thank you, Brindall. I cannot tell you how important this is. Be safe."

After several goodbyes, we follow Daylon along the hidden passage. Thirty minutes later, we make it to the main rail line. It's then that I realize I'm finally splitting up with two of my closest friends, and that thought hits me hard.

We stand on the boarding platform and face each other. Daylon walks away, giving the four of us time to say our goodbyes.

"I can't believe this is it." Vern grabs my arm, and I feel his hand shaking. Grish steps next to me and wraps her arms around my waist. Then Shiloc is there, and the four of us stand hugging each other for several minutes. I feel Grish start to heave. When I push back, I can see Vern's cheeks wet with tears, and Shiloe won't look at us. I feel my own eyes begin to well up.

"At least we can finally be away from this war, right?" Grish says with a sniffle.

"For a while," I say. "But it'll be here waiting for us when we return."

"I'm tired of it," Grish continues. "I'm tired of the fighting, the death…even the sound of those crows, for God's sake."

I grip the other three in my arms. "It's just a short while, guys. Get what you need and come back safe. Deal?"

Vern and Grish both nod but say nothing.

"Yes. Please, be careful," Shiloe finally says in a shaky voice.

Vern gives us a wide grin, which makes me miss him already. Then he takes Grish by the hand and pulls her with him, and they turn and hop on another train. Shiloe and I watch as it heads out of the tunnel and then rockets off toward the Western Theater.

"Tough sayin' goodbye, sometimes," Daylon says as she stands next to us. "And I guess this is it for us too, at least for a while."

"Good luck, Daylon," Shiloe says. "Thank you for helping us, and everyone else."

Daylon smiles, then turns and hops onto another rail line. Shiloe and I stand with our arms around each other and watch as the train bolts off toward the Eastern Theater.

"And then there were two," I say and give Shiloe a gentle shake.

"Yeah…and then—" But she doesn't finish the sentence. Instead, she turns and looks into my eyes. We stand facing each other on the busy terminal. People pass us, hurrying to their own destinations. Amidst the hubbub and chattering, only Shiloe matters to me. I hold her hands as she leans in closer. Like a dream, I feel as if I'm floating.

Then. She kisses me.

I hold her, my arms wrapped around her waist, and time seems to pause. I feel like I'm one with her, and the noise around us fades away like we are alone. It's the kiss I'd been waiting for my entire life, and nothing matters more than Shiloe at that moment.

Eventually, she pulls away.

"Thank you, Brin," she whispers. "Thank you for keeping us safe and looking after us. We owe you our lives."

Then she turns and pulls me with her, and we board the last train out.

The doors slide open, and the familiar smell of battle hits my nostrils.

I hate the fact that I welcome it.

In a strange way, I also hate the fact that I will miss it.

Inside the passenger cab are some fresh recruits and Agency spies, all heading toward the Central Theater. We're among friends now, but I know soon we'll be in dangerous territory.

Shiloe and I take a seat near the midsection and settle in. She leans her head on my shoulder as the doors slide shut. I feel the train lift, and the sound of electricity surges. The transport glides forward, and within seconds, we're rocketing through darkened tunnels to the next chapter in this war, one that may prove to be more challenging than anything else we've faced so far.

Thank you for reading *A Storm of Immortality*, book one of *A Charade of Immortality*. I truly hope you enjoyed it. If you don't mind doing me a small favor, please consider leaving a review on Amazon or your favorite website. Reviews are critically important to a writer's work and help get the word out. Additionally, please consider heading over to the website www.theskylightseries.com and sign up for updates, information and special offers. I'd love to connect with you and talk about this series and hear your thoughts and ideas. Once again, thank you. This would not be possible without your support.

J. Wint

www.ingramcontent.com/pod-product-compliance
Lightning Source LLC
Chambersburg PA
CBHW020457310726
48979CB00016B/2685/J

* 9 7 8 1 7 3 6 3 0 2 9 8 9 *